ALAN BAXTER

DEVOURING DARK

PRAISE FOR DEVOURING DARK

"*Devouring Dark* is a thrilling mix of crime and horror, a book that somehow defies either description yet embraces both. It moves like a juggernaut, thundering towards an intense, emotional conclusion. I devoured Alan Baxter's dark; you should too."

– Gary McMahon, author of *Pretty Little Dead Things*

"*Devouring Dark* is a powerful tale of crime and death, cleverly crafted and flawlessly executed. I'm a fan of Alan Baxter and *Devouring Dark* is a perfect example of why. Do yourself a favor and join me for some shivers."

– James A. Moore, author of *Seven Forges* and the *Serenity Falls* Trilogy

---

"Action-packed yet emotionally resonant, *Devouring Dark* held me to the last page."

– Kaaron Warren, World Fantasy Convention Guest of Honor and Shirley Jackson Award-winning author of *Tide of Stone*

Praise for the Work of Alan Baxter

"Alan Baxter's fiction is dark, disturbing, hard-hitting and heart-breakingly honest. He reflects on worlds known and unknown with compassion, and demonstrates an almost second-sight into human behaviour."

– Kaaron Warren, Shirley Jackson Award-winner and author of *The Grief Hole*

"Alan Baxter is an accomplished storyteller who ably evokes magic and menace."

– Laird Barron, author of *Swift to Chase*

"Alan's work is reminiscent of that of Clive Barker and Jim C. Hines, but with a unique flavour all of its own."

– Angela Slatter, World Fantasy, British Fantasy and Aurealis Award winner

---

"Alan Baxter has joined the ranks of talented authors who seek to push the boundaries of fantasy fiction."

– *The Manly Daily*

"Alan Baxter delivers a heady mix of magic, monsters and bloody fights to the death. Nobody does kick-ass brutality like Baxter."

– Greig Beck, International bestselling author of *Beneath the Dark Ice* and *Primordia*

"If Stephen King and Jim Butcher ever had a love child then it would be Alan Baxter."

– *Smash Dragons*

"Baxter draws you along a knife's edge of tension from the first page to the last, leaving your heart thumping and sweat on your brow."

– *Midwest Book Review*

DEVOURING DARK
ISBN-13: 978-1-940658-98-8
ISBN-10: 1-940658-98-5
Grey Matter Press First Trade Paperback Edition - November 2018

Copyright © 2018 Alan Baxter
Cover Artwork Copyright © 2018 Sabercore Art
Book Design Copyright © 2018 Grey Matter Press
Edited by Anthony Rivera

GREY MATTER
P R E S S

CHICAGO

Grey Matter Press
greymatterpress.com

Grey Matter Press on Facebook
facebook.com/greymatterpress

For my son, Arlo - a light so bright
he shines all my darkness away.

TABLE OF CONTENTS

DEVOURING DARK - 11

SHADOWS OF THE LONELY DEAD - 295
(THE AWARD-WINNING SHORT STORY THAT INSPIRED DEVOURING DARK)

ACKNOWLEDGEMENTS - 308

ABOUT THE AUTHOR - 310

ONE

MATT MCLEOD KNEW THE OLD ADAGE, that light is supposed to push away the darkness. But he also knew it wasn't true. Light sits on top, like a film of oil on water. The dark is still there underneath, deep, permanent, waiting. And usually it's enough, that surface skein of brightness, to keep a soul from the yawning black abyss below. But once the cracks appear, the fall is inevitable. And the darkness devours.

Knowing this truth, Matt often wondered how long he had left. Though he was convinced time was largely irrelevant. He was already falling, had been for years. How much damage he could do on the way down, who he could take with him, those were better concerns.

He killed the engine of his battered old car and silence descended. The dashboard glow winked out, leaving him in inky shadow, just the streetlights refracting through raindrops on the windscreen for company. Cold and wet, a classic London night. The alley across the quiet road glistened, like a throat ready to swallow. Sullivan would be along any time now.

Matt rolled a short, thin joint, just a sprinkling of weed to take the edge off. He didn't particularly enjoy being stoned any more, but the process hurt a little less if he was buzzing. Not really high, that would dull his reactions too much. It was a balancing act, like everything in life. Just enough self-medication, but not so much as to cease being what they call a fully functioning adult. Whatever the fuck that really meant.

The bluish smoke drifted lazily around Matt's head as he watched the alley, and then there Sullivan was, entering from the other end, parkland gloomy and dripping behind the silhouette of his bulk. Shit, but he was a big bastard. Not that size really mattered, muscles being no match for the dark.

Matt drew deeply of the spliff and it singed his fingers as it crackled away to almost nothing. Pressing the tiny roach into the car's ashtray, he readied himself, then opened the door and stepped out. The cold and persistent drizzle bit instantly through his warm comfort and only on leaving did he realise how safe and embracing the car had been. Another metaphor for life right there. He headed across the street for the alley, aiming to meet his target halfway down.

John Sullivan, thirty-nine, single, worked by day as a used car salesman—which made him a scumbag already—but his extracurricular activity was of far more interest to Matt. And why Matt was here. Sullivan paid no attention to anything as he trudged through the rain, hiding under a flat cap, hunched in a trench coat. Large industrial bins lined one side of the alley, various detritus, rubbish bags, broken bottles, littered and glistened among the puddles on the rough asphalt underfoot. Sullivan tramped through it all. When Sullivan was in the shadows just over halfway along, Matt stepped from the eyes of the street into the privacy of this ignored corner of the city.

"Mr. John Sullivan." Matt's voice was strong, not showing the nerves that rippled through him.

The man paused, looked up quickly, a moment of shock passing over his face before he settled back to his default of belligerent bastard. "What? Who are you?"

"I'm your comeuppance, old son."

The big man's eyes narrowed and he tipped his head to one side. A slight smile started and Matt could not stand for that. He began the litany. "Jeremy Roberts, aged eight, violated in the change room at the football field at Edgware." The man's smile faded. "Tony

Small, aged seven, same location. Justin O'Leary, aged eight, ran into you in the public toilets at the Argyll shopping centre and was never the same again."

"Who the fuck are you, ya short-arsed Jock?" Sullivan's demeanour wavered between horror and anger, his East London accent heightened. "What are you talking about?" He was confused by Matt's confidence in a frame only five feet nine and thinner than some lengths of rope. He must be sure he could shatter such a skinny body, but the things Matt was saying were discomfiting to him. As they were intended to be.

"Aye, you know exactly what I'm talking about," Matt said, letting his Scottish accent out more as it seemed to annoy the guy. "Shall I go on? Stuart Glenn, aged nine, your nephew's birthday party at your own brother's house."

Sullivan roared and rushed forward, anger winning. Matt braced and let the man grab him by the lapels of his thick, black donkey jacket. Matt's shaggy hair, soaked now with rain, fell across his eyes as he was slammed into the grimy wall, his scuffed black combat boots swinging a good two feet off the ground. The air rushed out of him and his vision crossed, but his hands found the big bastard's wrists and wrapped around them, skin to skin. It was all he needed.

The cracks opened, like Matt's bones were splitting and his flesh peeling off, and the dark came through. Even stoned it was agony. Matt grimaced, wondered why he never seemed to get used to it, but instead it hurt more every time. Short-term agony for long-term relief. But how long until he couldn't bear it?

"Dark attracts itself like iron filings to a magnet, mate," Matt said through clenched teeth.

Sullivan stared at his hands curled into Matt's jacket, trying to make sense of the blackness that swirled like ink in water through his skin. His forearms were exposed a few inches and the dark went that way, swimming up his arms, snaking towards his heart. "The fuck is this?" he managed.

"Ah, but it hurts, does it not?" Matt asked him.

Sullivan shook, his legs weakening. He staggered back, dropped to his knees, hands losing their hold on the coat, but Matt kept his grip on the thick wrists. Matt's breath was ragged as he let the darkness through, let it reach up from whatever nether region it inhabited. When his vision started to fail from the pain of the transfer he let go and stumbled away. The pain didn't ease.

The dark stretched between them, palms to arms, like tar. Matt backed off far enough to sever it and it writhed in the air like cut worms before it soaked back in. He forced it down, closed the connection, denied it the further release for which it yearned, his teeth gritted against the agony in his bones. He would have peace from it for a few months again now, assuming he could get it back under control.

Sullivan sat back on his heels, staring at his withered, blackened hands, like a crone's claws. He tore open his shirt to see the stain spreading across his chest as the skin sank tight over his ribs, up his neck, to engulf his face. His eyes filled up like empty vessels accepting oil, and those sightless black orbs turned briefly towards Matt before he shivered and collapsed face-first into the rain. His clothes, soaked, settled around him and clung to a suddenly wasted, skeletal frame. He twitched once, then stilled.

Matt sank to his knees, desperate to breathe away the pain through his body. The cost of his ability was getting higher, the hurt more intense and long-lasting. He needed to drag the body away to his car, take it somewhere and hide it. It was easy enough to break up those brittle remains, smash them into unrecognisable dust, but his hands shook, his legs trembled. He couldn't lift a kitten, let alone a man, even one withered by the darkness. For several minutes Matt gasped for air, wishing the pain to ease, and it finally began to settle just a little.

He couldn't stay long, someone might come any moment. Already he had pushed his luck too far. One of the large industrial waste bins stood nearby, half-open, and he knew there were no cameras here. He had done his homework, not only on the man himself, but on the chosen location of his comeuppance. The idea of hauling the corpse out to his car was too much, but Matt dredged up the strength to shoulder it off the ground. Though it was only bones in blackened skin, wrapped in sodden clothes, its weight was almost too much for him to bear. He had never been this weak after a delivery before. He managed to tip it over the edge into the skip. He snapped up the long limbs, folded the whole mess in on itself, then dragged cardboard and other detritus over the top to conceal it. Finally, he slid the cover fully closed, gasping for breath, and collapsed back to his knees, vision swirling and swimming. It would have to do. With any luck the body wouldn't be noticed until it went up into a garbage truck and got dumped to rot at the local tip. Hopefully it would never be seen again.

Tears streaked Matt's cheeks, lost in the rain. He looked to the black, rain-filled clouds and whispered, "Another one for you, Tommy. I'm so sorry."

He staggered to his car, turned the heater up full and drove for home. His hands shook like he had a palsy as he weakly gripped the wheel, willing the hurting to ease, his bones to close together again. Surely he would not be able to do this for much longer. The next one, maybe the one after that, must certainly kill him too. He drove slowly and carefully, in need of a large scotch and a hot bath.

* * *

Clancy Turner stood in shadows at the end of the alley, his tall, wiry frame easy to conceal in the dim corner, and watched the small Scotsman drive away. He realised his mouth was hanging wide open and snapped it shut, wiped a hand over his dark face to brush the rain away. What the holy hell had he just witnessed?

He replayed the video he had shot on his phone, cursing the weather that soaked his track suit and stuck it to his skin. It was all there. He thought he would be videoing a fight, something funny for YouTube, but had got so much more. He tapped up the notepad app and quickly wrote down the licence plate of the Scotsman's car before he forgot it. Then he cautiously approached the broken-up corpse lying in the bin and dragged aside the rubbish concealing it. Wincing, shaking his head in pointless denial, he nudged it with an empty glass Coke bottle. It shifted and settled back, like so many old branches wrapped in a trench coat. The head was still obvious, black, old leather stretched tight across the bone. It reminded Clancy of photos he'd seen of mummies in sarcophagi, ancient and desiccated. But he had watched this man walking just minutes ago, followed him through the park, wondering if he might be a good mark for a mugging. The guy had been big and strong-looking, Clancy was reluctant to chance it, even with the good knife he carried. Then, still undecided, he'd stopped at the sight of the small man's appearance. And everything he had seen after that still seemed dreamlike. Impossible. But right there in the dumpster was proof that he wasn't crazy.

Clancy smiled and snapped a few photos. This was some proper horrorshow shit. The Boss would be very interested in it, he was certain of that.

TWO

MATT GOT HOME AND POURED a generous measure of Laphroaig into a clean tumbler. He swallowed it in one then looked disdainfully at the empty glass. He couldn't afford to drink like that, not on a warehouseman's salary. He poured another, smaller measure, and sipped it. This was his true drug of choice, a good single malt. The ache had begun to leak away from his bones on the drive home to Finsbury Park and his one-bedroom basement flat, but he was hollowed out inside. He always felt that way after letting the dark through, but it was better than the sensation of constant fracturing that lived in him if he didn't give frequent release to the urges that plagued him. And he was doing good with it. Atoning.

Aye, keep telling yourself that.

He put the glass on the coffee table and went through to the bathroom, turned the taps on to fill the tub, then into the bedroom to strip off his wet clothes. He trudged back into the lounge room naked and shivering and flicked on the bar heater. He could hardly afford his electricity bill, but even Scotsmen got cold on London nights like this. And it wasn't really the cold that bothered him, but the driving icy wetness of autumn rain. It was no different back home in November. He always looked forward to the snow and the proper cold, infinitely preferable to damp chills.

He took his malt and slipped into the delightful relief of the hot bath, and let the warmth ease his muscles and joints. Out on the coffee table, his phone rang, buzzing as it vibrated across the wood. "Fuck it," he muttered, and sank deeper into the water until it lapped under his chin. He swallowed the last of the whisky, put the glass on the side of the tub, and closed his eyes.

He was startled awake by the phone ringing and buzzing again. The water was still warm, he couldn't have been out for long. "Fuck's sake…" He ground his teeth until the ringing stopped, then tried to settle again, but the moment had passed. "You could slip and drown, ya fucking bellend," he said quietly, and hauled himself into the cold air to dry off and get dressed.

Wrapped in worn and fluffy track pants and a thick woollen jumper, he stood and stared at his bookcases, covering two walls of the lounge. Spines criss-crossed the shelves, stacked horizontally atop those lined up in neat rows like literary soldiers, jammed in any available gap. Hundreds of novels, just as many reference books of the occult, the mystical, ancient history, superstition, all the things that had guided him along his life path since that day he opened himself to the dark when he was so very young. But all that knowledge hadn't helped him understand how to slow the dark's inevitable consumption of his being. He had found his methods, learned he could do some good on the way out, even if he would never really atone.

There were a lot of books, but none caught his eye. He was still too wired to read, and exhausted at the same time. That strange in-between state of too much and too little. Overfull and emptied out.

He slumped into the familiar comfort of the worn, brown couch. He'd bought it new, but it had been in this same flat for a long time, coming on eight years now, the same amount of time he'd worked in the big Tesco's warehouse. As soon as he'd got a job he got a place, and there he stayed. It sure beat the nearly two years he'd spent on the street and various hostels after running from Edinburgh at the age of sixteen. And he was happy here. As happy as he could be, at least. It was his, and the landlord was unlikely to kick him out any time soon, as long as Matt kept the rent paid on time, and he was faultless on that front. A home of his own, a private space, was about the most important thing to him. And it was all so temporary anyway, the dark would have him soon.

He switched on the television and instantly recognised *Terminator 2*. He grinned. "Say, that's a nice bike." His American accent quite convincing, even if he did think so himself. The movie was halfway through but would do nicely to unwind. His phone chimed again, a text message this time. He leaned forward to stare at it. Two missed calls, one text, one voicemail. All from Ben.

He opened the message.

me and the lads at the carpenters check your voicemail dickhead!

Matt grinned despite his fatigue. Ben and the lads were good people. On Matt's first day at the warehouse, Ben had introduced himself, instantly friendly and welcoming with his chiselled good looks and confident swagger. He had such a love of life about him, such an embrace of living, that Matt had been drawn in almost against his will, yin swirling into yang. Ben had introduced Matt to Gareth and Steve, and the four of them had been fast friends ever since. Matt keyed up the voice message and strained to hear over the noises of shouting and glasses in the pub.

"Matt, it's Benny. Get down to the Carpenter's Arms, mate. We're sinking a few and there's a stag do here with strippers and everything. You're missing out!"

Matt deleted the message and looked at the phone like it held greater wisdom than tits and beers. It was tempting, but he was done for. The time showed at the top of the screen, just after 9:30 p.m. Still early. It was only a five-minute walk back to Finsbury Park Tube, then a couple of stops to Holloway Road. He could easily be there by ten. As he was thinking, *Nah, fuck it, I'm comfy*, another text popped up.

come on twat your missing all the fun!

Matt sneered. He should go just to correct Ben's awful grammar.

John Sullivan withering away to a stunned, blackened skeleton flashed across his mind and Matt was up out of the chair in an instant. Dead tired or not, he knew he was unlikely to sleep soon, the brief nap in the bath notwithstanding. Moping at home with that memory still fresh was certainly not a good idea. Drinking with his mates absolutely was. He changed into jeans and jacket, pulled on his boots and was on the Tube to Holloway Road less than fifteen minutes after Ben's last text.

THREE

CLANCY TURNER ARRIVED AT STRATTON'S pub on the edge of Camden Town soaked and cold, but still excited about the news he had to share. Big Lou at the door nodded as Clancy slipped by and then went back to challenging three young men for ID. The Boss kept an honest premises and insisted it stay relatively free of violence.

Clancy walked through the main bar, slipping between raucous groups of drinkers gathered around dark wood tables, red velvet stools and benches adding colour to the gloomy interior. A young crowd mostly, a few old regulars in the far corner, watching from safety as the tide of frivolity ebbed and flowed to the bar and back. Clancy spotted Tracy among the staff scurrying about behind the ale pumps and dog-legged over. His news wasn't that urgent. He waved as he approached and she flicked him a grin as she juggled vodka bottles and glasses.

"Didn't know you were on tonight," Clancy said, talking loudly over the roar of dozens of other conversations, accompanied by "My Sharona" on the jukebox. Lots of Stratton's patrons were a bit old school.

"Brittany called in sick. Vince asked me to cover."

"Brittany's always sick."

Tracy rolled her eyes. "Too much MDMA will do that to you."

Clancy nodded at the wisdom of her assessment. Shit, he liked this girl. Really liked her, not just wanted to fuck her. Although he wanted that too. "Wanna grab a drink after your shift then?"

She twisted a half-smile that was part apology, part reluctance. "I'm pretty tired, and only going to be worse after tonight."

Clancy raised his chin, like it was no big thing, even as he cursed inside. "Another time then."

"Yeah, maybe." Before he could say more, she turned to the customer Clancy had been studiously ignoring. "Fourteen quid, love."

Clancy took one last lingering look at her cleavage in the low-cut T-shirt she wore and turned away. He wasn't going to give up on her any time soon. He headed for the door beside the far end of the bar, leading to the office and storeroom, and spotted Len Cartwright from the East End mob in one corner. The man dripped with gold jewellery, his blue silk shirt rippling with reflected light. The pub's concealed lighting shone off the man's insanely greased black hair too. Clancy went to him and reached out a hand.

"Great to see you, Mr. Cartwright."

Cartwright let Clancy hold his hand for a moment, not actually deigning himself to return the shake. That would be giving a lowlife too much respect, but he did glance at Clancy and offer the tiniest nod. Then he returned his attention to the man sitting opposite, opining on something about the Irish. Infuriating bastard, but there were some people you just didn't ignore. Etiquette and all that. Respect was currency and Clancy would never allow himself to be seen to be a pauper.

With a nod in return, Clancy released the limp hand and pushed through the back door into a cool concrete corridor that was stark after the warm welcome of the pub with its polished wood and soft furnishings. The short passage went by the storeroom and staff toilet, then doors out to the rear lane, before ending in a wooden door marked PRIVATE. Yelling came from the other side. The Boss was furious with someone.

Clancy paused, waiting to see if the rage would settle. The Boss was able to turn it on and off like a tap, but you most certainly didn't want to get caught in the flow.

"You fuckin' tell him that Vince Stratton is not some young fuckin' pup he can fuck around like that!" the Boss yelled. "I will not stand for it, and I will have the fuckin' hide clean off the back of any cunt who even thinks of crossing me, do you understand? *Do you under-fuckin'-stand?* Good. Then we are in agreement. You have until Sunday afternoon. If it gets dark outside on Sunday and he hasn't shown up right in front of my fuckin' desk, blood is gonna spill far and fuckin' wide. And it gets dark early this time of year, you remember that!"

There was a crash as the Boss slammed down the telephone receiver. Clancy was glad he wouldn't have to see any poor shame-faced bastard scurrying away. He tapped on the door.

"Come in." The rage had gone and Vince sounded calm as a librarian.

Clancy went inside, closed the door behind himself. "This an all right time, Boss?"

"Always got time for you Clancy, my boy. Sorry if you had to overhear that unpleasantness just then. Some people only understand a certain language, you know. Polite of you to wait."

The Boss didn't miss a trick, CCTV throughout the pub feeding directly to the desktop computer by his left hand. He stood, rising his full six-foot-two-inch frame from behind the mahogany desk, and moved over to an ornate, glass-fronted drinks cabinet in the corner. His broad, muscular shoulders stretched his fine Saville Row shirt. He might be entering his fifties, but he was still a hardass. Clancy was the same height as his boss, but half as wide and, frankly, terrified of the man. But it was a highly respectful terror, and he would forever be grateful to Stratton for what he'd done. Clancy's dad had been a useless piece of shit, gone before Clancy was a teen, but Stratton showed how a real man should act and comport himself. Clancy would do anything for him. All the boys shared that loyalty.

"Drink?" Stratton asked.

"Thanks, Boss. I'll have a brandy. Bloody frigid out there tonight."

"You look like a drowned rat, old son. Ever heard of this modern invention called an umbrella?"

Clancy laughed. "I should try one out maybe."

Stratton handed over a cut crystal tumbler with a generous measure in it and sat back behind his desk with a drink of his own. He perused Clancy for a moment, the expression on his pale, craggy face giving nothing away. "So what's news? Did you deliver to Carl's place?"

"Yes, Boss. Did that this morning. All good. Carl says hello."

"Well, hello back to Carl then. So what now? Just paying a friendly visit? I'm flattered, old son, but hardly worth catching your death for. You should be home and dry if you're not working."

Clancy nodded, sat opposite the Boss. "Well, that's just it. I was heading home when I saw the most bizarre fucking thing I've ever witnessed. This little Scottish bloke… Well, you know you always tell us to keep our eyes open, especially for anything unusual."

Stratton inclined his head. "The city is a big, strange place full of big, strange things. I've learned to be observant, and that's why I try to instil the habit in you boys."

"Right. Well, honestly, I don't even know where to start."

Stratton's eyes narrowed. "Try right at the beginning."

With a lot of stuttering, nervous laughs and apologies for insanity, Clancy finally got out the story of what he'd seen.

"He just withered away?" Stratton asked eventually.

Clancy moved around the desk and showed his phone. He played the video, then flicked through photos of the soaked and blackened corpse folded up in the large bin. "See, I'm not joking. He just left him there and fucked off. To be honest, he looked half-dead himself, like it nearly finished him, what he did."

"I wonder what the Old Bill are gonna make of that should someone find it," Stratton said.

"It's pretty unlikely to be found until the truck dumps it at the tip. And even then, it might go unnoticed." Clancy flicked apps and showed his notepad screen. "That's the licence plate of the car the little Scottish fella bolted off in. It was a dark blue hatchback, an old VW Golf, I think."

Stratton grinned and copied the licence plate down onto a paper pad on his desk. "Well done, lad, that's good work. Where was this alley?"

"Just off Liverpool Road, near The Angel."

"Sit down, son. This needs investigating. You done good bringing this to my attention. If what you say is true, I'd be very interested to talk to a bloke with those talents."

"I remember, Boss. I pay attention. You might be able to use him for your... You know?"

Stratton wagged one finger. "Don't dig, son. I look after you boys and you ask no questions, whatever you may suspect of me."

"Yes, Boss." Clancy returned to his seat and sipped high-quality brandy while Stratton dialled a number.

The Boss smiled over the phone while he waited, then said, "Detective Sergeant Collins, please. Thank you."

There was a few moments pause. Clancy sipped, Stratton idly cleaned his fingernails with an ornate letter opener. Then a voice sounded on the other end.

"Charlie, me old mate, it's Vince. Yeah, well, I'm sure I'm equally pleased to hear your dulcet tones, but I need some information. Yes, you *can* help me. I still have that video." He paused, listening, then, "Any unusual bodies cropped up tonight? Around The Angel maybe?" He laughed. "You say no, but do you mean yes, and you're not going to tell me anything. Or maybe now you need to check? In the bins in some alleys, maybe? I'm omnipotent around this town, remember? Never mind, not my business and you know me, I mind my own business." There was a bark of laughter down the line that Clancy heard clear on the other side of the desk.

"Anyway," Stratton went on. "I need a bit of help. Track down the owner of a car for me, will you?" He read out the licence plate. "Old blue Golf. No, nothing to do with any bodies, Charlie, don't be so paranoid. Maybe I'm just throwing you a bone in advance payment for this little favour. Because I'm a generous man, Charlie, old son. It's entirely a business thing. I just need an address for that car." He paused, a slow smile spreading. "Nah, I don't know anything about any bodies near The Angel or anywhere else. Ha! Fuck you too, mate. No problem, get someone to give me a call with that address. What? Yeah, you got my mobile, text it if you like. Cheers, mucker. We must catch up soon and share a few measures. Ta ra."

Stratton put the phone back in its cradle and grinned at Clancy. "Well, whoever it was you saw doing that crazy thing, we'll soon know where they live. Then you and a couple of boys can pop 'round and ask them to come and see me so we can have a little chat about it all."

"And if he doesn't want to come? After what I saw, I don't want to try to force him."

"Quite so. Well, we're not gangsters, Clance, you know that, but sometimes you do need to coerce someone with a shooter. Easier to do your coercion from a distance that way."

Stratton went to a safe and rummaged in it for a moment, then returned with a small revolver. He held it up. "You have this one, and take Dexter with you. He's got his own pistol, tell him to bring it. Take along some more boys if you feel like it. Not David though, he's too new. And do your absolute best to not fire this, and tell Dex the same. Just use them as incentive, understand?"

Clancy raised his glass in a toast. "Yes, Boss."

FOUR

MATT ARRIVED AT THE CARPENTER'S ARMS and immediately regretted his decision. The place was packed and thumping and he realised he would rather be in a nice, quiet pub instead of this cavern of rowdy drinkers and flashing lights. Or back at home after all. An impromptu performance space had been set up at one end where bad garage bands would sometimes play on a Friday night. A deck and light unit were working overtime as patrons hollered and whooped at a blonde policewoman in an unlikely miniskirt, gyrating under the disco ball. Matt reassessed his decision as she slipped out of the tight white blouse to reveal a fine lacy bra and decidedly impressive cleavage.

He shook his head. Big fan of a good cleavage though he was, he didn't need this level of celebration. He was whittled down by his night's work. This was a bad decision.

He staggered as his sleeve was dragged from one side and turned to see Ben grinning drunkenly. "Sit down, fucker!" Ben yelled and hauled Matt across to a table not far from the door.

The view of the stripper was still good and, once he was sat on a wooden stool, Matt felt a little less crushed by his surroundings. Gareth returned from the bar and scowled, the dark skin of his arms rippling with his well-developed muscles as he held three pints in a triangle grip.

"Bloody timing, mate!" He put the beers on the table, pushed one each to Matt, Ben and Steve, then turned to struggle back through the crowd to the bar, presumably for another beer for himself. Now that was good service and good friendship rolled into one.

Matt looked at the pint of lager, already condensing the glass, then up at the stripper as she leaned forward and made her breasts swing, teasing the crowd as one hand toyed with her bra strap. Well, maybe he would stay for one or two. He clinked glasses with Ben and Steve, the latter not removing his eyes from the show, doubtless for fear of missing any detail.

Ben and Steve couldn't be more different. Ben was classically handsome, square-jawed with olive skin and dark, thick hair, a wildly successful womaniser. Steve-O was hopeless with the ladies, skinny and awkward, long face like a sad horse. The rest of them tried repeatedly to train some confidence into him, but the gangly fellow was pretty useless.

Ben grinned at Steve's slack-jawed expression, then leaned in to Matt. "Haven't seen you much outside work lately," he said, voice raised over the noise of the whipped-up crowd. "Not since that great night at the club when we all ended up back at Steve-O's."

Matt laughed. "And Steve almost got off with that one bird, with the blue hair."

"Except he fucking passed out on his own couch and she went home with me!" Ben finished.

They shook their heads, laughing to themselves. Poor old Steve. One of these days.

"So where you been?" Ben asked.

"Not been feeling too social," Matt said. "Just laying low, you know." Close as he was with these boys—the full eight years he'd been at the warehouse he'd known Ben and Steve, working with them, and Gareth almost as long—he could hardly tell them where he'd really been. His investigations into John Sullivan had been slow and thorough over several months, but the last couple of weeks before he hit someone with the dark was always a time of intense focus, nothing but working and planning, leading up to the event itself. He tried to imagine what they might think of him if they knew the truth. Most likely they would run in horror. He preferred to keep his dark talent an absolute secret and live as normal a life as possible otherwise. His bones ached with the memory of Sullivan's recent demise.

"Well, it's good to see you, mate," Ben said, and clinked the glass in Matt's hand with his own.

"You too." Matt raised the toast, took a long draught. "What's new?"

Ben opened his mouth to answer, but it turned into a cheer of appreciation.

Matt turned to see the stripper had finally rewarded the patient masses and she strode back and forth twirling her bra high. She really did have a fine body. Gareth returned with another pint of his own and the four friends fell to drinking, laughing and enjoying the floor show. Gareth was a good sport, joining the frivolity regardless of persuasion, and then became particularly happy when it turned out to be an equal opportunity show, a well-endowed male copper taking his turn. All kinds of whoops and hollers accompanied his appearance, from the outraged to the celebratory.

Matt grinned. Perhaps this had been the right decision after all. These three guys were worth their weight in gold. They worked together, kept each other sane against idiot supervisors, often came out to drink and carouse. Good friends were important, even if Matt's time was limited. Maybe *because* his time was limited. If he was going to enjoy any of whatever life remained between now and the dark swallowing him down, he'd need friends to help him do it.

He skulled his pint and stood. "My round, boys. Drink up, ya weasels!"

* * *

Matt enjoyed the fresh air on the short walk from the Tube to his flat after the vomit stench that had accompanied him all the way in the train. Despite his misgivings he'd had a good night. Two more strippers had taken to the stage after the policeman. Whoever had organised that stag night had spared no expense and Matt was grateful.

He was comfortably pissed but not staggering drunk. Truth was, he seemed to have a capacity for alcohol that defied chemistry. He could get an enjoyable buzz happening, then continue to drink for hours without ever seeming to get any more inebriated. And he never passed out or had blackouts like his friends described, waking with no idea of what had gone on or how they'd got home. He felt mildly cheated by this state of affairs, but was happy not to have periods of time he couldn't remember. If he got so drunk he didn't know what he was doing, who knew what he might do with his dark talent.

He fumbled the key in the lock a couple of times, drunk enough to have lost some fine motor skills, and went inside with a bacon sandwich uppermost in his mind. His stomach rumbled audibly as he pushed the door closed. He stepped into the lounge room and started, ice filled his veins and sobriety crashed over him at the sight of three men, two holding guns levelled at his chest. He had rarely ever seen a gun, let alone been threatened with one. His knees became weak and trembled.

"What do you want, lads? You can have it." He pulled out his wallet. "You want money? I've not much, but you can have it all. Here, it's only about twenty quid."

Not men, these were little more than children. The tall, thin one in the middle wearing a pale blue track suit that was bright against his dark skin, waved his free hand. "No, no, nothing like that. Put your money away. We're simply being cautious. I'm Clancy, and these are my friends Dexter and Saul." Dexter had the other gun. Saul did his best to look mean without one.

"Right. Am I supposed to be pleased to meet you?"

"Not really, I suppose. My boss would like a chat with you, that's all."

The young fellow, he couldn't be more than seventeen or eighteen at most, did seem genuinely contrite. In fact, all three looked like nervous teenagers. "Serious fucking tools and numbers for an invite to a chat," he said. "Could you not have just left a note or something?"

"My boss is very keen to talk," Clancy said. "He wanted to make sure you accepted his invitation."

"It's after midnight and I'm pissed. I have to be up at six for work tomorrow. Can it not wait?"

"No, sorry."

"How about if I promise to come around wherever it is after work tomorrow? I finish at four."

"No, we really need to go now. We've been waiting here quite a while already."

Matt scanned the three faces. Dexter's serious, suspicious eyes, bright in skin darker than Clancy's. Saul's mean glare surrounded by freckles under a mop of red hair. Clancy with his polite manner and apologetic gaze. And something else. There was a genuine fear there that the other two didn't share, like Clancy knew something they didn't. All three, while nervous, seemed hardened and unforgiving. Tough kids with attitude that far outweighed their age or worth. They carried a weight of bitterness about them, a look of hurt behind the shields of assumed strength. "Who are you people?" Matt asked. "Who's your boss?"

"Better if he explains."

Matt felt idiotic capitulating to these children, even if two of them were armed. "What if I just say no? Are you really going to fucking shoot me?"

"I'll kneecap you," Clancy said calmly. "Then tourniquet your leg and take you to the Boss. You may lose the leg that way."

Matt's eyebrows rose. "Fuck me, lad. You're damaged goods, you know that?"

Clancy smiled and nodded. "The Boss saved me though. Saved all of us. You'll probably like him. Let's be off, eh?"

Matt threw up his hands, exasperated and thoroughly confused. He turned and walked back out the front door, sure the gun-toting teenagers would follow and direct him where to go.

FIVE

Amy Cavendish walked softly through the night-darkened corridors of Sally Gentle Hospice, feet silent on the deep burgundy carpet. In rooms to either side of her, afforded as much dignity as possible, people were dying. Amy enjoyed the night shift because it was usually quiet, and because most terminal patients seemed to slip away under cover of darkness. Even those who hadn't surfaced from unconsciousness for days or weeks seemed to somehow know when the sun was gone and shadows bathed the land, and they took that as their cue to leave.

Amy was no ghoul, hoping for death, but she wanted to be there when it happened. Her gift allowed her to ease that passing, just a little she hoped, and she could then use it for some kind of good. What the dying gave her, she had learned to pass on, to add a little justice to an unjust world.

She stepped into the doorway of Mrs. Ingrid Evangeline's room and watched the skeletal form under the light blanket. The old woman's breaths were a good fifteen seconds apart. Amy had been right. She moved to the side of the bed, sat in the visitor's chair and took Ingrid's long, thin hand between her palms. It felt like twigs and papyrus, thin as hope. The poor woman had no one to visit her, but hadn't woken for the last few days anyway. Regardless, Amy knew everyone died alone, even if they were surrounded by tear-stained friends and relatives. It was a journey of utter solitude. A good life, no regrets, was the best most could hope for.

Ingrid's breaths drew further apart every time, as if she must have died before a sudden, sharp, shallow gasp would buy her another thirty seconds of existence. Amy rested her head against the back of the old woman's hand and sensed the shadows rising. The darkness of her death, her suffering, began to move. *Here she goes*, Amy thought, and Ingrid hitched her last breath and died.

That shade of suffering swelled and Amy drew it into herself, stored it where she always had room for more. Where she could share it later with someone truly deserving. Maybe Amy's gift didn't actually ease the pain of the dying, or their loneliness, but she liked to think it gave them solace, something to recognise. A moment of sharing, a tiny legacy of what they had been. And when she passed it on, Amy wondered if perhaps the deceased were somewhere, with some inkling of the service they had provided through her. Though she doubted that last part.

But Amy had no choice in the matter. It was what she did, and along the way she was a damn good nurse too. Since she started in palliative care she had gathered the shadows of the lonely dead, for many years collecting them up inside, with no other purpose beyond the simple fact that she could. Then she fell in love with a burdened young man, Jake, abused and hurting. His story had filled her with a desire to exact some kind of revenge for him. And for the first time, it occurred to her that maybe she could let her stored shadows out, deliver them to someone deserving of the dark stain of death. Jake's abusive stepfather had been the first, had confirmed her suspicions. And she had found her calling, the reason for her gift. Collecting death from the innocent, delivering it to the wicked, where it would grow over weeks or months into consuming tumours and corruption, and hurry them from the mortal plane, horrified and confused. She had no idea where her gift came from, or why she had it, only that she did. And that it was her duty to use it.

She made a note of the time of Ingrid Evangeline's death, stood, and gently kissed the old woman's forehead. Then she left to start the paperwork, carrying the death shadow deep inside with all the others she had yet to release.

As she passed an open door on her way to the office a papery voice called out, "Hey, darlin'!"

Amy smiled slightly, shook her head. "What are you doing awake, Mr. Stratton?" she whispered from the doorway.

"Dying, love. Might as well make the most of life before I journey to that undiscovered country."

Amy's eyebrows rose. "Shakespeare, right?"

Old Terry Stratton shifted himself up a little on the bed, cleared his throat. "'For who would bear the whips and scorns of time,'" he said, his voice taking on a depth and sadness that grabbed at Amy's heart. "'The oppressor's wrong, the proud man's contumely, the pangs of despised love, the law's delay, the insolence of office and the spurns, that patient merit of the unworthy takes, when he himself might his quietus make with a bare bodkin? Who would fardels bear to grunt and sweat under a weary life, but that the dread of something after death, the undiscovered country from whose bourn no traveller returns, puzzles the will, and makes us rather bear those ills we have, than fly to others that we know not of? Thus conscience does make cowards of us all.' *Hamlet*, my love. Act three, Scene one."

Amy laughed softly. "Good grief, Mr. Stratton, you have hidden depths."

"So you got a bare bodkin, love? Maybe I'm not such a coward after all."

"I'm afraid not. But is there anything this side of suicide I can do to ease your comfort?" She kept her smile but winced inside. People should be allowed to let themselves out if they wanted to. If her chosen career had proven anything to be true, it was that simple fact of life. Of death. Dogs weren't allowed to suffer. But perhaps an injection rather than the bodkin.

The old man drew a bony hand back over his bald, liver-spotted brow. His eyes bulged in a sunken face, his cheekbones like shark fins through the receding sea of what was once a handsome visage. "Talk to me a minute, maybe?"

Amy walked into the room and sat beside the bed. Ingrid's paperwork could wait a while. "What would you like to talk about?"

"Anything, really. I just love to hear your accent. Where are you from again?"

"Sydney."

"That's right." Terry nodded knowingly. "I'm so glad you don't do that awful thing where you make every sentence a question. That horrible upswing on the last syllable."

"Oh, that bugs the hell out of me too," Amy said. "A lot of Aussies hate it."

"So why come to a pissing hole like London when you had that sunshine and ocean and Bondi Beach and all that?"

Amy smiled a little sadly. "I needed a fresh start."

Terry's eyes narrowed. "Love affair gone bad?"

"Very astute, Mr. Stratton."

"Tell me about it?"

Amy shook her head indulgently. "I learned a lot about myself in recent years, during a wonderful relationship with a guy called Jake. In some ways we saved each other, gave each other new purpose. But after nearly three years it kinda started to change. He has things he needs to go back and work out. We're still really good friends. Who knows what the future holds. But he needed space and I needed to get away for a while." She laughed. "Why am I telling you all this?"

"Cos I'm easy to talk to, love. And it makes me happy to think that people's lives are going on while I waste away. Your life has barely even started. What are you, twenty?"

"Don't be a flatterer. I'm twenty-seven."

"You don't look it, with that shiny blonde hair and smooth skin." He stared at her wistfully for moment, then looked away. "Forgive an old man. You make sure you live a good life. Don't let any opportunity slip you by for fear or a sense of duty, you hear me."

Amy tipped her head to one side. "Fear?"

"People could achieve so much, but they're fearful. They let it drag on them and they don't reach their heights. You make sure you don't give in to that kind of fucking inertia."

His words held the weight of time-earned wisdom. "Okay, Mr. Stratton. I promise."

"Call me Terry."

Amy patted his hand where it rested on the covers. "Terry."

"Vince didn't come today, did he?"

"Your son? He rang, don't you remember? Said he'd been caught up with business and would be by in the morning. Lots of hassles at his pub."

Terry nodded weakly, drawing a long breath in through his nose. "That's right. I get forgetful. All these drugs and things."

"But you remember Shakespeare."

"The Bard is eternal, my love." His eyelids fluttered. "I'm getting tired again. Bloody sleeping my way to death. Seems pointless. Sure you don't have any bodkins?"

"I'm sure, Terry. I'll let you rest."

"Thanks for talking with me."

"Of course. It's the least I can do." And she meant it. Interactions like these with the more lucid patients was time she truly valued, and she considered it an essential part of the job. "You sure there's nothing I can get you?"

"Nah, I just need to sleep." He opened his eyes and tipped her a crooked smile. "Fuck cancer, eh?"

Amy nodded. "Fuck cancer, Terry. Fuck it right in the eye."

He laughed softly, coughed and pressed a hand to his chest. With another weak smile he closed his eyes and was instantly asleep.

Amy watched him for a few moments more, wondering what he might have achieved in his eighty-six years. What did he let fear, or duty, prevent him from doing? And what did he do that no one else on earth before or since could ever do? She pulled his door quietly to and went to the office to start Ingrid Evangeline's paperwork.

* * *

A shadowy figure quietly picked the lock of Matt McLeod's basement flat and snuck inside, gently closing the door behind them. Using a small penlight torch, they began methodically scanning the premises, opening drawers and cupboards, looking between books on the overladen shelves. They found a laptop on the couch and sat down to peruse it, using a small USB thumb drive to crack the password encryption and access Matt's files. They copied several things from the computer's hard drive and moved into the kitchen, then the bedroom.

In a little under thirty minutes, they re-emerged into the cold night and clicked Matt's front door locked behind them. Taking confident strides up the ten steps to street level, they pulled a cell phone from the depths of a coat pocket and dialled Vince Stratton's number.

SIX

CLANCY UNLOCKED THE FRONT DOOR of a pub called Stratton's and led Matt inside. Dexter and Saul walked stoically behind. The drive out to Camden Town had taken a little less than ten minutes, but the whole journey had been done in tense silence. The pub was closed and dim, chairs on the tables and the smell of disinfectant and furniture polish ripe. Matt had never been to this bar before, and thought it might have been quite a good place for a drink under different circumstances. But with three angry teenagers guiding him through the empty space with their guns, it sucked balls. He was exhausted and adrenalised at the same time and quite frankly over everything. A long night was fast becoming interminable.

The young men sent him along a cool corridor at the back of the pub and a large, muscular middle-aged man with a full head of gunmetal hair stood in an office doorway at the end. He had a shadow of stubble on his pale face, a heavy brow, though his expression was welcoming. But despite the smile, and unlike the teenagers, this guy looked very dangerous.

"Mr. McLeod," the large man said. "So kind of you to come."

"Like I had any fucking choice."

"True, but thank you all the same. I'm Vince Stratton."

Matt jabbed a thumb back over his shoulder. "You know these

fucking children with hand cannons had me drive myself over here, all of us crammed in my little Golf? I'm a man with nothing to lose, you know. I seriously considered driving into a wall and killing us all. But it's London. I couldn't get enough speed up."

"I apologise. I can certainly recompense you the petrol money, perhaps?"

"Who are you people, the Gangster Mickey Mouse Club or something?"

Stratton laughed, quite genuinely. "Not at all, Mr. McLeod. And we're certainly not gangsters. These boys are the lost and the broken, in need of help, and I give them purpose."

Matt's eyes narrowed. "Oh aye? And what do they give you in return?"

"Nothing like that. They work for me, help me with business, and they get paid, board and lodging, a direction in life, if you will."

"Business? Running a pub?"

"This place is not my only interest, Mr. McLeod."

"Will you stop calling me that? My name's Matt."

"Of course, and call me Vince. Please, excuse me for a moment." He looked past Matt to the three milling in the corridor. "Dexter, Saul, thank you. Why don't you both head on home. It's late." They nodded and turned away. Stratton gestured into the office behind him. "Clancy, join us inside a moment."

Stratton walked ahead of them and casually pulled a gun from his pocket as he went. He gestured to draw attention to it and made an apologetic face.

"What is it with the fucking guns?" Matt asked.

"I won't bullshit you, McLeod. I know you're a killer, and I know you can finish me with a touch. Please come in."

Matt's knees went weak for the second time that night. How could this weird pub landlord and his band of merry munchkins possibly know about the dark? Just what the hell was going on? Reluctantly, as if he hauled his legs through wet cement, he walked into the office.

Stratton sat behind his desk, the gun still in his hand resting carelessly on a large ink blotter. He looked entirely comfortable with it, like he was no stranger to firearms at all. Completely unlike the three lads and their nervousness behind hard man façades.

Stratton indicated that Matt sit opposite him, then turned his attention to Clancy, held out his hand. Clancy handed over his pistol. "Not fired I take it? Mr. McLeod seems entirely unventilated."

"No, Boss."

"Good-o. Now, it seems a business opportunity has come up. Go to dead drop four and collect, will you?"

Clancy nodded. "Okay. Four's a long way out now, though, and this time of night—"

Stratton silenced him with a raised palm and pulled out his wallet. He rummaged and extracted a twenty pound note. "Get a taxi."

The gangly lad nodded and scurried off. Stratton returned his attention to Matt.

"Now then, we have much to discuss."

"Just who are you?" The man's easy confidence and casual manner frightened Matt. Combined with what this guy seemed to know, Matt had the feeling he was falling into a deep well from which he might never climb free.

"I'm just Vince Stratton," Vince Stratton said. "I'm certainly not about to tell you the extent of my business. Even my boys don't know that. It's what makes them useful."

"They do all your running around and have nothing on you if they get picked up by the law?"

Stratton smiled broadly, like a predator. "The law? Why would they get picked up by the police?"

Anger flared in Matt's gut. "Just stop fucking me around, will you. I'm drunk, tired, and thoroughly pissed off. The last thing I want to do is plumb the depths of your weird fucking Fagin-fetish lifestyle. What do you want with me? Why did you call me a killer?"

Stratton nodded. "If we're cutting straight through all the bullshit, Matt, that has to go both ways. You can kill with a touch. You were witnessed doing so, and I have evidence of the result." He held up his phone to show a photograph of John Sullivan's rain-soaked corpse lying in the bin. "You really should plan better and dispose of the body more carefully," Stratton said, mouth twisted in disapproval.

"I usually do, but sometimes it's not so easy. This one hurt a lot and I just had to get out of there. I've only ever left a body once before. It's not something I plan to make a habit of."

"You're a real amateur. Yet it sounds like you've done a lot of this."

Matt laughed. What was the point of lying, given everything Stratton clearly knew? "Of course I'm an amateur! It's not like there's a fucking university course for this shit or something. There are no apprenticeships for what I am. But I should have sucked it up and taken the body."

"Yes, you should. But you were spotted in action anyway, so as far as you and I are concerned, taking the body or not isn't the issue."

Matt rubbed a hand over his face. "So that's it. Clancy saw me, did he?"

"What makes you think it was Clancy?"

"Because of the three children you sent to pick me up, he was the only one scared of me."

Stratton raised an eyebrow. "Observant." He leaned forward, elbows on the desk, chin on his hands. "What the fuck are you, Matthew McLeod?"

"Like you said, it goes both ways. How about you start by telling me what you are, Vince?"

"I'm a killer too, Matt. Let's leave it at that. I recognise you, on a level deeper than skin, darker than night."

Matt flinched inside at the man's sudden and strangely poetic reference to the dark. But of course, it was a turn of phrase, not an actual knowledge. How much could he tell this guy about the details of his activities and get away without giving too much of himself? "I'm on a mission of redemption," Matt said slowly, the words strange. He had never vocalised before just what it was he did. He'd never needed to. "I'm dying, Vince, and I have no idea how long I have left. But I have this skill to atone and I'm using it. Simple as that."

"It really is quite something," the big man said "Clancy showed me his video—"

"Video?"

"Yes, you really were careless tonight."

Matt grimaced. What was wrong with him, to have messed up so thoroughly? Perhaps he was becoming complacent. Or just too tired of it all.

"You can do that at will?" Stratton asked.

"Sure. Not without cost. It hurts like fuck and I need time and isolation. I knew I was taking a bit of a risk with Sullivan, but I couldn't get close to him otherwise. I knew he always walked through that alley after his AA meeting. I kept an eye out, but your boy was obviously sneakier than I thought."

"Why Sullivan?"

"Because he was a fucking kiddie fiddler and that shit cannot be rehabilitated."

"So you executed him."

"Yep."

The two men stared at each other over the desk for several silent moments. Eventually Stratton nodded and stood. He went to his drinks cabinet and poured two generous measures of Talisker single malt scotch.

"I'm guessing you're a whisky drinker?"

Matt snorted. "Because I'm Scottish? You racist bastard." He reached for the glass anyway. He was a whisky drinker, but fuck this guy.

"No offence meant," Stratton said, resuming his seat. "How did you know Sullivan was a pedo? Why haven't the police taken him in?"

"Usual shit. Nothing could quite stick, no one would press charges. I spent months gathering information, talking to people. It's what I do."

"Fascinating." Stratton sipped his drink, seemingly lost in thought. "Let me ask you something else, Matt. Can you continue what you did there until there's nothing left?"

"What do you mean?"

"Well, your ability reduced that large man to little more than bones. Can you reduce someone further? To nothing?"

Matt's eyes narrowed as he considered where this might be leading. "Can I do that and leave nothing behind but clothes, you mean?"

Stratton nodded, lips pursed.

"Well, I've never tried. It hurts so much that once the body is a manageable collection of bones that I can easily break up, I stop. But theoretically, yes, I suppose I could." He chose not to mention that it would likely kill him too.

"Well, isn't that interesting," Stratton said with a smile.

"Can I go now?"

"No. Not yet." The phone on Stratton's desk rang and he smiled. "Perfect timing. Excuse me a moment, please." He kept his eyes locked to Matt's as he answered. "Yes. Righto, very good." He scribbled notes rapidly on a pad beside the phone and grinned. "Thank you."

Stratton's gaze was intense when he replaced the receiver, still grinning.

"What the fuck is your deal, man?" Matt asked.

"Your mother's name is Helen. She's a housewife. Your father is Daniel, he works for a construction business just outside Edinburgh. They live in a nice detached house in Longniddry."

Matt's blood ran cooler, but he ground his teeth and held his silence. It had been a long time since he'd seen his parents and his guilt weighed heavily. What did Stratton expect to gain from this implicit threat?

"No siblings, no partner, but I'm sure you love your folks," Stratton said.

"And?"

"And you'd like them to stay safe and well."

"What do you want from me?"

"Your services."

Silence descended between them again. Eventually Matt said, "I'm a dead man walking. I'll top myself before I work for a gangster like you."

Stratton frowned. "I told you, I'm not a gangster. I don't like the word or the people, though I admit I sometimes have to work for them to meet my bills. Regardless, if you kill yourself, I will kill your parents."

Matt ground the heels of his hands into his eye sockets until he saw dancing colours. "What services exactly?"

"I want you to kill for me, Matt. You don't tell Clancy or any of my boys anything about what we do. You work autonomously, do whatever it is you feel you need to do, for whatever reason. I'm not here to curtail your atonement."

"How very fucking magnanimous of you."

"But when I call on you and give you a target, you will take them out for me. And leave nothing behind."

"Or you'll kill my parents."

"And anyone else even vaguely close to you. Your friends, colleagues, girlfriend, should I find out about one."

Matt barked a laugh. "Chance would be a fine thing. It's not easy to pick up girls when you're in my position."

"Well. Even so."

"I only kill people truly deserving of a nasty death, Mr. Stratton." Matt's voice sounded wheedling and he hated himself for it, but he would do anything to be out of this situation. "I research in great depth and make absolutely sure, and only kill when I'm certain. I'm not cut out for random murder!"

Stratton leaned forward on his elbows. "My business is built on not asking questions, but simply acting on request. Naturally I assess risks, but I don't make any emotional or ethical judgements."

"I fucking do!" Matt shouted. "I can't do this for you."

Stratton grinned like a shark. "But you have to."

An abyss dropped open beneath Matt and all concerns fell into it. He tensed, about to leap over the desk and deliver the dark to this big, frightening bastard who claimed he wasn't a gangster. No more evidence was required after a confession like that.

Even as Matt's feet began to press against the floor to launch him forward Stratton whipped up the gun and pointed it right between Matt's eyes.

"The next to die after you hit my carpet will be your parents."

Matt sank back into his seat, muscles become jelly. He closed his eyes, frustrated and helpless.

"If I have to kill you, I *will* kill them right after," Stratton said calmly. "If you go to the police about me in any way, they will die.

I can have them killed even if I'm in a cell. If you do anything other than what I say, your parents will die slowly and painfully and they will know, during every second of their agony, that it's your fault."

Matt winced at the word 'fault'. So much in his life was his fault. So much was destroyed by his actions. He should have killed himself a long time ago and ended the prospect of further hurt to anyone, but he thought he'd been doing well. His atonement was actually having a positive effect on the world, however small that effect might be. But now this. "Fine." He would have to think his way around the problem and find a way out. Meanwhile, he hopefully wouldn't have to kill anyone too innocent. Whatever that even meant.

He looked up, eyes defiant. "It's not something I can do often, you know. You can't use me like a fucking machine gun. I killed tonight, it'll be days at least, maybe weeks, before I can do it again." It was the truth and he wondered if he would have been able to take out Stratton a moment ago, after all. Maybe the rage, the desperation, would have lent him strength. And it would probably have killed him. But so what?

"You need to recharge?"

"I guess so, something like that. And I only have a finite time left, a finite number of kills left in me. Any time one of them might finish me off. It might be the next."

Stratton nodded. "Fair enough. Well, you head home and recharge, and I'll get one good hit out of you, at least."

"Are you really an assassin outsourcing your fucking targets? Is that what's happening here?"

Stratton laughed, nodded. "I suppose so. But I'll save you for the most deserving. For a job that requires something a little special. Your particular touch."

"Oh, well, that's good then. But why? Why exercise this power over me?"

"Because I can. Because a hit with no body is very useful. Because there's so little new in my game that this is irresistible." Stratton took a mobile phone from his drawer and slid it across the desk. "We won't ever meet in the flesh again. This is a burner phone, untraceable.

Only I will call on it. Don't use it for any other reason. There's no credit for outgoing calls or texts anyway. When I need you, I'll call, so keep it charged."

Stratton stood and gestured with the gun. "After you."

"Oh, I can go now?" Matt jammed the phone into his jacket pocket.

"Of course. I'll look forward to…"

Matt didn't hear the rest as he strode from the room and down the cool corridor. He stomped out through the bar and kicked open the pub door hard enough to break the glass. He was disappointed when it didn't actually break. Maybe he couldn't kick as hard as he thought he could. Or maybe it was toughened glass. Bulletproof? The thought seemed both absurd and likely at the same time.

His Golf was parked at the curb and he climbed in. Just his luck, he'd probably be stopped for drunk driving now and lose his licence. As he gunned the small engine and peeled away from the curb, he saw Vince Stratton, a solid silhouette filling the pub entrance, watching.

SEVEN

DETECTIVE SERGEANT CHARLIE COLLINS sat in his penthouse flat staring at eight-by-tens. He sipped from a can of Special Brew and wished he was snorting some fine white instead. He would have to lean on the Yardies again and get a parcel for his ongoing protection. He knew he was kidding himself. They owned him far more than he owned them. Same with the mob, the Poles, the Russians. Every crooked bastard had a handle on Charlie Collins, but he had access like no other cop. Sure, he was bent, but he got shit done. Let the small stuff go and catch the big fish, the murderers, the paedophiles, the rapists. Mobsters could ruin each other ten ways till Sunday for all he cared. He'd concentrate on protecting real people.

Like the body in the photographs spread out on his coffee table. Who was this guy and what the hell happened to him? And why did Vince Stratton mention it? Talking of people who had Charlie over a barrel, Vince was a master. And Charlie didn't even know exactly what it was Stratton did, except protest far too loudly, far too often, that he wasn't a gangster. But he did like to wind up Charlie whenever he got the chance, like randomly mentioning this body lying all blackened and broken in an alley near The Angel. How had Stratton known? And why did he mention it, then ask for some random check on a car owned by…

Charlie shuffled paperwork. Matthew McLeod. A nobody warehouseman. Arrived in London from Edinburgh about a decade ago, same job and home for the last eight years. No record, no priors, no reason to matter to anyone. Was there a connection between the body in the alley and this seemingly irrelevant Scotsman? Had Vince Stratton's need to annoy Charlie caused him to inadvertently give away a nugget of useful information? If that was the case, he couldn't figure out what it was, and no doubt that was Stratton's comfort, but Charlie's innate detective senses were tingling. Something was going on here. Was there a connection between McLeod and the stiff? Or McLeod and Stratton? Or Stratton and the stiff? Or all fucking three?

Charlie shifted stuff around again and moved a different set of photographs to the top of the pile. He stared at the shots of a withered, blackened corpse in a toilet stall. The body had been found in the changing rooms of a sports field in Hendon a little over two years previously. The killer had never been found, the method unsolved. Several people wanted to put it down to a burning, but there were no scorch marks in the cubicle, no other damage, and the clothing was perfectly intact. A loose narrative had been created whereby the victim had been burned, then dressed and left in the cubicle to be discovered. But forensics said it really didn't bear the hallmarks of burning. More like the body had been drained of all moisture, desiccated like an Egyptian mummy, left somewhere dry for years on end. But something else had occurred too. A kind of disruption of the flesh and organs on a cellular level. The bones were brittle like chalk. None of the experts brought in had any answers, most were more than a little disturbed by it, and the ridiculous burning and dumping story persisted despite the evidence. Or perhaps because of the *lack* of it. When something remained unexplained for long enough, people tended to move on to other, more immediate concerns. Problems they could solve.

It remained an open case, but no one at the station ever expected it to go any further, like so many cold cases, unsolved murders, strange deaths, lost properties. But Charlie had a habit of remembering this stuff and when Stratton's strange tip-off, or slip-up, had led to an almost identical corpse, Collins had dug out the old paperwork.

The sports field had been empty of people at the time and the body discovered by a young boy who had run back an hour after his soccer training to pick up a shirt he'd accidentally left behind. Charlie picked up the witness statement:

> *I went back in because the changing rooms was still unlocked and I would of got in big trouble if I lost my shirt. I heard a noise and called out, "Anyone here? I left my shirt." A man suddenly appeared and he looked proper spooked and his face was all twisted like he was in pain or something. It really scared me and I lied and said, "My dad is right outside waiting for me! He's a big man and a boxer and he'll kick the crap out of you." He wasn't really outside, but he is a boxer and I was scared.*
>
> *So the man looked around in a panic, maybe thinking my dad was coming right for him then and there. Then he said, "Fuck it!" and legged it right past me and ran away. I was really scared but I snatched my shirt off the bench and was going to run away too, but I realised the man had gone and I was safe. I went to see where he'd come from and found the black body in the toilet. It was horrible. I screamed and ran all the way home and told my dad and he called the police.*
>
> *The man I saw in the changing rooms was short and skinny, not much bigger than me. He was wearing dark clothes and black boots. He only said, "Fuck it!" but I don't think he sounded like he was from London. He had a weird accent. His hair was black and a bit long and curly.*

Joshua Headley, age 12
Bell Lane, Hendon

Charlie Collins frowned. *He had a weird accent.* Scottish, perhaps? Was Matt McLeod a small fellow with lots of black curly hair? Without a record, Charlie had no way to check, but he did have vehicle details. He could check McLeod's driver's licence mugshot from records with the DVLA when he got back to the office in the morning. He glanced at his watch. Nearly 3:00 a.m.

"Bollocks," he muttered. It was almost time to get up and go to work anyway. He had more and more trouble sleeping lately. Always tired but never inclined to go to bed.

He dragged himself up, took a piss before he went to try a few hours of tossing and turning on his expensive sheets. Just some of the benefits of enhancing his police salary, but he was still a policeman and he still fought for justice. And he was definitely onto something here. Some connection between Matt McLeod, Vince Stratton and these two bodies, more than two years apart. Was McLeod a runner, dumping corpses for someone else? Why leave one in a sports field toilet and one in a dumpster? And why or how was Stratton involved? Maybe he was the killer. Or perhaps Stratton and McLeod's partnership was a new thing, in which case Charlie would have to figure out what they had to gain from each other. After all, Stratton had wanted the car owner traced, and that implied he had no knowledge of McLeod until tonight. So maybe the two men had never met and Stratton was tracking McLeod for reasons as yet unknown. That left the corpse an outlier, unless he could connect McLeod and the guy with curly black hair and a strange accent.

Regardless, Charlie had a bunch of puzzle pieces and he knew there must be a way to fit them together. He downed the last of the super-strength beer and scuffed through to his bedroom. He fell face-first onto the king-size bed and hoped some answers might come to him in whatever state of semi-consciousness or unconsciousness he managed before dawn.

EIGHT

Amy Cavendish quietly made a meal while her flatmate slept. Amy's shift finished at 6:00 a.m. and Carla wouldn't be up until seven thirty to get ready for her day job. They'd chat while Amy ate her dinner and Carla her breakfast, often the only time they ever saw each other on any given day. Strange for two people living under the same small roof, but it worked for them both.

Amy's chat with old Terry Stratton hung heavily on her mind. The way he quoted Shakespeare so eloquently, then talked of the inertia of fear. It rang true and Amy silently promised him again she wouldn't let fear hold her back from anything. Like fear held Carla back from dumping that idiot Quentin, for example.

As the pasta boiled on the stove, Amy opened her laptop and pulled up the password-protected files she kept under innocuous and meaningless names. Her research had led her to a few likely candidates for the next release of the shadows of the dead. She needed to decide who was most deserving and how she might get access to them, and an excuse to touch.

She flipped through photos and paused when she came to Arthur Prentiss, MBE. Her extensive research had made him her prime target. Businessman extraordinaire, one of the richest men in Britain, lauded for his entrepreneurism, fawned over by the wealthy and elite. But also a bastard who had twice got off with serious assaults on women, had several times been accused of ripping off the vulnerable and poor, and barely stayed within the law when it came to his business dealings. She had spent time digging and learned of a number of human rights abuses glossed over in his various international interests. Plus further assaults that hadn't made the mainstream media, and a number of deaths in sub-Saharan Africa the man had cleverly concealed. But legally, no one could touch him. The man was a grade-A evil bastard.

She scrolled through a document where she had gathered excerpts from articles detailing his extensive sweatshop operations, his almost occult tax avoidance methods, and a dozen other crimes that could never be pinned on him well enough to stick. Or were crimes in everything but legal name. No one became as wealthy and powerful as Prentiss without seriously screwing people over left, right and centre. It took a particular kind of arsehole to rise to Prentiss's level of influence and affluence, and he didn't even pay lip service to altruism with charitable trusts or donations of any kind. He was the worst kind of right-wing capitalist and embodied everything Amy considered wrong with the modern world, quite aside from his personal infractions. Amy's blood boiled at the very thought of his existence. How much misery did this man create for his own selfish ends?

She nodded softly to herself. This son of a bitch was the most deserving of her next excursion. She'd been watching him, looking for an opportunity, for months now. Time to check again if there was a way to arrange to meet him. She began some new searches.

"Arthur Prentiss?" Carla said from the kitchen door. "Why are you reading about him?"

Her heavy Spanish accent always charmed Amy, but this time it made her jump and she quickly closed the laptop and turned back to the stove. "Just scanning the news," she said.

"Who's he bought this time?"

Amy laughed. "Half the world, probably. You're up early."

"I couldn't sleep."

Amy stirred her pasta once with a wooden spoon then turned to Carla. "You okay? Worried about something?"

Carla winced, started to shake her head, then shrugged.

"Quentin Barker, maybe?" Amy suggested.

Carla let out a small, rueful laugh. "Yes. Of course. Isn't it always him?"

"What did he do this time?"

Carla moved to the counter to make coffee and put bread in the toaster. "We were supposed to go out for dinner last night. It's the one-year anniversary since we met. He booked a nice table at a fancy restaurant and everything. Like he was really trying, you know? Like he cared."

"What happened?"

"He was supposed to pick me up here at seven last night, but he called at six thirty and said he'd been held up with a difficult client and I should take a taxi to the restaurant, he'd meet me there at seven thirty. So I did. And at seven forty-five he texted to say how sorry he was that he was still running late and I should go ahead and order. Can you believe that? On my own in a restaurant looking like a complete loser."

Amy drained the pasta and stirred in a ready-made sauce. "Fucking loser. He's a big-shot lawyer, Carla. That makes him an arsehole by definition." She'd like to give him a taste of her talent, but he didn't really qualify. There were a million shitbags like Quentin Barker in central London alone. She needed to save her skills for the truly deserving. "So what happened?"

"I texted back and said that I would not order and when was he getting there. He didn't reply. So I rang and he didn't answer. At eight o'clock I rang again and he still didn't answer and I left. I was so embarrassed, all nicely dressed and stood up like that."

Amy put down her fork and stood to give Carla a hug. "I'm so sorry. He's such a dickhead. Why don't you just dump his sorry arse?"

"I should, I know."

"What did he say about you leaving? Anything?"

Carla shrugged, kept her eyes down as she buttered her toast. "He still hasn't answered my calls or texts. I have no intention of contacting him again until he does."

"And then what?"

"I don't know."

Amy hugged Carla once more, then returned to her meal. "You're a beautiful woman, great at your job, vibrant and wonderful in every way. You need to give him an ultimatum. Tell him to shape up or you're gone, back to Madrid. Or, if you want to stay in London and stick with the PA position you have, just dump him anyway. Guys would line up to date someone as hot as you, you know that!"

Carla laughed, but it was a slightly sad sound. "Shut up, Amy."

"You know it's true. And besides, who needs a man anyway? You're all those things on your own. And you're better off on your own than being dicked around by a loser like Quentin."

Carla nodded, chewing absently on toast. "I don't know why I put up with it. I know I don't need to. I know I don't need anyone."

"You want a drink tonight? You finish at five thirty, right? I don't start until nine. Let's have a few drinks in between and all the dickhead men can go and jump off a cliff."

"Thanks, Amy. Yes, let's do that." She kissed Amy's cheek and took her coffee and toast in hand. "I might take this back to bed. The Garrison at six o'clock?"

Amy grinned. "Perfect. I'll see you there."

"Thank you, Amy."

Carla went back to her room and Amy felt as though she had at least done a small thing to make the poor girl feel better. Quentin really was a bastard, she had no idea why Carla persisted. There must be something in it. Maybe he was amazing in bed. He was certainly rich and good-looking, but he knew it, and that was ugly. Still, she would enjoy a few drinks with her flatmate this evening before work and maybe she could press home her case for leaving him.

Meanwhile, she went back online and started researching the movements and engagements of Arthur Prentiss, MBE.

NINE

MATT DRAGGED HIMSELF TO WORK the next morning, clocking in for his 7:30 a.m. start. A heavy hand slapped his shoulder as he headed for the roster room.

"Good night last night!" Ben's wide smile and rested visage made Matt grind his teeth. But it wasn't Ben's fault.

"Aye," he said. "Some top entertainment was had by all."

"We should do it more often."

"Crash unsuspecting stag parties with strippers?"

"Well, yeah. But I just mean catch up and have a few beers, you know? You're a good bloke, McLeod. You shouldn't hole yourself up at home so much. How about we go out and score some good fillies next time? I reckon you could use a shag."

Matt grinned despite his fatigue. "I could at that. Not sure I'm up for going out on the pull tonight though."

Ben's eyes narrowed. "Yeah, you look really ragged. You hungover? We didn't drink that much last night."

"I'm more tired than hungover. Didn't sleep much."

"Ha! You should have drunk more then! Let's organise something soon, though, yeah?"

"Yeah, we will."

He watched Ben stride off for the forklift and his day's work. The confidence of the guy's swagger, arms held wide from his body, made Matt shake his head. All bollocks and armpits, as his dad would have said.

Thinking of his dad made Matt sag with fatigue again, and a dull anger pulsed in his gut. That fucking Stratton, threatening his parents. It was only a further weight on the burden of guilt that Matt kept so far apart from his folks. He genuinely loved them, but how could they ever love him if they knew? They still doted on him. He'd been a distant child after he let the dark in. Aloof, the counsellors called him. He seemed to attract trouble, always a loner, eaten by what he'd done. At sixteen, he'd said he needed to stretch his wings and had quit school as soon as he was able, and run to London. His parents called and wrote often, always emailing him pictures of their lives, enquiring after his, telling him they loved him. It twisted his insides. He loved them and now this apparently-not-a-gangster bastard was threatening their lives.

The ghost of Tommy drifted in Matt's mind. Tiny, innocent Tommy, the source of it all. Matt knew two things with absolute certainty. One, he had to protect his parents. Two, he had to continue to pay back Tommy. Vince Stratton was interfering with both those convictions. The man needed to be removed from the equation. Matt had the means, but Stratton was smart and wise to Matt's skills. Getting close would not be easy, but he had to. And the man deserved to die. Aside from the personal threat, he was definitely deep in the ranks of the truly bad. Matt could take him out, remove the threat to his parents, dedicate the kill to Tommy, *and* it would be a public service. He would fix his problems and be back on track. Or dead, if the next one did finish him, but things would be nicely wrapped up. Maybe his next kill would be his last, taking out Sullivan had been that hard.

He tentatively probed the darkness deep within himself. It lashed forward, hungry to be released, to consume. Weakness flooded his muscles as he pressed it back down. He was still far too weak to control it, needed more time to recover from the Sullivan hit. But he could use that recovery time.

He knew Stratton's place. He would stake it out, use the skills he'd developed with his previous activity and learn the bastard's pattern of movements. Figure out a way to get close when the big man least expected it. All he needed was a few seconds of skin-to-skin contact and the victim quickly became too feeble to fight back. The actual death always took a minute or two, but the strike was fairly quick. He wondered if he *could* push the power to reduce a person to nothing but dust as Stratton had asked. It wasn't something he'd considered before and he wondered why. After all, burning a pile of clothes was easy compared to getting rid of the rickety corpses his work usually left. It hurt so much to get that far that he had never pushed it further. It took a mind like Stratton's, he supposed, to consider the case for pushing harder. Maybe Stratton himself could be the lab rat in that particular experiment.

A powerful sense of purpose settled over Matt as he took his worksheet and headed out into the warehouse. Tonight he needed to rest, he felt as though he could sleep for a week. Yesterday had been ridiculous, but tomorrow he would start casing Stratton's pub and plan his next hit. And if the bastard sent word of a job before that strike of his own was ready? Wait and see. He could claim he wasn't charged up yet, incapable, until he was ready to hit Stratton himself. Matt smiled as he started work, feeling like he was taking back some control of the situation.

* * *

The early twilight of late autumn made everything gloomy as Charlie Collins sat in his Benz watching the row of old Victorian houses. The cold and wet persisted, but the combination of heated seats and hot air blowing from the dash kept him quite comfortable. The addition of a good dark rum was an unnecessary but welcome bonus.

The houses he watched had long ago been converted into flats and the one belonging to Matthew McLeod was murky behind its street-level, black anodised fence. The scrollwork atop the fencing was an interesting variety of curlicue, and the stone steps leading down to Matt's front door were scalloped with age. Collins wondered how many feet on what kinds of business had slowly worn that granite away. The history of London was fascinating to him, the idea that hundreds of generations had walked these streets, first dirt, then cobbles, now tarmac.

Movement down the road caught his attention and he stilled his wandering mind. A short fellow in dark boots and a heavy black donkey jacket strolled along, hands thrust deep into his pockets. He had shaggy, dark hair, slightly curly, a little over his collar. The guy looked dead tired, face ashen, head hanging.

Collins scanned the statement from Joshua Headley, age twelve, of Bell Lane, Hendon.

> *The man I saw in the changing rooms was short and skinny, not much bigger than me. He was wearing dark clothes and black boots... He had a weird accent. His hair was black and a bit long and curly.*

The guy in the donkey jacket couldn't be more than five feet eight or nine. A policeman's eye was well-trained to make accurate estimates on that stuff. And he was skinny. The clothing matched, as did the hair. When the small man turned and trotted down the steps to Matthew McLeod's basement flat and let himself in with a key, Collins allowed himself a small smile of satisfaction.

Stratton had screwed up in his boastfulness and let a little too much information slip. What the connections were was still a mystery, but Collins was convinced now that the body in the toilet stall in Hendon, the one last night near The Angel, and this McLeod guy were all somehow related. And those things also led back to Vince Stratton. He would pin something on that smug prick yet.

Keeping his cards close to his chest was key at this stage. Patience and careful observation were required. Collins jotted a few notes in his trusty Moleskine and put the car in gear to head home. Before anything else, he needed to gather every bit of information he could about Matthew McLeod, so it was time to call in some details from the DVLA, Social Services, and anyone else that might have a tiny

nugget of useful fodder to feed the growing profile he needed before he started cracking heads together to see what fell out.

TEN

Amy stared at the laptop with a smile, unable to believe her luck. After a little more research that morning she had grown tired and gone to bed, planning to learn more later. Now, sitting at the kitchen bench sipping coffee, she had discovered that Prentiss was throwing a huge industry gala the following night in a big hotel at Canary Wharf.

Prentiss had a finger in many industries and one of those was movie-making. He acted as producer on a wide variety of projects and regularly showed off his standing in society by hosting these lavish events, packed to the gills with celebrities and wealthy aristocrats, all fawning over each other and shoring up each other's need to be loved and validated. No doubt also sharing the latest exploitative money-making scheme, favours for the elite. She wondered how many of them were also getting away with literal murder like Prentiss.

Friday's event was to celebrate the deal to make another in the unfathomably popular *Hot Pursuit* franchise. Amy could only think of the movies as barely veiled homoerotic fantasies for rev-heads, but the films raked in millions, loved by men and women alike around the world. Each consecutive one had more stars, bigger stars, a more lavish budget, more insane computer-generated car chases around some of the world's most beautiful cities. This latest instalment, *Hot*

Pursuit: Berlin Burnout, sounded truly dire, but the list of big Hollywood names attached was impressive. And, of course, Arthur Prentiss was producer, raking in more dough. But by far the best thing about Friday's party was that it was being organised by Raven Events & Media. And Raven was run by Caroline French, one of Amy's few friends in London. Her patience watching Prentiss all this time had finally paid off.

Amy had done some hostess work for Caroline to make ends meet when she first arrived in the city after answering a temp agency advertisement. They had become friends and when Amy got the job at the Sally Gentle Hospice, they had kept in touch. Amy tapped fingertips to her lips, trying to figure out her best angle. Eventually she messaged Carla, suggesting they change their drinks that night from The Garrison to Scully's Bar. It was almost certain that Caroline would be at Scully's. She was there most nights she wasn't working.

Carla pinged her a text back almost immediately.

No probs. See you there in thirty.

Amy felt bad, shifting her focus this way, but she could still be a good friend to Carla and spend a few minutes buttering up Caroline while she was at it. The following night's party was too good a chance to pass up and there wasn't much time to get on top of things.

She got dressed and made up, put her work clothes in a bag and headed for her car. She found parking only two streets from Scully's and walked briskly to fight off the biting November cold. At least the rain had stopped for the time being. Sydney never had weather like this and it wasn't even proper winter yet. She was a little concerned about just how cold it might get and how she would cope. But she was a little excited by the prospect too. She almost walked straight into Carla coming the other way.

"Hi! Perfect timing."

Carla grinned, squeezed her in an enthusiastic hug. "Let's get inside. I'm freezing! I'll never get used to British winters."

"I'm looking forward to my first!"

Carla laughed, shook her head. "You wait and see."

They bought wine and sat on stools around a tall table in the trendy bar. The place was heated far beyond necessary in that truly

English way. Amy smiled to herself. Just like it would be air-conditioned to Arctic levels at the slightest hint of warmth come spring. Most Australian venues used the same overcompensations.

"Why did you want to come here?" Carla asked. Her expression betrayed her dislike of the place.

Amy gave in to the guilt. "Honestly, I'm hoping to bump into a friend who I need a quick chat with. I'm sorry, I hope you don't mind. It'll only take a few minutes, and otherwise I'm here just for you."

Carla flapped a hand. "Don't worry about it! I don't mind. It's nice just to be out. I'm happy to meet your other friends. But you couldn't just call her for a quick chat?"

"She's the kind of person who responds well to face-to-face interaction. And she hardly ever answers her phone or messages without a several day delay. I need to ask her a favour before the weekend."

Carla nodded. "Fair enough. She sounds interesting."

"That's an understatement. So any word from dickhead? I mean, Quentin?" Amy gave an evil grin to show she was joking, but they both knew she really wasn't.

Carla grinned back, then her face fell. Her big brown eyes were suddenly wet.

Amy jumped up and ran around to hug her. "I'm so sorry! Are you okay?"

"It's all right. It's not your fault. He did message me. Called me a stroppy bitch for flouncing out of the restaurant and not waiting for him."

Amy kept an arm around her friend. "Seriously? Those are the words he used?"

"Yes. Stroppy bitch and flounce. These are words uniquely British and so chauvinistic."

"They really are."

"He said I embarrassed the hell out of him because he arrived at the restaurant about ten minutes after I left and was made to look a fool."

"He left you sitting there on your own for an hour!"

Carla nodded, took a long swig of wine. "I know. I rang him and told him that. Told him he was a selfish, insensitive bastard." Carla put the glass to her lips, but paused, looked over the rim at Amy. "And I told him he could get fucked, we're over."

Amy jumped and clapped her hands. "I'm so sorry, Carla, but I'm so happy for you! He really is a bastard and you don't need him. You're better off without him."

Carla smiled sadly, nodded. "I was kinda dreaming about marrying him and living among his wealth and privilege, you know? I liked the idea of joining the aristocracy. His family is old Britain."

Amy returned to her seat and lifted her glass in a toast. "I get that, but I guarantee you can find someone else far better than him. British aristocracy is not all it's cracked up to be." She thought of Arthur Prentiss as she spoke. "And even then, I bet you can find a way into the aristocracy without resorting to shits like him, if that's what you really want."

Carla clinked glasses. "I know. It was a silly dream, blinding me to the horrible truth. I feel, I don't know, lighter. I feel better than I have in months!"

Amy tapped glasses with her again. "I will drink to that!"

She caught a glimpse of long, platinum hair and a tight leopard-print dress. A triumphant *Yes!* nearly escaped her lips. "I'll get us another round," she said. "I can't drink too much before work, but your news needs celebrating. And I just saw my friend come in. I'll be one minute, okay?"

She slipped from her stool and cut through the rapidly thickening crowd. Thursday was the new Friday in London, and bars were usually packed before seven. A place as currently in vogue as Scully's especially. She caught Caroline's eye and waved.

"Amy!" Caroline grabbed her in a tight hug, all hip bones and sharp shoulders.

Caroline was a great person, but she existed almost solely on stress and cocaine. Amy wondered how long she could last in this business.

"How are you?" Amy asked. "It's been too long!"

"Oh, you know," Caroline almost sang, "Busy, busy, making sure everyone is sucking the right dicks."

"But still frequenting Scully's!"

Caroline laughed, looked distastefully around the space, all mirrors and chrome and faux decadence. "This place has about three months to go before it's just another washed-up wine bar. But for now, it's still the place to be seen. Not really your scene though."

Amy made an apologetic face. "Actually, I was hoping to bump into you."

"Oh? You need something?" Caroline winked expansively.

"Not like that! I saw that you're hosting the Arthur Prentiss thing tomorrow night."

Caroline winced as theatrically as she had winked. "*Hot Pursuit.* Honestly."

"I know, right? But I'm a huge fan of that new girl in the franchise, Caitlin Halliday?"

"Are you really?"

"I would *love* to meet her."

Caroline laughed, shook her head. "Sweetie, consider your name on the door!"

Amy squealed and gave Caroline another hug. "You're the best! Will I see you there?"

"Of course. I'll be very busy, but we'll have a drink, yes? You want a drink now?"

Amy did her best to look contrite. "I'm with a friend who's going through a break-up—"

Caroline waved a hand. "No need to say more. You're a good person. We'll catch up tomorrow and share all our news. I look forward to it. It'll be a nice break from the despicably wealthy."

Amy thanked her again, not buying for a moment that Caroline didn't love every second of her work. But it would be good to catch up and have a drink, and now she had her direct path to Arthur Prentiss. Everything had come together beautifully. And all she needed to do was shake that bastard's hand. She bought two more wines and headed back to Carla, determined to give her friend her undivided attention until she had to leave for work.

ELEVEN

Vince Stratton leaned back in his large chair and observed his boys. Seven of them lounged about the office, his current crew in their rich and varied splendour. "Let's be having it then," he said. "What have you got?"

Clancy, leaning against a metal filing cabinet, raised a hand, ever the one keen to please. It made Stratton a little sad inside. It was going to become a problem. "Yes, Clance?"

"I was chatting with that Berkeley guy, from the West Ham crew?"

"And?"

"He let on that they're hitting one of the Russian places sometime this week, apparently. Always bad blood between them two crews, of course, but they hear tell of a big stash of coke."

"They plan to relieve the Russians of some cocaine?" Stratton asked.

"Apparently."

"Jesus. There will be blood."

Clancy nodded, eyes wide. "I know, right? It'll be open warfare if the Russians pick them for the hit."

"Which they will."

"You think so?"

Stratton laughed. "Of course they will. Because the Russians are not stupid, but that bunch of muppets from West Ham have barely one whole brain between them. This will mark the end of them, you'll see."

"No great loss," Dexter muttered.

Stratton wagged a finger. "Don't be so sure. No one will miss that pack of cum stains, for certain, but anything that thins the ranks of hoodlums in this town means it's harder for people like us to slip around the edges and make our money. And others will pour like water into the gaps left behind. Things will shift and we'd better stay aware of that."

"So does that mean you're going to interfere?" Clancy asked. "Protect West Ham somehow?"

Stratton laughed louder still. "Fuck me, no! It's all far from being my work, but I do like to make it my business. We'll see how it all shakes out. Once the West Hammers are wiped out, there'll be a scramble to pick up their turf and operations, paltry as those things are." He turned to David Westley, a fourteen-year-old hardnut recently attached to his operation, not long out of the Genest Detention Centre. "You're not far from there, right?"

"Other side of Stratford," David said. "Not too far."

"Make yourself busy around the estates," Stratton said. "Ask around, not too pushy, see if there's any dissent among the West Ham crew about hitting the Russians. Maybe someone there has a brain, might give us some insight. Remember, boys, knowledge is power."

David nodded, eyes a little nervous, darting around the group. The kid still had to prove himself. Stratton saw Clancy's annoyance at having his news passed over to someone else to follow up, even though he knew young David needed breaking in. Definitely he was going to become a problem.

"Anyone got anything else?" Stratton asked the room in general. There was a shaking of heads and low murmuring. "Righto. Well, Saul, I need you to go to dead drop two and pick up."

"Yes, Boss."

"Everyone else, off you go. Ears to the ground, eyes open. Anyone need any money?"

Two of boys stepped cautiously forward and Stratton handed them a couple of twenties each while the rest filed out. The pair pocketed their allowance, slipped away, leaving Stratton alone except for Clancy, still leaning against the filing cabinet, eyes hooded.

"Out with it," Stratton said.

"Why give it to that new kid? I picked up the rumour."

Stratton smiled, but it was mirthless. "And that's why someone else has to learn more. Word gets around, you know that. You talking to the West Ham muppet and then asking around the area? How obvious is that?"

Clancy hung his head. "I s'pose."

"You got to use your noggin, sunshine. We're silent as sharks in this town, boy, seeing and hearing everything but leaving not a ripple."

Clancy nodded.

"You go to four like I asked?" Stratton had dead drops all over London, changed them regularly and leaked the information of their locations through his boys. He never went near them himself. It was a method that had worked for years and no one knew who he was, yet all the mobs and gangs around the country knew the best hits came via that ever-changing network of anonymous communication.

Clancy brightened up, dug inside his shell suit and pulled out an envelope. "Here it is. Feels quite bulky, more than just a letter maybe?"

Stratton stared with narrow eyes, not taking the package. Clancy's hand began to tremble slightly, standing awkwardly, one arm out. Stratton let him hang, let the discomfort build.

"Just sayin'," the boy muttered eventually, unable to handle the silence any longer.

"What did I tell you about asking too many questions?"

"You just told me to use my noggin!" Clancy almost shouted.

Stratton nodded slightly, took the package. Clancy slumped back against the cabinet in relief. "I told you to use your noggin when it comes to the business of availing ourselves of other people's information. But I have always, *always*, reminded you to never avail yourselves of information pertaining to me. Have I not?"

"It's just that—"

"Have I not?" Stratton yelled and Clancy jumped, nodded vigorously. "My business is my own and it's best built on a solid knowledge of everything that goes on in my town. You boys, you run information and errands for me, you keep me connected, but you stay out of my business. It's very simple."

"I just want to do the best job for you I can," Clancy said, almost a whisper.

"Then you will do as I say and nothing more, yes?"

"Okay."

"Good lad. You need any money?"

"Nah. That twat from West Ham I was talking to? I lifted his wallet. He had three hundred quid in there!"

Stratton chuckled. "Good boy. Off you go then. Buy yourself something nice."

"Yes, Boss."

Clancy slunk off, his shoulders low. The boy was far too smart for this job, and Stratton wondered if there was some way to farm him out somewhere. If only he could rein in his curiosity, stop idolising Stratton so much, he might settle down. But it felt too late for that already. Time would tell, and any action would be very saddening, but business came first.

Young David, he had problems like all the boys, but he might turn out to be more grounded if he could manage his anger. Stratton had high hopes for him. Now Dexter, he had a powerful abandonment complex and that always led to issues of trust. If Stratton could convince young Dex that he would never be let down in this outfit like he had been at home, well then Dexter would become a solid asset. Same with Saul. He was already a more solidly based kid, more a rebel than really damaged goods. Of course, they all had their broken parts, but Saul was less shattered than the rest. And all the time Stratton gave Saul the extra cash to help his junkie sister, that line would remain tight.

Stratton sighed. There were the others too. If Clancy did fail, despite all the work Stratton had put in, it wouldn't be the end of the world. His little crew was always in flux and always would be.

That was the nature of the business and, in truth, it worked better that way.

He opened the envelope and read through the note inside. It was from Albert Stoker, the boss of the West Ham crew. He was buying a hit against Vladimir Potolkin, the best hitman the Russians had in-country. Covering his arse before the cocaine hit, maybe? Perhaps these West Ham muppets weren't so stupid after all. Stratton ran a thumb over the wad of bills the letter had been wrapped around. It was a generous down payment, but hitting Potolkin would be no easy thing.

He rang one of his boys on the kid's burner phone, young Suresh. Now there was a kid with all kinds of problems and Stratton honestly didn't expect him to last. Abused by an absolute shit of a father and over-smothered by a compensating mother. Gods forbid the woman would protect the poor boy from his predator father. Stratton had made it clear he could arrange to have the man removed from the family home if requested, but Suresh would have to request it willingly. Give him time. If it worked, Suresh would be properly on the hook and a great asset. The kid answered on the fifth ring.

"Boss, sorry I didn't hear the phone over the traffic. Did I forget something?"

"No bother, lad. Just got a little job for you. You free for it?"

"Of course."

"Good boy. Pop around to Vicarage Lane, you know where. Just nose around and make sure Albert Stoker isn't compromised."

"Yes, Boss. Call back in about two hours. I'll know by then."

"Good lad." Stratton hung up and pursed his lips. Always good to double check that a client wasn't under arrest and giving up some juicy information in some plea bargain or other. It was unlikely. If Stoker had been touched up by the cops, Stratton was sure to have heard of it, but extra caution was worthwhile. Measure twice, cut once, his old dad always said. It was as applicable to crime as it was to carpentry.

The letter included an email address, set up specifically for this job alone. Stratton opened a browser and logged in to the account, wrote a note and saved it as a draft. Nothing would be sent, so nothing could be traced. Stoker would check the account regularly and see the draft. He'd read it, delete it, then save a draft of his own with his response. Wasn't technology a marvellous thing? Stratton smiled, wondering if Stoker would have anything close to the money he was asking for to whack Potolkin. Of course, he hadn't said anything about the job, or the cost in actual numbers, but Stoker would understand the code. And if the old gangster did accept the cost, he was obviously planning to boost an awful lot of cocaine. Stratton poured himself a drink and chuckled quietly. He loved these idiot gangsters, they were so profitable. Time for bed soon, and he knew he would sleep well.

TWELVE

CHARLIE COLLINS SPENT THE MORNING gathering what information he could and only succeeded in frustrating himself. So often a case was like trying to catch smoke. You could see it, smell it, you knew it was there and all connected somehow, but taking hold of it was elusive, impossible. You needed to find the fire and capture that. The smoke wasn't the case, just the product of its existence. Trouble was, most good crims were experts at keeping the smoke to a minimum and the fire virtually non-existent. But he had no choice. It was in his bones, this situation, and he needed to keep digging and scratching and picking.

Other cases took up some more of the morning, but he dealt with them haphazardly. Vince Stratton was lodged in his head like a fish hook in a carp's cheek. By eleven he couldn't concentrate any more. Time to poke the hornet's nest.

He parked the Benz across the street from Stratton's pub. The place was a couple of streets removed from the hustle of Camden High Street, but the pavements were busy enough and the traffic a steady stream. He looked up at the building, three stories occupying a busy corner. The dark wood double doors were set where the corner of the building itself was cut back to flatten the edges. Maroon tiles covered the lower two metres or so of the ground-floor walls, big windows with leadlight panels ran both sides. The second and third stories were simple white stucco with boring modern double-glazed windows in white aluminium frames. Clearly it was a front for something, but what? Stratton was far more than a simple publican, and records showed he owned this building, having bought it in 1994 from the previous owners, one of those awful pub-food chains. Stratton had turned it back into the classic London pub. The kind that could hardly turn a profit and stay open. The transaction usually went the other way, publican families selling up to Wetherspoons or Firkin or whoever the hell else was slowly destroying the real personality of the city.

Collins shook his head and winced at the ache it set in motion. Lack of sleep and too much booze seemed to be his defining state lately. He jogged across the road between two shiny black taxis and narrowly missed being taken out by a bicycle courier.

"Fucking blind cunt!" the skinny man yelled, wiry legs pumping, blond dreadlocks streaming behind.

Collins took a deep breath and stepped onto the pavement. He pushed open the door to the pub and walked into the familiar smell of stale beer and wood polish. He remembered when pubs used to smell of cigarette smoke too and he missed that. The modern world, forever disinfecting itself against life. There'd be nothing left soon.

He ordered a pint of Kronenbourg, then thought better of it and ordered a double scotch.

"Instead of the beer?" the pretty bar girl asked.

He paused, then shrugged. "No, as well as."

She nodded and served him the drinks, took his money. He'd swallowed the double scotch in one by the time she came back with his change and he took the frosty pint to a table in the corner. He sat with his back to the wall, surveying the establishment. A couple of early lunchtime drinkers sat on stools at the bar, ties loosened as they chatted. An old geezer stared into a pint of bitter, alone at a table on one side. Collins looked away as a flash of his future self became a little too close for comfort. If he ever actually reached old age.

There was no one else in the place except himself and the bar girl. She was smoking hot, wearing tight black jeans and an equally tight black T-shirt with STRATTON's emblazoned in cursive script across her full chest. His mind began to address scenarios where she was stripping that tight black attire off for him, but he caught himself and looked away. She could barely be half his age. That didn't stop a man's desire, of course, but he felt like a proper sad sack sitting there fantasising about it.

He scanned around the ceiling, counted four different CCTV cameras mounted surreptitiously in the corners. He was wondering how many more there might be that he couldn't see when a door beside the bar opened and Vince Stratton strolled out. The bastard didn't look anywhere near Collins, but it was obvious why he had emerged now.

Stratton went to the bar and chatted to the bar girl. She smiled, a little awkwardly, and Stratton leaned on the bar and lifted her chin with one forefinger. Her smile forced itself wider and she nodded slightly as he said something else. Relief flooded her face when she turned away and reached for a tumbler. She poured a measure of Talisker from the top shelf behind the bar and handed it over.

Collins seethed a little inside, wondering how much abuse this girl and the others who worked here might cop at Stratton's hands. Should he ask her? Offer to hear any case of sexual harassment or assault? It might give him something over the big bastard, but the girl was unlikely to risk her job or personal safety by saying anything.

Stratton turned from the bar and pinned Collins with an icy glare. Collins tipped two fingers to his temple in a lazy salute then took a sip of lager. *So it begins.*

"Doesn't seem like this is your sort of place," Stratton said, sitting opposite.

"Oh? What do you think *would* seem like my sort of place?"

Stratton lifted his glass casually, raised his other hand beside it. "I don't know. Maybe the back room of some West Indian gang's headquarters. A dark alley with Andreyov and his minions. Something like that."

Collins allowed himself a crooked smile. That Stratton knew of his close associations with organised crime was not news. His life of jumping fences between the legal and illegal, ignoring a lot of things to get scores in other places as he lined his pockets along the way, was no revelation. Internal affairs had never been able to pin anything on him yet, and he was barely more crooked than half the detectives he worked with. He was just better at it. But it irked him that Stratton would open with such a tasteless display. He chose not to rise to it. "So we found an interesting corpse over at The Angel."

Stratton raised one eyebrow. "Did you now?"

"How did you know about it?"

"Don't know what you're talking about, officer."

Collins smiled. Officer. Like it was an insult. "I know there's a connection between you and that corpse."

"Again, Mr. Collins, I really have no idea what you're talking about."

Collins watched Stratton's eyes carefully. "And Matthew McLeod," he said levelly.

A twitch at the corner of one eye, tiny, almost imperceptible. "What about him?"

"You had me check into his address right at the same time as you were crapping on about bodies at The Angel. So what's the connection?"

Stratton leaned back, stared at the wall behind Collins. "There is no connection. You're being paranoid. That McLeod caused a bit of a ruckus in here the other night, then roared off in the car I mentioned. I wanted to know where he lived so I could send one of my boys around to collect for the damages. Which I did last night and now everything's sorted. Nothing for you to worry about."

Quick thinking there, or maybe Stratton had already come up with that line of bullshit in case of an event just like this. He was a wily bastard, after all. But Collins intended to keep pushing. "I do worry about it though, you see. Because that's my job. There's a connection between McLeod and The Angel stiff. And that makes me think there's a connection to you as well. So I plan to figure out what that is."

Stratton swallowed his drink and stood. He looked down on Collins, tried to be intimidating. "I still have that video, Charlie. You with that fetid whore bouncing on your tiny cock, cocaine all around, you snorting it off her rather impressive tits. Honestly, it's all very sordid and just the sort of thing the media love these days."

Collins sucked his teeth. "But you'll never really use it, will you? And lose your direct line into the police and my valuable assistance?"

"If you don't back the fuck up, Collins, I will most definitely use it. You think you're my only source among the law? Do grow up. You need to drop this and fuck off. Right now."

He turned and stalked away before Collins could reply. The detective leaned back and sipped his lager, a satisfied smile twitching his lips. Stratton was rattled. He knew the man meant it about using that fucking video footage. He'd been such an idiot that night and would no doubt pay for it for a long time yet. Maybe it would cost him his job. But his work here was done for now. He would appear for all intents and purposes to back off as instructed. But Stratton would almost certainly try to cover his arse and Collins intended to be watching his every move from a safe distance.

THIRTEEN

MATT FINISHED WORK AT THREE on Fridays, something he always appreciated though he could think of no earthly reason why such a strange practice persisted. He had three shelves left to catalogue, which he could easily have finished had he stayed until four like every other weekday. But the warehouse closed up at three on Fridays because that's how it had always been and who were they to change anything?

A heavy hand landed on his shoulder as he headed to the machine to clock out. "You're looking better today, mate!" Ben's teeth were white in his wide grin.

"Aye, I went home last night, fed myself and then just fell into bed. Slept about fourteen hours straight."

"Sweet! So you're all revved up and ready to come out on the pull with us tonight then, yeah?"

Matt made an apologetic face. "Shit, sorry, man. Not tonight. I've a couple of things to do."

"Really? More important than wetting your wick?"

"A bit more, yeah." He realised Ben wasn't going to take no for an answer. "Where are you guys off to?"

"We're gonna start at the Carpenter's, get a few in early and lay the foundation. Not likely to be too many fillies there, of course, but you never know. Then we're gonna head over to the Cactus Club."

"Seriously? That place is full of fucking teenagers, man."

"And your point is?"

"Ah, right. With you. Well, tell you what. I'll get onto these er-rands I need to run and probably come and meet you there. Text me when you're leaving the pub for the Cactus?"

Ben slapped his back, his grin wider than ever. "That's the spirit, you horny wee fucker! I'll do that, aye."

Matt winced. "Honestly, how many times? Please don't try to do the accent. You're worse than fucking Scotty off *Star Trek*."

Ben laughed and strode away. "I'll text you!" he yelled back over his shoulder.

Matt waved and nodded, then clocked out. He had every inten-tion of ignoring that text. Hopefully he could make it up to Ben and the others before the weekend was out. He really did feel bad letting them down, but this situation with Stratton was a lot more import-ant. He was having trouble thinking about anything beyond it.

It wasn't a lie about the big sleep, and he did feel quite rejuvenated. It may be entirely possible to call up the dark again at a moment's notice if he had to. Maybe if he could get close to Stratton it could end here and now. But he had learned that caution was the key, a slow and steady gathering of details. Although he did plan to test some boundaries too. And if the opportunity arose, he would leap on it.

He reached deep inside and let the dark rise a little. It thrashed and strained, desperate for release, and Matt crammed it down, pulled his mind away quickly as his skeleton threatened to split and shatter like glass. Maybe not so ready yet after all. Or maybe there were no more kills left in him except his own. Perhaps if he had made it across Stratton's desk and sent the dark into the bastard it would have finished them both off. And he couldn't help thinking that might not have been such a bad result. Maybe it could still be the upshot of all this. Time would tell.

He went home, changed, and was driving out to Camden Town before five o'clock. He parked a couple of blocks away from the pub and made sure his baseball cap was pulled low over his eyes. He turned up the collar of his donkey jacket and pushed hands deep into the pockets against the biting cold. At least it wasn't raining.

He walked casually to the junction where Stratton's pub stood and kept going, passing on the opposite side of the street. It was fairly busy, both on the pavements and inside the pub. Early winter dark had fallen, and the lights inside made strange criss-crossed TV screens of the windows. Patrons sat or stood inside in groups, drinks clutched in their hands, faces happy and indulgent. Everyone enjoying that end-of-the-week drink, where the possibilities are endless and Monday morning seems like a dream, so far away. Yet it always came around so damned quickly, made it hard to ever believe a whole weekend had in fact passed since the last time a body dragged themselves to one hateful place of employment or another. Matt grinned. Perhaps his own frustrations were colouring his perceptions. It was entirely likely a lot of the folk in there were genuinely happy with their lives and jobs, and good for them.

He turned the corner away from the pub and walked all the way around the next block in order to pass by again coming back in the other direction. He went around the corner, noting that the pub had two back alleys, one on each street of the corner on which it stood. Presumably they met each other behind the building. It was a big structure, taking up a good quarter of the block.

Matt crossed the road and headed into one of the alleys. It was relatively clear, a couple of cars parked in bays marked Resident Pass Only, some big industrial bins along the back wall of the pub. There was enough room to drive a small delivery truck through, and several paired doors led into other buildings that shared the access. Back windows of the pub, that Matt felt pretty sure would be Stratton's office, glowed with light from within. But the windows were about three metres off the ground, the back of the building a lot lower than the front. Steps led up to the main doors on the corner and the place would have a big cellar, cool and full of metal kegs and plastic pipes.

Matt slowed as he passed the window, glanced up cautiously without stopping. There were heavy duty bars, a cage standing only six inches from the glass. Enough for a small window to be cracked open for a breath of fresh air, at least as fresh as it ever got in Camden, but most definitely no access.

He turned the right angle of the alley, heading back for the main street around the corner. Double access doors, smooth and featureless on the outside. More windows three metres up, but these were dark and equally protected by one-inch-thick metal bars. And then he was back among the bustle and traffic. Definitely no easy ingress other than the front doors. The double doors at the back didn't even have a lock to pick, not that Matt had any idea how to pick a lock anyway.

He sighed and crossed the street, leaned in the shelter of a dark shop doorway to stare at the impenetrable edifice of Stratton's. There would be no sneaking in and catching the bastard unawares. So perhaps it was time to push those boundaries a little bit. This was an entirely new situation, after all.

Taking a deep breath, trying to still the trembling nerves in his gut, Matt trotted between the traffic and pushed his way inside. Stratton's pub was warm and welcoming, the sudden burst of chatter and clinking glasses a pleasant juxtaposition to the cold and engine noise outside. He went to the bar and ordered a pint of bitter.

There weren't many places to sit, all the tables packed with people, and knots of folks stood around between them. But both long windows had high, narrow tables and bar stools along them. A couple of the stools were free and Matt picked one, leaned back against the narrow ledge of table and sipped his beer as he watched the throng. "Once in a Lifetime" by Talking Heads was blaring over the jukebox and Matt smiled crookedly. "This is absolutely not my beautiful house," he muttered to himself.

The door beside the bar led to Stratton's office, he knew that from his previous visit. There was another door behind the bar which no doubt led to some kind of storeroom. Those dark windows he'd seen in the alley, he presumed. When he'd ordered his beer, he'd seen an old-fashioned double trapdoor in the floor which would lead down into the beer cellar. A similar arrangement was mounted at an angle beside the pub doors out front, for deliveries from the street. The pavement between the kerb and those doors was chipped and battered from decades of barrels being bounced and rolled back and forth. Could he perhaps find his way into the cellar from outside?

Slip in while a delivery was taking place, hide out until things were closed up, then find his way up into the pub later to catch Stratton unawares. Be bloody typical if he managed to pull that off only to find the trapdoor behind the bar locked shut and himself trapped in the cellar all night. Matt was under no illusion when it came to his skills. He was no superhero or Navy SEAL.

On occasion he'd managed to break a house and get to a victim, but his usual method involved finding a way to reach the target outside somewhere, out of sight, but easily accessed. He shook his head. The Sullivan hit had supposedly been like that, but he'd fucked up and that kid Clancy had seen everything. He'd checked so carefully before stepping into the alley, was sure no one had been around. It was inevitable, he supposed, that he would fuck up eventually. Maybe he'd been lucky until now. What a bloody mess. He'd simply have to do his best to fix the situation. But this pub was more tightly locked up than a house, and perhaps he would need to find a way to cross paths with Stratton out in public after all.

The door beside the bar opened and Matt stiffened, bracing himself for Stratton. This was the boundary he was hoping to push, see how much he could unsettle the man. He frowned when Clancy emerged, his young face set as he headed directly for Matt.

He stopped a metre or so away. "I'm going to give you a note."

Matt raised an eyebrow. "Okay."

"You don't fucking touch me, right! Just the paper."

Matt couldn't help himself. He jerked forward on his stool, flexed his free hand open like he was throwing something. Clancy leapt backwards and crashed into a group of drinkers. Glasses fell, beer spilled, and shouting and annoyance erupted in an instant.

Matt sat laughing, occasionally sipping his beer while Clancy made copious apologies and ran to the bar to organise replacement drinks as quickly as he could. His face was thunderous when he had finally sorted it all out several minutes later. He stood at arm's length and held out a folded piece of paper.

"Slowly, you fucker!" he said.

Matt reached out in mock slow motion and plucked the sheet from Clancy's grip. The kid turned and pushed through the crowd without another word. Matt unfolded the note and frowned at the neat handwriting, clearly done with an old-fashioned fountain pen.

You've been lurking around outside, casing the joint and creeping about in the alley out the back. Now you're in here having a fucking drink like you don't have a care in the world. You need to leave and never come back, or that threat I made will come to pass quicker than you can squeeze out a fart. Now go and wait for my call.

V.S.

Matt smiled and raised his glass, gestured around at a couple of the CCTV lenses he could see near the ceiling. He downed the pint and left, the night darker and colder after the raucous warmth of the pub. *Boundaries pushed*, he thought.

He hadn't achieved much, but he knew now just how omnipotent Stratton's observations around his place were. He would never get near him in there. But he intended to keep watching and figure out the man's movements outside his place of business, and perhaps he had the big man a little bit rattled and that couldn't hurt. He hunched into his coat and headed back down the road for his car.

* * *

Charlie Collins sat in his Benz, the heater blowing warmth into his face. The shadowy side street in which he was parked gave him a fairly decent view of at least half of Stratton's pub, and one of the back alleys. He watched Matthew McLeod emerge from the pub, a crooked grin on his face. What was the Scotsman doing there? And why was he so pleased with himself?

Collins had watched the guy stroll back and forth for fifteen minutes, then case the back alleys. If Stratton and this McLeod were working together, why was the guy acting like he planned to rob the joint? And then he'd gone in and sat at the window as casual as you like and enjoyed a damn pint.

Collins pursed his lips. McLeod had left after talking to that young black kid that Collins had seen around Stratton a lot. It was an open secret that Stratton kept a cadre of young lads in his employ, had them running all kinds of errands. Collins had tried several times to track one of the kids to get to Stratton himself, but the bastard was always one step ahead. Collins checked his notes. Clancy Turner, that was it. And Clancy had looked positively terrified of McLeod and then McLeod had left. Collins hissed through his teeth in frustration. The waters were getting murkier. Just what the hell was going on?

He made a couple more notes, to lean on Clancy Turner, check out more of Stratton's boys, maybe try to track their movements again if time allowed.

Then he put the Benz in gear and rolled out of the street in the direction McLeod had been walking. He got lucky and saw the old blue Golf pull out in front and he tailed McLeod easily all the way back to his dingy flat. Collins sat outside for twenty minutes, but McLeod didn't emerge again. Annoyed, he headed off towards the river and Deptford. It was a fairly long and traffic-jammed drive on a Friday night, but he needed to stand on the Irish over there and collect some money. It was either that or actually investigate the hit against the Barking crew, and he was fairly sure O'Halloran would rather avoid that unnecessary ugliness. And with the money, Collins could stock up on some white and head home to think more deeply about this whole Stratton and McLeod thing.

FOURTEEN

AMY USED HER PHONE'S FRONT CAMERA to check her make-up as the cab pulled up to the kerb outside the Marriott. The big Prentiss gala event was being held high up in the hotel, an entire floor seconded for the function. If Amy knew anything about Caroline French and the events she organised, it would be glitzy and glamourous to an obscene degree. The few things Amy had worked on while she looked for a palliative care job in London had been difficult. In some ways, that kind of silver-service waitressing made a person a kind of modern-day slave, ignored at best, actively despised at worst by the so-called cream of society. It could be an ugly process, truly inhumane that such things existed, highlighting the ridiculous inequality in what was supposedly an advanced, first-world civilisation. She couldn't fathom Carla's desire to join that set. Or perhaps it was just Amy's old hippy philosophy coming out, her colonial rebel heart. When you worked in palliative care, it became quickly apparent that everyone was the same in the end. Those with more money than they could spend died just as scared and alone as people who had barely had enough to live on all their lives. Death was the only great equaliser and it came for everyone in the end. Now and then she helped to address the great universal balance by ushering it in a little sooner for some she considered most deserving.

But tonight Amy was on the far side of the divide, an interloper among the elite. She looked good, but her dress was a little black number, straight off the rack. She knew she had the figure to make it look better than it was. Her hair was self-managed, but her natural blonde always glowed under lights. Hopefully she wouldn't stand out too starkly among the manicured, coiffured and fashionista-dressed inside. She paid the cabbie and hopped out, gasping against the icy breeze. Her knuckles were white around her diamanté clutch as she hurried across the pavement. A uniformed attendant opened the hotel door and said, "Good evening, ma'am."

She smiled. "Hiya."

One elevator among the many in the lobby was marked off with fabric tape and a short red carpet. A giant of a man with deep black skin and tight cornrows, wearing a fine suit that stretched to bursting over his muscles, stood just inside the barrier. His eyes were like steel shutters, his face an impressive wall of expressionless professionalism.

Amy approached the man, slightly intimidated. "The Prentiss event?" she asked. "*Hot Pursuit* launch party?"

"Your name?" the bouncer asked, giving nothing away. His voice was like rocks rolling in the bottom of some unfathomably deep canyon.

"Amy Cavendish."

He flicked the screen of a small tablet, scanned a list. When he looked up again his demeanour was entirely different, open and friendly. "Welcome, Miss Cavendish, so glad you could make it." His voice was just as deep and resonant, but now it was warm too. He'd switched from terrifying to really quite alluring in an instant. That was quite a skill.

Amy allowed herself a flash of fantasy, imagined taking him home afterwards, then stopped quickly as she felt her cheeks colouring. "Thank you," she managed lamely.

The bouncer unhooked one end of the tape barrier and pressed the elevator button. The doors opened immediately. He gestured her inside and said, "Press for the West India Ballroom."

The button was clearly marked and moments later Amy found

herself shepherded into a huge reception space, buzzing with chatter and the hint of a string quartet somewhere at the far end. Millions of pounds worth of fashion and jewellery glittered and swished all around her. Waiters and waitresses like penguins scuttled everywhere with trays of champagne and *hors d'oeuvres*. Ridiculous tiny food, salmon and capers, things on sticks, rice paper wrapped around prawns and garish, bubbling fish-egg concoctions.

Amy snagged a champagne flute and sipped quickly, determined to steady her nerves. She couldn't imagine anywhere she would be more out of her element, but she was here for a reason. Large oyster lights in the ceiling were set to a low ambient glow, sconces around the cream walls equally dim, creating a soft, almost dusky vibe. Wood panels and expensive paintings between the wall lights softened the edges of the space, the sculpted ceiling like an inverted arctic landscape above her. Amy stepped onto the deep, fern-green carpet and tried to look like she belonged.

A dozen Hollywood A-listers were within touching distance already. Who knew how many more were scattered around the crowd. She spotted two megastars she recognised like old friends, though they were anything but. Both of them Australian actors from long-running soap operas back home, made good in the big, wide world. It was surreal to see them in this context, and she smirked at how short they both were in real life. She shook her head. As if this was real life. Scores of society darlings buzzed and twittered, the sound of fake laughter ringing through the air like alarm bells.

The string quartet played on a raised stage at the far end, and Amy began winding her way through the mass of people towards them simply to be moving rather than standing near the doors like a stunned mullet. She hadn't got halfway before a high-pitched and drawn out, "Amy!" sent waves of relief flooding through her.

She turned into the vigorous hug and air kisses of Caroline French, Raven Events and Media CEO, alive in her natural habitat.

"So glad you could make it," Caroline said, as if Amy hadn't only yesterday blagged herself an invite. "Isn't it just *effervescent* in here?"

Amy nodded, smiled. "It really is. Thanks for getting me in."

"No problem. It's wonderful to see you. So tell me, what's the goss?"

Amy laughed. "There really isn't any. I'm still working palliative at Sally Gentle. Living with a wonderful Spanish girl called Carla."

"She's the one going through the break-up?"

"Good memory! Yes, she just dumped this complete dickhead who was treating her terribly. Some blueblood old-money fool. Quentin Barker."

Caroline pursed her lips, stared up at the white scallop light fitting above. "Barker, Quentin Barker." Her gaze snapped back to Amy. "Yes, Quentin, son of Reginald Barker, who's cousin to one of the last generation princesses, Fergie or Anne or someone. I'd have to check. Blueblood indeed."

"Is there anything you don't know?" Amy asked with a laugh.

"About society, darling? Good god, no. Reginald Barker likes to fuck little boys, you know. Your friend is very well off out of that nasty clique of old toffs."

Amy's eyebrows shot up. "Well, I'll be sure to let her know about her narrow escape."

"You do that. Now then." Caroline looked around the room. "You wanted to meet Caitlin Halliday, yes?"

Amy winced inside. It was her cover story, but she had to brace herself for it. Halliday was the latest plastic Hollywood darling. Not a bad actor, by any means, but no Streep or Blanchett. She had the right look and the bucketload of luck that made her a current favourite. She tended to show up on all the talk shows espousing her latest role as the ambassador for some Third World charity or other. Amy couldn't help wondering just how much of it was managed PR, if any of it was genuine. But it was her way in. "Yes, I'd love to meet her. The Rwandan appeal stuff she's been doing is just amazing."

"Isn't it, though?" Caroline grabbed her arm and almost dragged her off her feet across the room. They bore down on Caitlin Halliday like a conjoined missile. "Caitlin!" Caroline declared. "You absolutely must meet my dear friend Amy Cavendish."

Amy was thrust forward and she reached out a hand. "Such an honour to meet you!"

"Lovely to meet you too," Caitlin said, slipping easily into her role, as though she was genuinely enchanted. She reached out one dusky hand, the skin a soft cocoa in the warm light, offset with perfect bright red nails. Her hair was glistening black, straightened, with a blonde streak down one side.

Amy shook hands, Caitlin's touch light, but firm, and so warm. Not usually star struck, Amy was a little stunned at how beautiful Caitlin really was, even more stunning in person than she appeared in film. That had to be a rare occurrence.

"Amy is involved in similar work to your Rwandan stuff," Caroline said, completely missing Amy's point. Or choosing to manufacture something for them to talk about. She flicked a wink at Amy and said, "We'll talk more." Then she was gone, as though she had never been there.

"You're involved with First Vision too?" Caitlin asked.

Amy trawled her memory for anything to do with Third World aid, any detail of her earlier research of Halliday, and managed to keep the conversation rolling. She did send money to charities fairly regularly and she set the record straight, admitting she wasn't nearly as involved as she'd like to be, that Caroline was being unnecessarily generous. Caitlin quickly proved herself to be a genuinely nice person, and Amy berated herself for assuming the woman was just another vapid starlet.

Others in the small group were equally engaged and it wasn't long before Amy decided that Caitlin's interests were absolutely sincere, and she promised herself that after this bizarre party she would endeavour to make some of her truth-bending actual fact. At the very least she knew a decent slice of her next pay cheque would go to Caitlin's favoured cause, and she would try to see where volunteering might fit in. But she did already provide one particular public service for which she was uniquely qualified and that was supposed to be her focus here. She needed to remember that her worth was measured by her own means, not other people's achievements.

After a good twenty minutes of vibrant conversation that moved from charity to homelessness to domestic violence and more, a natural lull finally developed. Amy took the opportunity and said casually, "So I haven't seen Arthur Prentiss yet this evening."

"Oh, he's here, the dear man," Caitlin said. "Would you like to meet him?"

"I would, very much." Amy wondered if everything she had recently come to believe about Caitlin was undermined by the simple act of calling Prentiss a dear man, but the actress had a variety of obligations to fulfil and not bad-mouthing the source of her enormous salary was probably one of them.

"Come with me." Caitlin put a hand behind Amy's upper arm and guided her across the room.

Moments later, Amy found herself standing among a group of Hollywood stars that would make any fan faint. Though she had certain issues with the superficiality of it all, she had to admit it was cool as hell to be mingling shoulder to shoulder with these icons of the big screen. But directly across from her was Arthur Prentiss, her target. She took a deep breath, steadied herself and drew her attention down to all the shadows of the dead that lived inside her. This was her calling, her reason to be. This was why she had the ability she had. Time to focus.

Since she was a teenager she had been drawn to the dead, always knew she would work in palliative care. The events in Sydney several years ago, with Jake and her discovery of her purpose, had shown her why. Her life had always included a desire for some kind of justice where she saw inequity. She had begun gathering the shadows when she realised she could, without any inclination of why she could. Then that grand discovery of delivering a fast-creeping death to Jake's abusive stepfather and she had finally come into her power. The thing she had been born to do. Since that first time with Jake's despicable stepfather, she had collected and released the shadows many times, adding a little more balance to the world, doing her own dark charity. Now it was time again.

As Caitlin made introductions around the group, Amy gathered the hungry shadows and let them rise. She shook hands with celebrities, Caitlin's words, "My new friend Amy!", a kind of distant soundtrack, like a TV on in another room. Then Caitlin was introducing Arthur Prentiss. Amy smiled, heart pounding, took his hand, and let her shadows go.

The sensation began deep in her gut, as it always did. A ripple of pleasure that spread out into her groin, up into her chest, not unlike an orgasm dialled low. The shadows gusted out of her, from her palm into his, soaking rapidly into his body like ink spreading through tissue paper, though invisible to the naked eye. She felt exactly their passage and often wondered what it would be like to see, but was glad the lack of any evidence made her calling easy to perform in public. Prentiss felt it too. He shuddered slightly, glanced down at his hand in hers even as he said, "A pleasure."

Amy didn't let all the shadows go. She had learned to keep some in reserve for next time, as much to avoid the empty whiteness of their total absence as anything else. But she gave him a good dose. The stain of lonely death washed up through him, into his heart, lungs, gut, balls, brain. Symptoms would appear quickly, probably within the next few weeks, maybe a couple of months at most. He would visit a doctor who would look with narrowed eyes and creased brow, *I've never seen anything present so quickly.* Tests would be done, treatments started almost in a panic. Within another few weeks the medical professionals would be shaking their heads, offering empty apologies, *I'm sorry, I've never seen tumours grow and spread like this. This is the most aggressive cancer I've ever witnessed.* The blooming blackness of a dozen different deaths would be in Prentiss, like birdseed scattered through his organs. He would shrivel and shrink and decay from the inside out. Amy gave him three or four months, tops. If he was strong. One victim had keeled over in only three weeks, and that had shocked even her. She couldn't track the progress of some, but this man, this mogul, would be across the news, his rapid decline documented for the world. His last great production, Amy Cavendish, Executive Producer.

He trembled slightly as he disengaged the handshake, cleared his throat a little self-consciously.

"It's an absolute pleasure to meet you," Amy said, smiling with her mouth while her eyes drilled venom into his. She let her smile expand into a predatory grin. "I'm so glad I got to shake your hand."

As his brow creased, one hand pressing absently at his chest, she let the look melt off her face and turned to Caitlin. "I can't believe I'm in such august company!" She flapped and gushed, the small group laughing and flickering their eyebrows at each other, the moment gone before it had even really started. But it was done.

Amy knew she could relax now, actually enjoy the party and the free booze. She certainly needed it. The release of the shadows always left her tense and drained, as though she'd run a marathon or climbed a mountain. But there was a thrill too, the same as with those other endeavours. The warm glow of achievement, of a goal conquered. She would be buzzing for hours, and a few champagnes and maybe a little dancing later would be the best possible follow-up. Did people like this even dance at these parties? The string quartet lost at the back of the room were hardly pumping out bangers. Maybe she'd move on to a club later. She imagined taking Caitlin Halliday with her, maybe that big, handsome fellow outside the elevator too. She realised she was grinning a little, the thrill of the hit electrifying her core, so she took a deep breath to steady herself, dial it down.

She glanced over at Prentiss again, his face still slightly uncertain even as he tried to shake off the strange feeling that had passed through him. Amy caught her breath. Behind Prentiss, looking directly at her over the mogul's right shoulder, was a dark smear of presence. At once the shape of a man and not, man-sized but somehow emanating the containment of multitudes, of gargantuan manifestation. It exuded icy menace, total malevolence. It brushed one hand gently across Prentiss's left cheek as it stared at her. Even with no features, just a black impression of a head, she knew it stared *directly* at her. Into her.

The last couple of times she had released her shadows, she had immediately afterwards sensed some kind of presence near the victim. The last time she had seen a kind of smoky shape, a cloud drifting around the victim's back and head. This time it was clearer than ever, most definitely there, most definitely a human-like shape of darkness and unimaginable depths. Some kind of entity drawn by her action, surely. Attracted to it, or created by it? And it was focussed intently on her. Her buzz drained away like cold water down a drain, the smile slid off her face. A chill rippled up through her gut.

Prentiss shook himself, literally vibrated his shoulders and waved his arms, and the thing swirled and dissipated like ebony mist. But not before its attention had drilled deep into Amy, absolutely making itself known.

As it went, so did its cold threat, and a second later it was if it had never been.

A hand fell on Amy's shoulder, startled her slightly. "You okay?" Caitlin asked. "You look like you've seen a ghost!"

Amy forced a small laugh as they took a step away from the group. "Sorry. Must be the heat in here or something. I just came over a little funny for a moment."

"You need some air?"

"I think I need a drink."

Caitlin raised her eyebrows, blew out her cheeks. "Good call! Me too."

Amy glanced around, fixed Caitlin with a serious look. "You really think he's a dear man? Prentiss?"

Caitlin grinned crookedly, checked no one was too near. She leaned close to whisper. "Honestly, the man's a cunt. I'm not supposed to say that, but I feel like you get it. But, you know, this is my job." Her eyes narrowed. "Why are you really here?"

"You can see right through me, eh?"

"Of course. We're like that, us superstars." She rolled her eyes. "I figured you were one of those people who loves to mix with the stars, you know? And fair enough, we get a lot of that, it goes with the territory. But you're not. You don't care about us at all!"

Relief washed through Amy. She was so pleased to know her initial impression of Caitlin had been accurate. "Oh, it's not that I don't care. I mean, you're clearly lovely and that makes me very happy. It's just that I know Caroline. I used to work these things for her, and I fancied a posh night out with plenty of free grog. So I blagged in. Sorry!"

"Don't apologise! That's excellent. I fucking hate these ridiculous events." Caitlin took her arm again, steered her away. "I'm so glad you're here. I have to come to these things, but if I hang out with you, I can avoid…them! Let's get drunk and sit in a corner and talk shit about all these idiots."

Amy smiled. She really liked this Hollywood starlet. It seemed they had a lot in common. And she was certainly glad for the distraction of a new friend. The memory of the apparition behind Prentiss haunted her. Was it just an apparition or had it really manifested there? She had felt a chill from it. Prentiss had appeared to feel it too, to literally shake it off. She drew a deep breath. "A fine plan!" she said. "And maybe when we've drunk all the champagne, we can slip away and go clubbing?"

Caitlin laughed, high and genuine. "Fuck, yes! What a great idea."

They headed for a table covered in glasses of champagne, wine and beer.

FIFTEEN

CHARLIE COLLINS SAT IN HIS CAR and stared at the façade of Stratton's pub. He sniffed, pulled a small baggie from his jacket pocket and tapped out a line onto the back of a London A to Z. In these days of GPS, it seemed he only ever used the old book for coke any more. He straightened up the line with his police petrol card, then rolled up a twenty and snorted it in one. He breathed out slowly, leaned his head back and sighed. This was good stuff. The money from the Irish had been put to good use. He tipped his gaze back to Stratton's. He was like a dog with a bone and he knew it. He also knew it's what made him a good cop. He could have gone home, as planned, to think and make notes and worry about what the hell was really going on. But something niggled at him, some sixth sense that he had learned to trust. So after scoring, he had come back to watch. Waiting here, staring at a dull building, annoyed him. But something…

He glanced at the clock. Nearly 1:00 a.m. Stratton clearly had extended licencing, but Collins wasn't sure how long. Maybe until two, as it was Friday night. The pub was still busy inside, but not packed like it had been before. People milled around the street, traffic still crept by, both far less dense than before, but Camden never really slept.

Collins sat up a little straighter, the rush of the drug coursing through his veins, at the sight of Vince Stratton strolling past one of the front windows. So the man did show himself among his patrons sometimes. Charlie wasn't sure if that meant anything or not. But this whole situation was static. Stratton had not gone anywhere through the afternoon, hadn't responded to the lunchtime nudge. Maybe Collins was being impatient, but he felt the urge to push something to get closer to this McLeod mystery.

Emboldened by the coke and driven by frustration, he hopped out of the car and jogged across the street. The lights on his Benz flashed as he pressed the remote lock and trotted up the front steps of the pub. A burly bouncer stood in the doorway. The man looked him up and down, then shrugged and stepped aside.

"Much obliged," Collins said with a grin. He quickly flexed his jaw, made a mental note not to let himself chew on the invisible gum of good drugs, and pushed the door open into the warm pub.

He went to the bar and ordered a pint. When he turned from the bar he found Stratton staring daggers at him from across the room. He raised his glass in a toast and Stratton strode over like a predator locked on prey. Charlie took a deep breath. The man was certainly intimidating, but he would not be scared. Thankfully the coke gave him an edge of confidence he might not have otherwise had.

"Did I not tell you to fuck off?" Stratton asked in a soft, friendly voice that belied the words.

"A man can't come to the pub for drink?"

"Not this man." Stratton jabbed him hard in the chest with one thick forefinger. "And not this pub. This is police harassment, you little cocksucker. You think you're going to intimidate me or something? For what?"

Charlie barked a laugh. "Police harassment? Is it? I really think it's just an off-duty copper enjoying a pint. If anyone's being harassed…"

"You're never off-duty, we all know that."

"Just enjoying a drink."

"Why are you so obsessed with me all of a sudden? Because I heard a rumour on the grapevine about a body and was kind enough to casually pass it on to you? Anyone would think you'd be grateful, offering to buy *me* a drink. But no, you're here like a bad fucking smell, stinking up my pub with your bollocks."

"My stinking bollocks? I'm not sure we're well enough acquainted for you to make such a personal assessment, Mr. Stratton." Charlie suppressed a giggle. This coke really was too good. It was making him act like a dick. But he did intend to pressure Stratton a bit, so maybe this approach would work.

"How many pints have you had?" Stratton leaned in, stared into Charlie's eyes. "Ah, perhaps you've enjoyed more than mere alcohol? Honestly, officer, getting high and harassing law-abiding citizens is no way for a representative of Her Majesty to act."

Time to put more pressure on. "Let me tell you what I know, Mr. Stratton."

"Please fucking do."

"I know that you wanted information on Matt McLeod. I also know that there's a connection between McLeod and that stiff at The Angel. And I know of at least one other similar corpse connected to the man."

Stratton raised his eyebrows. "Do you now? I can't imagine why there would be any connection with a young troublemaker who happened to come in here *once* and any dead bodies at all."

Collins paused, watched the thoughts racing behind Stratton's eyes. The man had not known about at least some of what he had just shared. Perhaps Stratton was trying to find out more just like he was. But then, the question of why still persisted. Was Stratton planning to use McLeod for something? Was he standing over him for something? Or did McLeod have something over Stratton and the landlord was trying to get himself out of trouble? "And I know McLeod was here this afternoon," Charlie said. He nodded, smiled, then drank deeply of his pint.

Stratton's eyes narrowed. "You seem to know entirely too much irrelevant information, Detective. All of this means nothing to me and I wonder why you're pushing so hard? What do you hope to achieve?"

"I enforce the law, Mr. Stratton."

"When it suits you."

Collins inclined his head, allowing that one to pass. "And I intend to enforce the law with regards to you. You're up to nefarious shit and one day I'll be bringing you down."

"And you've forgotten again all about that horrible video footage I have of you?"

"Not at all. But you won't use it. Not yet, at least."

"Won't I?"

Collins smiled. "No. Because you're intrigued. You can always give me this McLeod and an answer to those weird blackened corpses, and then you and I can go on to spar another day. That would be a nice result. I could close up a couple of cold cases."

Stratton laughed, seeming to relax slightly. "Is that what this is? You want me to give up McLeod somehow?"

"I don't like those dead bodies, Mr. Stratton. I don't want to see any more of them. And I think McLeod is involved. You and I will come to a head one day. Maybe you'll bring me down with that video, maybe not. Who fucking cares, honestly. But there's a strange state of affairs happening here, don't you think?"

Stratton nodded, stroked his chin slowly. "I most certainly do think, yes. But I have no intention of helping you. I do not play games, Detective."

Collins downed the last of his pint. "Fair enough then. Just as long as we understand each other." Without waiting for a response he turned and left.

Let Stratton stew on that for a while, see what it shook loose. He had meant it when he said that he and Stratton would come to a head one day, but he was sure that day wasn't coming any time soon. They orbited each other, trapped in each other's gravity. People like Stratton and Collins needed one another to exist, and while it would bring him enormous pleasure to bring Stratton down, he wanted to nail the bastard for something massive. Meanwhile, maybe Stratton would recognise the mistake he'd made in connecting McLeod and The Angel corpse and pass something over. Stratton was smart enough to give something up and get the heat off, free himself up to party another day. The man was a professional, after all. And Charlie had meant it when he said he'd be happy to tidy up McLeod and the strange corpses, save Stratton himself for another day.

As he strolled down the front steps, hunched against the biting cold, movement across the street caught his eye, not far from where his car was parked in shadow. He paused, wondering if some lowlife was scoping out the Benz for an opportunistic theft. He crossed the road, heading towards the side street, and the figure moved in the shadows and began strolling quickly away. Collins smiled, pleased he might have been just in time to scare off a hoodlum, then his grin froze. It was McLeod.

So that was why the old sixth sense had been bugging him, hassling him to come back at this late hour. It never failed, his psychic cop power. Maybe he could play these two bastards off against each other.

McLeod was walking altogether too casually away from Stratton's, up the side road past Charlie's Benz. Collins cleared his throat and took the plunge. "Mr. McLeod?" he called out.

The Scotsman stiffened but kept walking. He didn't look around, quickened his pace.

"Matthew McLeod, I know that's you. Can we talk a moment?"

McLeod stopped. After a moment, he turned. "You've got the wrong man, pal. Not sure who you think I am."

"You're Matthew McLeod. You were here earlier this evening, you talked with Clancy Turner. Then you left and went home. I couldn't let it go and came back, and it seems like you did the exact same thing."

Even in the dark, Collins saw the Scotsman's face blanch. "What the fuck do you want?" McLeod asked.

"I'm a police detective. I want to bring down the criminal who hides behind the supposed legal business of that pub." He jabbed a thumb back over his shoulder. "Perhaps you and I could share some information?"

"Not a clue what you're on about, old son. Sorry. My name's not McLeod."

Collins smiled and pulled a business card from his pocket. "Right. Of course. Sorry about that." He handed over the card. "But if you do decide your name is McLeod after all, and you'd like to tell me anything about Vince Stratton, why don't you give me a call?"

McLeod took the card and stuffed it into a pocket. "Aye, right. Maybe if I take this you'll leave me alone?"

Collins nodded and blipped the remote on his car. He turned back to it and climbed in, watched McLeod in the side mirror as the small man hurried away down the night-shrouded road. It had been well worth coming back here after all. Now he had them both to watch and see what shook down. Maybe one or other would make a mistake, or make a move that he could follow up. Maybe McLeod would even give something up on Stratton, but Collins had to admit he'd be a little disappointed if that happened. Whatever, it had been a good night's work. He could go home and rest easy for a while.

* * *

Matt sat in his car three blocks from Stratton's and stared at the business card in his shaking hand. Detective Sergeant Charles Collins. How the hell had the man known his name? And how did he know about what Matt had been up to that afternoon?

After sitting at home and stewing for an hour, Matt hadn't been able to settle, so he'd ignored Ben's texts about the Cactus Club, as he knew he would, and come back to watch Stratton's some more. He had intended to see if Vince left the pub at closing time and went somewhere else. He imagined the man living in some big, fancy house in a northern suburb or something. But then this Detective Collins had just shown up out of nowhere. And he still didn't know if Stratton ever left the protected castle of his fucking pub.

He pocketed the card again and started the engine. So much for following Stratton home tonight. He had no intention of getting too cosy with the police for any reason. He had a trail of corpses in his personal history after all, and could do without any police scrutiny. He was in no doubt that Stratton would have the upper hand there too. With any luck, he'd be able to figure out a way to get close to Stratton without this Collins noticing. Surely the bastard left the pub sometimes. But it was all extra hassle he could really do well without.

He got another text from Ben.

disappointed mate really hoped you'd come out with us

Matt grimaced against genuine contrition.

Really sorry, man. Next time, I promise. Did Steve-O get laid?

He stared at the phone for a moment, then it pinged with a reply.

HAHAHAHAHAHAHAHAHAHAHAHA

Matt grinned, sent back a smiley face in reply, and pocketed the phone. He drove for home, planning on a few drams of good malt to maybe help him sleep.

SIXTEEN

AMY STUMBLED INTO HER APARTMENT at nearly three in the morning, breathing deeply as she worked hard on staying upright, determined not to wake Carla. It turned out that Caitlin Halliday was a hell of a good person, a sexy good dancer, and Amy felt like she'd made a real friend. She was under no illusions about how much they might see of each other. Caitlin had been born in Stockholm, educated in London and now lived in LA. She had a schedule most actors would actually kill for, and her star was showing no signs of slowing its rise any time soon. But they had shared cell phone numbers and email addresses, and were already hooked up on Facebook—Caitlin's personal page, not, as she called it, her awful Hollywood star page bullshit. Caitlin had insisted they hang out whenever they were both in town. She'd already texted while Amy was in the cab home, reinforcing her pleasure at her first *real night out* in ages. Amy texted back a happy face and *Can't wait to do it again!* She had made a genuine friend.

She closed the front door quietly then walked straight into the hall table and knocked the bowl of keys and loose change to the floor. It clattered and all manner of low-level noisy items rattled off the radiator. Amy paused, wincing, waiting for Carla to come out of her room, maybe a baseball bat held high. Should she say something to let her flatmate know it wasn't an intruder?

There was no further sound and Amy breathed a sigh of relief. Carla's door stood half open and Amy leaned near, listening for sounds of heavy breathing. There were none. Soft orange light coated the bed and Amy realised the curtains were open allowing streetlight in, and the bed was vacant. She laughed aloud. All this creeping about, and failing in the attempt, and Carla wasn't even home to be disturbed. She must be on a good bender, it wasn't like her to be out this late.

Amy winced again, thinking of the lateness. A day off was a strange curse for a shift worker. While she had enjoyed her night immensely, and delivered the shadows to a very worthy recipient, her own life continued unabated. She was on the afternoon shift the next day, working 2:00 p.m. until midnight, then back to the nightshift on Sunday. She squinted as she counted up in her head. Eleven hours until work started. She was very ready to crash now so she could sleep for a good nine hours and hopefully not have too bad a hangover and plenty of time to get to work. Maybe it wasn't so bad.

She took two preventative Ibuprofen tablets with a pint of water, then went to strip off clothes and make-up and have a shower. The hot water and steam helped to start the sobering-up process and she didn't feel quite so wasted as she turned off the taps and pulled the shower curtain aside. She had forgotten to hit the switch for the extractor fan and the bathroom was a thick mist of steam. As she stepped from the tub and flicked the switch, a shadow filled the still-open bathroom doorway. Amy jumped, crying out involuntarily.

"Carla, you scared the shit out of me!"

She grabbed a towel, wrapped it loosely around herself and stuck her head out into the hallway. There was no one there.

"Carla?"

No answer. Amy shook her head. Had she imagined it? Swirls in the steam or something. The vision of the dark presence behind Prentiss after she'd delivered the shadows swept through her mind and a wave of ice caressed her body at the same time. Whatever the hell that thing was, it scared her. Her gift had always been so straightforward before, but lately it was becoming complicated. To the point where swirls of steam made her scream like a schoolgirl on a ghost train.

If nothing else, the quick shock had hastened her sobriety. She refilled her water glass, downed it, then filled it again to take to bed with her. She would be up a dozen times in the night to pee, most likely, but better that than a heinous headache.

She pulled on undies and a baggy T-shirt, I ⊠ SYDNEY, put the glass on her bedside table and switched off the light. As she lay down and pulled the duvet up to her chin, the sense of relief was palpable. One of the best things about a good night out was getting home to the comfort of your own bed. The streetlights outside were never entirely doused. She couldn't remember the number of times she had promised to buy herself some blockout linings for the curtains. But the soft orange glow had become familiar and she didn't mind so much, the wardrobe and dressing table, and her small bookshelf, awash in a soft glow like an artificial sunset. Her door was pushed almost closed, a giant poster of the Sydney skyline on the back. A gift from her mother, *To remind you to come home one day.* The details were spectral in the dim light, but the Harbour Bridge and Opera House so iconic she was sure she would recognise them in pitch darkness.

She breathed in deeply, let her eyes flutter closed, then suddenly sat up, staring in wide-eyed shock at the doorway. It was wide open, the poster lost against the wall, and a dark silhouette filled the space, icy and malevolent.

"Carla?" Amy said weakly, knowing without a doubt it wasn't her flatmate.

The presence seemed to swell and reduce in the doorframe, like it pulsed in time to some beat far slower than her currently racing heart. Again she felt the presence of multitudes contained in the vaguely man-shaped smear of blackness. Trembling wracked her body as her knuckles tightened on the edge of the duvet. She stared, a soft, keening wail escaping her lips.

It reached forward, one arm rising then seeming to elongate, to stretch into the room. It covered the space between them interminably slowly even though it appeared to move quite fast, as though the room expanded even as the arm lengthened. It pushed a frozen wave of air before it, made goosebumps spring up along Amy's exposed arms. As the weak wailing continued, her breath clouded and wisped around her face.

The black arm reached further and she saw ripples and reflections in it, as though it was made of undulating tar, somehow held into the rough shape of a limb, but the limb bore no hand, no fingers, just a jet black, scintillating stump.

Amy drew icy breath deep into her lungs and screamed, her piercing voice carrying all her fear and rage in the face of her utter inability to do anything about the entity reaching for her, about to wind her into itself. She scrambled back up the bed, pressing herself into the wall.

A bang like a gunshot echoed through the flat, the front door hitting the hallway wall, and Carla was running towards her, crying, "Amy? Amy what's wrong?"

The black presence in the doorway shattered and spiralled away in a million shards of night as Carla burst through it into Amy's room. The Spanish girl's face was flushed, her eyes wide in alarm. She wrapped her arms around herself, looked left and right.

"It's so cold in here! Amy, are you okay?"

Amy nodded, tears on her cheeks, gooseflesh still standing tall. She gasped one, two ragged breaths, so thankful for Carla's appearance but at a total loss for something to say.

Carla ran to the bed, sat and stroked Amy's hair. "Oh, Amy, I thought you were being attacked!"

Amy nodded again. "Me too."

"A dream?"

"I guess so." But she knew it had been no dream. Something was coming for her. Something she had released along with the shadows she put into Prentiss.

But it had started before then. The last few times she released shadows she had sensed it there, rising nearer. Only this time had it appeared so completely, so solid, in a vaguely human shape. And it had followed her home. If not for Carla coming in, it would surely have had her. Amy couldn't stop shaking, terrified at the thought that maybe it was here now and there was no stopping it. But the sensation of icy malevolence had dissipated, the flat felt normal again, warm and homey.

"I'll make tea," Carla said. "You need a cup of tea."

Amy smiled weakly, followed Carla from the room. "I think I do. Lots of sugar."

As she passed through the door she braced herself, but there was nothing, no sensation at all. Maybe it had clung to her since the delivery earlier to Prentiss, then picked its moment when things were quiet enough, and then Carla had inadvertently saved her. If her flatmate had been even a minute later coming home… And now it was gone forever. She had no way to know that, but Amy decided she would have to believe it because any alternative was too terrifying to consider.

SEVENTEEN

MATT ROSE EARLY, particularly for a Saturday. Working a regular job, forty hours Monday to Friday, meant he usually enjoyed his weekend lie-ins. But though a few whiskies had helped him fall asleep, his dreams had been grim and twisted, fuelled by anxiety and stress. By 7:00 a.m. he knew he was wide awake and staying that way.

He hauled himself from bed and set about making coffee and toast with Rose's orange marmalade just like he'd had almost every day growing up. His mother wouldn't consider a different brand. He flinched at the memory of her. As if his guilt wasn't black enough, what he'd done to the family, running out so young, hardly being in touch and generally a godawful son. Now they were directly at risk from this Stratton fucker despite his distance. How the hell had he got so entangled so quickly? All because he had been careless with the Sullivan hit.

No, not careless. Weak. Too broken by the act to take care of the body, too fatigued to pay attention and spot someone watching him. He could have just run away and not been followed, come back for his car later, and Stratton would probably never have got his claws in. But that was pointless thinking. "There's nae use fretting what's already done." His mother again, in her infinite wisdom, would say that all the time. A pragmatic woman. How he missed her. Even as distant and aloof as he'd been, as difficult and troubled, pushing his parents away, they did everything they could to include him, embrace him, nurture him. And he only loved them more for that, and it only made the remorse cut more deeply.

He shook himself, gulped coffee. Fuck that and fuck Stratton. He had to do something, be proactive. And he had to avoid that copper while he was at it. He still hadn't quite figured out what was happening there, but the guy was easily spotted with his big Mercedes and fancy clothes, shiny leather shoes.

Matt tidied away his breakfast things and got dressed, then called Steve-O. The phone was answered with a curt, slurred, "Y'ello? Matt?"

"Hey man, sorry to call so early. Thought your phone would be off if you were sleeping."

"Must've forgot."

"Sorry about that."

"Hmm. What's up?"

"Can I borrow your moped?"

Steve seemed to wake up very quickly, his voice clearing. "What for?" He loved his little white Vespa, treated it like a lover. Which might be as close to a relationship as the poor bugger was likely to get unless he built up some confidence. Matt and the others were not giving up on destroying Steve's virginity. In the pub the other night Ben had outlined a plan for a couple of weeks hence, but Matt couldn't remember the details through the boozy haze. It would come up again. If the plan had been for last night at the Cactus Club, Ben's last text confirmed it hadn't worked.

"I need to run some errands today and my bloody car's broken down." In fact, it might get recognised by Stratton or Collins, but Steve-O didn't need to know that.

"You'll have to Tube over and pick it up."

"Aye, I'll do that. Thanks, man, you're a lifesaver."

"You pay for anything that happens, even a tiny scratch!"

"I will."

"I know every square centimetre of my bike."

Matt laughed. Bike! Steve acted like he was a Hell's Angel on a vintage Shovelhead. "I know that. I'll treat her like a proper lady."

"All right. I'll put the kettle on."

"You're a top man, Steve-O. See you soon."

Matt hung up, grinning. Steve really was a great bloke. One day some lucky girl would notice him and she would be treated like royalty, loved and respected and looked after. Not many people were the genuine article good guy, but Steve was.

Still feeling guilty at letting his friends down, he tapped out another text to Ben, again apologising for ducking out of the night before. He suggested they organise something decent for next Friday. As much as anything, it gave him some focus to knock this Stratton situation over in less than a week. *Maybe we should make a weekend of it,* he texted to Ben. *Like we did last year, go down to Brighton. I'll see Steve-O today and run it by him. You check in with Gareth and let's go hard.* He sent the text and stood staring at the phone, imagining a run-in with Stratton in the meantime, another agonising delivery of the dark. He hoped he would live to see the following weekend.

A little after 9:00 a.m. Matt sat drinking tea with Steve-O in is little estate flat, one of hundreds just like it in a forest of dull concrete blocks. Matt was anxious to be moving, but tried to remain calm, casual. They talked about nothing in particular. Matt suggested Brighton the following weekend and Steve was into the idea. He said he was catching up with Ben and Gareth for the football that afternoon and they'd start looking for a place to stay down there. Matt had to excuse himself from joining them at the game.

"What's so important about these errands?" Steve asked.

Matt shrugged. "Just a bunch of shit I've been putting off. It'll all be sorted soon."

"You okay, mate?" Steve asked, his eyes concerned.

Matt nodded, trying to think of the best reply, when he was saved by a knock at the door. Gareth came in, bulging in training gear straight from the gym. "You're up already? Sweet. Thought I might be out there banging for ages to wake you."

"What's everyone doing up so early?" Steve asked, slumping back into an armchair.

"I'm always up early," Gareth said. "And we're going to the markets before the football, remember?"

"Yeah, but I didn't expect you this soon," Steve said. "You're a nutter."

"Early rise and straight to the gym. Best hangover cure in the world, mate," Gareth said with a bright grin. "Assuming you survive the first ten or fifteen minutes without chucking up." He looked at Matt. "You all right, man? Where were you last night? It was bloody good!"

"It was!" Steve confirmed. "You missed a cracker."

"Yeah, gutted," Matt said. "But I have to go. Steve, tell him about next weekend."

"What about next weekend?" Gareth asked, already smiling. He was always up for a party.

"Tell you in a minute," Steve said and then reminded Matt how important the moped was as he handed over the keys to the lock-up. "You remember which one?" He stood, pointing out the window of his tenth floor flat. Across the road were dozens of lock-up garages, and beyond them a two-metre-or-so-high wall that masked them from a busy dual carriageway, a scraggly collection of trees marching down the slope between. Just another scruffy urban corner.

"Aye, it's end of the first row on the left. Easy as. And thanks again."

"No problem. Be careful."

"I will!"

It only took a minute or two to walk around Steve's building and across the road to the collection of lock-up garages. Several long rows of dozens of roller doors facing each other with concrete aprons between, a gutter full of leaves along the centre of each row. Matt walked down the first row to Steve's lock-up right next to the end wall. Traffic roared from the dual carriageway on the other side. The key protested in the rusted lock for a moment, then the handle twisted and the door marked with a big painted number 12 rattled up. Matt retrieved Steve's helmet from atop a pile of boxes and wheeled the small Italian bike out into the day.

Just before 10:00 a.m. Matt parked the Vespa in a side street and strolled to the junction opposite Stratton's, keeping to the shadows of the surrounding buildings. He had one eye on the closed and darkened pub, the other on the lookout for Collins's expensive car. The detective didn't appear to be anywhere around, so Matt found himself a deeply concealed doorway with a good view of the pub and slumped down to wait. The stone step was ice cold, even through his jeans, and a vague aroma of piss drifted around. He pulled his knees up and wrapped himself tightly in his thick, black coat. Anyone passing would think him some homeless loser and this city was famous for ignoring those people. Matt had more than enough first-hand experience of that from his first two years in London.

After a couple of hours getting colder and stiffer, Matt began to wonder if his idea was idiotic. Perhaps Stratton did live in some big house somewhere and there was no one in the pub to watch for. Maybe the bastard had left last night after Matt had been spooked off by Collins.

At close to noon, Matt slipped from hiding and trotted a block away to a café. He ordered coffee and a bacon sandwich, standing in the doorway while he waited for his food to keep an eye out. He could only just see the pub from this vantage, but hoped he could see enough. Once served, he went back to his spot, the hot coffee and delicious crispy bacon positively heavenly.

Another hour passed and Matt began to regret the coffee as the urge to piss became ever stronger. Trying to ignore it, half-dozing, half-daydreaming, the front of Stratton's had drifted into an out-of-focus blur while his mind wandered. Then movement caught his attention. All the lights were still off inside, but the front door opened and Stratton stepped out, well-dressed in slacks and a tweed jacket. He looked like a regular gentleman, his gunmetal hair combed back and slicked in an old-fashioned wave. He had a phone pressed to his ear and was chatting lazily, a smile tugging at his lips. So maybe he did live in the pub after all. Maybe the upper floors were some lavish flat. Matt imagined it like something out of a Sherlock Holmes story, all wingbacked leather chairs and dark wood furnishings.

Stratton hung up the phone and pulled a long cigar from his inside jacket pocket, fired it up with one of those mini jet engine lighters. He leaned against the wall, puffing thick smoke up into the grey day, as if he was waiting for something. Matt trusted the camouflage of his shadowed corner, patient. After a few minutes Clancy jogged across the street with a wave. Stratton pushed himself forward off the wall and the two chatted for a few minutes. Eventually, Stratton handed Clancy an envelope and sent him off with a slap on the shoulder. Clancy walked back the way he'd come, affecting a faintly ridiculous swagger like he was an LA gangster, almost dragging one leg behind as though crippled by an unfortunate car accident. Stratton watched him go then gave a slight shake of the head, but his smile was warm. Maybe he really did care for these boys.

Matt had to lean out of hiding as Stratton wandered away to the north. He didn't go far before unlocking a shiny Rover 3500. Matt grinned. It was a classic old gangster car, back when gangsters lived in the 1970s. But Stratton's car was immaculate, beautifully restored and cared for. The V8 engine roared and revved, exhaust fumes clouding the cold morning air. The pale metallic green vehicle would be pretty easy to follow, there weren't many on the roads any more, particularly so polished. Matt slipped from the doorway, ran back a block and hopped onto Steve's Vespa. He pulled the helmet on and started the thing, its engine whine no better than a hair dryer as he hurried forward again. It might be weedy, but in London traffic it would zip and zoom all over the place easily.

At the junction Matt prayed he hadn't lost sight of Stratton already and was rewarded with the sight of the car making a right turn a couple of hundred metres up the road. Matt followed and pushed the local speed limits a little to catch up. After a couple more turns, just managing to keep the old car in sight, he had settled into a comfortable tail. The Saturday traffic was heavy and Matt hoped his riding position gave him a better view of Stratton than the bastard had of him. Regardless, he stayed well back, very nearly losing the Rover on several occasions. Twice a lucky guess put him back behind it after he'd lost it at a junction. They drove for nearly twenty minutes, Matt's hands numb with cold by the time Stratton indicated and turned into the large gravelled car park of a care home.

Matt pulled up a hundred meters or so back and parked. He hooked the helmet onto the handlebar and tried to vigorously rub some life back into his cold-whitened hands. He walked carefully up to the main gate and snuck a look in. Stratton's car was parked in a visitor bay but the man himself was nowhere to be seen.

He looked up at the sign: SALLY GENTLE HOSPICE, PROVIDING PALLIATIVE CARE AND SUPPORT FOR PATIENTS AND THEIR FAMILIES.

Matt frowned. Who might Stratton be visiting? A family member or friend with a terminal illness, presumably, but who? And could they give Matt any useful information? It was a clue, so he determined to follow it up. A small park, little more than a ten-square-metre patch of grass with flowerbeds all around it, was directly across the road from the hospice. A big oak tree stood in the middle of it, leafless now, its branches dark scribbles against the slate sky. There were a couple of benches, one on each side. Matt went and sat on the far bench, obscured by the tree and scrubby shrubs. He could see the front of the hospice, but anyone on that side of the street was unlikely to see him in any detail. The urge to piss had become unbearable after the cold ride and sitting on a frozen bench was the last straw. Hoping no one would notice, Matt stepped up behind the oak tree and released his bladder, sighing up to the clouds in blessed relief. Thankfully, no one else came by to see him and he returned to his vigil on the bench entirely more comfortable. Though no less cold to the bone.

It was another hour before Stratton's Rover crunched across the gravel and drove back towards Camden Town. Matt had long since decided that he had had more than enough of being cold. He'd spent more than four hours sitting around in the late autumn chill and wanted to be warm, but he remained in place a while longer. Just in case Stratton had spotted him, just in case Collins was around. Paranoia was a valuable asset when people actually were after you.

He gave it twenty minutes then decided that he'd been careful enough. He crossed the street and entered the Sally Gentle Hospice. He was immediately enveloped by calm and warmth. Almost too warm, the air thick and cloying after the sharp chill of outdoors. Deep pile carpet covered the floor, the lights and other fittings were expensive, almost ostentatious. The place was clearly well, and privately, funded.

A middle-aged woman with a greying bun and oversized blue plastic glasses sat behind a reception desk. "Can I help you?"

"Aye, er…" Matt had no idea how to proceed. What was the best course of action? He'd sat on that bench trying to decide and had come up with nothing. No angle. Might as well just spit it out. "Was Mr. Stratton here?" he asked.

The woman smiled. "He still is, the dear man. You'd like to visit?"

Matt licked his lips, nonplussed for a moment as his mind raced. Mr. Stratton was still here, but he'd seen Vince's car leave. And he'd seen Vince at the wheel. So another Mr. Stratton. Palliative care. Vince visiting. The bastard's father? An uncle? Surely he was too old for a surviving grandparent. "I would, yes, if that's okay."

"No problem. Terry gets very tired, so he may not wake. He had his son visit not long ago, so he'll be a bit worn out. And he's easily confused these days."

Father then. Interesting. "That's okay, I'd still like to see him."

"You're family?"

"Err, yeah, nephew." The woman's eyes narrowed. *You're too fucking young!* Matt's mind screamed. "Grand-nephew, actually," he quickly added, "but I call him Uncle."

"Well, aren't you a sweet young man. He's in room five, along the corridor there on your left."

"Thanks."

"Sign in first, please."

"Oh, aye." Matt scribbled a signature that looked like a drunk's doodle and wrote Paul Stratton in the box beside it. Who would check?

Heart hammering uncomfortably fast, Matt walked away before she could ask or say any more. He poked his head cautiously into the door of room five and saw the drawn old man lying on the bed, eyes closed. The head of the bed was propped up about thirty degrees and a drip stand stood beside the man's shoulder, clear tubes hanging like strange decorations in the dimly lit room. A television on the wall beyond the foot of the bed burbled softly. The room stank of white lilies, the long established flower of the dead with its thick, choking perfume that mugged and subdued any other smell, even the slow decay of the still-just-living.

Rather than stand half in the corridor like a prize lemon, Matt stepped into the room and pushed the door to behind him. What the hell now? He checked the cards on the table beside the bed. A whole bunch of names that meant nothing to him. The room was otherwise empty but for the paraphernalia of life support and a few trappings of comfort.

A door in the corner led to a private bathroom. Despite his public piss against the oak tree, he already needed to go again and had no intention of holding it as long as before. He crept over and shut the door. When he went back into the room, Terry Stratton's eyes remained closed. Matt turned a slow circle in the dim room, wondering just what the hell he had expected to find here. Maybe he could talk to the old man when he woke and ask questions. If the guy was easily confused, perhaps he could coax some secrets about Vince that he could use for leverage.

"'Thou know'st tis common; all that lives must die.'"

Matt jumped at the soft, papery voice. He turned to the old man.

"'Passing through nature to eternity.'" Terry smiled. "*Hamlet*. Act one, Scene two."

"You like a bit of Shakespeare, eh?" Matt asked.

"Who are you then?"

"Friend of your son. Thought I'd drop by and say hello."

"That right?"

"I know what it's like. People don't visit much, you spend a lot of time on your own. Thought you might like a chat, pass some time."

"My son doesn't have friends," Terry said, his voice a little stronger. "You're one of his boys, obviously. Don't pretend to be something you're not." The man sounded disapproving, but not unkind.

"Fair enough. Sorry about that." That was close. Matt forced himself to breathe easily.

"You're older than most of his runners. You been with him a long time."

"We have a fair history, aye."

"I've never really understood everything Vince does, but I know he's the kind of entrepreneur who gives you lads a chance, uses you for his errands and stuff. So at least there's still some good in him. You owe him a lot, yeah?"

Matt thought of Clancy and Dexter and the others and wondered what they might owe Vince Stratton. "I guess so."

"Sent you 'round cos he couldn't come, did he?"

Matt pulled the chair closer to the bed, sat down. "He was here earlier today, don't you remember?"

Terry's brow creased, his face drawn tight to the skull like he was already a cadaver, long since put in the ground. The sickly sweet smell of death drifted around him, stuck in the back of Matt's throat despite the lilies. "Ah, fuck, son, I don't remember much any more."

"That Shakespeare sounded pretty right to me."

Terry laughed, a single thick, bubbling cough. "'Aye, but to die, and go we know not where, to lie in cold obstruction and to rot.' That's from *Measure for Measure*, Act three, Scene one."

"Is it?"

"Yeah, it is. I don't remember my nurse's names or who came around an hour ago, but I remember that old stuff. Funny thing, the way my brain is going." He sniffed. "I've loved Shakespeare all my life, and memorised a bloody lot of it. Played a lot of parts on the boards through my youth and middle age. I know for a fact I'm right about that line. My brain is turning to pea soup, son, but some bits refuse to give in and seem to only get stronger."

"You were an actor?"

"I was a teacher, lad. English teacher. But I was also into amateur dramatics and got a few decent parts. Even entertained the idea of going for the fame and glory once. Managed to get good enough to understudy for a couple of big names."

"What happened?"

"Life."

Matt nodded, lips pursed. "Seems a shame."

"Family comes first."

"Vince needed you?"

Terry barked his wet laugh again. "Vince? Can you imagine him needing anyone? He was independent before he started school, that one. His mum, with her illness. I couldn't keep the hours of an actor and look after her."

"Oh right, that makes sense." Matt wondered how he might find out more about the woman. And what good it might do.

A tear breached the old man's eye. "Who'll look after my Maisey now, eh?"

Still going then. Maybe he could use that. If Stratton was going to threaten Matt's mother, maybe he could return the favour. "I'm sure Vince has it covered."

"That's what he tells me, but it's not the same. All this time, convinced I would end up a widower, and here I am and she's still going strong. She'll be seventy-seven next birthday. She'll wither without me. It sounds conceited, but it's true. You can't know a love like we had. I remember all about that. She's even managed to visit me here once or twice, that's how strong her love is. Despite the crippling pain. I remember that too."

Matt swallowed, genuine grief thickening his throat. How could Vince be such a dick when he had a father like this? "I'm sorry," he muttered.

"What's your name, son?"

Matt felt a strange urge for honesty, sure the old man would forget anyway. If he couldn't remember his nurse's names, he wouldn't remember this. "Matt," he said. "Matt McLeod."

"Tomorrow, and tomorrow, and tomorrow," Terry said, his voice stronger than ever. "Creeps in this petty pace from day to day, to the last syllable of recorded time." He coughed, drew a deep breath, then carried on. "And all our yesterdays have lighted fools the way to dusty death. Out, out, brief candle! Life's but a walking shadow, a poor player that struts and frets his hour upon the stage, and then is heard no more. It is a tale told by an idiot, full of sound and fury, signifying nothing."

Matt kept quiet. He had no response to that.

"Macbeth," Terry said, his voice reedy once more. "That's one for you lot, eh? The Scottish Play. We're never supposed to say its name for fear of bad luck."

"I've heard that. Didn't know if it was true or not."

"Full of sound and fury, signifying nothing." Terry said, voice still weak, but bitter. "Go on, fuck off. I'm tired. Unless you know a way to end my suffering, you can go now. Thanks for your effort and tell

Vince thanks, but I don't need extra visitors. I'm nearly dead, so let's just let that be, shall we?"

Matt stood quickly, shocked by the sudden strength of the man's rancour. "I'm sorry." He reached out a hand and took Terry's that lay limply on the coverlet, shook it gently. Here lay a fine soul dying. "Whatever happens, you're a good man. Everything about this is utterly fucking unjust."

Terry narrowed his eyes for a moment, then he nodded. "Yes. Yes it is."

Matt left the room and walked back to the reception. The woman behind the desk looked up. "Everything okay?" she asked, her face soft, eyes sad. It was clearly a well-practised expression of sympathy.

"He's very tired," Matt said. "I'll come again another day."

A nurse stepped out of the office behind the desk and paused, eyes locked with Matt. His breath caught in his throat. She was quite beautiful, long blonde hair tied back in a loose ponytail, fine nose and emerald eyes, but he saw far more than that. She seemed to be cloaked in darkness, a curling mantle of shadows, tendrils blacker than night that she wore like a glamourous dress and flowing tresses of hair, winding in and around her physical form.

And she clearly saw something in him too, her eyes widening, mouth falling slightly open. But where he saw beauty and dark promise, a power and confidence, her expression betrayed that what she saw was shocking, frightening, even disgusting.

"Hi, I haven't seen you here before," she said, like she hoped to never see him again. Her voice was soft, accented. Australian, Matt realised.

He managed a quick nod, swallowed hard and hurried from the hospice. He desperately wanted to know more about what he had seen surrounding her, but couldn't bear to spend another second under her horrified gaze.

* * *

Amy stood behind the desk as the young man almost bolted from the hospice. She breathed deeply, tried to think clearly. She had never seen anything like that before. Outwardly he appeared to be a craggily handsome, smallish man in his late twenties, shaggy, dark hair, no taller than her, quite skinny. But around him, over him, clinging to his back and shoulders like a parasite, was a cloud of blackness that seemed to suck in the light around him. It was not unlike the shadows she took from the dead, but it was blacker, deeper, enormously more malevolent. And he wore it like a burden, a suffering weight.

She should be terrified of him, but while his blackness was terrifying, the man himself seemed sweet and entirely normal. He had been quite embarrassed to see her and it struck her that he had appeared to look *around* her as well as at her. Could he see something similar? Did she carry a dark passenger like he did? The shadow on his back reminded her of the presence in her doorway the night before, but it didn't seem to be a threat to him. Could he help her understand the rising malice of her gift? Was he like her? She had never come across anyone else in her life with whom she could even discuss her power, let alone someone who might share it. She had to see that man again.

"Carol, who was that?" she asked, leaning over to look at the visitor book.

"Mr. Stratton's grand-nephew, would you believe?"

Amy shook her head. "No, that's not possible."

"Why?"

"I've had long talks with Terry during the nights. Grand-nephew? That would have to be the grandson of Terry's brother or sister?"

"Yes."

"Terry doesn't have any brothers or sisters. We've talked about it because I'm an only child too, like him."

Carol frowned. "Well, that doesn't make sense." She turned the book around. "Says here his name was Paul Stratton."

"Why would he make something like that up?" Amy hurried from the desk and went to room five. She had to know more. Terry was snoring softly as she entered. Frustrated she stood by his bed, wondering what to do.

His eyes flickered open. "Like Piccadilly Circus in here today," he said. "But I'm most glad to see you, my Sydney beauty."

She grinned. "Charmer! You had visitors today."

Terry frowned. "Feels like it, but I don't remember."

"A young Scottish man," Amy said, remembering his accent as he talked to Carol. *He's very tired. I'll come again another day.*

Terry's eyebrows rose. "Full of sound and fury, signifying nothing." he said with a soft laugh.

"What's that?"

"Macbeth. That was his name."

Amy shook her head, smiling slightly. "His name was Macbeth?"

"No, wait. We talked about Macbeth because he was a Mac... Mac... Fuck this melting brain, love, don't ever get old and cancerous."

"I'll do my best."

"McLeod! Fucking Matt McLeod! I actually remembered something."

"How do you know him?"

"I don't. One of my son's boys."

"His boys?"

"Employees."

"Ah, your son employs that young man? Matt McLeod?"

But Terry was asleep again, faded, almost translucent he was so close to death. Amy put a hand to his forehead and felt gently for his shadows. She would be collecting those before long, he had a few more days at most. Poor old Terry Stratton, she would miss him.

But Matt McLeod, employed by Vince Stratton. She tapped that information into the notepad app on her phone so she wouldn't forget. Vince usually visited his father once a day. She'd have to ask him about Matt next time, find out how she could meet the dark-bearing Scotsman again. He terrified her, but she had to talk to him.

EIGHTEEN

VINCE STRATTON LOOKED UP at a knock on his office door. He'd been lost in an article about a tribe in Papua New Guinea who still practised a form of cannibalism. Fascinating stuff. A glance at his screen showed Dexter waiting outside, a shadow in the dimly lit corridor. He was a good boy, despite his damage. He looked at everything with the suspicion that it would let him down, which is what he'd been conditioned to expect. Everything in his life thus far had fallen apart and left him lost and lonely. And angry. He intended to ensure Dexter found purpose that would reward him, rebuild his confidence in the possibility of achievement and self-actualisation. They may be buzzwords, but they were real. Stratton would never use the words out loud—he didn't want to sound like some idiot Anthony Robbins buttercup—but he believed strongly in the concepts nonetheless. He simply needed to take his time building that trust with Dex, not scare him off like a deer bolting from a snapped twig in a quiet forest.

"Come in, lad!" he called out.

Dexter pushed the door open and stepped inside, eyes checking left and right. He was like a cat, always checking the corners, looking for an exit.

"Come in, lad," Stratton said again. "Shut the door."

The young boy did as he was told and approached the desk. He clutched an envelope in one hand. *Business time*, Vince thought to himself. Another missive that had found its way to him through the convoluted network of dead-letter drops and unsent emails. It was a process that eventually went beyond retrieval, the client setting things in motion that were impossible to stop. Whatever series of drops they might have used to trigger Stratton's involvement would be gone now, moved or finished with. The envelope Dexter carried looked thick enough to contain the cash he was expecting. The final confirmation. Whoever that money related to was a dead man already. They just didn't know it yet. Vince had two jobs on the go, and was fairly sure this would be Najdovski, a Macedonian mobster from the East End. And someone he might just have a new and interesting way of dealing with.

"What do you have there?" he asked.

Dexter looked down like he was surprised to be carrying something. The boy had attention issues too, strangely enough. Vince would need to train better focus into him. "Pick up from three like you asked, Boss."

It was Najdovski. "And you destroyed the drop after collecting?"

"Yep, all gone."

"Good lad."

Vince took the envelope and thumbed through the cash inside. A great big wad of notes was something he never grew bored of seeing. And this particular one was exactly the cost of Aleksandar Najdovski's life. And it offered an opportunity to play with that weird Scotsman's skills before Vince took him out. Najdovski's was a complicated hit and the lack of a body would be perfect. Then Vince would indeed take out the Scotsman, a freebie he'd be only too happily indulge. Use the man then end the man. Simple. There was a temptation to keep him around, but tidying up behind himself was more important.

He pulled a couple of fifty pound notes from the envelope and handed them over. "Good work, Dex. Take this and enjoy yourself."

Dexter looked at the money, back up to Stratton. His eyebrows rose. "You sure?"

"I've told you, lad. You do right by me and you'll be looked after."

Dex nodded to the wad still in Stratton's hand. "What's that for?" he asked, his voice nervous.

Vince pursed his lips, head tipping to one side. Disappointing. But give the boy time, he was still quite new. Not new like David though. He should really know better. "Golden rule, remember? What is it?"

"Don't ask questions."

"Right. So why are you asking questions?"

Dexter shrugged. "Just wondering, you know. What it is you do. What I do."

"You're a valuable asset to my many and varied business interests. That's all you need to know. As time goes by, you may well learn more. But do as you're told and ask no questions, then you'll continue to have a room provided, money in your pocket, three squares a day and all the other comforts I offer. Not much of me to ask, is it? That you don't question me?"

"No, Boss."

"You're happy in that house with Clancy and Saul?"

"Yes, Boss."

Dexter seemed disappointed, even annoyed. In a way, Vince respected that, but it couldn't be allowed. He was still confident Dexter would fall into line and prove himself to be the asset he hoped for. More so than Clancy anyway.

"Good lad," Vince said with a broad smile. "I promise you, those things are fixtures if you do right by me. They won't be taken away." Dexter nodded. Still not trusting, but starting to hope. The hook was starting to catch. "Off you go then. I'll call when I need you next."

Dexter scurried away, closing the door quietly behind him.

Vince stared at the cash in his hand for a moment, then took it to the safe in the corner. He tossed up again the wisdom of using McLeod for this hit, though he knew it was something he would have to do. He'd been wondering about a method for Najdovski since the job had first surfaced, so the appearance of McLeod was as fortuitous as it was unusual. Stratton was a meticulously careful man and his career was built on professionalism and attention to detail, so he was also well aware of his only weakness. And if he was honest, he was indulging that weakness. He had a compelling desire to kill with as wide a variety of weapons as possible. Usually a fairly safe foible. But after learning of McLeod's existence and his skill, Vince knew he would have to use the man as an extension of himself. If it were really true that the Scotsman could kill with a touch, hard as that might be to believe, Vince had to use him as a weapon. And he had seen the video evidence that it was no fantasy. Vince had few challenges in life any more, but this was one he had to rise to. And it solved the problems of Najdovski's corpse. The hit had the instruction that Najdovski disappear, leave no body, no trace. There was an element of fear being deployed, an uncertainty to destabilise Najdovski's crew. Of course, taking the man out and leaving no trace was not beyond Stratton's own skills, but McLeod's method was uniquely suited. Stratton smiled to himself. He was using that loose reasoning as an excuse to use McLeod as a weapon, he knew. He wasn't without self-reflection enough to fool himself. But it all worked out nicely and added a little spice to his life. And then he would get rid of the Scotsman, to ensure that dangerous and unnatural talent didn't ever get anywhere that might compromise Stratton himself.

Vince would watch McLeod's work, stay nearby. He would be ready to correct any errors. And if he could genuinely pull off a job using McLeod's skills? What a truly great moment in his career that would be. Then he could take McLeod out and get on with business as usual. It was a safe enough adventure.

Najdovski had a restaurant on the edge of Soho, not far from Oxford Street. Since this job had been initiated, Vince had begun his groundwork and decided the best place for the hit would be there. Najdovski had a habit of staying back late on his own most nights. The man was an idiot really. Or had no idea he was making enemies. But that also made him an idiot, so the first assessment stood.

With a smile, Vince opened Word on his desktop and typed up a document, printed it off. It had the restaurant address, a suggested time, all the details McLeod would need. Vince then printed a slightly grainy but perfectly serviceable photo of Najdovski. Using surgical gloves, he retrieved both pages from the printer and put them into a standard letter envelope. At the bottom of the instructions, capital letters spelled out BEFORE TUESDAY.

He grinned. That would put the panic into the bastard and ensure the job met the specifications for which Stratton had been handsomely paid. He rang Saul's mobile number and the young lad answered on the second ring.

"Boss?"

"You at the pub?" Vince knew he was, but it paid to let the lads think they had more autonomy than they did.

"Sure am."

"My office, please."

Moments later the freckled redhead knocked and Vince told him to come in. He handed the envelope with McLeod's instructions over, still wearing his surgical gloves. Saul paid no attention, used to the habit.

"Dead drop two, please, right away."

"No problem."

"How long do you need?"

Saul pursed his lips to think. "Twenty minutes, tops."

"Good. And here." Vince handed over a fifty pound note. "For your sister. How's her rehab going?"

Saul grimaced. "She checked herself out again."

"Hmm. Terrible corruption comes from heroin, lad, of the body, heart and mind. Give her the money, get her comfortable, talk her into trying again, yeah?"

"Thanks, Boss. Why are you so interested in helping her?"

Vince smiled, a shark to a seal. "Because you're under my wing now and she matters to you. So she matters to me. I've told you that before, so take it as gospel, lad. Off you go."

As Saul left, Vince's smile faded. The sister would be dead soon, and he had to hope he'd secured Saul's loyalty before then. It should be time enough, the boy was already largely hooked. He checked the time. Nearly 5:00 p.m. On a Saturday. The pub would start to get busy soon, it was already quite crowded. He rang Clancy's burn phone, watched on the monitor as Clancy extricated himself from chatting up Tracy at the bar. Vince smiled. Poor kid was besotted with that bar girl and he didn't have a chance. Shame he didn't have the same kind of leverage Vince himself enjoyed. He'd availed himself of Tracy's charms a few times. Maybe he'd do that again a little later on, the girl had a fantastic body.

"Yes, Boss?"

Vince shook off his speculation. "Dead drop two at five thirty. Destroy the drop afterwards."

"No problem. Back to you?"

"No, it's a delivery." Vince checked his notes and read over McLeod's address.

There was a moment of silence. On the monitor, he watched Clancy's brow creased in thought. Bloody kid was thinking again. It really was getting to be a problem.

"That's where we picked up that bloke the other night. The Scottish guy with the—"

"I know very well what it is," Vince said. "Just do as you're told."

"Yes, Boss. No problem."

"And no engagement, no chatter. Put it in his hand and leave without conversation."

"If he's not there?"

"Wait until he is. Call me when it's done."

"Yes, Boss."

Vince rang off and watched Clancy check his watch, decide he had a bit of time in hand, and return to Tracy at the bar. She smiled politely, but her brow creased with subtle annoyance.

Vince turned to a locked metal cabinet in the corner and pulled a bunch of keys from his pocket. He opened the doors and stood looking at the vast array of handheld weapons inside. He had extra-curricular work to do this night and needed to pick just the right tool. Something old school for this target.

NINETEEN

Matt finally returned to his flat a little worse for wear. He hadn't been able to face going home directly from the strange encounter with the girl at the hospice. He'd needed time to think, to try to figure out what the hell he had actually seen. So he sat in a non-descript pub, somewhere he'd never been before, and pondered the situation over several pints. And got nowhere except a bit drunk and very hungry. Rather than waste more money on overpriced, over-fried pub food, he headed home to make an omelette.

He stopped short at the top of the old stone steps leading down from street level to his front door. "What do you want now?"

Clancy looked up, his eyes suddenly wide. "Don't touch me." His voice was stronger than his expression belied.

Matt shook his head. "Fuck off then, and I won't."

Clancy held up an envelope, normal letter size, plain white, nothing written on it. He put it down on the bottom step and hurried up to the street, squeezing against the metal railings to stay as far from Matt as possible.

Matt stepped back to make it easy for the spooked kid, even though his own stomach had gone liquid. "What's that?"

Clancy stood a few feet away and stared.

"Yer a fucking weirdo, you know that?" Matt said. "Why do you associate with a fucker like Stratton anyway?"

Clancy kept his lips pressed together, his eyes locked on Matt's.

With a sigh, Matt walked down the steps and picked up the envelope. He looked up to Clancy and the boy nodded once and hurried away.

Matt let himself in and put the envelope on the coffee table. He didn't want to open it, but knew he would have to. It wasn't something he could ignore, however strong that desire might be. On top of that, nerves had made him nauseated, but he had to eat or he'd only feel worse, though his appetite was ruined. He put bread in the toaster, stared at his reflection in the chrome while it browned. When it popped up, he spread some butter and stood mechanically chewing. The toast was like cardboard and dust, but he robotically filled the hole in his gut, soaking up the alcohol and giving some fuel to his trembling muscles.

When the food was down, he returned to the lounge and sat on the sofa, staring at the envelope in front of him. Eventually, with a sound not unlike a quiet sob, he picked it up and opened it.

A photograph came out first, a man around forty or forty-five maybe, short dark hair, a long, sharp nose and eyes a little too close together. He looked mean and angry, but his expression in the photo was as much responsible for that perception as his features. It was the kind of shot a private investigator might have taken of an adulterous husband stepping out of a seedy motel. Then there was the printed sheet of instructions. Matt read through, twice. Nothing about what he was supposed to do, but of course, that was obvious given who the delivery boy had been. Details of a location, habits, times, the man himself and two words at the bottom which made Matt's trembling double.

BEFORE TUESDAY.

It was already Saturday night. That meant Matt had to go to this restaurant and kill this poor bastard, whoever he was, either the next day or the day after that. No bracing time, no planning time. Stratton was deploying him like a fucking bomb, with no regard for process or organisation. It simply wasn't possible. The page of instructions rustled as it vibrated in his furious grasp and he dropped it onto the coffee table like it was burning him.

No, simply not possible.

A buzzing on the bookshelf made him jump and Matt looked over at the burn phone, glowing in the shadow of the shelf above. The phone Stratton had given him. He went and picked it up, but the ringing had stopped. He realised it hadn't been ringing, it was a text arriving. He opened the message, the sender's number blocked, but it could only be Stratton.

My boy tells me you have your instructions. You will at this stage be refusing to accept the situation. You will be thinking about coming to my place and railing about how it can't be done. But I'm sure you remember my reward for your failure. You remember who will pay. If I see you anywhere before Tuesday, they get what I promised. If you don't do the job before Tuesday, they get what I promised. If you involve anyone else… I'm sure you get the picture. By the way, I'm not at my place and won't be until after Tuesday. There's no way out. Do the job.

Matt roared in incoherent fury and threw the phone against the wall. It exploded into a shower of plastic and electronic components that bounced and pinged off every surface. All he wanted to do was stride right into Stratton's pub, grab the bastard, and deliver all the dark he had, finish this even if it meant finishing it in plain sight of everyone there. A hit like that would kill him anyway, given how hurt he had been after the last one. The one that got him in all this trouble in the first place. So what did he care? End everything, end himself, save his parents. They didn't need to know anything, he was a shit son anyway and always had been. They'd be better off without him, there was no redemption from his life.

But through the fog of rage, Stratton's words came back to him.

By the way, I'm not at my place and won't be until after Tuesday.

Of course the prick had anticipated Matt's death wish course of action. He knew Matt had nothing to lose, and the bastard had thought of everything. Breathing heavily, fists clenching and unclenching at his sides, Matt's mind turned over and over with every conceivable option. But there were really very few. It all led back to the same thing. He had to do what Stratton asked or his parents would be killed. And another death like that he simply could not allow. His whole family? No way. Anything but that. So he would have to do the hit. And he would try to survive it, and then take whatever dark he had left and deliver it directly into Stratton's face, whatever that might cost him. There was no other choice.

TWENTY

CHARLIE COLLINS TRIED A COUPLE OF TIMES to get the key into the lock of his penthouse, smiling sardonically as he did so. It had been a while since he was just drunk and the sensation was rather pleasant. But he had that good coke inside, so he'd soon be supplementing the buzz. Having set things in motion with the Stratton and McLeod situation, he had allowed himself a bit of time off. After a Saturday morning catching up on reports and other office bullshit that couldn't be avoided forever, he had gone to the dog racing and done quite well for himself.

The money wasn't as important as the rush of winning, but that was the same for all of life. And yet the money was a necessary extra, one that paid for his lavish lifestyle and indulged his extravagant tastes. He was a vain man, impressed by material things, and entirely self-aware of his superficiality. And he didn't care. There was depth to him too.

He flicked a switch inside the door and a few standard lamps around the place swelled in a soft glow. He hated bright lights at home, preferred the comfort of dimness and gloom. He threw his jacket on the back of a large leather armchair and went into the kitchen, swallowed down a tall tumbler of water and left the glass in the sink before heading to his bedroom. In the bedside drawer was the baggie of fine white powder. He slipped his notebook from his jacket pocket, dropped it into the drawer, and took the coke back into the front room, sank into another opulent chair and pulled a small glass-topped table up close. He tapped a generous line out onto the smooth surface, used a wooden coaster to straighten it up, and took a ten pound note from his wallet, rolled it up.

He paused. This Matthew McLeod was frustrating. Charlie couldn't quite place him in the scheme of things. He didn't like a puzzle part that didn't fit and McLeod was the perfect example of an oddly-shaped piece. The young man's desperation around Stratton's place, his nervousness. It was beyond obvious he didn't belong there. He was a rogue moon in Stratton's orbit, and surely Charlie could somehow leverage that. He was impatient for the players themselves to trigger new moves.

With a sigh, he sat forward and expertly snorted half the line, switched nostrils and finished it off. Man, this was good stuff, thickening in the back of this throat instantly, the buzz powerful and immediate and growing quickly. He sat back in the armchair, and his widening smile froze at the sight of something dark and looming above him.

He went to leap forward, but was an aeon too late as a sharp, cold line tightened around his throat and wrapped all the way to the back of his neck. He kicked and yelled, but the icy thing only bit tighter so he stilled, terror rising as quickly as the cocaine rush, turning his body to jelly. He pissed, warmth spreading across his lap and running back up the crease of his arse.

"The wonderful thing about a garrotte," Vince Stratton said from behind the chair, "is that once it's in place, it's already too late for the victim. But it gives the killer all the time he wants."

Collins gasped, the biting pressure of the wire across his larynx hurting more by the second, turning from ice to a line of fire. He scrabbled at it, but it was buried deep in the skin of his neck and he only scratched himself with his fingernails. Looking left and right as far he could showed Stratton's hands, each holding an end of the piano wire taut. It crossed at the back of Charlie's neck, entirely encircling him, gouging in as Stratton moved his hands fractionally further apart. "Wha...?" Collins managed, but couldn't think of words even if he'd been able to say them. Lights and colours danced in front of his eyes, blood rushed in his ears, his pulse deafening against the inside of his skull, the coke pounding his senses in wicked unison with adrenaline. Yet Stratton's voice was clear above it all, even though the man whispered almost lovingly.

"I told you, I am not in the business of playing fucking games, Detective. You honestly think you can come into my pub and push me around? You think you can put some kind of pressure on me and I'll crack? I'm very fucking disappointed in how much you underestimate me." The man's bulk was a shadow above and behind the armchair, his face lost in the gloom of the dimly lit apartment.

The pressure of the garrotte eased marginally and Collins swallowed desperately, his Adam's apple on fire. Clearly Stratton expected an answer. Charlie's mind raced. He needed to talk fast to get out of this. "I misjudged you, clearly," he said, his voice a rasping growl from fear and the still not insignificant tightness of the wire. "But we can sort this out like sensible men."

"Can we really?"

"You want me to back off, fine. No problem. This is obviously a very sensitive subject. I thought we both understood the game, that we'd been playing each other for ages, that we'd continue to do so." The fucking coke was making him a rambling idiot. He needed to find a point, quickly. One that would actually appeal to the psychopath behind him. His mind reeled.

Stratton sighed. "The *very* first thing I said to you just now is that I am not in the business of playing games. *This* is not a fucking game. You're a corrupt, drug-addled fuckwit of a man, Charles Collins. You have no honour. No code. And now, you have no more time. You should have left me the fuck alone."

"No, wait, we can ta—" The words were cut off as Stratton yanked his hands apart and the thin wire bit through Charlie's trachea. The pain was instant and electric, his entire neck lit up with a bolt of fire. Nerves shot down into his shoulders and up into his brain as liquid flooded his hands and chest. Scarlet, even in the low light of the expensive penthouse. Charlie watched his life pour out.

Everything gone, all for nothing, his entire existence a blip of insignificance snuffed out by this fucking gangster. This two-bit London mobster, taking Charlie's life, how fucking dare he? Fury tore through the pain, but it was weak and fading as soon as it rose. Just like that, it was all over. Done.

Last thoughts fluttered in Charlie Collins's mind as he sank into despairing blackness, time drawing out like warm taffy. All the criminals, the dozens of murderers and paedophiles he'd put away, would be his legacy. People like that TV arsehole Jim Harrison, and all the kids he'd abused. Charlie had finished that fucker. All those kids, now adults, got some closure while Harrison rotted in jail. Dan Butler, the serial rapist, he was down too, never coming out. Charlie had worked tirelessly on that case, found what others couldn't. Lionel Chang, the East End Butcher, Charlie had put him away too. That sick fucker won't kill any more. For all his corruption, all his alignment with dodgy dealers, at least he had contributed to the greater good of society. He'd made a difference, hadn't he? The good outweighed the bad by a significant factor. Didn't it? Blackness closed over him like tar.

* * *

Vince Stratton held the garrotte tight for a good minute or two after Collins had gone limp and shit himself, even though it had cut through everything but the man's spine. Just to stop the bastard suddenly thrashing around and flicking blood everywhere in some last-ditch display of determination, some pointless final fight to live. But it seemed Collins had accepted his death at the end there, his eyes gone almost thoughtful as he slipped away.

Vince, leaning over the chair to watch the man's face even as he held the killing weapon in place, was mildly impressed. It always fascinated him how people died, and he'd watched an awful lot over the years take that final journey into what his old dad would call the undiscovered country. Some railed and thrashed and Vince hated that. Messy and undignified. Some simply melted in fear and denial, which was weak, though at least they went quietly.

But now and then someone would go calmly, not overtly terrified or furious. Of course, they may well start that way, as Collins here had, but then a calm would descend. An acceptance. Vince thought it might have something to do with a person whose regrets were greatly outweighed by things they were proud of, things they could gladly leave as their stamp on the world.

He smiled as he carefully extricated the wire from the depths of Collins's neck. "Good for you, old son," he said quietly. "You were a fucking idiot really, but at least you think you did okay before you left. Who knows, maybe you did."

He moved back from the chair and wound the garrotte up into a tight circle and lowered it into a plastic bag, waiting open on the floor, careful not to touch the furniture or anything else. Once the weapon was inside, he stripped off his surgical gloves and dropped them in too. He took another pair of gloves from his pocket and snapped them on, then closed up the bag. He stepped away from the chair and moved next to a standard lamp to look himself over closely. He smiled. A clean job, not a drop of blood on him, even though old Charlie and the chair he sat in were soaked in the stuff. He pocketed the bagged weapon and pulled a balaclava over his face, then a hat down low over that. It would mask not only his appearance, but hopefully the fact he was wearing the mask too. His gloves were dark green and no other skin was visible anywhere. He hunched down in his oversized coat to make his profile wrong, make him seem several inches shorter than he actually was. Any image he left on the security cameras in and around the building would give up a man of indeterminate race, fatter and shorter than Stratton's tall bulk. He had come in the same way. Sometimes, when people paid very little attention, it was all too easy.

TWENTY-ONE

Amy sat at the kitchen counter drinking coffee. She couldn't get the sight of that poor man out of her head, the blackness sitting on his shoulders like a hungry demon, coiled around his neck and face. She tried to imagine what he might have seen in her, what it was his eyes betrayed. He seemed both entranced and shocked. How many others like them were out there? It was arrogance of the highest order to think they were the only two in the world and their paths had crossed in London. Then again, she had travelled to the other side of the planet for that to happen.

She had always considered herself somewhat unique, often wondering if others shared her power but not having the first clue how to find out. She never dreamed it would be as simple as seeing the shadows literally lurking on and around a person, assuming that's what it was. It stood to reason there had to be others out there and, if she was interpreting properly what she'd seen, she knew now she would be able to identify them. But given he was the first she'd ever noticed, they were obviously few and far between. It was possible she'd never see another in her lifetime.

Regardless, there was one right here in London. The man pretending to be Paul Stratton, but whose name was actually Matt Mc-

Leod. And therein were even more questions. Why was he pretending to be someone he wasn't? Terry had said the guy worked for his son, Vince. She needed more time to think, to figure it all out, but there was one clear path to the man, and that was via his boss.

Amy checked the time. Eleven o'clock. It was a kind of day off, as she had finished at midnight the night before and went back on night shift in ten hours. But Vince usually came to visit Terry during the day, often around lunchtime. They had only met on a couple of occasions, given that Amy almost always worked nights. She'd had a good sleep, and knew the fatigued transition back to nights would run her down regardless. She might as well accept the fact that she was up now and unlikely to sleep again before the end of her shift, at 7:00 a.m. the next day. Then she could crash hard. So she had from now until work started at 9:00 p.m. to track down Matt McLeod.

She remembered one of the occasions she had bumped into Vince and they made small talk like people do, pretending the man lying right beside them wasn't dying. The way people skirted the subject of death even as they stared it in the eye never ceased to amaze Amy. And all the euphemisms, like "passed away" and "lost", like the people were a ship on the horizon or a bloody wallet. If only folk would face up to the stark inevitability of it all, talk about it openly, discuss it while the vigour of life still burned inside them, she was convinced the whole thing would lose a lot of its barbed sting.

There was no compensation in death, though, no closure. Every death was simply another open wound those closest to the dead bore and learned to live with. Time heals all wounds, according to popular mythology, but that was bullshit. The wounds don't heal, it just takes time to learn to get on with life regardless, continue to live and ignore those gaping holes of loss.

Vince had said something about being a publican. *Bloody lovely joint, it is,* Terry had chimed in. Amy wracked her brain. He had said where it was, or something about it. It had stuck because it was somewhere she had recently visited, somewhere famous... Camden Markets! That was it. She had been to Camden Lock and the markets not long before that encounter with Vince, been thoroughly charmed by the area, even though it was a battle of seedy London reality versus manufactured tourist centre these days. But Vince had said his pub was in Camden.

She pulled her phone over and opened the browser, tapped VINCE STRATTON PUBLICAN CAMDEN into the search bar. Loads of results instantly for Stratton's in Camden Town. She grinned. Well, that had to be it. She decided it was time to visit that particular location again.

By just before 1:00 p.m. she was following the maps app on her phone to the address of the pub. Her stomach rumbled, not helped by the number of cafés and other eateries she'd passed. It would hopefully only take a moment to find out a contact number or something for McLeod, then she could get herself a bite. The man might even be working in the pub now, given he was one of Vince's employees. Perhaps she could invite him for lunch and they could talk honestly about their shared nature. It made her nervous, but it was too important a thing to dance around, especially given her recent experience of the lurking shadow creature in her doorway, reaching for her. If it wasn't for Carla... And the thing haunted her still, though for now only in her mind. Was it coming back?

She tried to put the thought away, best not to even consider the possibilities. At least it seemed for now it was gone. Had it missed its chance and gone for good? Would she be safe if she never let the shadows out again, but give it another opening if she let them go, doing her good for mankind? That seemed hardly fair. Maybe this McLeod guy would have answers, or something that might help at least, some insight or experience.

Stratton's loomed on the next corner and she smiled. Nice-looking place, Terry was right. Big too. She pushed open the front door and was enveloped in warmth and the welcoming aromas of beer and hot chips, chicken schnitzels and steaks, roast beef and pork and over-steamed vegies. There was a busy lunchtime crowd, the traditional pub Sunday lunch in full effect, a great British pastime.

Several young women and one twenty-something man milled busily behind the bar, but none of them were McLeod. She worked her way through the throng, hunger chewing holes in her as she passed tables laden with roast dinners and gravy. Maybe she'd have to indulge herself here. The fare did look pretty good.

She got to the bar and a pretty redhead who couldn't be more than twenty years old turned a smile on. "What can I get ya?"

Amy smiled at the accent. "Fellow Aussie! Where you from?"

"Shepparton. You?"

"Sydney most recently, but I'm working here indefinitely now. I'm Amy."

"Which pub?" the redhead asked with a laugh. "I'm Emily."

Amy laughed along, well aware that the first question you asked any Australian in London was which pub they worked in. "Actually, I'm a nurse, but I know that breaks the mould."

"Good for you, that's a fine thing to be. Nice to meet you. Sorry to rush you, but we're a bit flat out."

Amy grinned. "Sorry, of course. I'll have a half of Kronenbourg and the roast beef, please."

The bar girl tapped the order into the cash register nearest her. "Well, haven't you assimilated!" She handed over a number on a metal stand. "That's for your lunch. Put it on your table and they'll bring it over." She moved away, poured the half pint of French lager and brought it back. "Here you go."

Amy took the drink. "Thanks. Say, you know a Matt McLeod, works here?"

Emily shook her head. "Doesn't work the bar that I know of."

"I'm pretty sure he's one of Vince Stratton's employees."

Emily's face twisted into disapproval. "Well, that's a bit different maybe. Who the fuck knows what Vince and *his boys* get up to. It's all a bit dodgy, you ask me. Anyway, I wouldn't know. See that guy at the end of the bar, cap too big for his dumb head?"

Amy leaned forward to see past the crowd and grinned. "Shell suit and everything," she said.

Emily laughed. "Yeah, he's the full cliché. Anyway, he's one of Vince's boys, so he'd know maybe."

"Great, thanks!"

Amy looked around the busy pub for a place to sit, but nothing was free. Carrying her drink and order number, she approached the young man Emily had pointed out. He looked at her, one eyebrow raised.

"Hi. I'm Amy."

He grinned and went all sort of floppy, like he'd suddenly contracted a palsy. "Well, hey. I'm Clancy."

Amy realised too late the fool thought she was coming onto him. Good grief, he could barely be out of school. He had to be at least ten years younger than her. Still, full marks for confidence. She wondered if he was even old enough to legally be in the pub. Better head off the lust before it was too far gone.

"Emily told me you might know where I can find Matt Mc-Leod."

Clancy seemed to suddenly stiffen, his eyes momentarily wild before he pulled his composure back by sheer force of will. "Oh yeah? Why you want him?"

"Long story, but I know he works for Vince, so thought I might find him here."

"Works for Vince?"

"Doesn't he?"

Clancy looked at the order number in Amy's hand. "You've got some food coming?"

"Yeah."

"Well, neither Vince or Matt are in right now." He got up, offered his seat. "Bloody busy today, so you might have to eat here at the bar."

"That's fine." She took the stool, wondering why things suddenly felt a little off-kilter.

"You enjoy your lunch," Clancy said with a wide smile. "I'll go and give Vince a call and ask when Matt might be around next."

"Great, thanks."

The tall, lanky kid loped off and disappeared through a door beside the bar. Amy sat sipping her lager, feeling like a fool. Clancy's reactions to everything had put her on edge, but she couldn't pin down why. It was only a few minutes more before a harried-looking young man came up with her plate of roast beef, potatoes, vegies and gravy. It was a hearty serving, way more than she would be able to finish. But that was the English pub way.

"You expecting anything else?" he asked.

"No, just this."

"Enjoy." He grabbed the number and swept away.

"Thanks," she called half-heartedly after him.

Her hunger hadn't been lying and she polished off a lot more of the meal than she thought she would have managed, but was right that she couldn't finish it. The whole time she wondered what had happened to Clancy. Only thirty seconds after she put her knife and fork down, he appeared beside her like the genie from the bottle. Had he been watching her eat?

"Vince can't come to the pub right now," he said. His eyes betrayed a kind of suspicion, a wariness. He didn't get too close, spoke more loudly than he needed to, if only he'd take a step nearer. "But he says he can give you a number for Matt. He's at a coffee shop across town, if you'd like to meet him there."

"You can't give me the number?"

"Nah, sorry. Employer confidentiality or some shit."

The whole situation stank. Every nerve in Amy screamed at her to be alert, be alarmed, get the fuck out of there. Just what was going on with these people? "A coffee shop?" she asked.

"Yeah. Swanky new place called Beverley's. Here." He handed her a scrap of paper with the address on it, snatched his hand away the second she took hold of it.

Amy stared at the scrawled handwriting that would have made a doctor proud. It was a public place, at least. And she really needed to talk to McLeod. If they were setting her up somehow, so be it. All the time she was in sight of other people, she'd play along, even if she couldn't figure out their game. "Okay, thanks. I'll go there now."

"Right." Clancy stepped back but kept watching her.

She swallowed the last of her beer and left, very grateful for the cold, fresh bite of the late autumn air outside. The warm and welcoming pub had quickly become oppressive. She tapped the address into her phone and watched the map calculate a route. Ten-minute's walk. Not so far.

She'd only gone about two blocks when she realised Clancy was following her. Useless kid, all limbs and obvious clothes, he was pretty rubbish at tailing someone. Never mind, the whole staying in public thing still applied. If her route led towards anywhere quieter than these busy streets she would abort immediately.

But the streets remained busy and she soon found herself outside a black and gold extravagance of a café advertising Arabica blends and vegan, gluten-free health snacks. She shook her head. Fucking hipsters. But the Vince Stratton she had met was old school London, definitely not part of this set. As she stood frowning at the window, the door opened and Vince himself leaned out.

"Amy!" he declared, all smiles. "The same Amy from Dad's hospice. I wasn't expecting you."

"That's me." She was a bit lost for anything else to say.

"Come in, I'll buy you a coffee. It's crowded, but I've got a table." He ducked away before she could answer.

She glanced back and flicked a short salute to Clancy across the street. The goof jumped and tried to pretend he hadn't seen her, that he was fascinated by the product range of the lingerie shop he found himself looking into. She had to laugh.

Inside, the café was way too hot, but the aroma of coffee enticing. Vince sat by the door and gestured to a free seat at his table. "What'll you have?"

"Cappuccino, thanks." She scanned the place as she sat, wondering if there were other employees at other tables, pretending to be patrons. She had to shake off this feeling she was in a spy novel or some Jason Bourne thriller.

Vince stood, spoke briefly at the counter, then returned. "You're after Matt McLeod."

"That's right."

"Why?"

The cold-faced simplicity of the question stumped her for a moment. Then she began to spin a tale. "Truth is, I wanted to ask him out."

"That right? He's a lucky guy then."

Creep. "If you say so. I wasn't expecting all this running around the city though."

"Why did you come to ask me about him?"

"He works for you, right?"

"What gave you that idea?"

"That's what your dad said."

Vince sat back, one forefinger rubbing his chin. A woman came over and put a coffee down in front of Amy. "Thank you, Beverley," Vince said, before Amy could speak. Then he said to her, "My dad?"

"Yeah."

"And why would my dad say that?"

The roast dinner recently consumed became a cold rock in her gut. This was all wrong. "Why are you being so weird about this? Matt came to visit your dad, I saw him there, fancied him, asked your dad who he was. He said he was Matt McLeod and Matt worked for you, so I thought you might have his number. Honestly, it's really not worth all this bloody trouble." She stood up to leave, frightened by Stratton's cold perusal.

His face broke into a warm grin, the frosty look dropped from his eyes. "Sit down, sit down. Enjoy your coffee."

She sank back into the chair reluctantly.

"So Matt came to visit my old dad, did he?"

"Yeah."

"That's nice of him, isn't it."

The words and the delivery were at odds. Vince might as well have said, *That's the last thing he'll ever do.*

Amy knew beyond doubt that she'd made a terrible mistake. She had thought maybe Stratton and McLeod were both playing her somehow and she wanted to find out, still keen to talk to McLeod, but that wasn't it at all. It seemed obvious Stratton hadn't known anything about Matt's visit until now. And that would explain why he had signed in as a Stratton rather than under his own name. He must be up to something and she'd blown it for him. Did he do shadow work like she did, and was he setting up Vince as his next victim?

And here Vince sat with murder in his eyes, affable on the outside but frozen granite within. She had made a horrible error of judgement and was sure it was going to be very bad for Matt McLeod. And potentially for her too. If she didn't get away now, it might all go south more quickly than she could deal with.

She stood up, bumping a person passing behind her, but didn't even acknowledge them. "Sorry to waste your time, Mr. Stratton. I have to go."

She turned and fled the café. Clancy was outside the door and she glared at him, ready to punch his dumb kid's face if he so much as uttered a word. A black cab with its orange light blessedly bright on top passed across the street. She ran out, yelling for it. A horn blared and she leapt backwards from an old Vauxhall that nearly wiped her out. An angry woman inside yelled and gesticulated. Amy waved a frantic apology and leapt into the cab as it slowed.

The driver, a friendly-looking Sikh man with a bright blue turban and long black beard, looked her up and down over his shoulder, face furrowed. "You in trouble, love?"

"Abusive boyfriend," she said, hoping it was a good enough cover for her panic. "Please, just get me away from here."

His eyes widened. "You got it!" He stamped on the accelerator and the cab lurched away. Out the back window she saw Stratton and Clancy standing outside the café, staring after her.

What the hell had she done? And how was she going to warn Matt?

TWENTY-TWO

IN THE FACE OF EXHAUSTION AND DRUNKENNESS, Matt's fury had not lasted long. He needed rest more than anything else and had fallen into bed, but sleep eluded him for a long time. He tossed and turned, thoughts tumbling over each other as he tried to think of a way out of his current predicament. It surely couldn't be as hopeless as it seemed.

Eventually fatigue won out and he'd fallen into a troubled, restless sleep. He woke briefly around dawn, stumbled to the bathroom, and returned to bed, his very bones weary. Just another hour or two then he could plan, think more clearly.

He awoke with a start, knowing a lot of time had passed, and cursed aloud at the sight of his bedside clock reading 2:28 p.m. He only had two days to sort out the mess his life had become, and he'd bloody slept through half of one of them. Idiot!

But his head was clearer than ever, finally rested. As he made his way to the kitchen and put coffee on, plans began to drop into place. Of course, step one was the least pleasant in many ways. Without giving himself too much time to think about it, he pulled out his phone and hit the number for the house that hadn't been his home for many years.

"Hello, McLeod residence."

Matt squeezed his eyes shut at the sound of her voice. "Hey, Mam."

"Matthew! Oh, where have you been? You've no' called for weeks."

"I'm sorry, Mam, really. But I'm calling now."

"You are, and thank you. How are you? When will you visit? I can barely remember what you look like."

It had been years since he had last made time to see his parents, and only then because they had come down to London. The guilt weighed too heavily, though he knew his absence only added to their pain. And that further burdened him, and the awful cycle continued. "Mam, I'll be honest with you. I'm in a spot of bother."

"Do you need money? What do you need? How can we help? Come home, son. Come home."

"Mam, please, calm down. I need to talk now and it's not easy. I wish I could explain more, but I can't. I need you and Dad to go away for a week or so."

"Away? Away where? Why?"

"Mam, please listen. I'm in some trouble, but I'm going to sort it out. It'll take a little while, that's all, and I need you and Dad to be away, somewhere no one will find you."

"Who's looking for us, Matt? Are you in trouble with the police?"

Matt laughed. "I wish it were that simple. I'm so sorry, but I've got caught up with some criminal types and they've threatened you."

"They've what?"

"I'll sort it, Mam, I promise. But please, just pack up and head off for a week. Don't tell anyone where you're going and make sure you're not followed."

"Matthew, your father and I have work. We can't just up and leave. And what do you mean followed?" Her voice rose in pitch, panic setting in. "Who's going to follow us, Matt? And why?"

Matt rubbed a hand over his face. His parents weren't the kind of people who could run away at the drop of a hat. This wasn't some movie where people took the word of the hero without question. What was he thinking, trying to get them to leave?

There was a scuffling and muffled voices, then his father, rough and angry. "What the bloody hell is going on, son? Your mother looks like you told her you're going to die."

"I'm really sorry, Dad. I'm in some trouble and I'm going to fix it, but I need you and Mam to go away for a week."

"We bloody well will not. If someone has a problem with us, I'll give 'em what for, son, you can count on that!"

"Dad, these people are dangerous criminals…"

"Oh, aye, and you're going to fix them up, are you? You're a bloody gangster now, are you?"

Matt sighed. Step one of his new plan and it had all turned to shit instantly. "Dad, listen. I know this sounds ridiculous, I know it's hard to take in, but I really need you to trust me here. These gangsters know where you live and they've threatened to kill you if I don't do what they want."

Silence hung heavy for a moment. When his father spoke again, the man's voice was subdued. "Are you serious, son?"

"Aye, Dad. It's a bloody mess. But I'm going to the police, I'm going to get everything sorted out. I just can't be sure how much they mean their threats or how quickly they can get to you. But I have to take them seriously, so you have to take *me* seriously. I'm so sorry."

"Are you going to be okay, Matt?"

"I don't know. But yes, I think so. I have a plan. I have a police contact. I'm going to act fast and get it all fixed. But please, for my peace of mind, you and Mam take off for a week. Even just a few days."

His father drew a long breath, slowly let it out. "We'll call in sick to work, head to—"

"Don't tell me! Don't tell anyone. Just slip away, somewhere you've never been. Mam has work?" he added stupidly.

"Aye, couple of days a week in a shop in town. She enjoys it."

"Ah, good for her."

"You'd know that if you called more. Were around more."

"I know. I'm sorry. After this is all over I'll come and visit." Matt realised he meant it and grief tore at his chest. "I'll be around more, I promise."

"Okay, son."

The sudden calm acceptance broke something inside Matt. The weight of being a parent fell on him vicariously through the fatigue in his father's voice. He needed to make things right, somehow. "I'm a fuck-up, Dad, I know that. I made so many mistakes." Tears breached his eyelids, silently traced his cheeks. "I can't begin to tell you how, but I absolutely will try to be better. I'll fix this and I'll come and see you and Mam."

"We'd like that, Matt. We know you have…burdens. But we can't help you unless you tell us what they are. We really want to help you, son."

How could he possibly tell them what he'd done? But if nothing else, this ridiculous situation he found himself in had sharpened to razor clarity his need to do something to atone beyond the delivery of the dark. His gift, cursed though it was, killing him though it might be, was only part of his penance. Now his encumbrance had come full circle and ensnared his entire family and he owed them the truth if nothing else. Uncontrollable, one sob barked forth from his chest before he could swallow it down again.

"Go away for a few days, Dad. I'll fix this!"

"How will we know when to come back?"

Matt paused, lost for an answer for a moment. Eventually he said, "Does Mam still have a mobile phone?"

"Aye. I cannae stand them."

"I know, Dad. Tell her I'll text when it's okay. If you don't hear from me in a few days, go to the police and tell them everything."

"There's precious little to tell them, son."

Matt nodded, knowing the truth of that. He would either get Stratton fixed or do the bastard's hit, then go after the son of a bitch himself. By the end of the week, one or other of them would be dead. Or both. If it was Stratton, Matt would be able to tell his parents it was safe to come home. If Matt didn't survive… "I'll send you more info as and when I can. For now, I just want to know you're safe."

"We have to leave right away?"

"Yes, please, Dad. And make sure you're not followed."

"Jesus, son, what have got yourself into?"

"It's a mess. But I'll sort it. I will. I have to go."

"Okay, son. Call us as soon as you can."

"I will."

"We love you, son. We always have. You know that, don't you?"

"I do. And I love you too." Another sob breached and Matt stabbed the END CALL button before it gained voice. He dropped the phone onto the table while he bawled.

Ten minutes passed before he finally calmed down enough to think clearly again. It was messy as hell, but he hoped his parents were safe now, at least in the short term.

The next step was to find out if that copper, Collins, had any real hold on Stratton. If Matt could offer some information, get Stratton put away, it might help him avoid all this unpleasantness. But he'd need to play his cards carefully. Stratton had said he could have Matt's parents killed from a cell, but surely getting the fucker arrested would buy time and space to fix things properly.

After copying all the relevant information from the instructions Clancy had delivered, Matt repacked Stratton's envelope. He found the business card from Collins and checked the station address. With the evidence from Stratton thrust deep in his cost pocket, he headed out.

It didn't take long to get to the police station and Matt's nerves were strung tight by the time he trotted up the front steps and pushed open the glass doors. The main lobby was a large space with a table and magazines, cheap plastic chairs. Doors led off to either side, and in front of him was a reception desk, sheltered behind thick glass that rose to join the ceiling. There were a couple of grills in the glass, several police officers milling around a busy-looking admin area behind. Matt stepped up to one of the grills and waited.

An officer noticed him, came over. She was good-looking, but hard-edged, her eyes suspicious. He supposed a job like hers was enough to trim the forgiveness off anyone. If you had a job where most people you met were criminals or victims of crime, it was maybe hard to see anyone and not think of them as a lawbreaker. Hell, if only she knew what he'd done.

"Help you?"

Matt swallowed, hoped she couldn't see the trembling in his hands. He flashed the business card. "Here to see Detective Collins."

The woman's eyes narrowed, the area behind her suddenly still, several pairs of eyes turned to regard him. "You have an appointment?" the policewoman asked. He noticed a badge on her chest read Parker.

"Err, no, I don't. Just wanted to talk with him about something."

"About what?" Parker's demeanour was colder than ever, the half dozen or so others behind her silent, watching.

Matt knew he'd made a mistake, but couldn't figure out why or what to do about it. "We bumped into each other a couple of days ago, that's all. He asked me about a thing he was working on. I thought of something last night that might help, was in the area today, so thought I'd drop by and chat." He was rambling and couldn't help it. He wanted to leave, but turning tail and bolting from a police station was close to the most self-damning thing imaginable.

"Can you tell me what it was with regards to?" Parker asked. "And exactly when you saw him?"

Matt took a breath, thinking frantically. If he told her anything about Stratton, or even the location, he knew for reasons he couldn't explain that it would almost certainly be bad. As he drew breath to speak, a door at the back of the admin area popped open and a detective in a sharply cut skirt and suit jacket walked in. She looked harried, short-cropped black hair in disarray, the dark skin of her brow creased in what looked like a permanent scowl.

"They're moving Collins's body in half an hour," she barked at one of the uniforms at a desk. "I need you to—" She stopped, belatedly aware something was amiss.

Matt didn't miss the acid look one of the other uniforms shot her, or Parker's stiffening shoulders. Collins's body? Fuck it all, the man was dead? It was too much of a coincidence to consider it might be a different Collins. Matt simply could not risk that assumption. The detective had been watching Stratton's, so another thing Matt refused to ignore was the possibility that it was Stratton himself who had done the killing. He didn't know why, but he didn't need to. He needed to be away.

Trying to pretend he hadn't noticed the uncomfortable moment in the back he said, "It was last Wednesday, days ago. Your man Collins was investigating something about a break-in over at Hendon. I work nearby and told him I didn't see anything, but then I remembered. I saw a young bloke, white, maybe twenty or so. He was loitering in the shop doorway about half an hour before. No idea if it's relevant, but I was passing by here and thought I'd drop in and let Detective Collins know. Maybe you could just pass that on for me." He gasped a breath, sure he was gibbering like a fool.

Parker nodded slowly. "Height and weight?" she asked.

"What?"

"The suspicious guy you saw. How tall? Fat, thin?"

"Ah, right? Er, maybe five ten or so, quite skinny. Wearing jeans and a black puffy jacket." Who the hell wore puffy jackets any more? Surely she'd see right through the lie.

Parker scribbled on a pad. "Anything else?"

"Nope. That's about it. Listen, I have to get moving, I have an appointment down the road in a few minutes. But you'll see Detective Collins gets that information, aye?"

Parker drilled him with her gaze for a second and Matt held her eye, smiled softly, as casual as possible even though he was roiling inside.

"We'll make sure the information gets passed on. Thanks for your help. Can I just take your name and a number, in case we need more?"

"Of course. It's Peter Dudley." Matt rattled off a made-up phone number and wondered what poor bastard might soon be getting an unexpected call from the police. "I have to run now. Thanks!"

Without waiting for a goodbye he turned and walked away as calmly as he could manage, pulled open the door. No challenge forthcoming, he glanced back and flicked a wave over his shoulder. Parker nodded in return, her face more relaxed than it had been. Maybe he'd pulled it off. But the detective in the back stared at him with unbridled scrutiny, like she was trying to see through him.

Thankfully his car was several streets away and he walked a long way around to it, ensuring he wasn't followed. His mind churned in a panic the whole way. Collins was dead. Perhaps the poor bastard had died in a drug shootout or something. It didn't have to be related to Stratton, but Matt had to assume it was. He couldn't take the risk to think any differently.

He also had to assume the police were now useless to him. If he brought up anything about Stratton with any other officer they would either decide to connect him to Collins's death or they would need to investigate Stratton. That would only bring a world of heat down on Matt, and things would move far too slowly. Collins might have already had something, might have been able to act quickly. He might even have had eyes on Stratton and known where the bastard gangster had gone to ground. Was that perhaps why he died? Did Stratton find Collins on his tail?

Regardless, it was all academic now. Matt knew he was on his own. And that meant he only had one choice left. He had to do the hit like Stratton wanted. That was the only way to get to the man and finish him too. Matt just hoped he had the dark and the strength to do both. It was one neat solution to everything, except the ever-increasing weight he carried for his parents. He wanted more than ever now to keep his promise to see them again soon. He doubted he would ever be able to come clean about his deepest guilt, but he needed to see them if he could. Even if he was successful taking out Stratton and that finished him off too they might never hear from him again, but at least they would be safe. Maybe that wasn't such a bad result.

His phone buzzed in his pocket as he slumped into the driver's seat of his car and started the engine, got the heater going. He pulled it out to read the text message.

The phone I gave you keeps telling me it's turned off. I told you to leave it on. You need to know some things. 1. I think it's sweet you suggested your dear old mum and dad have a holiday. They left with a couple of suitcases and very sad faces not half an hour ago. I know exactly where they are. 2. What the fuck are you doing visiting my father? You're canny, I'll give you that, but you made a big mistake there. Your pretty blonde lady friend might suffer for it now. Do not fuck me around, son. You have a job to do.

Matt stared at the words, his stomach loose, pulse drumming in his temples. The fucker was already watching his parents. How far was his reach? And he had Matt's personal mobile number. And he knew Matt had been to the hospice. Did he have spies there too? And who was Matt's pretty blonde lady friend? He wracked his brain for a full minute before a cold realisation dawned. The girl with the beautiful shadows. Had she seen something in him too, tried to find him? Like a dickhead, he had told Terry his real name. Did that nurse ask about him and Terry remembered? The one bloody thing his dying brain retained except fucking Shakespeare? The nurse must have gone to Vince looking for him and now she was in trouble. Stupid bloody woman! There was no other possible connection.

"What a massive fucking mess!" Matt yelled at the world in general.

He drove hard for home with only one thought in mind: kill Najdovski and bring Stratton out of hiding.

TWENTY-THREE

As HE DROVE, Matt sent a message by return text, one eye on the road. *Phone broken. You win. I'll do the job tonight.*

A horn blared and he swerved back into his lane. Be bloody typical to kill himself in a car crash. Maybe it would be the easiest result. But he was sure Stratton would kill his parents and that nurse purely out of spite. Matt had them all to protect now.

As he sat fuming at a red light, he looked up the number of Terry Stratton's hospice and dialled. When it was answered he realised he had no idea who to ask for.

"You have a nurse there, mid-twenties maybe, long blonde hair in a ponytail, green eyes. I can't remember her name."

"You mean Amy Cavendish?" the soft-spoken receptionist asked.

"I'm afraid I don't know. I only met her very briefly. Does anyone else fit the description?" He remembered something else from that brief and disturbing encounter. "She's Australian, I think."

"Yes, that's Amy."

"Amy Cavendish?"

"That's right."

"She there?"

"I'm afraid not. She doesn't start until nine tonight. Shall I take a message for her?"

Matt swerved again, narrowly missing a cyclist who yelled and flipped the bird. Matt ignored him, thinking hard. He had to get a message to this Amy sooner than that. If Stratton already had her, it might be too late, but if she was at home... Did Stratton know where she lived? It was possible, the fucker seemed to know everything about everyone. But more likely Stratton would intercept Amy on her way to work, just to get at Matt. His blood rushed with a sudden realisation.

"Hello? Can I take a message for Amy?"

"Aye, sorry. Listen, it's really, really important that I talk to Amy before she goes to work tonight. I realise you can't give out personal information, so I won't ask you for it, but you have her mobile number, yes? Can you please call her and give her my number. Ask her to call me urgently?"

There was pause, then, "I suppose I could do that. Is everything all right, sir?"

"Oh, yes, certainly. I just...err...I just need to talk to her before she leaves for work as I need her to bring something with her." It seemed all he did was come up with bullshit cover stories on the fly lately, and they all sounded ridiculous to his ears. But people were buying them. Maybe he'd missed his calling. Was there any work in being a professional bullshitter? Politician or real estate, he supposed. Used cars maybe.

"I'll tell you what," the kindly woman said, but her voice was a little less patient now. "How about you give me a message and I'll text it to Amy. After that, it's all up to her, yes?"

"Perfect, thank you! Can you please ask her to call Matt McLeod urgently?" He spelled out his name, rattled off his number.

"That's it?"

"That's it. Thank you."

"You're welcome, and I hope you have a good day."

Matt laughed before he could help himself. "Let's just say I hope it gets better instead of worse." He hung up, knowing it was likely to get anything but better.

He threw his phone onto the passenger seat, finally giving all his concentration to the road. He had no choice at this stage but to go ahead with planning the Najdovski hit. He glanced at the phone, willing it to ring. If Amy called, maybe there was another possibility. If Stratton didn't know where she lived and planned to pick her up on her way to work, maybe Matt could intercept him.

The idea of using Amy for bait made him feel a little queasy. Amy Cavendish. She swam in his mind's eye, beautiful to behold, a real stunner. Even wearing that shadow like a mantle, like some hugely cowled, magnificent dress from a fairy tale, curling up over her, wrapping around her, cascading down her shoulders. It was a mesmerising thing. He had barely given himself a second to look, so shocked he'd been, but it was burned into his memory. Was she like him? His own dark felt so much heavier, more malevolent. He couldn't imagine it presenting like that to anyone else. And if he could see hers, why couldn't he see his own. It certainly seemed as though she had seen something about him. Could she see *her* own darkness?

So many questions, so many possibilities. He really needed to talk to her, for them both to compare their lives, but Vince fucking Stratton loomed over everything like the biggest shadow of all. The same course of action was all that remained. Plan the Najdovski hit.

Matt grimaced, glanced at the inert phone again. "Please call me, Amy! Please call."

* * *

Detective Abela Farouk stood by her desk, staring at the papers scattered across it, but seeing nothing. Nothing physical, at least. She saw her memories, skittering past her mind's eye in unbidden profusion. Charlie Collins at his own desk, scowling. Collins at the markets, buying her a red silk scarf. Collins in her bed, smiling with the self-satisfaction of a man who knows he's done a good job. And he did do a good job in bed, for all his other faults.

Now he was dead, his head almost removed by what the forensic coroner had thought might have been a garrotte. Who the hell killed with a garrotte any more?

Abela owed Charlie Collins nothing. Their relationship had been torrid, intense, incredible. But after six months she couldn't look askance any more at the side deals, the backhanders. She knew a lot of cops were a little bit crooked, even though she kept her own slate fastidiously clean. She could have ignored a little extra-curricular activity. But not the degree to which Charlie pushed the boundaries. His opulent penthouse apartment was testament to how far he was willing to go. And now that apartment was soaked in his blood. Something bad had caught up with Charlie Collins, as so many people had said it would.

And talking of catching up, that young man in the front office earlier had been asking after Charlie and there was something amiss there. A sense of disquiet, of discomfort, hung around the lad. From what he said, it all appeared unrelated, but her career had given her extrasensory skills she had learned to listen to. The way he'd stiffened when she had mentioned moving Charlie's body, then pretended not to have heard. She was annoyed with herself that she'd stumbled like that. Charlie's death had her wrong-footed. Maybe that young fellow had something to do with this after all, despite his story about information on a break-in somewhere in Hendon. She would file his name and description for potential future use. She knew damn well none of the others in the department would.

Most of the station had just shrugged and moved on when news of his killing came in. They didn't care about someone who daily risked their lives and careers with his blasé ostentatiousness. "Fuck him," Sergeant Patel had said. "He had it coming."

Abela couldn't really argue that point. He did have it coming. And she knew the department would do all it had to in order to make the crime of his murder go away. Sure, they'd catch someone if they could, but they would happily bury the case too if all the boxes were ticked. Legend was the police would never stop until they'd nabbed the killer of one of their own. Unless that one happened to be Charlie Collins.

But she couldn't let it go. She loved Charlie, agonised every day that she'd had to walk away. It had been the right decision, but crooked or not she loved him. She couldn't let him end like this. Abela owed Charlie Collins nothing, but she knew she would have to see this one through.

"When you know a thing is right, to ignore it is to burden your soul." Her father's advice, his traditional Egyptian upbringing showing through in the eloquence of his lessons. But his sensibilities were universal. She doubted he had ever considered a case like this when he gave that advice, but he gave it often and she could easily apply it here. She might have been born in London to her immigrant parents, but their home country strictness paid off more often than not. They despaired of how English she had grown up, but that would ever be *their* burden. They were the ones who had emigrated, after all.

She turned and strode to the superintendent's office, knocked, and stepped inside.

He smiled up at her, his lined face friendly under neatly trimmed grey hair. "You want the Collins case." It wasn't a question.

She started, but did her best to cover it. "Er...yeah."

"You two had a thing, right? You sure it's appropriate for you to take it?"

"It wasn't a serious thing." She was a little shocked at how easily she lied, when it was still a thing as far as she was concerned. But too late for that. It had always been too late for that. "But I don't think the others care."

The superintendent pursed his lips. Then he nodded. "Okay. It's yours. But don't make too many waves, okay? Be subtle."

Don't stir up a mess of organised crime that would have repercussions across the force, is what he meant. She understood where that came from. "I'll just find his killer if I can."

"Be careful, Farouk."

She smiled. "I will."

Back at her desk she found herself at sea. Where the hell did she even start? She sniffed and grabbed her keys to drive over to Charlie's apartment.

TWENTY-FOUR

AMY HAD LET THE CAB DRIVE HER generally away from Camden for about ten minutes, then paid the fare and jumped out. The driver was concerned, tried to get her to open up the whole way, offered to take her to the police or a hospital. The man was very sweet and genuinely concerned, eyes wide in his lined face, brow creased under the tight blue edge of his turban.

Amy had insisted she would be perfectly fine, she just needed to get away and he'd helped her do that. His face was anxious, like a puppy sad to be left at home, when she climbed from the cab with one last heartfelt thanks.

Once he'd driven away, she just walked. What had she done? How much trouble was McLeod in now? She'd thought it was all so simple. The man worked for Stratton and she was smart and had found a way to him. All she'd found was a way directly into heaps of trouble.

The roast dinner she'd had at Stratton's pub still sat in her gut like a stone. A calming cup of tea would help. She crossed the road to a quiet-looking café, sat at the window so she could watch the street in case Stratton or that gangly idiot boy of his, Clancy, came looking. She was fairly convinced she was well beyond their reach, but paranoia became a healthy default state when you felt like you were in a world of danger.

Stratton's eyes when she mentioned Matt had seen Terry. Like a shark's, flat and glistening, emotionless. But a cold, predatory calculation seemed evident beneath, ticking away, making plans. Murderous plans, even as the man sat quietly sipping black coffee.

She needed more than ever to get word to Matt, but was clean out of options. The only angle she'd had turned out to be a treacherous dead end. Now what? If only the sign-in book at the hospice asked for a contact number or something, but it would never be that easy. And McLeod had used a fake name, so he'd certainly have used a fake number too. She sighed, sipped at hot, relaxing tea. She'd blown it, no more options. Some super spy she'd made. She let out a bitter laugh, shook her head. All those thriller novels she enjoyed, imagining herself at least as good as the protagonist, capable and powerful, taking on criminals and international organised crime, winning the day. Especially with her secret dark ability, something even Bond or Bourne couldn't boast. And it turns out she couldn't even track one man in one town. Life wasn't like books and movies.

All she could do was hope that Matt McLeod could handle himself better than her and perhaps be the match of a bastard like Stratton. She paid for her tea and walked a couple of streets over to get a bus back home. Maybe at some point McLeod would come by the hospice again and she'd get a chance to talk to him. Then a cold thought hit her. Stratton knew where she worked. He had immediately recognised her as Amy from the hospice. If he was pissed off, would he harass her at work? His father only had a few days left at most, but he gave Stratton every good reason to be there. Maybe if the big bastard did hassle her, she would just have to be honest. She genuinely had no idea where McLeod was and that's what she would tell him. If he got too much up in her face, she would call the police. Whatever was between him and McLeod could stay between them.

What a mess.

And along with the dark presence of Stratton suddenly clouding her life, the other dark incident still lingered. The one Carla had shattered, just in the nick of time. Would that thing return? Unable to resist, she glanced back over one shoulder as she walked from the bus stop and her heart skipped a beat at the sight of a tall, lean, blackened shape drifting behind her. She spun around, sucking in a ragged breath, and a lanky teenager emerged from the shadow of a brick wall, cast her a suspicious sidelong glance.

"I'm not following you," he said, and pointed to a building over the road. He trotted towards it, looking back once or twice. His expression seemed pained, like he was concerned he had scared her. Truth was, she had scared herself.

But if she blurred her vision at the edges of shadows, she thought she could see reaching black limbs, questing, feeling their way out. She sucked another quick breath in, then turned and walked briskly for home.

She put the key in the front door of her flat, thinking she'd get a bit of sleep before work after all, but wondering if she wasn't perhaps too wired to rest. As she pushed the door open, there was a crash inside and her gut froze. The front door led onto a hallway that went directly into the combined kitchen and lounge room of the small, two-bedroom apartment. Three doors led off the hall, one to the bathroom and the other two for her bedroom and Carla's. On a chair in the middle of the lounge, where the coffee table used to be, was Carla, wild-eyed and furious, tape over her mouth, thrashing against more tape that bound her to a wooden chair. The crash was from the glass-topped coffee table smashing where she'd kicked out at it as the front door opened. Stratton was a menacing bulk behind her, one meaty hand grappling to hold the crazed girl still while his other held aloft a broad, shining knife.

Amy observed it all in a fraction of a second, her mouth opening to scream. One thought flashed through her mind. *Run!* Run and call the police. That's why Carla had kicked out, it was a warning. One chance, run for help.

Amy spun in the doorway and crashed directly into the skinny, gangly chest of the idiot boy, Clancy. He grabbed her shoulders and tried to push her back into the apartment.

"Now, don't struggle, beautiful," he said, grinning like she was the child. His teeth were strangely bright in his brown face, the corridor dim behind him.

Amy froze, Clancy's hands like clamps.

"I came to chat some more," Stratton said from behind her, his voice calm like it was the most reasonable thing in the world. "When you weren't here, I decided to wait. Now, let's be civilised about this, shall we?"

Clancy smiled at her still, tried to push her back again. The thought of letting her shadows out passed through her mind, but they weren't an attack like a gunshot. They were slow-acting, insidious and creeping. Absolutely fatal, but no use in a moment of crisis like this. Or could they be used that way? She always simply let them flow out. She had never considered gathering them first and striking with them like a dark punch. Now might not be the time to experiment, but did she have a choice? The image of the dark stranger in her bedroom doorway flashed through her mind, its malevolent presence. Would she bring it back if she used her shadows again? Her mind spun in panic.

"Come on. Inside!" Clancy said, and pushed again. He was taller than Amy, but skinny, and only a little boy, for fuck's sake.

"Amy! Run!" Carla had obviously worked the tape over her mouth loose and her terrified, high-pitched entreaty spurred Amy into adrenalised action.

"Fuck you!" Amy screamed. She pushed up onto the balls of her feet, leaning back as she went, and slammed her forehead into Clancy's nose. A purely physical escape seemed the best option.

A wet, brittle crunch, louder than seemed possible, accompanied the sensation of collapse through her skull. Clancy howled, staggering backwards, letting go as he cupped both hands over his streaming face. Scarlet flooded his pale blue, shiny shell suit. Taking no risks, Amy swung a foot up between his legs with enough force to lift him to his toes. He made a sound like a cough and a gag combined and hit the deck, curled up like a startled armadillo, and whined.

Amy didn't wait to see anything else. Incited by Stratton's roar of rage behind her, she leapt over Clancy and bolted for the stairs. She felt sick, gasping for air as she powered down step after step, flight after flight, hanging onto the bannister to swing around and keep going, just keep going. The slam of Stratton's giant feet on the stairs behind her was like a countdown, a ticking clock to her demise. He yelled after her, but the words were lost in the rush of her blood and the pounding of the pulse in her ears.

She wanted desperately to look around, but feared the huge knife plunging into her back if she so much as glimpsed it again. Finally the last flight of stairs and the building lobby beyond, a glass-fronted oasis of light and normality, the busy street beyond populated with oblivious pedestrians and indifferent cars.

She hammered open the door at the bottom of the stairs, and it bounced back off the wall and startled old Mrs. Carver from the first floor. The woman turned, eyes wide, mail forgotten in her hands. Her mail slot stood open.

"Amy, dear, whatever's the matter?"

Amy skidded across the lobby, spun around to look back up the stairs. Stratton was on the last flight, looking through the window in the stairwell door, his eyes burning with a cold fury. Amy pulled out her phone, dialled 999, making sure he could see.

"Amy, dear?" Mrs. Carver said again. She leaned around the wall to look and Stratton quickly hid the knife behind his back.

"Stay back, please!" Amy said. She rose her voice to a shout. "I'm calling the police!"

She backed up to the front doors of the building, pulled one open and stood in the gap, clearly visible to the street behind. "Mrs. Carver, please come and stand over here. That man is dangerous."

Carver hurried over, expression terrified. "What's happening?"

Amy didn't answer as the line connected.

"Police, fire or ambulance?"

"Police, quickly!"

There was a click over the line and then, "Police, how can we help you?"

Amy rattled off her address and then, "There's a man in my apartment with a knife. He's holding my flatmate hostage. She's tied up in there!" Her voice was high and panicked, Mrs. Carver's gasp of horror beside her strangely calming in spite of the situation.

"There's a car on the way," the voice on the other end said. "Are you safe?"

"For now, yes, but my flatmate isn't!"

"I understand. Do you know who the intruder is?"

"Yes!" Amy raised her voice again. "It's Vince Stratton. He owns Stratton's pub in Camden Town!"

Stratton, still watching impassively from behind the door, slowly shook his head. He turned and jogged back up. Surely he wouldn't hurt Carla now, would he? That would be insane. Unless he intended to kill her to make sure there was no witness and then come after Amy herself. Did he have an alibi for this period of time? He must have a dozen people who would testify that he wasn't here. Had she made another terrible mistake? She was totally not cut out for this stuff. Had she just got Carla killed?

She realised the voice at the other end was becoming urgent.

"Sorry, what?"

"I said the car is two minutes away. Are you still near your apartment?"

"I'm in the lobby."

"And you're safe there?"

"I think so. For now."

"Are there any other ways out of your building?"

Ice dropped in Amy's gut. "Yes! There are back stairs to the rear lane, where the bins are and everything."

In a panic once more, Amy stabbed to end the call and ran. The police were coming, but what if they were too late? Surely Vince was the kind of criminal well-practised at protecting himself. From each floor, residents could take the lift in the middle of the landing, or one of two flights of stairs. The front led to the lobby, the way Amy had run, and the back led to the rear lane, full of refuse and the stink of piss. Amy pounded up the front stairs to the first-floor landing, bolted past the lift and slammed through the door into the back stairway. She heard the door to the back lane creaking and her heart leapt into her throat. Thinking nothing of her own safety, suddenly desperate to protect Carla, she ran down the back stairs and saw through the glass panel in the door. Stratton had Carla, still bound up but screaming and thrashing, over his shoulder like an old carpet. Clancy limped beside him and they reached a big, pale green car. Stratton threw Carla onto the back seat and climbed in, Clancy falling into the passenger seat.

Amy pushed open the door and met Stratton's eye as he started the engine. He lifted the knife for her to see, then leaned his head out of the window.

"Let's not involve the police any further, eh? If you want your friend to be safe, you tell the police you made a terrible mistake, you made the wrong identification. Turns out it was just a new boyfriend of your pal here. You feel so foolish and you're terribly sorry for wasting everyone's time."

A siren rose some distance away, getting louder.

"And you leave everything else well alone," Vince went on. "Forget about McLeod. He works for me now. Your friend here will be back, safe and sound, in a couple of days if you simply shut up and leave everything well alone. Understand?"

Amy swallowed, lost and confused. He was really taking her. He was kidnapping Carla to make sure Amy did nothing more.

"You'll let her go? Really?" Her voice was weak, cracked.

"I will, *if* you leave me alone, *and* leave McLeod alone. She'll be home in a couple of days. But you'd better tell the police what I told you."

"I don't even know how to reach McLeod. You were my only lead."

"Good. Keep it that way."

Without waiting for further conversation, the big car revved and backed up rapidly. Clancy's eyes were murderous from the passenger seat, one hand still pressed over his ruined nose. The other probably cupped his balls. Stratton swerved at the end of the lane and powered away down the street.

Amy stood, numb, tears trickling over her cheeks. The siren grew louder. She turned and went back through the building, into the front lobby as two uniformed police ran in. Mrs. Carver still stood where Amy had left her, bewildered.

"I'm so sorry," Amy said mechanically. "I made a terrible mistake."

"A mistake," one of the officers asked.

"I'm so embarrassed," Amy said, her chest tight. She wanted desperately to tell them the truth, but was in no doubt Stratton was capable of terrible harm to Carla. And, somehow, almost certain to get away with it. All she could do was exactly as the fucker had suggested and stop everything. Leave it all alone. She had to trust he would let Carla go again and then they could decide what to do, if anything. McLeod was on his own.

"Embarrassed?" the policeman asked.

"It wasn't an intruder. It was…a new boyfriend I'd never met. I interrupted them doing some S and M stuff, you know?"

The policeman smirked. "Seriously?"

"Yeah. They didn't expect me home. When I saw them I panicked and ran."

The policeman barked a short laugh, but his partner frowned. "You told dispatch there was a knife," she said.

"Yeah, sorry. It wasn't a knife. It was… It was a dildo. A chrome one, you know."

Mrs. Carver gasped again, muttered a constricted, "Good grief!" But her face was twisted in amusement.

Both police were smiling now and Amy couldn't believe how easily she'd sold such bullshit. "I'm really sorry," she said again.

"No problem," the policeman said, still chuckling. "Better safe than sorry, eh?"

"Dispatch said the intruder was someone called Vince Stratton," the policewoman said. "That right?"

Amy forced a laugh. "No, I thought it was. But that was just my panic. He's…he's half Stratton's age. His name is Dave apparently."

"Dave?"

"That's right."

"So what made you think it was this Stratton?"

"He runs a pub in Camden, called Stratton's. I was there last night. Didn't like the man when he acted all sleazy to me and my friends. In my panic, I thought it was him. I'm such an idiot. I'm so sorry."

"So everything's okay?"

"Everything's fine." Everything was far from fine. Amy's stomach roiled, her head pounded. Maintaining the casual façade became harder and harder. She just wanted to curl up on the spot and cry her eyes out.

"All right, then," the policeman said. "Perhaps you'd better organise your comings and goings with your flatmate more carefully in future?"

"Oh yes. We'll have a chat about that, don't worry."

"Good."

The police turned and left, chatting as they walked across the pavement to their car.

"What an exciting life you lead!" Mrs. Carver said with a cheeky smile.

"I'm so sorry if I scared you."

"That's all right, dear. There's not much excitement left at my age, so I don't mind."

Amy smiled and put a hand on the old lady's shoulder, gave it a gentle squeeze. She turned back to the stairs, walked as casually as she could back up to her flat, and then ran for the bathroom to vomit. Panic, fear, stress, it all came out with her bile, a debilitating, terrifying expulsion. What the hell was happening to her life?

Finally she sat back, exhausted. It was done. She would do exactly as Stratton asked and leave everything well alone. The man wouldn't be foolish enough to go back to his pub or take Carla there. Whatever he was doing, wherever he might be, he had said he would send Carla back in a couple of days. What other choice did Amy have but to wait and hope he was telling the truth? She would simply forget McLeod even existed. Nothing was worth Carla's life, even learning more about her own secrets.

In the corner of the bathroom, something seemed to move. She looked quickly at it, but there was nothing there. Like stars too pale to see if she looked directly at them, the shadowy figure appeared again to her left. As she slowly panned her vision, she got the impression of a shadowed man, reaching forward blindly, searching, but the distance between them seemed endless. Whatever this thing was, it was trying to find her again. A sob escaped her.

She leaned against the cool tiles of the bathroom wall, closed her eyes, and her phone beeped. It was a text message from work.

Amy, a gentleman by the name of Matt McLeod rang and said it was very urgent that you call him right away. I said I would pass on the message.

And there was McLeod's number, right there. Amy stared at the text for a moment, read it again. "What the fuck do I do now?" she whispered at the ceiling.

TWENTY-FIVE

VINCE STRATTON SAT CARLA ON THE BED in the spare room of his safe house not far from Hampstead Heath. She glared at him, her wet brown eyes burning with hatred. He held the knife up for her to see and she flinched.

"I'm not going to hurt you. Okay? I'm going to cut you free. Don't do anything stupid."

She didn't answer, but Vince knew she would be compliant for now, too scared, too lost, to resist. Her fire would come back, she was full-blooded, that was certain. Her craziness kicking that table, fucking everything up. She was a fighter. But for the moment she was thankfully subdued. He slit the tape at her wrists and pulled it free from her mouth again.

"You fucker!" she spat, her accent strong.

"Yeah, I hear that a lot."

"Why can't you leave us alone? Let me go. I'll go back home, never tell anyone anything. It can all be over."

"I'm sorry, I need you. Let's call you my insurance policy. Now listen, this is important. If you stay calm and quiet, you'll be in this room for a couple of days and then I'll send you home. It has an *en suite* over there, so you've got all the facilities you need. We'll bring you food and drink regularly, look after you like it's a five-star hotel, all right? You just promise me you'll be calm and peaceful until then and all this unpleasantness ends. Okay?"

"And Amy?"

"Same for her. She stays out of my business for a while and everything is sorted. That's what you're my insurance *for*, in fact."

Her eyes were still full of fire, but she nodded. "I have no choice but to trust you, do I?"

"No, I suppose not."

"What's happening? What's Amy done?"

"Nothing for you to worry about."

She stared daggers at him.

He smiled. "Be good now. I'll get you some food in a little while."

He left and shut the door, her furious eyes fastened on him the whole way. He secured the lock. She would try to escape, no question. It was clear she wasn't the kind of person to do as she was told for long. But the door had a sturdy lock, the window, bars. It would take only the barest degree of care to keep her contained. And he would kill her when he knew he didn't need her as a bargaining chip any longer. This whole bloody mess had rapidly spiraled out of control. McLeod had been to see his dad, for fuck's sake. The Scottish bastard was more of a problem than Vince had ever considered. But he had other, more immediate, concerns.

Clancy sat on the floral sofa in the lounge, a packet of frozen peas pressed to his face. He winced as Stratton came back into the room, as well he should, the bloody fool. Talking of fighters, that Amy Cavendish had flattened this fucking idiot. Part of Vince had to respect that. He had been too furious to speak in the car on the way, too consumed with thoughts and plans. And his silence would have given Clancy time to think about his position. Now it was time to have it all out.

"So what do you have to say for yourself?" Vince demanded.

"I'm sorry, Boss." It came out muffled, like Clancy had a terrible cold.

Stratton shook his head, genuinely disappointed. "We'll go over there and scare her, I said. Make sure she stops fawning over McLeod so there are no complications."

"I know. Sorry, Boss."

"So you said. She beat you up, you useless fucker!" Stratton exploded, spittle flying from his lips. "A bloody woman half your size fucking beat you up!"

Clancy recoiled from the sudden verbal assault, his eyes going wide. "She surprised me. She's more than half my size, Boss. She's very strong."

"She's a fucking woman and she beat the shit out of you and called the police. And now we have her fucking flatmate locked up in there. We had to kidnap the bitch, you useless fucking idiot! What do we do now?"

Clancy pushed himself further back into the sofa, shaking his head dumbly, side to side like a lowing cow. "I can help," he said eventually.

Vince laughed. "Can you really?"

"I know what's going on. I can help. I want to help."

Vince narrowed his eyes, fury turning to a deeper concern. Had it finally come to the thing he had long feared? This was supposed to be the chance for Clancy to redeem himself. To become questionless and obedient, show his allegiance. "You know what's going on?"

Clancy pulled himself up, took a deep breath. "I know you don't like questions, Boss. I get it. But I've figured it out. I don't need to ask questions." When Vince said nothing, Clancy ploughed ahead. "I know you're a hitman. I know we move the messages around and you're untraceable that way. I know you want McLeod to kill Najdovski for you. He's that Macedonian mobster, right? That fool with the restaurant in Soho?" Clancy frowned, looked down. "I'm not sure why you want McLeod to do it. Maybe you and him came to an agreement, him with that weird fucking thing he does." He looked up again. "Anyway, I checked the instructions you had me deliver to McLeod because I knew I had it right, and that confirmed it."

"You read a delivery?" Stratton asked, very quietly.

Clancy nodded vigorously. He knew he had broken all the golden rules here, but the fool pressed on. "But it's okay, yeah? Because I'm down with it. I want in."

"You want in?"

"Let me be your apprentice. Teach me. Use me. This Amy Cavendish? I'll take her out. Prove I've got what it takes. You want her dead now, right? While you concentrate on McLeod and Najdovski."

Stratton sighed, rubbed a hand over his face. This whole thing was out of control. It was what he got for trying to inject a bit of excitement into his career. He should have known better. He *did* know better, and had ignored himself. But it was Clancy who had first brought McLeod to his attention and here it came full circle. He needed to tidy up all these loose ends before everything unravelled. He had Carla to keep Amy quiet for the moment. She had said she had no other idea how to reach McLeod, and that fool wasn't going to risk going anywhere near Vince's father again. Time to close it all down. Keep Carla locked up for now, go and take out McLeod first. He was the most volatile. Then finish off Amy Cavendish. She would be at her flat and submissive, or he could intercept her going to or from work. Once McLeod and Cavendish were dead, he'd come back and finish off that furious Spaniard in the spare room. Get rid of all those bodies and that was an end to it. He shouldn't have tried to use McLeod in the first place, it was foolish. His desire to use as many weapons as possible was a fine hobby, but it could never be allowed to compromise The Work. The Work was everything, always the first priority.

So yes, kill McLeod, kill Cavendish, kill Carla. Get back to business as usual. That only left one other loose end.

The bag exploded and frozen peas flew everywhere as Stratton's mighty fist smashed into Clancy's face. A bloody shame, he genuinely liked this boy.

Clancy rocked back with a howl, blood pouring out again from his already ruined nose, fresh red over the drying brown down his front. Before the boy could recover, Vince grabbed him by collar and waistband and lifted him from the couch to slam him face-first onto the swirling brown patterns of the 70s carpet. Clancy woofed as the air was forced from him and Vince sat heavily across the poor lad's lower back. He looped one arm around under Clancy's chin and hauled his head back, then slapped his free palm over Clancy's mouth. He used his forefinger and thumb to pinch Clancy's swollen nostrils closed and held on tight.

Clancy's mouth worked and sucked against Stratton's wide hand, but there was no air to be had. He *hicced* and flinched, eyes wide and white and panicked, began to thrash but Vince's weight had him pinned. He quickly weakened, his resistance flowing away like rain on dry earth, and he sank to the carpet, limp.

Vince laid over him, locked in place for another minute to make absolutely sure. Clancy's head was turned to one side, his wide eyes staring glassily at the wall, showing nothing but the remains of panic. When Vince finally pulled his hand away it was covered in blood and snot and spit. He wiped it across Clancy's back then stood astride the boy, staring down.

"Bloody shame," he muttered. "Real bloody shame, you foolish young man. You could have been something."

He lifted the long, limp form and carried his ex-boy into the flat's other bedroom and laid him on the floor beside the bed. A red and orange blanket covered the mattress and Stratton pulled it free, tipped Clancy's body left and right to tuck the blanket beneath him, then wrapped the two sides over the top. Clancy lay there shrouded like a 70s mummy. The blanket would soak up any external blood and Vince would burn it when he got around to disposing of the body. He needed to organise tools for that, but it could wait for a day or two until the rest of this mess was fixed. For now, he needed to head to McLeod's place for stage one of Operation Tidy Everything The Fuck Up.

* * *

Abela stood in the middle of Charlie's lounge room, staring in horror at the blood-soaked armchair. It wasn't that she hadn't seen blood before. She was a homicide detective after all. She'd seen plenty of atrocious shit and had decent methods of distancing herself from it. And a damn fine police-financed therapist. The horror was that all this particular blood had, until recently, been inside Charlie.

"You fucking twat!" she spat at the empty chair, fury roiling with grief in her gut. Charlie had been a good cop, he'd pulled some serious collars. But he couldn't resist the temptations presented to him. It helped him get closer to the real criminals, he told her. But that was rationalisation of the most self-deluding kind. Beyond the bravado and the risk, he was a kind and caring man. "I fucking loved you!" she yelled, tears finally coming for the first time since the news had arrived.

She found herself gasping, sobbing, and reined it in quickly. *Abela means breathing! Live your name.* More of her father's old-country wisdom. He would tell her that even when she was small, a toddler wailing over a scraped knee. But again, it was good advice. She hauled in a deep breath, wiped at her eyes and nose. Then she breathed again, and again. She was no less angry, no less upset, but a moment of catharsis had passed with the tears. Charlie was over, gone. That was a finished chapter. So sudden, so pointless. But final. All she could do was maybe give him one last posthumous collar. Catch his killer.

The chair was nothing but his place of death, and the body had nothing of interest on it. There had been coke on the table and that had been impounded. Abela dreaded to think what else toxicology might turn up, but none of that mattered now. She had his car keys in an evidence bag and would search the Merc later. But she knew Charlie, he was a note-taker. He would jot things down, write them in a variety of ways and stare at his notepads for hours, trying to fathom connections. He operated by staring at words, looking for patterns. So whatever he had been working on last would be written down somewhere, long before he transferred the relevant details to official reports.

She turned and looked into the bedroom. Her mind wandered to the games they'd played in there, the fun they'd had. She saw herself on her knees on the black silk sheets, naked, riding Charlie like a wild mustang. She certainly missed that. But she remembered nights curled together too, holding him, or Charlie holding her, talking quietly. They slept well together, fitting like moulded parts of a similar height. And she remembered him waking regularly in the night, grabbing a notepad from his bedside drawer to stare at one page or another with a furrowed brow, or to frantically scribble cryptic words that he would decipher and process over coffee the next morning.

She went into the bedroom and opened the drawer. Sure enough, a pad was there. Unable to face the chair full of blood again, she sat on the side of the bed and started leafing through the thin pages. They were crammed with Charlie's tight, sharp scrawl. She didn't know what genuine handwriting experts would make of it, but to her it always looked like a mind going too fast, a sports car revving into the red. But it was thorough, in its way.

For a while the names and places and questions were all a bit disparate, but Abela knew Charlie. She knew his method. When they had been together they had regularly bounced cases and ideas off each other. After ten minutes, she began to lock into his voice and rhythm and his notes began to make a coherent music.

After half an hour, she had a twisted but somewhat organised idea of where he had been going. Two main threads presented themselves. One, a Scotsman called Matthew McLeod, connected with a death two years ago and one recently, somewhere around The Angel. Deaths which apparently presented the most disturbing of corpses that Charlie had described in his notes as "unnatural" and "maybe something inexplicable", whatever the hell that meant. She would look up those case files later. She paused, remembering the uncomfortable young man at the station earlier. He had been a Scotsman. And, according to the notes, that whole situation was also somehow connected with Vincent Stratton, infamous landlord of Stratton's in Camden Town. That name made her blood run slightly chilly. She imagined everyone in the service knew at least something about Vince Stratton. She had crossed paths with him a few times, and the man was a frictionless eel. Nothing would ever stick. But Charlie had been determined to take him down and seemed to think this McLeod was his lead-in. Plus, McLeod was connected to those bodies somehow and Charlie seemed to think he could nail both men through that, but he had wanted something more solid on Stratton, something bigger.

THAT FUCKING VIDEO!

Almost at the end of the notepad was that strange and confusing entry. What video? Was it something Stratton had over Charlie? Abela wouldn't be surprised. But her path seemed clear enough for now. She needed to talk to both Stratton and McLeod and see if she could figure out the connection Charlie hadn't laid out too clearly in his notes. But given Stratton's reputation, she would most definitely start with McLeod. And all his details were written down right there in her hands. She'd check Charlie's car to see if there were any other details to be found, then head over to McLeod's house in Finsbury Park.

TWENTY-SIX

MATT SAT ON HIS COUCH, the information from Stratton on the table in front of him. He'd need to go out soon, drive by the Najdovski joint and try to get a feel for it. The sketch Stratton had badly drawn, using some awful desktop app, gave a rough layout of the restaurant, but he had no sense of scale, of location. How would he get in? Was there a back door he could knock on to draw Najdovski out when the man was alone? Maybe that would be the best option, and then just grab the poor fucker and whack him on the spot and leg it, leave Stratton to deal with the fallout. But that meant Matt would have to scope out all the possible CCTV cameras in the streets around, anything the restaurant used for security. He may have to go inside after killing Najdovski and wipe any footage if they had cameras overlooking his approach or his chosen area of attack.

He cursed and sipped a whisky. He usually took weeks to plan these things, not hours.

His phone rang and he grimaced, imagining more harassment from Stratton. But his phone displayed a number he didn't recognise. His heart skipped.

"Hello?"

"Matt?" A woman's voice.

"Yes, this is Matt McLeod."

"It's Amy Cavendish. You wanted me to call."

His mouth dried up and he could think of nothing to say. His heart raced, tears forced themselves into his eyes, betrayers of his fragile state of mind.

"Matt? Are you there?"

"Yes. Yes, sorry. I'm so glad you called."

"I nearly didn't. I want this all to be over."

Over? All what? "I'm afraid I may have got you in some trouble," Matt said. "A man called Stratton—"

"Vince Stratton broke into my flat and abducted my friend," Amy said, her voice flat, strangely emotionless.

"You what?"

"He took her as insurance, he said, and will hold her until this is all sorted out."

"Jesus fuck." Matt moved quickly around his flat, grabbing anything he thought he might need. Wallet, phone charger, a penknife that was about the most useless weapon imaginable with its three-inch folding blade, but it was all he had. "This kinda changes everything." He looked around, wondering what else he might need and realised nothing was any use to him now. He just had to be away.

"I really don't give a fuck about what's happening," Amy said, fear and sorrow breaking into her voice at last. "I just want to be left alone. And I want Carla back."

Matt pulled on his coat and left the flat, pausing on the stairs leading up to the street to look and listen intently. "If he's done that, then everything's changed," he said, trying to keep his voice strong, for both their sakes. "I thought if I did what he wanted I could manoeuvre this around to all being over, but that's clearly not the case." He walked to the street and looked around again. Nothing. He ran to his car, jumped in. "He'll be coming for me now."

"What do you mean?"

The car barked into life and Matt floored it, roared away from the curb heading anywhere that wasn't his flat. "I fucked up. I went to see Terry thinking I was being smart, but I was an idiot. I've blown everything to shit. He'll not wait for me to do the job now, I'm sure of it. He'll be coming for me."

"Then you have to get away. Go to the police."

"I can't do that. Amy, I'm already away, I'm driving now. Where are you?"

"I'm not telling you that! I told you, I just want all this to be over."

"It won't. I'm so sorry, but it won't."

"Stratton said that in a couple of days he'd let Carla go and this would all be over." Tears were clear in Amy's voice now, her throat tightening her words. "All I had to do was leave you and him alone. I shouldn't even be calling!"

Matt took a deep breath. He felt like a bastard of the highest order. "He won't let her go, Amy. Stratton is a cold-blooded killer, it's as simple as that. He'll come for me, and when I'm dead he'll use your friend to get back to you, then he'll kill her too."

"What? Why?"

"He won't leave any loose ends, I'm sure of that."

"No, no, no. He said he'd let her go. I just need to stay out of his business."

"There is no way out of his business. Once you're in, you're his or you're finished."

Amy didn't reply but he could hear her breathing, hard and fast.

"We have to get together and talk," he said. "Let's meet. Somewhere public, a pub or café or a park. I'm no threat to you, but we have to talk."

"I'm going back to the police. Surely they can fix this!"

"Amy, no! Even if they manage to arrest him, Stratton has connections. He has my parents on his fucking kill list. He has your friend and his little fucking boys who work for him. I'm sure he's slippery enough to never get arrested, but even if he were he'd still manage to kill us all from inside. He'd do it out of spite if nothing else. Think about him. You know I'm right."

"So what the hell do we do?" Tears were being replaced with a high tone of panic in Amy's voice, but there was a strength there too. Anger. Matt was glad to hear her determination to not give in to fear.

"Let's meet. You and I have more than this going on, right?" Matt swallowed hard. "You saw my dark." It wasn't a question.

She was silent again.

"I saw yours," he said. "It…it was beautiful."

"What the fuck is happening?" she demanded, and it was the most absurd question he had ever heard, but he couldn't blame her for asking it.

"I'm in a car. I can get to you. Where shall we meet?"

"There's a shopping mall not far from me, it has a food court on the third floor. There's a Chinese joint there called Bamboo Station. I'll sit at the tables in front of that place and we can meet there. We'll be completely lost in the crowd, it's always packed."

Relief washed through Matt. At least together they could look out for each other and plan some kind of way forward. "Great. Give me the address."

* * *

The mall was five massive floors, each the size of a city block. Marble and mirror and light and chrome was everywhere, shop after shop of fashions and electronic goods, books and computer games, travel agents and hairdressers and a thousand other things. Tinsel and baubles hung from every available space, a fake plastic Christmas tree stood sentry to consumerism at least once every thirty metres or so. In the centre of the place was a massive atrium and the god-emperor of all Christmas trees filled it, towering at least twenty metres high, bedecked with hundreds of glittering balls and twinkling lights. At its foot, a grotto made of plastic fencing and cotton wool snow housed a giant red Santa in a giant red chair, with a line of families stretching off and around it, each awaiting their turn at the jolly man's lap and a photo.

"Not even fucking December yet," Matt muttered to himself, wincing against the carols being piped through every invisible speaker.

Thankfully the food court was largely decoration-free and the hubbub of voices drowned out the seasonal muzak. He saw her right away, spotted her shadows before he noticed the Bamboo Station sign behind her. She hadn't noticed him and he took a moment to stare.

She was well-curved in her jeans and fitted jumper, her face smooth and gorgeous. Blonde hair sat over her shoulders in tumbling loose curls. And around, above and through it all, that delicious blackness. It was alive around her, even while she wore it like the most ostentatious dress, it seemed to swell and shift gently with purpose, writhing, lace-like edges and tendrils of it curling softly in the air around her, like it wrapped her up and guarded her. There was menace to it, a contained power, but it seemed somehow to capitulate to her presence, its caress loving, not like his own darkness that tried to constantly consume him. That he needed to hold always in check. He couldn't imagine his looked like that. Could she release hers like he did?

She glanced up and saw him, winced. His wonder was shattered in that all too honest reaction to his arrival. He raised a hand and went to sit opposite her at the white, plastic table. A thousand other people around them went about their mundane lives, oblivious. For several moments they sat and simply stared at each other, around each other.

"Tell me what you see," Matt said eventually.

"You first."

He shrugged. "Okay." It took him a few minutes to describe it as best he could, her face growing ever more surprised.

"It's really that clear?" she asked when he ran out of words.

"Aye. It's not something I've ever seen on anyone before."

"Me either."

"You can't see your own?" he asked.

"No, I see nothing around me. But I see yours clearly."

"Same," he said. "But mine's not like yours, is it?"

Amy frowned, shook her head slightly.

"It's okay," he said. "I know mine's evil. It always has been."

"What do you mean?"

"Tell me what you see."

Amy looked him up and down, seemed to concentrate a lot on his shoulders and over his head. Eventually she said, "You described mine as like something I wore. Yours is more... Yours seems to wear you. No, maybe that's not right. It's more like it rides you, sitting on your back like a giant… Fuck, I don't know. It has no real shape. It's just this huge presence that seems to hold you by your head and shoulders, and sits wrapped around your back, like you'd shake it off if you had the slightest opportunity and it refuses to let go."

Matt coughed a humourless laugh. "Sounds about fucking right. I'd be rid of it in an instant if I could."

"Why?"

"You wouldn't?" he asked her, aghast.

"No. It's my gift."

"Mine is fucking killing me." When her eyebrows shot up, he said, "I think maybe we have something very similar to each other, but fundamentally different somehow. What do you mean, your gift?"

Amy sat back in her chair, her expression thoughtful.

"Please, let's both be one hundred per cent honest with each other," Matt said. "I think we owe each other that."

She nodded. "Yeah. Okay. Well, I've always been drawn to the dead and dying. I didn't know why for years, until I began work in palliative care and was present for so many people at the moment of their death. And I realised I could ease that passing by taking some of the shadow of their death into me. It doesn't ease their pain, or reduce their fear, but in some way they know, right at the very end, that someone is there, sharing that darkness. As they fall into the black unknown, I take a little of that shadow into myself and they know they've left a tiny legacy."

Matt had never heard anything so wonderful before, or so frightening. "And you just collect it?"

"At first, yes. I wondered if I had a purpose beyond the simple gathering, but I didn't know what. Then, a few years ago, it occurred to me that maybe I could pass the shadows on. Let them out in the opposite way to how I take them in. I was with a guy whose stepfather had abused him horribly. I thought maybe that bastard deserved some of my darkness. So I paid him a visit, shook his hand and found I did have the ability to give my shadows to people deserving of them." Her eyes narrowed.

Matt realised this was maybe part of the story she was reluctant to tell, not knowing him at all. "So what happened?" He took a leap. "You can tell me. I'm a killer too."

Her face blanched, but a kind of relief seemed to flow through her gaze.

"I only kill bad people," Matt added. "I'm not some psychopath. But I'll tell you mine in a minute. Finish your story."

She leaned forward again, forearms crossed on the table. "What happened to him? He developed a violently aggressive cancer and died eight weeks later." She stared deep into Matt's eyes. "So I'm a killer too, I guess. When I pass the shadows on to people, the darkness of it invades their body. Corrupts them. They very quickly develop cancers or some debilitating and terminal illness. I haven't been able to track them all, but most. And those I've watched never make it more than a few months before they're destroyed by what I gave them. Some of them barely make it a few weeks. It depends how much I give, how strong they are, who knows what else."

Matt smiled. "Well, yours is far more manageable than mine!"

"Is it?"

"Who do you give it to?" he asked.

"Anyone I think deserving. People who hurt others and get away with it."

"And how do you do it?"

"Just like with Jake's stepdad. I arrange or engineer some kind of meeting and shake hands. That's all it takes, skin-to-skin contact, and I let the shadows through." She laughed, shook her head. "I've never told anyone this stuff before. I can't believe I'm telling you."

"But you can see we're similar."

"Exactly. Honestly, it's a real relief. I thought I was alone in this."

Matt nodded, smiled. "Me too. So where did your…your gift come from?"

"It's always been there. I guess it just grew from my affinity with the dead. But I've always had it, I think. You haven't?"

Matt stared at his hands clasped together on the table. His knuckles were white and he realised most of his body was tensed like he was about to leap up and bolt. He took a deep breath, tried to relax.

"Come on," Amy said. "I showed you mine. You're not gonna chicken and run, are you?"

He grinned, not surprised she'd seen through his fears. "No, you're right. It's an amazing relief to have someone to talk to about this."

"Go on then."

"Is that everything about yours?" he asked. She seemed to be nervous. Perhaps it was simply opening up, but he had the sense there was something she was keeping back.

"Maybe not quite all," she admitted. "But that's the most of it and all I'm telling you for now. So what about yours?"

"Mine is very different. And very unpleasant."

"That's okay, you can tell me."

He looked up, held her gaze with his. "If I'm honest with you, it's likely you'll think a hell of a lot less of me. So I need you to promise me one thing first."

"What?"

"Whatever you think of me, we finish this Stratton situation one way or another. If you want to never say another word to me after that, fine. If you're disgusted by me, I need you to swallow that and get this mess cleaned up first."

She tipped her head to one side, brow creasing in concern. "It can't be that bad, can it?"

"Maybe it can." The look on her face beguiled him, she was so wonderful to behold. And finally, someone who could understand his darkness. He couldn't bear the thought she would be horrified and run from him. But she may well do exactly that. He briefly entertained the idea of lying about his situation, then quickly realised the most powerful thing they had was honesty. Nothing else would do.

She nodded. "I promise. Whatever you tell me, we'll talk about the Stratton thing too."

"Okay." Trembling started in his belly, made his knees shudder. He clasped his hands tight together again to mask their shaking. "I know exactly where my darkness came from. When I was four years old, my mother gave birth to a little boy, my brother." His voice cracked and Amy put a hand over his. He pulled away. "Don't. You'll not feel sorry for me soon. His name was Thomas. Tommy. And I hated him."

Her eyebrows rose and Matt nodded.

"Aye, I warned you. I'd been the only one, you see. When my mam told me she was pregnant I was horrified. I didn't want someone else coming along and taking away my attention."

"But I think all kids feel like that when they get a sibling," Amy said. "It's perfectly natural."

"But most kids don't do something about it. I killed Tommy." His breath caught and he concentrated only on keeping the tears from falling.

Amy stared at him, her mouth slightly open. "Killed him?" she said eventually.

"When he was just over three months old. I'd had enough, I suppose. He would get all the attention, he would wake at night, my mam and dad were exhausted. Of course, now, looking back, I know they were doing all they could to make sure they didn't ignore me. They didn't love me any less, they were just parents struggling with a newborn. But I was four, I was selfish, I was fucking atrocious. I snuck into his room almost as soon as they moved the cot from their room into Tommy's own nursery. I took my pillow with me and I wrapped it over his tiny face and held it there until I knew he was gone."

Amy gasped. She clapped a hand over her mouth, eyes wide.

"I woke up again in the early hours to my mam screaming. It was put down to SIDS. You know, cot death."

"Sudden Infant Death Syndrome," Amy whispered, like she was trying to make sense of it. She never would, he knew that.

"Aye. It was horrendous. I couldn't believe what I'd done, but at the time I was satisfied too. I was amazed at the power I'd discovered in myself. She screamed and my father pounded along the hallway, and then I heard his barking sobs of grief. I sat there in the darkness of my room and I knew it was all me. I had created that horror. I had killed Tommy. I was simultaneously elated and broken open by sudden grief. And the darkness reached up and it took me. It wormed its way into my bones and lived there, slowly eating me up from the inside. It spread out and surrounded me. I'd opened a portal to raw death and it had moved in. I knew it was slowly taking me away. I quickly realised that, and I also realised it was exactly what I deserved."

Amy shook her head, brow creased again. "No, Matt. No. It's horrible, but you were just a child. Your parents?"

"They never knew. They still don't. Oh, I forgot from time to time, managed to be normal here and there for short periods of time. But I was a sullen and distant child, always pegged as a weird one. Mam and Dad tried all kinds of things. Took me to counsellors and tried to engage me in any way they could. They thought maybe the grief of losing my baby brother had affected me, but of course, they had no idea exactly how. And I lived in the shadow of my dark the whole time."

"Matt, this is tragic."

"No less than I deserved."

"Don't say that!"

"It's true!" he almost shouted. A few people nearby glanced over and he glared until they looked away. He dropped his voice again and their words were once more lost in the volume of the place. "I'm sorry. I've never told this stuff to anyone. It's hard."

"Of course it is. So what happened? You said it was killing you, but you're still here."

"It was killing me. Still is. I've no idea how long I've got left, but I found a way to use it. To extend myself and atone, at least in part, for a little while."

"This is the bit about how you're a killer," Amy said. "But you're not like me in that, are you?"

"No. When I was fifteen, I was playing football for a local team. I used to do a lot of sport, though I was never very good at it. The physical activity, exhausting myself, seemed to lessen the pressure of the dark. After a match one day, late autumn, it was already night as I was walking home. It was strangely warm for the time of year, and there was light rain too. Weird, but not unpleasant. I took a shortcut across a playground not far from my house and as I got to the other side, a car pulled up at the curb. The driver leaned over the passenger seat and pushed the door open, called me over, asking for directions. He pointed to a map on the passenger seat to ask me if he was looking at the right streets. When I leaned in to look, he grabbed me and hauled me into the car and roared off."

"Fucking scumbag."

Matt smiled weakly, nodded. "But he picked the wrong boy. I was small for my age. Still am, I guess, and skinny. He must have thought I'd be an easy mark. But I was terrified, as you can imagine. He had a knife, like a kitchen knife, and he held it between us as he drove into this housing estate and parked up in a dark corner, in the shadows of a bunch of garages. There was no one around anywhere. He undid his trousers with his free hand and his cock was already hard, this short, stubby fucking thing, poking up out of his fly."

Amy grimaced, but her eyes burned with fury. Matt was pleased to see that, at least, but she wouldn't have forgotten everything else he had said. She would still hate him, he was sure.

"Anyway," he went on. "He points to his cock and says, 'Suck this and I'll no' cut you. Then you can go. Simple.' And you know what? In a way, it was simple. He might even have meant it. But I was just not going to do it. I couldn't think what I was going to do, but no way would I put that cunt's filthy prick in my mouth. And that's when I felt the dark straining against me. In a way, the evil presence of it was exulting in this awful situation, you know? For the first time, I sensed a kind of intelligence to it, and it wanted this horrible thing to happen. I felt it straining against me in its joy and I thought, 'I can let it go. I can let it out.' I had no idea what might happen, but I just… let go.

"It was horrendous. I'd never known such pain, like my bones were splitting apart to release it, and the dark was pulsing out through my flesh and skin like acid. I started screaming and thrashing. That bastard pedo's face fell and he was yelling at me as I thrashed and foamed at the mouth. I thought I was killing myself and who knows what he thought. And the pain! Fuck, it was blinding me. In a raw panic, I grabbed at him, thinking this evil child raper would somehow be able to help me. I just wanted someone to make the pain go away. And as soon as I touched the skin of his arm, the dark flooded out of me in a wave and rushed into him. His hand blackened, then his arm, and it spread over his face. He was howling in agony, trying to shake me off, but my fingers were wrapped onto him like a vice. I remember seeing that disgusting little cock of his blacken and wither, and I laughed at that, and then I felt a sudden moment of control. That little bit of mirth broke through the pain and I realised I had to push the dark back down or it was going to consume us both. And I forced it away. I refused to let it have any further free rein, insisted it fuck off back into the deepest, darkest part of me and stay there, where it had always sat, slowly eating away at me. And it did. I was strong enough. It retreated, almost satisfied. Sated. The pedo was little more than a blackened skeleton, his skin stretched taut over his bones, all his flesh sunk away, his eyes like fucking raisins in his skull. I still burned with pain, but I leapt from the car and I ran and ran through that weird warm, wet night until I got home and I fell into bed and passed out.

"The next morning I woke up and felt better than I had in years, like the dark had been repressed a little bit. It was still there, still eating me, but I realised I could use this new-found skill. I could periodically let it out to consume any deserving bastard I could find. Maybe, I thought, each fucker like that pedo I killed might be a tiny bit of recompense for taking Tommy's life when it had barely begun, and along the way the pressure of my dark was lessened for a time. I left home not long after that night, came to London. I lived on the streets for a while, eventually found a job, got a place. I've been on my mission ever since. It's still destroying me, but I've been taking a few out along the way before it finally finishes me. I don't think I have many left."

Matt sat back in his chair, exhausted from the telling. It was catharsis like he'd never known before, pouring it all out to someone. Finally admitting everything, all the things he'd never told anyone. But it was not the kind of story to make him any friends. Girding himself against her disgust, he looked up to see Amy's face.

She was crying openly, staring at him with the most unguarded sorrow. He shook his head slightly, confused.

"You poor, poor man," she said, almost too quietly for him to hear.

"What?"

She reached out, took his hand. He was too stunned to do anything about it, basked in the warmth of her touch.

"Look at you," she said, "lost in this all-consuming guilt. It's not your fault. Matt, none of this is your fault!"

"Of course it is! I smothered my tiny brother to death!"

She nodded, tears glistening on her cheeks in the bright fluorescent lights. "Yes, you did a *horrible* thing. But you were just a child. Not many would act on their jealousy like you did, sure, but the depth of your guilt shows you're not a monster. You made a mistake."

"Big fucking mistake!"

"Maybe. I wonder what would have happened if you'd admitted to what you did, back then when you were four."

Matt laughed bitterly. "I can't even imagine. Stop and think about it for a moment, about what that would have been like. How my parents would have looked at me then. Their lives were already shattered. Imagine then learning it was their surviving son who was responsible! Bad enough they lost one son."

"But it sounds like maybe they kinda lost you too anyway."

The old guilt stabbed at him again. "Aye, that's maybe true. But at least they think Tommy's death was a horrible bit of bad luck. Natural, at least."

They sat in silence for a long time, both crying softly, Matt's hand still resting in Amy's warm grip.

"You really think your dark is killing you?" Amy asked eventually.

"No question. Before long, I'll let it out and it'll finish me too. Or I won't recover from the kill afterwards. I can feel it gaining on me."

"What about if you stop using it?"

"Same thing. Might take a bit longer, but it'll break me down eventually. At least by using it, I'm doing some good in the world before I go. Atoning a little bit for Tommy."

"I think maybe you've long since made up for that."

"Do you? I don't. Nothing can make up for what I did. No amount of bastards taken out of the world."

"How many have you killed?"

He looked into her eyes again, those deep green gems. They were soft with concern.

"Twenty-two," he said eventually.

Her eyebrows rose. "Wow. That's impressive."

"Is it? What about you?"

"I only realised I could release my shadows about five years ago. I've given them to nine people since then."

"Seems we both average a couple of fuckers a year."

They both laughed, but it was sad, slightly broken laughter.

"Hey," Matt said, realising a positive at last. "At least yours isn't killing you. Your whole thing about gathering your dark—no, you call them your shadows?" She nodded. "Aye, well, the way you deliberately collect and distribute them is all benevolence. You're doing good work."

"So are you."

"Maybe. But mine is born of horror and it's killing me."

She looked down at their hands intertwined and gently removed hers. Matt was disappointed at the retraction of her touch. "Maybe mine is too," she said quietly.

"Is what?"

"Killing me."

"What do you mean?"

Amy told him all about the strange presence that had been released with her most recent delivery of shadows. How convinced she was that it meant her harm. "Perhaps," she concluded, "it's been gaining strength every time and finally got free. I'd sensed it in the background on a couple of occasions before, but this time it actually seemed to manifest somehow, and it definitely came for me. If Carla hadn't interrupted it…" She winced, swallowed hard at the mention of her friend's name.

"But you think it's gone now?" Matt asked.

"I'm not sure. I think so, but then I sense something, feel it lurking just out of sight. I keep looking over my shoulder, jumping at shapes in the night. Maybe it's just regathering its strength. I have no idea. But if I deliver my shadows again, I'm sure it'll be back, stronger than ever."

"So is this the end of your career dispensing shadows of justice?"

She smiled crookedly. "Shadows of justice. I like that. But I don't know. I don't want to stop. It's my reason for being, you know? It feels like what I was born to do. But I don't want that thing to get me."

"Our conditions seem so similar, yet so different. You reckon they're the same?"

"Maybe. I don't know if I could do what you do."

Matt stared at the tabletop, thinking. "I think maybe you could, if you chose to. But perhaps we share different forms of the same thing. You seek out your shadows, collect them and use them. It's entirely more controlled. I let the dark into myself long ago and it lives in me now, feeds off me."

"I wonder if you could collect more like I do."

He laughed ruefully. "That might just kill me more quickly."

"I guess we need to think about it, compare notes, maybe see what we can learn by what we see in each other." She shook her head, looked away across the sea of strangers. "I've wanted to try to figure out more about the manifestation I triggered, but I haven't had much chance."

Matt nodded, sat up straighter. "Which brings us to more pressing and immediate concerns."

"We need to talk about this stuff a lot more," Amy said. "But you're right. We have other issues at hand."

"You don't hate me?" Matt asked, nerves tickling his gut.

"No. And I'm not going to run away and refuse to speak to you again. We only know each other with this thing, and need to talk about it more. But later. Right now, what about Stratton? I have to save Carla, and if that means waiting for him to release her, that's what I'll do. You might be on your own there."

Matt shook his head. "It definitely won't go that way. Like I said, he has people on my parents, he has Carla, and he has all kinds of strengths. Even if we put him away, he'll get all those people killed just because he can."

"So what do we do?"

"I was thinking about exactly that on the drive over here. There's only one way out of this. *We* have to kill *him*."

"Scriously?"

"Sure. And I can do that. It might be the last thing I ever do, but I'm okay with that. It'll take that fucker out, and he certainly deserves it. The bastard is a hitman! And it'll save my parents and your friend. We just have to work out how we're going to do it."

TWENTY-SEVEN

VINCE STRATTON APPROACHED MCLEOD's basement flat fuelled by anger. But he was a professional, his career defined by patient, careful planning and ruthless attention to detail. These latest details were troublesome but easily fixed. His anger at Clancy's snooping had transformed into a rage that he'd had to do away with the foolish boy. Bloody fool. It would burn him inside for a long time, that particular necessity. Apart from the inconvenience of the whole thing, lads like Clancy were hard to find. That balance of smarts and obeisance. Clever enough to do everything that was required of them, but dumb enough to follow orders blindly and never ask questions. Of course, Vince reminded himself, Clancy hadn't been like that after all, which is why he had to go. Vince didn't need another one like Clancy. He needed someone better. Now he would concentrate on making Dexter the one. If he could get over his innate distrust of everything and accept Stratton for the benevolent dictator he was, then yes, perhaps Dexter.

But there were more important concerns in Vince's immediate vicinity. Clancy was dealt with, the body could be taken care of later with the efficiency a person of Stratton's experience thought nothing of. Next, McLeod. That was another thing that smarted, that niggled at his sense of who he was as a person and as a professional. He really wanted to use McLeod as a weapon, to add to his ever-growing array of interesting and original hits. But ruthless attention to detail dictated other things, and the McLeod situation was getting very close to being out of control.

If Vince were a lesser man, if he was stupid, he would insist on seeing his plan through. He would let McLeod do for Najdovski and then take McLeod out the instant it was done. Do all the tidying up himself. He had seriously entertained that idea for a fair while before accepting the simple truth. It was too risky. When control started to slip, it needed to be snatched back instantly. The further it slipped, the less likely it was to ever come back.

Vince paused on the pavement, looking down the worn steps to McLeod's front door. The night had begun to settle, even though it was still before 5:00 p.m. Autumn daylight so short, but it suited him. He operated best in the dark, and the longer the night-time hours, the more he could get done. The light in the front room was on, glowing softly through thin curtains that turned everything inside into a hazy miasma of not-quite-visible habitation. The television played, flickering away in one corner. Vince smiled. He knew there was no other exit for McLeod, the old building built long before modern safety considerations. The place was a death trap, should someone be in the back when a fire broke out in the front.

For a moment Vince paused, considering an arson angle. But no, it wasn't certain enough, not by a long way. He wanted to watch the life leave McLeod's eyes, but he needed to make sure he stayed well away from the bastard's deadly touch.

He crept down the steps, kept low as he shuffled silently over to the window, lost in deep shadow. He peeked up over the sill, scanning the front room. Beyond the glow of the television and the general outline of furniture, he could see no detail. But there was no movement either. He saw enough to know that no one sat on the couch or in the armchair in one corner. A low table stood before the couch, but it was bare. No tell-tale coffee cup or plate. Three doors led from the main room. He saw the kitchen through one door, the light on in there too. The other doors—he assumed a bedroom and a bathroom—were dark. So McLeod must be in the kitchen, maybe organising one last feed before he went after Najdovski. *I'll do the job tonight,* he had said. No you won't, old son, Vince thought, and grinned.

He pulled his lock-pick kit from a pocket of his dark grey canvas jacket and went to work on McLeod's front door. He was silent and swift, a simple Yale lock no challenge at all. He held his breath as he swung the door open, hoping it was well-oiled. There was no creak to give him away.

Too easy.

He stepped inside and pushed the door to behind him, then stood up, shook himself. Quick and ruthless, no fucking about. He slipped a silenced automatic pistol from his inside pocket and only took his eyes off the kitchen door for a second while he checked the weapon over. He knew by touch that it was ready, the safety off, but a professional double-checked everything.

"Mr. McLeod," he announced in a strident voice. He aimed the pistol at the kitchen door, expecting the bastard to leap through it instantly. "I'm afraid we have to talk."

Nothing.

Vince grinned. Canny bastard. Hiding inside, hoping Vince gets close enough to be touched. There was a thrill to that, when the prey actually engaged in the hunt. "Good for you, McLeod."

Vince crept to the wall beside the kitchen door and sank into a crouch. Of course, there was every chance the bastard wasn't in. Wouldn't that be a hoot. Vince tucked and rolled into the tiny kitchen, came up on one knee and swept the gun barrel left and right. No one. He barked a short laugh.

"Fucking hell," he muttered to himself. "Where the fuck have you gone?"

He moved swiftly but carefully into the bedroom, took a torch in his free hand and swept it across the dark space. Empty. He flicked on the light to confirm, checked the corners, then repeated the actions in the tiny bathroom. Nothing. The place was empty. Clearly nothing could be straightforward with this Scottish bastard. Maybe he was already on his way to do Najdovski. Surely he wouldn't try to hit him while it was so early, everything busy. The man would be alone after closing time, nice and easy. Maybe it would come to that plan after all. If he couldn't be traced, Vince would have to intercept the bastard before he hit the Macedonian, then he could take care of Najdovski himself. Everything nice and tidy. Then finish off that Amy Cavendish, and finally get rid of the Spaniard in his safe house.

A professional moved with the flux of chaos, Vince reminded himself. React with positive confidence, not anger or frustration. Those things led to mistakes. He took a deep breath, swallowed down the rage that threatened to rise.

"Move with events!" he said loudly to himself.

Stratton often imagined himself a sword-wielding hero, always at war with his anger. As a teenager, he had been to a few counselling sessions after one too many fights and one too many run-ins with the law. *You don't want to be in trouble, do you?* the counsellor had said, a mousey woman with thick glasses and a mop of curly brown hair. But she was cute and teenage Vince had lusted after her despite her annoying habit of trying to fix him.

No, I want to avoid trouble, he had said, offering the answer he assumed she wanted to hear.

Well, that's good. And you know, it's your anger that gets you into trouble. Your anger exists. You can't deny it, but you can address it. You can think about what makes you angry and try to change things. And in the meantime, you can refuse to let your anger rule you. When you feel it rising, challenge it. Don't let it take control. You *take control. Anger is a beast you can slay with determination.*

Vince had laughed at that, but her words had resonated. *A beast? Like a dragon?*

Sure! she said, genuinely pleased with his comparison. *And you can be like Saint George, yes? You can stand tall and slay that dragon.*

Ever since, Stratton had pictured himself as Saint George, in shining armour astride a muscled white charger, lance and sword in hand. He had to laugh, even still, but it worked. He pictured his anger as a dragon rising up, and he slashed and stabbed at it and slew the bastard time and again. Not because he wanted to avoid trouble. He enjoyed a bit of that. But because he didn't want to get caught for his trouble, and a person got caught when they got sloppy and made mistakes. And when he got angry, and frustrated, he made mistakes. And Matthew fucking McLeod was making him so fucking angry right now. He needed to finish that bastard and take back control.

"Pull it together!" he told himself in a harsh whisper. He pictured a dragon with McLeod's face rearing up. He saw himself, armoured and strong, and he swept a mighty sword around and took the head off that dragon. He breathed deeply and slowly, and smiled softly. The rage began to subside.

He left McLeod's flat, pulled the door shut behind him, and peeled off his surgical gloves, stuffed them deep into a pocket. The street was fairly busy, the neon glow of shops bathing the dark pavement a hundred metres further up. It didn't take long to find a place selling pre-paid mobiles and he bought a cheap, base model and a sim. A pub across the street offered warmth and a seat, so Vince went in, bought a scotch and dry, and sat in a corner. It was a quiet place, the kind of pub that existed solely for the benefit of a few local regulars. Quite charming in its own way, but a world of difference to his own busy establishment.

He dug around in his pockets and pulled out a scrap of paper with McLeod's mobile number on it. He must be sure to take that phone away from McLeod and destroy it when he finally caught up with the slippery Scots bastard and finished him. There would be records, of course, modern technology with its irritating habit of helping the police in all kinds of clever ways, but that shouldn't matter. With Collins dead, there shouldn't be any connection between McLeod and himself. He put in the number and tapped out a text message.

Bit of a complication with the job. Do not go ahead. Repeat, DO NOT go ahead. I need to give you further details. Message me back on this number and we'll talk.

Vince sent the message, put the phone on the table in front of him and sat back, drink in hand. He sipped and stared at the phone, willing it to buzz and light up with a response from McLeod. If nothing came in the next hour, he would have to go and stake out Najdovski's place and hope things didn't get any messier than they already were.

He breathed deeply, sipped scotch, and pictured the slaying of many dragons.

* * *

Detective Abela Farouk sat in her car watching Stratton as he sat in the pub, and she agonised over what to do next. She had arrived at McLeod's place and parked, just about to hop out of the car, when a large man she instantly recognised as Stratton had appeared and snuck down the steps to McLeod's front door. *Interesting*, she thought, and decided to watch and see what they talked about.

Then Stratton had picked the lock and crept inside. So maybe they weren't working together after all. Or perhaps they were, but Stratton had ulterior motives beyond anything they might have agreed upon. Regardless, it only made the situation murkier. So she continued to wait. Patience was always a virtue, many people other than her father thought that, though it had been one of his regular reminders too.

Then Stratton had emerged again looking furious, bought a phone, and gone to the pub just down the road. Abela remained in her car, having moved it a hundred yards up the street, and watched the publican through the window. He sat there drinking, staring at the new phone on the table. She felt she could almost hear his grinding teeth from where she sat, the fury etched on his face like a mask. There was no way she was going to get between that anger and McLeod, whom she assumed it was directed at. Whatever caper Charlie had been onto, perhaps a part of it was playing out here. But it had got him killed and she still held Stratton as the most likely candidate for that murder, though they had never been able to pin even a parking ticket on him before. Maybe she could give Charlie two last gifts—the capture of his killer and the closure of the cases he had dug up. Those inexplicable bodies, McLeod's connection. Her timing coming to McLeod's had been fortuitous, and she didn't want to blow whatever lucky chance she had. So she relaxed into the warm comfort of the velour seat and the heater of the company Ford, and waited.

TWENTY-EIGHT

MATT HELD UP HIS PHONE FOR AMY TO SEE. She read Stratton's message, raised an eyebrow.

"I'm guessing he's just been to my flat and found me not home. I'm glad you rang when you did, cos I would have been there otherwise."

"So I saved your life? I'll remember that."

Matt grinned. "Gallows humour? That's good. We need that. Now what the fuck are we going to do?"

He had told her all about what Stratton had asked of him, how he had control. Amy seemed to be getting both more scared and more angry with every piece of the story. The fear was healthy, the anger was good. She was strong, that much was apparent from the outset and only becoming more obvious. He was so pleased to have an ally in all this, at least someone to simply talk to. And someone to share the burden of his darkness, just by being able to tell her. He was still struggling to accept that she didn't hate him, despise him for what he'd done to bring the dark into himself. But she seemed genuinely sympathetic. It was hard to credit. But how could he use her help without risking her life?

"You're not still going to go after this Najdovski, are you?" she asked.

Matt shook his head. "It's pointless now, I think. Stratton knows it too. He wants to meet to finish me off, I'm sure. I don't imagine for a moment that he actually has any info about the hit. He knows I went to Terry. He knows you were looking for me. He knows things are more complicated than ever. I don't expect he meant to abduct your pal, Carla, but things got out of his control there too."

Matt smiled inwardly, remembering the story she had told him of escaping Stratton's clutches. What she'd done to that young idiot, Clancy. She was strong indeed.

"But that's why I'm convinced Carla won't be let go. She's only alive until I'm dead. And honestly, I think he'll use her to draw you out and then kill you too." Amy winced and Matt raised a hand. "Which is why we have to finish him quickly." He tapped his phone, sat on the table between them. "Which is why I'm going to do what he asks."

"What?"

"He wants to meet. So I'll meet him. I only have to get in grabbing distance and it's all over for him, even if it kills me too. Then my parents and you and Carla are safe."

"We need to know where Carla is though. She could be locked up anywhere."

Matt pursed his lips. "True. And it might be hard to get that out of the bastard. I need to simply destroy him instantly."

"We can't just leave Carla to rot!"

"Let me think."

Amy looked around the busy food court. "Despite everything, I need to eat. You?"

Matt realised he was ravenous. "Yes, actually."

"You like Chinese food?"

"Sure."

She stood and joined the queue for Bamboo Station. Matt watched her butt in her tight jeans for moment, more than impressed, then pulled his attention back to the issue at hand. What a total mess. And she was right about Carla. The fact the poor girl was locked up somewhere in London, almost certainly to be killed before long, was entirely Matt's fault. If he hadn't followed Stratton and gone to see Terry, then he would never have crossed paths with Amy. She wouldn't have come looking for him and fallen foul of Stratton. Carla would be happy and getting on with her life, as would Amy. It was all his fault, and he had to fix it. By the time she came back with food for them both, he had a plan. An audacious, ridiculous plan, but it was the best he could manage.

"Stratton wants me dead," he said around mouthfuls of salty noodles and chicken. "You're almost certainly not going to like what I've come up with, but given the situation and the lack of time, it's the best I can think of."

She frowned at him. "That doesn't fill me with confidence."

"Me either, if I'm honest. But can you think of anything?"

"Not really, I guess."

"Give me a second here. I have to message my mam." Matt pulled his phone out and tapped a message to his mother.

"What did you tell her?"

"That she's being watched and to go directly to the police and ask for protection. If they don't take her seriously, do anything to get arrested. I hope they take me at my word. If I try to draw Stratton out, he might have them killed just for the fucking sport of it."

Amy's eyebrows shot up. "Draw him out? Really?"

"I have to. I'll arrange to meet him, but I'll insist on setting the location. He's sure to bring his boys along, hide them as sentries to warn him when I'm coming. He's also sure to keep me at arm's length. Wouldn't surprise me if he tried to shoot me dead from a sniper position before I even see him if he has the chance. So I'm going to have to use your help and call in a few favours I really haven't earned. I just hope people will help me."

"I hope you know what you're doing, Matt."

"I have no fucking idea what I'm doing, but here's the plan. It's gonna take some setting up and a lot of sitting around waiting."

He jumped as his phone rang, buzzing on the table in front of him. BEN CALLING...

Matt pursed his lips, nodded. "Synchronicity," he said to Amy.

She looked confused, but he held up one hand as he answered the phone. "Ben, mate."

"Hello, Matty! So me and Steve-O and Gareth have just got down to the Carpenter's for a few, because you know the only way to start work on a Monday is hungover, right?"

"So you've suggested before, aye."

"Right. Well, where the fuck are you then? Surely you're not going to stand me up again, mate. You gonna come down and join us?"

"I'm afraid I can't do that, Ben, but I'm glad you called. And I hope you haven't had too many. I've got a *really* big favour to ask you guys."

TWENTY-NINE

VINCE STRATTON DRANK COKE because too much scotch would dull his edge. The rage he kept trying to slay had become a fury and he was about to give up on hearing from McLeod and go to the Najdovski location when his phone finally buzzed.

He stared at the message, nonplussed. He blinked, read it again. *Lock-up garage No. 12, midnight. Come alone.*

Followed by a street address. Vince shook his head. The weaselly little bastard was setting the terms now? "Oh no, old son," he muttered to himself, hot anger roiling his gut. "On no, not at all."

He tapped out a reply.

You don't call the shots, boy. You'll come to me, where I decide, or your father dies while your mother watches.

Being so blatant was certainly taking a risk, but the dragon that was Matt McLeod filled Vince's mind and needed slaying, metaphorically and in the flesh. This had to end, right now. His phone immediately flashed a response.

Try it.

Stratton gasped, hand trembling as he stared at the tiny digital words. Ridiculous. Just insane. He fumbled in his pockets and found another phone. "Gonna get fucking cancer carrying all these bastard devices around with me," he said under his breath. He opened a new message to an old, reliable contact.

Act three, Scene one. Just the male lead, while the leading lady enjoys the show. Message when complete.

He sat back, knowing it would take a while now for his man on the job to move in, take McLeod's father and kill him while his wife watched. Once word came in that it was done, he would ensure McLeod had the opportunity to speak to his mother and then things would swing inexorably Vince's way again. Taking back control. He lifted his glass to sip his Coke but was interrupted by the phone flashing back into life.

Performance delayed. Can't access players. The law have them safe inside.

Stratton growled deep anger and the glass shattered in his hand. Sharp pain accompanied half a dozen tiny lacerations that leaked blood quickly between his fingers. With a bark, he dropped the remains of the glass, shook his hand. Several people in the quiet pub had turned to look at him and he stared them down. "Mind your own fucking business!" he shouted.

Eyebrows raised, some faces turned away, others continued to stare. The barman looked up, "What's happening out there?"

Drawing far too much attention, Vince stood, gathered up his phones and strode out of the bar. He stalked along the dark streets until he found a quiet corner, a low brick wall encircling a scrubby attempt at some urban greenery. This end of the road was dim and still, quiet in the night. He sat on the wall and drew long, deep breaths, hands clenching and releasing as he forced some control back into his heart and mind.

You clever little shit, he thought.

If McLeod had gone to those lengths, sent his parents to the police, then unpleasant scrutiny was likely to fall on Vince any time. Nothing he couldn't shake off, but the more loose ends there were remaining, the harder it would be to smooth everything out and get back to business as usual. McLeod was playing an end game, forcing events along. His parents couldn't hole up in the police station indefinitely, and the police would come looking for Stratton if McLeod had given them names. He could wait it out, but then details would be hard to know. Patience was always a virtue, but sometimes things needed to be tidied away quickly before they could spiral away.

Well played, McLeod. He would have to go along with the bastard's plan after all. He supposed that was all he could expect. McLeod wasn't dumb enough to really accept Vince's last text as truth and ask where Vince was. It had been worth a try, but fine. He didn't buy it and he'd set up a stalemate. Vince would have to move with the momentum of events, roll with the punches. He had definitely lost some control of this situation and the best way to wrest it back was to let the other party think they had the upper hand.

A lock-up garage. Strange location. McLeod clearly had a plan, but it didn't matter. All Vince needed to do was get sight of him and pull a trigger before the bastard could lay a hand on his flesh. Pretty straightforward. But McLeod was proving time and again that he wasn't stupid. Caution was required.

Vince pulled out his regular phone and tapped up the maps app. The location was non-descript enough, beside a large dual carriageway, blocks of flats surrounding its other sides. Quiet, residential, urban, one of the shittier London housing estates. He rang Dexter.

"Hello, Boss."

"Hello, Dex. Get Saul and David and get to the address I'm going to text you ASAP. Don't do anything but watch and remember anyone you see. I'll be along presently, about midnight, but you get there right now and wait."

"Will do, Boss," Dex said.

"Good lad."

"What about Clancy?"

Vince shook his head sadly. Foolish Clancy. "What about him?"

"I haven't seen him all day. He missed a catch-up. You think he's okay?"

"Don't you worry about Clancy. Now get along, quick as you can. And report anyone you see coming and going by text as it happens, right?"

"Yes, Boss."

Vince hung up and texted his young protégé the address. If Dex was the better boy to train up, perhaps tonight would be a good test of his character. He took out another phone, his new burner, and typed a reply to McLeod's demand.

You're playing a dangerous game, son. You've chosen a quiet place. You got designs on me, have you? I'll be there at midnight. Do not make me wait for you.

He sent the message then paused to wonder if McLeod might have the means to get a weapon. Would the Scots prick set him up for a sniper shot? It was entirely possible the boy was going to try something like that. Vince couldn't discount the possibility he might have contacts. What exactly was McLeod thinking right now? Vince smiled. They were locked in a brutal chess match, a battle of wills and strategies, each with uniquely different weapons and skills. But Vince had something that could not be beat. He had experience. He'd been around these strange blocks many times and no snot-nosed twenty-something troublemaker was going to out-think him. He would get to the location early, stay hidden, and scout all around, find McLeod if he was lying in wait somewhere nearby. And perhaps McLeod would be waiting for exactly that, watching from a distance for Vince to arrive. Well, so be it. Game on.

* * *

Abela sat in the warmth of her Ford and frowned. Stratton had surged out of the pub like he meant to kill someone within seconds, only to then sit on a dark wall a little way down the road and juggle phones and facial expressions. He seemed to be running a gamut of emotions, but had eventually settled with some kind of resignation. And now he was striding purposefully back towards McLeod's place.

Abela watched in her mirror and then slowly made a U-turn once Stratton was far enough away not to notice. She purred along, parked again when Stratton paused and rummaged in his pockets. He pulled out keys and climbed into a big green Rover parked at the curb. The car rumbled to life and he drove away.

Shaking her head, unable to do anything but watch and wait, Abela followed.

THIRTY

Blind in total shadow, Matt started slightly as his phone flashed alive. Stratton was coming. That could only mean his parents had managed to get themselves somewhere safe after all. The first terrible gamble had paid off. Relief washed through him, closely followed by rising anxiety.

Stratton was coming.

Matt had forced a confrontation and he had no way of knowing how Stratton would respond to it, or how it might play out. And it could get all his friends killed. He had to hope his desperate measures worked. The meeting they'd had, the plans they had made, all seemed so ridiculous, but choice was thin on the ground. Sitting in Steve-O's flat, going over everything, their faces at first twisted in wry amusement. *This some kind of wind-up, mate?* Ben had asked. Strangely, it was Gareth who first realised the truth of it. Matt had watched his face smooth out, shocked and concerned. Slowly, with Amy's help, he'd convinced them the danger was all too real. And they'd stepped up, assured him they would help. True friends. How much would they remain friends based on what they might see this night?

"Mate, if you're in trouble, we're here for you," Ben had said finally, his face fixed in a mask of outrage and determination.

"There'll almost certainly be guns," Matt said, reluctant, but knowing he couldn't lie to them, even by omission.

"We've got your back," Ben repeated. Gareth and Steve-O looked less certain, but they both nodded all the same.

"You can't call the police?" Steve asked, not for the first time that evening.

"I wish I could explain more, mate, but I can't. Police are no good here right now."

Steve looked down at his scuffed white trainers, nodded again. "Fair enough."

More grateful then he could possibly express, Matt thanked them and went over the details of his plan, his ridiculous ideas. He just had to get close enough to grab the bastard. They didn't need to know why, but he could tell they were sceptical. No matter, as long as they helped. And he knew they would. They'd keep their word.

From the depth of his shadows, he sent a message to Amy.

He's coming.

It was just before eleven p.m. They would be lying in wait still for an hour, possibly more. It was likely Stratton would be late to show some kind of arrogance, some semblance of control. They'd talked of the possibility.

She texted back, *Okay.*

Matt nodded to himself in the pitch darkness and messaged Ben.

It's on. He's bound to send his boys first, so look out.

The response came almost immediately.

if this is some candid camera prank bollocks

Matt couldn't help but smile to himself, but there was no time for levity.

It's not. Deadly serious. Please be careful.

Ben's response was almost instant again.

its cool we got you

Matt took a deep breath, flexing his muscles in the dark and cold. He didn't need to get stiff while he was waiting, but he couldn't risk moving around too much. Stratton was certain to somehow case the area, check it out before he came too near. Matt swallowed his nerves and hunkered down.

He was trembling from the late chill biting into his bones when his silenced phone flashed to light again. Another message from Ben. *three likely lads just turned up and are wandering around the lock-ups. all young, one stocky black kid one ginger and one skinny little muppet doesn't look old enough to shave*

Matt nodded to himself. The black kid would be Dexter, as Clancy was tall and rangy, not stocky. The redhead would be Saul. He remembered them only too well from that fateful night when they'd appeared in his flat with guns and Stratton's demand to meet. The night everything had turned to shit. Really not so long ago, though it felt like a lifetime. The younger kid was a new player, but it didn't matter. How the hell many young boys did Stratton have under his wing anyway? Thankfully only three were here now. That was even odds. But Clancy might show up yet, and he was potentially the most volatile of them all, the most unpredictable. And he had a score to settle with Amy. Maybe other boys would come too. Matt texted back.

That'll be Stratton's boys. Watch them. Keep an eye out for any more.

Texts went back and forth as Ben reported from his clear view, looking down over the lock-ups from the window of Steve's flat. Eventually things settled down with Dexter loitering at the end of the row of lock-ups and Saul and the new kid each waiting in the shadows on either end of the block. They watched the road and generally looked like your average London malcontents, according to Ben.

The night ticked along. As midnight approached there was still no sign of Stratton and Matt's nerves began to jangle. Amy texted equally anxious concerns and he mollified himself somewhat by constantly reassuring her. Ben regularly checked in to report that Stratton's boys were still in their chosen spots. Occasional residents wandered past, but not many this late on a Sunday night. Some hobo pushed a shopping cart along and back, Ben convinced he could smell the horrible old man from the darkness of Steve's closed window ten floors up. A couple of times a woman Ben described as a "dusky beauty" wearing a skirt and jacket walked by, looking completely out of place. *far too corporate for this shithole*, Ben had messaged, but who knew what people got up to or why. *probably a social worker, lost looking for a flat. looks the official sort,* Ben concluded. Apparently Steve and Gareth were growing impatient and annoyed they'd missed a night's drinking right at the end of the weekend. Matt begged them to please be patient. And please be careful. Midnight came and went.

And still the night ticked on.

THIRTY-ONE

Vince Stratton, for all his size and slowly advancing age, was a bloody good assassin, and in damn good shape. He hadn't continued as long as he had without developing serious skills, and he deployed many of them as he cased the crappy estate where McLeod had insisted they meet. He moved unnoticed in shadows, circled the block and checked the side streets. He hunkered down in a stinking coat and broken shoes, disguised as a foul tramp pushing a broken trolley along and back, and even his own boys didn't recognise him as he scuffed by, head covered in a tattered woollen hat that shadowed his face.

Dex stared, not taking his eyes off until Vince was well past and the boss was pleased with his boy's attention. Dex was certainly the one to watch, to train. He'd misjudged Clancy, but he wouldn't make the same mistakes with Dexter. It was all about the right personality.

He shuffled around behind the lock-ups and climbed over the wall that divided the estate from the dual carriageway, busy even this late at night, an artery into London. There was about a two- or three-metre strip of packed earth populated with dozens of thin, sick-looking trees before the ground sloped sharply down to the bright road about ten metres away. All kinds of junk lay dumped among the trees, bottles and cans, packets and plastic bags, torn strips of old tarpaulin, and rain-stained cardboard boxes. An orange glow leaked up from the streetlights below, making thin, angular silhouettes on the wall from the tree trunks. The white and red lights of the traffic flickered between the trees, the combined hum of hundreds of tyres on asphalt a constant white noise. No one stood in wait in the shadows. For several hundred metres in either direction it was just gloom and detritus and no one to be seen.

Vince stripped off the tramp disguise, revealing jeans and bomber jacket underneath, and pulled the oversize, ragged boots off his light running shoes. He checked his gear. A shoulder-holstered nine millimetre, another at the small of his back. A knife at his hip and another at his calf. Garrotting wire in one pocket, a solid steel knuckleduster in the other. He checked his watch. Twelve twenty-five. Still no reports from his boys. McLeod must be inside the lock-up, probably had been since before he'd even given the address to Stratton. That's how Vince would have done it too if he wanted to get hands on with someone, as McLeod clearly did. No doubt the bastard wanted him to approach the garage and get close enough to be rushed. Well, maybe he'd have to play some of McLeod's game, but certainly not all of it.

He slipped the steel wrap over his left knuckles and unclipped the strap on the butt of the shoulder-holstered pistol. He smiled softly. *Let's play.*

* * *

Matt's phone lit up, a message from Ben.

big bloke, grey hair, looks like a right hard bastard, talked to the ginger on the corner coming to the garages now

Matt's heart hammered. He sent a message to Amy and Ben.

Game on. Please be careful everyone.

THIRTY-TWO

STRATTON WALKED THE LONG WAY AROUND, passing each row of garages and looking along its length before he got to the one in question. No one was visible anywhere except his boys, the streets still and cold, almost as though they slept like most of suburban London did this late. He reached the end of the row where Dexter waited, scanning left and right, watching for any movement, any flash of metal or glass. His back itched, the thought of a weapon trained on him from some hidden corner. It was possible he had grossly underestimated McLeod's resources, and that's why his back crawled, but life was chance. The odds were stacked heavily in Stratton's favour as far as he was concerned. And he had to admit, he was enjoying the rush of the gamble a little bit. It had been a while since he'd fallen into something with variables like this. But as much as McLeod might be providing some rare distraction from Vince's regular activities, the bastard needed shutting down.

He nodded to Dexter. "Nothing?"

"Not a peep, Boss. A few people moving around the streets, not many. None in the last ten minutes or so."

"Hopefully it's late enough that most folk are tucked up in their beds, eh?" Stratton looked up, scanning the ugly, grey blocks of flats in rows like giant gravestones in the night. "Could be anyone watching from up there," he mused. He shook his head. Many things were beyond his control, so he had to keep a tight grip on anything that was his to manage. "You armed?"

Dexter patted the pocket of his jacket, nodded.

"Saul and David?"

"No, just me. They don't have their own guns and you weren't around to sort 'em out."

"Okay. Keep it out of sight unless absolutely necessary. But use your judgement, right?"

"Yes, Boss."

"And don't get fucking excited and shoot me."

"Of course not."

"Right." Vince sniffed, looked up along the row of roller doors. "Here goes. As soon as there's any shooting, which I'm fairly convinced there will be, we have to consider that some busybody might call the law. Place like this, maybe they won't. Keep their heads down, stay out of it. But don't stick around long enough to get picked up, especially as you're packing."

"What if you get hurt?"

Vince smiled. "Please! But like I said before. Use your judgement."

He walked about five metres into the space between lock-ups and called out, "Mr. McLeod? You here, son? Let's have a little chat."

There was no response. The area was dead, as if it had been abandoned by all life except himself and Dexter, the strange emptiness of a city at night. Brighter, more central parts of town would be buzzing with people and traffic. The roadway beyond the concrete wall hummed, but these urban places sank into stasis as the night drew on. Plenty of denizens of the dark would be creeping around here and there, he was in no doubt of that. Derelicts and drug dealers, hookers and feckless youth. But right here, right now, nothing moved.

Vince took a few more paces in, eyes narrowed. No way he was getting within spitting distance of the door at the end marked number 12. "McLeod!" His voice was louder this time, strident. "This is where I stand. Your move." He slipped a hand into his jacket, rested his palm on the reassuring cold weight of the nine millimetre, not taking his eyes off the garage door.

There was a rattle and knocking, sudden and echoing in the concrete and metal enclosure. Vince slipped the pistol loose, held it close to his body as door twelve shook and began to roll up. He stared, tensed and steady. As soon as his target was clear, he would fire and *bang!* That would be it. Done. Anything else was clean-up. The door travelled very slowly.

"Come on, McLeod. You started this. Let's be having you."

Something didn't feel right. He had expected any number of possible plays, and there was no way he could know which way things would go, but something was about to go wrong. He could feel it.

As the door got halfway up he saw slim legs in jeans in the inky shadows. A woman's voice rang out, Australian accent. "Please don't do anything rash, Mr. Stratton. I have a message from Matt."

The door rolled all the way up and Amy Cavendish stood in the weak streetlight, hands palm out before her chest.

Then several things happened at once. Dexter yelled out, "Hey, who are you?"

At the same moment, a woman's voice, loud and clearly scared, shouted, "Above you to the right!"

Vince caught sight of a good-looking woman in a tight skirt suit standing beside an angry Dexter. Stratton spun around, eyes everywhere, and there the bastard was! McLeod legging it along the roofs of the garages behind him, not five meters away. He whipped out the pistol and fired.

* * *

As soon as Stratton had called out the first time, Matt's phone lit up with a message from Amy. *He's here!* Huddled under a wet and stinking sheet of canvas tarpaulin on the sloping grass by the busy road, several hundred metres from the lock-ups, Matt's heart began to pound. He threw off the heavy concealment, wincing against stiff muscles, and ran up the scrubby embankment, ducking left and right between the straggly trees. The garages seemed so far away.

Panic chewed at his gut. He'd had to hide a long way out to not be seen, but had he picked a spot too far, down near the noisy road? When he spotted a pile of clothes right by the wall he gulped down nerves, vindicated. They had definitely not been there a couple of hours before. Stratton had been here, casing the location before making himself known.

Matt didn't bother to spend any time thinking about it, but clambered up the wall, the sound of his movements masked by the traffic below. He gained the roofs of the garages in the second row and bolted across, knowing he would only get one chance, if that.

As the garage door rattled up and Amy said she had a message, Matt reached the other side and saw Stratton standing halfway along the concrete apron. He switched direction, about to launch at Stratton from behind. He had his chance, his moment. It was all he needed and he bloody had it! Then a woman ran into view at the end of the alley and yelled out, pointing up at him.

Stratton turned, pulling a gun from inside his jacket. Stratton was too good and too quick to be distracted by Amy for even a second more, the woman in the suit giving the gangster all the guidance he needed. Was it the copper from the front office of Collins's nick? Cursing his stupidity, Matt launched himself through the air. If he broke every bone in his body it wouldn't matter as long as he managed to get a hand on the bastard.

Stratton's gun flashed and its report shattered the night, bouncing back and forth off walls and doors. White-hot pain seared into Matt's ribs as his feet left the edge of the garages and his vision crossed. He was shot. The fucker had got him. That woman had doomed him, spoiled the one chance he had, against all odds, managed to engineer.

From the corner of one eye he caught sight of Dexter pulling out and raising his own gun, the woman in the suit staring wide-eyed, one hand coming up to her mouth, and then Ben smashed into Dexter from the side, crash-tackling him to the ground. Dexter's gun went off and the woman in the suit buckled over like she had been punched in the gut and face-planted to the pavement. Matt hit the concrete where Stratton had been standing, but Stratton had moved far aside. The pain was blinding, something in his shoulder popped and cracked. Amy screamed. Somewhere far away, Stratton was laughing.

"Fucking hell, son," he said. "That was incredibly dumb! Dexter, get the Aussie bitch."

Matt rolled over onto his back and looked up into the tunnel of Stratton's gun barrel, just beyond reach.

"I'll give you points for bollocks, McLeod, but that was really, really stupid."

They were all dead.

Matt realised his last thought would be the knowledge that not only was he dead, but Amy next, his friends, Carla, eventually his parents, the policewoman Dexter had shot—why the hell was she even here? Death was a mountain he had brought down on everyone he knew.

But Amy was still screaming, somewhere close by.

Stratton yelled out again, "Dexter, you bloody—" then looked sharply to his left as a huge wooden giraffe sliced through the air, Amy grimacing as she swung it. He got one arm halfway up to block, but only deflected it slightly before it cracked into the side of his head. Inanely, Matt knew it was a souvenir Steve-O had brought back from a holiday in Indonesia, then stashed in his garage because it was ugly as fuck and they'd all taken the piss out of him for it. Stratton hadn't realised Dexter was tackled by Ben and it had bought them one or two precious seconds.

Stratton staggered sideways, but squeezed the trigger anyway. Matt twisted away as concrete exploded beside his cheek and stung his eye. Half blinded he took the only chance he was going to get and scrambled forward, grabbing for Stratton's leg.

"Where the fuck are you, Dexter?" Stratton hollered. His arm swung up and he fired again, but not at Matt this time. Amy yelped, high and shocked, then spat a blistering stream of mostly incoherent vitriol littered with obscenities. Was she hit?

Stratton back-pedalled rapidly, but desperation drove Matt forward across the ground and he grabbed Stratton's left ankle in his left hand, but was greeted by a long sock. He needed skin! Stratton swung back his free leg for a kick and Matt shot his right hand into the man's trouser leg, crying out against the pain in his battered, surely broken shoulder as he stretched. He reached up, up, up, then flesh. Stratton howled like a whipped dog as he felt the contact and Matt exulted in the touch of hairy body.

He let the dark go.

If he thought the bullet wound and the impact with hard ground had hurt, the pain as the dark opened was a whole new experience. His bones flexed and cracked, his skin felt as though it had flayed away in incandescent flames. The dark swirled out of his hand and into Stratton's pasty flesh and snaked away up the muscled leg.

Stratton shrieked in agony and then his kick landed, caught Matt under the jaw, snapped his head back. Stars exploded and yet another new flavour of pain blossomed. Matt's grip was lost and he rolled instinctively away from the hurt, vision swimming in clouds of grey and flickering colours.

Voices shouted, Amy's among them. At least she was still alive. With nothing but pure determination to survive, Matt hauled himself onto his knees, trying to uncross his vision to look around.

Steve-O and Gareth sat on a thrashing Dexter at the mouth of the lock-ups, the policewoman motionless on the ground beside them. Ben was hammering along between the roller doors, his eyes looking past Matt.

"The fuck is happening here?" Ben yelled, the whites of his eyes clear as terror gripped him, but he ran on regardless, a real friend.

Matt turned. Amy sat against one closed garage door, clutching her shoulder as blood streamed between her fingers. The stupid giraffe lay in two pieces not far from her. Matt's gaze found Stratton.

The big man staggered left and right, moaning deeply in pain, a primal, wounded animal sound. His mouth hung open, tongue lolling, eyes rolling. Half his face and his left hand were withered and blackened, but still the bastard stood, stronger than sin. The gun was in his right hand and he raised it, tracking Ben who still yelled disbelief at all he saw.

"No!" Matt drove himself to his feet and ran directly across Ben's path. Pain stabbed and sliced in every part of him, then Stratton's gun boomed and another explosion of agony ripped into Matt's arm and spun him around a full three-sixty as he ran. But he refused to give in, not now, not this close. His vision closed to a stygian tunnel and all he saw was Stratton's face, half-blackened, twisted in pain and horror, disappearing down that shadowed hole.

So Matt focussed on that twisted visage and nothing else. He reached his hands forward, desperate to clasp them either side of Stratton's evil fucking head and give him all the dark he had left, finish the job.

Distantly he registered a punch in the gut and realised it was another bullet. His legs became tissue paper. He lunged forward but Stratton was miles off, far at the end of that darkening tunnel, and the big man turned and staggered away. He crammed the gun into a pocket and used his good arm to haul himself up the wall between them and the busy road. Matt marvelled at the bastard's strength as Stratton went over and vanished from sight. Matt realised he had fallen, concrete hard beneath him, grit grinding into his cheek, hard and cold. And then he was tumbling down an endless chasm of night.

He distantly heard Amy yelling, "Where's Carla?"

Ben shouting, "What the fuck, man?"

Then everything went dark.

THIRTY-THREE

AMY GASPED, sure she would never breathe properly again and simply drop dead on the spot. She couldn't take her eyes off the horror not three metres from her, Matt lying still in a pool of blood. So much blood! Stratton was gone, bent under the pain of Matt's incomplete attack. And the man's face… Half-blackened skull, the skin like old leather tight over a cheekbone, teeth exposed, his arm and leg seemingly withered to thin sticks in his loose clothes. But still he had shot Matt down and managed to scale the wall and get away.

Matt must surely be dead. Ben stumbled around in circles, his face white, muttering over and over, "What the fuck, man? What the fuck?"

Pain burned through Amy's upper left arm where a bullet had bitten out a chunk of flesh. Her mind spun uselessly, knowing only death and pain and that the world was a hideous and broken place.

Then a face swam into view, handsome and strong, but terrified, the olive skin paled to grey, topped with thick black hair. "Amy! You have to help me!" Ben's eyes were wild, terror barely held at bay somewhere in there. He needed her. He needed support.

Ben pulled up his jacket and ripped away his T-shirt from underneath. Amy got a flash of smoothly muscled torso, then he was wrapping the material around her arm, pulling it painfully tight.

"That'll hold the bleeding, right?" he said. "We have to help Matt!"

Amy staggered to her feet. "Thank you." She had no idea how bad her wound might be, but it was not life-threatening in the short term. She had to take charge here, had to do…something.

Ben let out a strangled sob. "What the fuck is happening here? What happened to that bloke?"

As Amy's senses came back online, she realised Ben wouldn't be able to hold it together much longer. The terror in his eyes was dangerously close to the surface.

Shouting from the end of the garages caught Amy's attention, Dex struggling to get up, Gareth and Steve-O calling out, asking what was going on. A woman lay there, still in a spreading pool of blood. That bloody woman had ruined everything. Matt was so close, then she had appeared and given him away. And died for it, by the look of things.

"Wait there!" she called. "Don't let that kid go!" Then she turned back to Ben. "Help me."

They grabbed Matt and carefully rolled him over onto his side.

"What did he do to him?" Ben said, his voice an octave higher than it had been.

Amy felt a strange calm descend. She needed to fix everything. They had a lot to do. "I'll explain later, if I can. We need to help Matt."

She crouched down beside him, deeply concerned at the amount of blood soaking through his clothes, pooling beneath him. There was hardly a part of him not sodden in it, almost black in the wan streetlight. His face was swollen, his lip burst, nose bleeding. She rushed to the lock-up and grabbed a pile of clothes she'd seen in there while she had sat waiting. She wadded up shirts and used trouser legs to tie them over Matt's wounds, hoping he hadn't already lost too much blood to survive, using Ben's help to hold things in place. The gut shot was the worst, but it was low down, maybe missed any vital organs. The shot across the ribs was a mess, but clean. His right arm looked broken just below the shoulder from the bullet that had punched through there. But if she could stem the blood loss, maybe he would live. His pulse was weak, but present. His breathing shallow, stuttering. Amy was a trained nurse and she could surely help. She had to! "You came in a car, right?" she asked Ben.

"Yeah. It's on the other side of Steve's block."

"Okay, I've got this now. Go and get your car. You have to get Matt to Emergency."

As Ben stood and hurried away, Dexter's voice yelled out again. "Let me go!"

Amy glanced over her shoulder and saw Steve and Gareth still struggling with Dexter, who pulled against them. "Bring him here," she shouted. She needed to talk to him, he was her last chance.

Steve, Amy realised, his face pale as milk, held a pistol between finger and thumb, like it might bite him, one of Dexter's arms in his other hand. Gareth, his dark face drawn and shocked, had a tight grip on Dex's other arm. Dexter seemed very small between them, just a child. She tried to ignore the woman lying on the road.

They dragged the boy towards her. Amy kept damming up the blood wherever she could. Thankfully Matt's chest continued to hitch with laboured breaths, his eyes flickering beneath closed lids. She felt his pulse again, and it was weak but still there. He was hurt badly, shadows stalked the edges of his mortality, but Amy's talent was good enough to tell her he wasn't dying just yet. He didn't have long, but maybe long enough to get to hospital. Where the hell was Ben?

Dexter stood beside her, looking down, no longer resisting. "This isn't right," he said stupidly.

"No," Amy said. "It's not. But it's real. Where are your friends?"

"Chickenshits bolted when the shooting started. They're a bit new."

"So you're on your own here."

"Guess so. What the fuck did he do to the Boss?"

Amy shook her head, not looking up. "That's not something I can explain. But surely you realise your boss is bad news, right?"

"He's got his flaws, but I know the score. He looks after me." There was a waver of uncertainty in his voice that Amy clung to like a life ring.

"You really still want to be associated with him?"

Dexter sniffed, looked up towards the wall over which Stratton had vanished. "He gonna survive that? Whatever happened to him?"

"I don't know. I hope not." Amy looked up, locked her gaze to Dexter's. "You really want to be around him now?"

"Everyone fucking lets me down," Dexter mumbled, almost as though he was talking to himself. "He hasn't. Hadn't. Yet."

"I'll help you, Dex. I'll look out for you." She had no idea how, but she genuinely meant it if only the kid would help her. She'd find some way. "I really need to know where my friend is."

"Your friend?"

"Stratton took her, kidnapped her. He has her stashed somewhere."

Dexter's jaw hung a little slack, his eyes haunted. "I don't know if I believe any of this."

"He really took my friend."

Dexter huffed a humourless laugh. "Oh, I believe that. I don't know if I believe…" He gestured to the wall Stratton had scrambled over.

"You're not dreaming, Dex."

The roar of an engine made them jump and Ben pulled up. He climbed out of the fancy Volkswagen, as new and shiny as Matt's was old and rusted, she noticed, and hollered to Steve-O and Gareth for help. They let go of Dex and between the three of them manhandled Matt into the back of the car, then piled in with him. Dexter stood numbly staring.

"We'll get him to the hospital," Ben said. "All…all this," he gestured around vaguely, "is your problem."

"The police will ask about bullet wounds," Steve said from the passenger seat. He stared at Dexter's gun, still in his hand, then Gareth grabbed it from the back seat where he cradled Matt.

"Give me that," Gareth said. Then to Ben, "We have to go!"

"Don't tell them anything," Amy said. "No names. Tell them… Tell them you found your friend, attacked and left for dead. The attackers were nowhere to be seen. Yeah? Something like that. Claim ignorance."

Steve shook his head, eyes round and white. "I don't know, man, this is so fucked up!"

"What about her?" Gareth pointed to the woman lying not far away.

Amy ground her teeth. "She's dead?"

Gareth shrugged. "I don't think so. She was moaning before."

"Fuck!" Amy stared, lost, too many things to think about. But they couldn't just leave her to bleed out, whoever she was, however much she had cost them. "Can you take her too?"

"We'll deal with it!" Ben snapped. "Let's go."

The car doors slammed and Ben reversed dangerously fast. He braked hard and Steve-O swung open his door, somehow hauled the shot woman up onto his lap in the passenger seat, and then Ben peeled away, tyres screeching. Amy was pleased Ben seemed to have pulled himself together, purpose giving him strength. She stared at her blood-soaked hands, the dark pool in front of her as she knelt on the cold concrete, then looked up at Dexter, glad he hadn't taken the first opportunity to run. They were the only two left in the strangely quiet and still aftermath of fury and blood.

"Why should I help you?" Dexter asked, his eyes still a little blank, shocked.

She had to admit it was a good question. "Please," she said. "You're not a bad kid, I can see that. This has happened, Vince is surely as good as dead. I really need your help to find my friend. Don't let her die, alone in some warehouse or wherever he put her."

"He might go back for her now."

Panic washed through Amy, but she had to put that thought aside. "I can only hope he's got enough to deal with, even if he's still alive. He's probably dead. I can't leave her to rot."

Dexter turned to scan the flats behind them. "Could be plenty of people up there saw stuff happen. Could be someone up there with a mobile phone right now, videoing it all."

"Then turn your fucking face away!"

Dexter moved slowly, sluggish. "Could be no one saw anything and everyone ignored the fighting and the gunshots. Estate like this, no one has much respect for the police. Let people do what they like, innit. Keep your head down and all that."

"Here's hoping," Amy said. Dex was clearly in shock, robotic and numb. Though he no doubt acted like a hard man, maybe this was the first really serious violence he had seen. Or perhaps the first time he'd been so close up to it.

"That bloke made me shoot her. I didn't mean to."

"I know."

"I'm not going down for that."

"Did you come in a car?" Amy asked, desperate to change the subject back to Carla.

"Yeah, Saul got his licence. They fucked off though."

Amy stood, ignoring the searing throb in her arm. Her sleeve and the T-shirt wrapped around it felt soaked, but she refused to look and check. The terrifyingly large pool of blood on the ground where Matt had lain, and a smaller pool out by the road from the woman Dexter had shot, was all that remained of the horrible scene that had unfolded. Blood and a broken giraffe. And herself standing with a child, desperate to find her friend. She glanced at the wall. Could Stratton have survived? He had clearly been in so much pain, but a crazy bull strength had driven him on. She prayed it couldn't last. Surely he *had* to be dead. Matt's ability so violent, so sudden, so powerful.

"We have to go in case the police come around." She kicked the broken giraffe back into the lock-up, closed and locked the door, then turned back to Dexter, knowing she had to keep cajoling him while she could, while shock kept him pliable. "Matt's car is parked a few blocks away." And his keys were in her pocket.

Look after these for me, he had said. *So I don't fucking jingle when I sneak up on him.*

Sneak up on him! How hideously wrong that had gone. But not entirely wrong. Perhaps they could get out of this yet. Perhaps Matt would survive, and Stratton would die. But in her gut she knew it almost certainly wasn't over yet.

"What do I care?" Dexter asked woodenly.

"Please care!" Amy begged. "Please! I know you're a good guy. I need your help." She stared into his flat gaze, tried to find something to catch his attention. *Everyone fucking lets me down.* That's what he'd said. "Do you have somewhere to go?" she asked softly. "Now that Stratton is…is most likely not going to be around any more."

Dexter glanced up at her, then dropped his haunted look back to the pool of blood. "I can go back to the pub first, check on the Boss. I still have my place he pays for…" His voice trailed off, his eyes rising to find Amy's once more.

"If the Boss is dead, no one will be paying for those digs," she said. She kept her tone soft and neutral. Factual, not judgemental. She gestured back towards the wall. "Seriously, you think he's going to survive that? You want to be around when things start getting investigated?" He winced, his brow settling into a frown. She pushed on. "It'll be a mess, right? Are you old enough to avoid care? Social services? And the woman, I know you didn't mean to shoot her, but that's complicated, right?" She hated to play with his fears, but she needed him. Carla needed him.

"Back to the street then. Won't be the first time."

"If you help me, I'll help you. You can stay at my place, for as long as you need."

He huffed another of his humourless laughs. "Why would you do that?"

"Because I know you're just a lost kid, Dex. You're tough and smart, but you need help. I'll take care of you, help you get back on your feet. For as long as you need. You deserve that, right?"

He frowned at her, measuring her sincerity. "You just want my help finding your friend."

"Yes! I do. But I will genuinely help you in return. Like Stratton helped you, but he's dead now. Please, Dex. I promise I won't let you down. *Please* help me find my friend. Do you know where she might be?"

Dexter looked back to the pool of blood the woman had left behind. "I didn't mean to shoot her."

"I know. I'll help you get rid of the gun, and if the police get involved I'll tell them it was Stratton, not you, who shot her."

Dexter squinted up at her.

She pressed the advantage, playing him as well as she could. "I'll be your alibi. And Stratton's dead, so her getting shot will be finished with. And then I'll take care of you, help you find your feet."

"My alibi?"

"You'll need one."

Dexter shrugged, sighed. "There's some places I know. Boss has a few safe houses around. I don't know 'em all." He looked over at the wall again. She thought maybe he was on the verge of tears, but they would never fall in her presence, she knew that. "What happened to him?"

"Something terrible," Amy whispered.

"*Can* he survive it?"

She shook her head. It was entirely possible that Stratton was strong enough to live through Matt's attack, but this kid needed to believe differently. As did she for that matter. "No. I'm *sure* he can't."

Dex returned his vacant gaze to her. "Probably dead in the road out there somewhere."

"Probably."

There was silence for a moment, Amy anxious to get away, but the situation was too delicate. "Might Carla be in one of those safe houses you mentioned?"

"Might be. Probably."

"Okay, come on! I promise I'll help you." She tugged his arm, sick of talking, of trying to motivate him. Thankfully he stumbled alongside her.

After the first hundred metres or so he found his feet and jogged with her. It only took a minute to get to Matt's car, and she was flooded with relief to be away from the scene of the violence. Her arm pulsed with pain and dizziness made her vision swim. She reached into the back seat and pulled out an old shirt scrunched up in there. Nausea rose and fell as she slumped into the driver's seat, wondering how much blood she had lost. Her sleeve was soaked, but it wasn't running freely from her fingers. Basic nursing told her she still wasn't in a life-threatening situation and if she could keep the bleeding under control she'd be okay in the short term. She might need stitches, and infection was a risk, but she had some time. She pulled away the soaked strips of Ben's T-shirt and dropped them into the footwell. They landed with a wet slap. She shrugged off her jacket and finally looked at the wound. It was ugly, but not nearly as big as it felt. Already the blood was thickening, slowing. She'd have a good scar, but beyond the pain it was no real threat. With a sigh of relief, she used torn rags of shirt to re-bandage it, doing a far better job than Ben had in his panic and haste. Once the material was tightly in place it felt better, even while it still burned and throbbed. Dexter ignored her the whole time, sagging in the passenger seat, staring dead ahead.

She finally turned to him. "Okay, now please help me. Where do you think we should go first?"

"I wonder what will happen to the pub."

"What?"

"Stratton's."

She drove away, desperate to be gone from anywhere near the scene of the crime if nothing else. Maybe the locals had ignored everything, but her skin crawled at the thought of the police appearing any moment. She turned onto the main road and headed quickly out of the estate, but carefully stayed within the speed limit. "What about the pub?"

"I wonder what'll happen to it. Where I'll live now, if he stops paying rent on our house. Maybe he left a will or something."

Amy shook her head, confused. Had he heard anything she'd offered? "Yeah, maybe. He might have left the pub to you boys. You like the idea of running a pub, Dex?"

"I'm not old enough to go in one, let alone own one."

Amy frowned. "How old are you?"

"Sixteen."

She shook her head. Poor kid, to see all this at his age. To see it at any age, but especially so young. And what kind of childhood had he endured to have been led to this? "You know what?" she said. "Time will tell, yeah? I mean, we know Vince is dead, but officially he's just disappeared, hasn't he? Missing." She needed to plant a new truth early. Maybe it would stick.

"He's bloody dead," Dexter said.

Amy swallowed, glad he had accepted that. She hoped it were true. "Yeah, but if the police come asking around, are you going to tell them that? How would you explain all this?"

He looked at her for the first time. "They wouldn't believe any of it."

"Of course not."

"I got no proof of anything."

Amy smiled at him, tried to sound kind, reassuring. "Right. So if they ask, you don't know. He's just gone. Disappeared. Didn't tell you or the boys anything. It'll be a while before anything is sorted out. Before his absence is even reported or investigated, probably."

"Yeah, I suppose so." Dexter stared vacantly at the road ahead once more. "Wait and see, I guess."

"Yeah. Wait and see. You may not even have to talk to the police if you stay away. They don't know you were even here. Stay with me. I'll take care of you, Dex, I promise. And you can talk to your friends, keep them up to speed on what's happening, right? Without getting too close?"

"I guess."

"Right. So, you'll be okay. But, please, Dex. For now, can we find Carla?"

"Maybe try the place in Holloway first. But we'll have to go back via the pub to get the keys. If the Boss left them out, of course."

Amy chose not to consider the possibility that something as simple as inaccessible keys might stymie their search and headed for Camden.

THIRTY-FOUR

THE NIGHT DREW TOWARDS DAWN and Dexter's shock started to abate. Amy did her best to keep a lid on her panic. Three safe houses, all run-down flats in tatty housing estates, had come up empty. The keys had been in the cabinet in Stratton's pub, thankfully easy to get to, and that had given Amy some hope. And Stratton hadn't been there, even though the possibility had horrified her as they made their way in. Dead. He had to be dead.

But as the night wore on, driving all over London with location after location proving to be fruitless, Amy's hopes leaked away.

Hours ago she'd had a text from Ben. Matt was alive but critical and had gone into surgery. The woman Dexter had shot was alive too, but she hadn't passed that news on yet. Dexter might worry she would recover and recognise him. Or he would be glad she hadn't died and stop helping Amy. The police were apparently asking questions because the hospital was obliged to report gunshot wounds, but Ben assured Amy that he and the boys had left her out of it entirely, said he'd explain more later. She'd heard nothing since.

"So where now?" she asked Dexter.

"There's two more places I know, but I'm tired."

"I get that. I'm tired too." Not to mention that her arm had sunk into a dull, burning ache and her fingers were slightly numb. She had no idea what damage might be happening under her hasty bandages, but she was sure there was nothing serious going on. She grabbed a bottle of water from the back seat and swallowed two more painkillers, hastily purchased from a service station when she'd stopped for petrol. Her jacket covered her bound arm again, and she decided that out of sight, out of mind was best. But the throbbing wouldn't let her truly forget about it. She willed the painkillers to kick in quickly. And she had a pounding headache, her eyes felt swollen and filled with grit from fatigue. Maybe the pills would ease that too. "Please, you said two more places. Let's try those and then I'll take you to my place. You can rest, eat my food. Anything."

"I can't remember where they are exactly."

"Can you ask someone?"

"Clancy should know."

Dexter pulled out a phone and dialled, listened, then hung up. "Voicemail. He wasn't around all day yesterday either."

Amy realised, from her conversations with Matt, that Clancy was the one who had been with Stratton when he took Carla. The one she had smashed. For sure that kid would know where her friend was. "Could he be sleeping? Is that why he's not answering?"

"Nah, phones always on. It's a rule."

"So it would ring and wake him?"

"Yeah, that's the idea."

"So why isn't he answering?"

Dexter laughed bitterly, turned a glare at her. "I don't fucking know."

Amy took a deep breath, steadied her nerves. She had to keep Dex on side. "Okay, sorry. Anyone else you can ask?"

Dex nodded, tapping at his phone. "I think Saul might have been out there before." He paused, waiting for an answer, then, "Shithead. Find somewhere safe to run off to, did you? Yeah, well, thanks for leaving me in the fucking lurch. No, everything is not all right." Dex cast a quick glance at Amy, then looked out at the road again. "I don't know what happened to the Boss. He left, but said nothing. No idea where he went."

Amy breathed a sigh of relief. There had been a lot of quiet time in the car as they drove around, Amy happy to let Dexter sit and think. Maybe it had been good for him. It seemed as though he'd decided to go with the disappearing boss story. It was the best for self-preservation, after all, because she couldn't imagine trying to explain to the police everything that had happened, and she was sure Dexter didn't like the prospect any more than she did. Or explaining it to his friends. So often when things were very complicated or frightening, it was best to know nothing about them, or at least to feign ignorance. She supposed others would continue to manage the pub for a while at least, open and close, work the bar, as they always did. Dex was smart enough to know when to keep his head down.

"Anyway," Dexter went on. "He'll turn up, like always. Meanwhile I have to go to the flat near Hampstead Heath. Yeah, that one. But I forgot the address, do you remember it? Right, and what about the one at Deptford?"

Amy winced, Hampstead Heath and Deptford were on opposite sides of the city. She'd potentially be driving around for hours yet.

Dexter hung up and said, "I've got the Hampstead address, but he doesn't know the Deptford one."

"Hampstead Heath is on this side of the river, at least," Amy said. "Let's go there."

A cold drizzle drifted through the orange street lights as they walked towards the block of flats a little before 6:00 a.m. Dexter led them up to the fourth floor and tried several keys from Stratton's large, jangling bunch until one turned. As the front door opened onto a living room straight out of a seventies sit-com, a muffled screaming burst out from somewhere inside.

Amy's heart leapt. "Carla? Is that you?"

A door across the room flexed in its frame as Carla pounded against it. "Amy? Jesus, Amy get me out of here!"

With a cry of relief, Amy surged to the door and rattled at it.

"It's locked," Carla said, tears in her voice. "There's no handle this side."

The door was padlocked from the outside. Amy stared at it a

moment, then turned to ask Dexter if one of the keys might fit it. He was nowhere to be seen. "Wait a minute," she shouted. "I'll get you out."

She ran back into the hallway to find Dexter standing in another doorway, strangely motionless. She moved beside him, opening her mouth to ask if he was okay, but the words died in her throat. Dexter stood staring at a body lying on the floor in the small bedroom. Clancy's body, his face a bloody mess, his eyes stark and wide in his dark face, staring back up at Dexter, seeing nothing.

"Fucking hell," Amy breathed.

"Stratton did that," Dexter said.

"You think so?"

"Of course. Who else? In this place?"

Amy realised he had to be right. The safe house where Stratton had brought Carla. She gasped. "I beat him up," she said. She pointed. "Clancy, I mean. When Stratton came to my flat, to get me, I beat Clancy up and got away, which is why Stratton took Carla."

Dexter didn't take his eyes off his friend. "You beat him up?"

"Well, he grabbed me, tried to give me to Stratton, so I fought back."

"And you beat him."

"Yeah."

Dexter nodded. "So Stratton killed him."

Amy swallowed. She couldn't think of any other explanation. Hatred raged in her, the thought of what Stratton was doing to these young men. "I'm sorry, Dexter."

"Me too." He turned away, shut the door on Clancy, and went into the kitchen. He opened a cupboard and pulled a small red fire extinguisher out from under the sink. Its cylinder body was metal and heavy. He returned to the bedroom where Carla was trapped and smashed repeatedly at the padlock and hasp with the base of the cylinder until he'd split and splintered the wood and forced the whole thing free of the door.

He swung the door wide and Carla stared at him for a second, then rushed into Amy's arms and the two friends hugged tightly. Amy couldn't remember anything feeling so good before.

"I thought you were dead," Carla said, crying into Amy's hair. "And I thought I would be next."

Amy squeezed, wincing at the throb of pain in her arm. "I'm so sorry this happened to you."

"How did you find me?"

"It's a long story. A very messed up story, and you should thank Dexter." She turned to introduce Carla properly, but the kid wasn't beside them any longer. Amy frowned, turned back to Carla. "You're safe now."

"We should go, before that big bastard comes back." Carla's eyes were wide, looking over Amy's shoulder like she expected Stratton to come blundering through the door any second.

"Yeah, let's move," Amy said. "But you're okay. Please don't ask me any questions, but I don't think he's coming back. Not ever."

Carla leaned away, stared a moment into her friend's eyes. She was clearly frightened by what she saw there but eventually she nodded. "Maybe you'll tell me about it one day?"

"Maybe one day."

"I'm so hungry, Amy. They left me there all night, no food."

"We'll get you something." She turned away. "Dexter?"

He didn't answer, nowhere to be seen. She moved to the front window of the flat to look down into the street, Matt's car parked on the other side about fifty metres along. As she stared, Dexter walked out the front of the block and off down the road, away from the car. He had his head down against the drizzle, hands thrust deep into his jacket pockets. Amy watched him for a moment until he turned a corner out of sight. She was sad he couldn't take her at her word and accept her help. She'd meant it. But perhaps her offer had been enough for him to do right by her, even if he'd ultimately decided to stay on his own. And who could blame him? She hoped something would go his way and Stratton would disappear, that the bastard had made some provisions for his precious boys. She determined to go by the pub once all this was over and see if Dex was still around. If he was, she would try to help him, keep her promise.

Amy put an arm around her friend's shoulders and led her down to the street and towards Matt's car. "Let's get you something to eat, then I'm going to drop you home." She paused, paranoia thrilling through her. "Maybe not home, not yet. We need somewhere not connected to either of us, just until we're sure."

"Sure of what?"

"Sure it's all over." Amy stood, motionless in thought. They couldn't use a hotel, or anywhere that a credit card might lead Stratton to them, just in case the bastard wasn't dead. She needed something completely unconnected to any of this. A thought occurred to her and she decided to take a chance. "Give me a second here." She pulled out her phone and dialled the newest number in there. It rang a couple of times, then a blurry voice answered.

"Amy? You okay?"

"Caitlin, I'm so sorry to wake you. Please don't think I'm a psycho. I know we only just met and I'm loathe to lean on a new friendship like this, but I'm in a bit of trouble."

"What kind of trouble?"

The Hollywood starlet's voice had straightened out immediately. Amy imagined her sitting up in bed, suddenly alert. "It's hard to explain, but I have a friend in need of something to eat and a safe place to stay for a day or two."

"She's in danger?"

"We both are." Amy's voice hitched, the weight of events pressing down on her.

Caitlin's voice gained strength again. "Say no more. Come here, I'll help."

"Really?"

"Of course. In my job, my psycho metre is finely tuned, and you don't make it blip, Amy."

"Thank you for trusting me."

Caitlin laughed. "If you were another weirdo I'd have known and not enjoyed our time together. I'll text you my address."

"Thank you so much! See you soon." Amy hung up and smiled at Carla. "There's somewhere we can go, where no one will think to look. You can stay for a day or two until we know the threat is gone."

THIRTY-FIVE

CAITLIN'S LONDON HOME was a huge penthouse apartment in a swanky inner-city suburb, with impressive security in technology and in personnel at the thick glass frontage. Amy immediately knew she'd made the right decision in coming here, beyond grateful her new friend had taken her at her word. The actress greeted them at her front door, dressed in sweats, her hair tied back loosely.

Carla looked from Caitlin to Amy and back again. "This… This is…"

Amy grinned. "I know. Long story. She's a friend."

"I've got a pot of coffee on," Caitlin said. "You want bacon and eggs?"

"Yes, please!" Carla said. "I haven't eaten for a long time."

"I'll skip it, thank you," Amy said, though her gut rumbled with hunger. "I have to keep moving."

Caitlin looked them both up and down, paused at the tear in Amy's jacket sleeve. "Come on in, for a moment at least."

While she cooked, Amy gave her a brief outline of the situation, leaving out all the weird stuff she couldn't, and didn't want, to explain. Enough that a gangster was threatening her and her friends. Caitlin was attentive, concerned.

"I know people. I can get you help."

Amy smiled. "Thank you. I'll ask if I need it, I promise. But I think it's okay. I just need to see my other friend in the hospital, make sure everything is taken care of. Then we'll be fine. As long as I know Carla is safe in the meantime. I have to get going."

Caitlin put a plate of food in front of Carla and laid a hand on her forearm. "You can stay as long as you like. I leave for LA in a few days, but I'll give you a key if you still need a place. Sisters got to look out for each other, right?" She turned her attention to Amy. "You want me to look at that arm?"

Amy frowned. "You saw that, huh?"

"You're favouring it, clearly in pain. What is it?"

Amy took a deep breath. "Gunshot." When Caitlin and Carla both gasped, she quickly added. "But it's a graze, really, nothing serious."

Caitlin insisted Amy let her clean and redress the wound. It was ugly, but already starting to dry out. With it properly bandaged from Caitlin's first aid kit, and more analgesics swallowed, Amy was confident it would present no real threat beyond discomfort. She thanked Caitlin, genuinely moved by her trust and generosity, and kissed Carla.

"This is nearly over, I'm sure of it." Though she wasn't sure at all. "I'll keep in touch."

She rode the lift back down, jumped into Matt's car and headed for the hospital. She'd only driven a few hundred yards when her phone beeped with a message from Ben. She pulled over to read it.

out of surgery. still alive the tough prick. you coming?

Amy bit back a sob of relief and tapped a reply.

He's going to be okay?

Ben's response was less than encouraging.

dunno he's still listed as critical doc said have to wait and see

Amy replied that she was on her way and pulled back out into the heavy early morning traffic. Her medical training gave her no room for respite or hope in news like that. Still critical and waiting to see meant Matt was in a bad way indeed. Like the news reports of terrorist attacks reporting things like "ten dead and more than thirty injured." The dead were simply that, but the injured could be anything from a few bruises to traumatically amputated limbs, destroyed internal organs, faces blown off, massive brain damage. "Injured" was such an inadequate word to describe some of the desecration possible to a human body. And often the injured count reduced and the death count rose, when those people supposedly injured had actually been killed, but it took their body a little while to realise.

Matt's gut shot gave Amy the most concern. Who knew what kind of damage he had sustained there, what kind of long-term complications he might have to live with even if he survived, even physical disability if the spine or nerves had been compromised.

She shook her head and cast the thoughts aside. It was too easy to fall down a deep hole of worst-case scenarios if she speculated. Just like the doctors said, wait and see. She cared deeply about Matt already, but in a strange and unfamiliar way. He was the only person in the world she was aware of who could have any idea what her life was like. And he'd admitted the same, she was the only person he knew with shadows and darkness like his own. They needed each other. To have found him in circumstances like this only for him to die now, so soon, would be the worst kind of injustice.

She resisted the urge to look back over her shoulder. During all the panic after the debacle with Stratton, she had managed not to think about the dark entity she had conjured. Now, thinking about Matt, she felt it lurking again. Held back, somehow, as if by some intangible but impenetrable barrier, but nonetheless right there. Close enough to reach out, to touch her. All it needed was for her to use her power again to bring down that barrier once more. Maybe for the last time. Well, it could stay there, lurking. She had no intention of letting it out again any time soon.

She finally fought her way across the city to the hospital, then rolled around and around a huge multi-storey car park to eventually find a vacant spot on the roof. It was well after 9:00 a.m. by the time she headed along corridors, following signs for the Intensive Care Unit. Her running shoes squeaked on antiseptic-smelling linoleum, watery sunlight battling stark fluorescent lights in the clinical passageways. When she finally pushed through one side of a double door into the ICU waiting area, the first thing she saw was Ben, scrunched into an uncomfortable-looking plastic chair, his head tipped back against the wall, mouth open.

A nurse behind a desk looked up. "Help you?"

"I'm here to see Matthew McLeod."

"You're Amy?"

"That's right."

"Matt's brother said you'd be along." The nurse glanced at Ben, then gave her attention back to Amy. "Poor love has refused to go anywhere."

Amy smiled, nodded. His brother? She needed to talk to Ben and learn what yarns he'd been spinning. "Can I see Matt?" she asked.

The nurse, it said SANDRA on her name badge, nodded. "Yes, but not just yet. As I told Ben, it's only family at this stage—"

"But I'm—"

Sandra held up a palm. "I know, Ben told me. You're engaged and that counts. I'm just letting you know the rules in case anyone asks you. As his fiancée, of course you're welcome to see him, but right now the doctor is in there, doing his rounds. He shouldn't be long. Wait with Ben and you'll see when the doctor leaves." Sandra pointed to a door with a reinforced square of glass in it halfway along the corridor. "Number three, love."

A blind was pulled down over the window, the room beyond a mystery, Matt so close but unattainable. "Thank you," Amy said, and went to sit by Ben.

He was awake when she joined him. He nodded and smiled sleepily. "You're here. You found your friend?"

"Yes, thank you."

"That's good." Ben tipped a sideways nod towards Sandra. "So you got all that?"

"You're his brother and I'm his fiancée. That's the story you spun to allow us to stay?"

He grinned impishly. "Yeah. Stepbrother, of course. He and I couldn't look more dissimilar really. They don't really care as long as you help them tick the right boxes, you know?"

"Thanks, Ben. Really. For everything."

"Steve-O and Gareth left right away last night. I checked in with them and they've both gone off to work today. They don't want to know any more. Told me to tell you and Matt they were done with it."

"Can't blame them."

"Nah, not really. But they'll come around given a bit of time. We've all been mates for years. They'll help again if need be. They're good boys."

"What about you?" Amy asked.

"What about me?"

"You stayed all night, made up stuff to stick around. You're not done with it?"

Ben laughed softly, but it was a tired and empty sound. "I'm not done with it. I figure you guys need all the help you can get. Besides, someone had to stay and fill you in on the story."

Amy's eyebrows rose, realisation coming back. "The police! What did they ask?"

"They wanted to know everything, of course. Gunshot wounds. We kept it really simple, told them me and Gareth were over at Steve's flat for a few Sunday evening beers. Matt was supposed to be there too. He hadn't arrived yet when we heard yelling and gunshots. We wondered what had happened but chose not to get involved, you know? Like most people on that estate, hopefully. Then Matt rings my phone, he's barely conscious, says he's been mugged right outside, tried to fight back and they shot him. Some other woman passing got shot too. So we ran down, found him like that near Steve's garage, and rushed him and the woman to hospital. Asked him if he saw anything, who attacked him, and he said two blokes in balaclavas. That's all he saw. But he was unconscious by the time we got here."

Amy nodded, thinking it over. "That's good. Nice and simple."

"That's what I thought. Unless the woman wakes up and starts messing up the story."

"She's alive, you said."

"Yeah, but still unconscious after surgery. I keep trying to check, but I'm not family, so I can't learn much. But I did learn one thing. She's police."

Ice bit deep in Amy's gut. "Shit. What was she doing there?"

"No idea. Maybe followed Stratton?"

"So she really could wake up and screw up the story."

Ben sniffed, sat up a little straighter. "She could. I'm planning to keep an eye and talk to her ASAP. She's in there." He nodded to a door a few along from Matt's.

"Before the police do?"

"If I can."

Amy nodded. "Steve and Gareth are okay to stick to the story otherwise?"

"Yeah, like I said, they're good lads. It's all good."

"And the police bought it?"

Ben grinned, impish again. He clearly enjoyed a bit of mischief. "Yeah, they nodded along all through like it was exactly what they expected. Said they'd come back when Matt woke up to see if he could tell them anything else. They're confused about the copper too though. Farouk, her name is. But we have to make sure we have a quick chat with Matt first and hope he can remember what we tell him."

It was all a bit tenuous, but what else could they do? "Is he going to wake up, Ben?" Amy's voice cracked as she spoke. She swallowed. "Is he going to be okay?"

Ben's grin slid away. "Dunno. He's pretty messed up. I got to talk a little bit to one doctor last night and he reckoned they'd done a pretty solid job, but the operating surgeon was already in another theatre. He's the bloke who really knows what's what."

"And he's in there now?"

"Yeah. We need to catch him on his way out."

They fell into a companionable silence. Fatigue hung heavy off Amy's bones, dragging at her like anchors. She wanted more than anything else to curl up and go to sleep, but at the same time felt far too energised, mentally, to even consider closing her eyes. She startled awake, shocked she'd dozed off in the chair after all, when Ben quickly stood.

"Hey, Doc! What news?"

Amy blinked, rubbed her eyes and moved to join them. The

surgeon was a bear of a man, well over six feet tall with a massive, rotund belly and thick beard. His smile was wide and welcoming. "The brother and...?"

"Fiancée," Amy said, and it sounded too weird, but she tried to appear convincing.

"Aha. Good-o. I'm Doctor Sturgess. Well, there's good news and bad news, but the good outweighs the bad." The surgeon gestured to the chairs and they all sat. Sturgess perched on the very edge of the plastic, barely two per cent of his ample behind in touch with the seat. He leaned forward, elbows on his knees, palms together like he was preparing to pray. He wagged his fingertips as he spoke. "There were three primary wounds and a variety of superficial ones of varying degrees. The three worst, of course, are the gunshots. Honestly, Matthew is very lucky to be alive."

"He's tough as nails, Doc," Ben said.

Sturgess barked one short, overloud laugh. "You're not wrong. Well, of the other injuries, most are contusions. The worst are a broken nose and dislocated jaw. He was rather badly beaten, it seems. The jaw is set and he won't be eating solid food for a while, but full function will return there. His right shoulder was badly broken from a considerable impact. Presumably he was thrown to the ground or something similar. That bone has been set, though I fear his shoulder may never move quite as freely again as it used to, and it might be a cause of ongoing discomfort for him as he ages."

"Not serious impairment, though?" Amy asked.

Sturgess shook his head. "Not unless he chooses to take up shot-put or professional tennis."

"You said there was bad news, Doc," Ben said. "None of this sounds all that great, but I'm guessing this is the good news?"

"Yes. These things he'll recover from almost entirely. Of the three gunshots, one left a flesh wound and a cracked rib. Another broke the humerus of his right arm, which only added to the complications of the broken shoulder. The humerus has been pinned and set, so that should be okay in the long run."

"What's the humerus?" Ben asked.

Amy tapped her upper arm. "The one in here."

Sturgess smiled, nodded. "As I said, he'll have ongoing difficulties with that shoulder, but hopefully nothing he can't deal with. Is he right-handed?"

Ben pursed his lips, nodded. "Yeah, he is."

"Ah, well. Perhaps he'll learn to use his left a little more in the short term."

"But the stomach shot?" Amy pressed. "That's where the bad news is?"

Sturgess nodded, brow creased. "We had to remove a significant section of lower intestine and make some surgical repairs to his right kidney. There was extensive internal bleeding, but I'm fairly confident we've managed to repair all the blood vessels. As far as I can tell, we've also done a bang-up job on the kidney, even if I do say so myself. The problems are potentially twofold. One, the kidney could fail after all, and two, the gut could refuse to start working again properly. The digestive system triggers a kind of shock stasis after events like this. It usually wakes up and begins working slowly, but his may or may not. As I said, there was considerable damage in there and we removed quite a lot. He may need external assistance for life if that doesn't all come back online."

"A stoma and bag?" Amy asked.

Sturgess nodded.

"What's that?" Ben asked.

"A hole in his gut," Amy said, "and a bag hanging outside to collect his waste. It's inconvenient and unpleasant, but thousands of people live with them for life, no problem."

Sturgess turned a raised eyebrow to her. "Medical training?"

She smiled. "Palliative care nurse. I work at Sally Gentle."

"Ah, good for you! Well, you'll have seen plenty of those then."

"Yeah. How likely is it?"

Sturgess smiled sadly, shook his head. "We have no way of knowing yet. Let's all keep our fingers crossed that tough-as-nails Matt recovers fully. There is every chance he will, notwithstanding lots of scarring and some movement issues in that arm, but we won't know for a few days at least. And aside from all these individual things, he's lost an enormous amount of blood and has all kinds of shocks to his system. Recovering from this amount of physical trauma is going to take a long time and there's the risk of secondary infection and so on. He's a long way from out of the woods yet. He won't be leaving ICU any time soon, I'm afraid. When's the wedding?"

Amy jumped. "Oh, er, no idea. We haven't set an actual date yet."

Sturgess nodded, put one meaty hand on her knee. "Maybe you should. Talk to him about it, make plans. Positive mindset is very important after this kind of trauma. Give him stuff to look forward to. We'll do all we can physically, medically, and of course we'll have counsellors, but you two need to be his knights *and* squires, yes? Help him, fight for him, and convince *him* to keep fighting."

"We'll do that, no problem," Ben said.

"Can we see him?" Amy asked. "Is he awake?"

"He woke briefly while I was in there and we shared a couple of words. He's heavily sedated and very uncertain of anything, as you can imagine. But yes, you can see him, and he may well wake again. When he does, remind him of the call button and the morphine self-administer button. He needs to use that as much as he feels necessary for pain management."

"Thank you, Doctor. Thank you for saving him."

Sturgess grinned broadly, nodded once to each of them. "We've a long way to go, but the worst is hopefully over."

Without another word he stood and strode away, paused briefly with the duty nurse, and then pushed out through the double doors. Amy and Ben watched him in silence, then turned to look at each other.

"That's mostly good, right?" Ben said. "I mean, living with a fucking bag is horrible, but if that's the worst result of all this?"

"Yeah." Amy bit her lower lip. "Let's hope that really is the worst. And let's hope he doesn't even need that. Like you said, tough as nails, right? You weren't lying about that?"

"No way! He's a little bloke, but he's like old boot leather."

Amy leaned forward, hugged Ben tightly to her. "Thank you, for everything."

He squeezed her back, then put his hands on her shoulders and pushed her away. "You're welcome. So's he. He's a mate. But you and I will be having a very serious conversation before too long about exactly what the fuck I saw last night."

Amy nodded, unable to hold Ben's gaze, angry and terrified as it was. "Of course. I don't know how much I can explain, but I'll tell you everything I can."

"Right. Now let's try to get our story into Matt before the bloody cops come back."

Amy took a deep breath in the doorway at the first sight of Matt. He wasn't a large man, only slightly over the same height and build as Amy herself, but on the white bed, under blankets stamped with the hospital name, he looked reduced almost to a child. His face seemed more drawn than the day before, like he'd been sucked dry overnight. An image of Stratton, his hand and face sunken, shrunk and blackened, flashed in her mind and she pushed it away. A clear plastic oxygen mask covered Matt's mouth and nose, a tube ran from one nostril and from a cannula in each arm. Various bags hung on stands either side of the bed, further wires emerged from the sheets to monitors flashing and beeping softly. She checked the drips. Antibiotics and nutrition mostly, nothing out of the ordinary.

"Jesus," she whispered softly.

Ben looked up from the bedside. "I know, right? Looks pretty terrible."

Amy moved to the other side of the bed. Matt's eyes were closed, but the lids flickered slightly with movement. His left hand lay palm down on the covers, the right heavily bandaged and cast, a half sling holding it immobile.

"You really are one tough son of a bitch," Amy whispered.

"Fucking Scotsman," Ben said with a smile. "They're made of rocks and foul temper."

"Racist," Matt whispered, muffled by the mask, and restricted by his injured jaw.

His eyes flickered open and he smiled weakly, glanced at Ben then Amy.

Amy leaned forward, clasping his left hand. She kissed his forehead. "Hi there."

"I feel fucking awful, so I'm clearly not dead."

"Not yet, mate," Ben said. "You're gonna be fine. But it'll take some time."

Matt's eyes tracked from Ben to Amy. "He knows fuck all about anything, but you're a nurse. Am I going to be all right?"

Amy smiled, squeezed his hand. "You'll be in intensive care for a while and you have to do everything the docs and nurses tell you. But yeah, you're going to be fine. Just keep strong and keep fighting."

"Aye, I'll do that."

"Mate, listen, this is important. The cops have been around and they're coming back."

Matt turned his attention back to Ben. "Okay. What's our story?"

Ben grinned, flicked Amy a knowing look, then said, "You were coming to Steve-O's for beers with me and Gareth, but you got mugged outside. Two blokes in balaclavas, there was a fight and they pulled out a gun. That's all you remember."

Matt's eyes slowly closed again, tightly in pain, not sleep. He made a soft grunt. Amy grabbed the morphine button, pushed it into his left hand. "Press this, it'll ease the pain. It's managed. You can press it as often as you need to."

Matt's thumb squeezed down, his eyes still closed. He sighed weakly.

"Matt, did you hear me?" Ben asked. "It's important, man."

"Two cunts in balaclavas mugged me and shot me. Outside Steve's. Beers."

"Yeah, you got it. Say it again, make sure it sticks."

"Two cunts," Matt said, his voice almost inaudible in the clear plastic. "Muggers. Steve's. Beers…" His eyes relaxed, his chest rose and fell evenly.

"He's out again," Amy said.

Ben nodded, moved away from the bed and sat in a plastic-covered armchair. "Yeah, I think he got it though."

"So now we wait," Amy said. She glanced over her shoulder to a door behind her. "Bathroom?"

"Yeah." Ben grinned again. "Got his own room with a fucking *en suite.*"

Amy turned towards it when Matt gasped. She spun back. His eyes were wide open, frightened. "Matt, it's okay, we're here."

"Stratton!" Hs voice was tight, still barely above a whisper, but his urgency was clear.

Amy took his hand again. She flicked a glance at Ben, then said, "He's dead, surely?"

Matt swallowed, shook his head. "He climbed over the wall. Got away."

"But he'll die after…after what you did. Won't he?"

"I don't know. Not certain. And if not, he'll come for me."

"Here?"

"Probably."

Ben stepped up to the bed again. "That fucker really going to hunt you down in a hospital?"

Matt took a deep breath, his eyes half-closing, popping open again. "We have to assume so," he managed.

"He won't get past the desk," Ben said. "The staff will stop him."

But Matt was out again.

Ben looked across the bed at Amy. "This is some seriously fucked up shit. Who is Stratton?"

"It's a long story. I'll tell you later. For now, I think I need to prepare."

"Prepare what? He won't get in here will he?"

Amy sighed. "He's a professional killer, Ben. I think he can get anywhere he wants to. And if Matt thinks there's a chance he'll live and come for another shot, we have to assume he will."

"So how do you plan to prepare for that?"

"Ben, I really need you trust me for a while here, okay? Matt and I are a little bit alike and there's maybe something I can do. I need you to stay here. Don't leave Matt alone for anything until I get back. I need a couple of hours. And maybe try to talk to Farouk?"

Ben stared at her, mouth half-open, for several long moments. Eventually he dropped his gaze and nodded. "I'm not going any-where. Bring me some food when you come back."

"I will. Thank you, Ben."

Amy gave Matt's hand one last squeeze then went to the bath-room. When she came back out Ben was sat in the armchair, his expression one of determination, but something else lived there too. Annoyance? And probably a measure of fear.

"You said he was hard as nails," Amy said. "So are you. You tackled one kid with a gun, ran at Stratton when he was shooting, got Matt here, stayed here to take care of him. You're a fucking hero, Ben. I mean it."

"He's a mate. That's important to me. But this shit is stretching my ability to cope."

Amy nodded, lost for any response. Eventually she said, "Thank you, Ben. I'll be back as quick as I can. What food do you want?"

"Surprise me."

"Okay."

Amy hurried away, her mind churning with the possibilities she considered. Things she wasn't sure she was even capable of, or what they might cost her, but there was no choice.

THIRTY-SIX

PAIN HAD TRANSCENDED a physical sensation and become an almost spiritual enlightenment. Why he hadn't passed out from the agony, Vince had no idea. Why he wasn't dead was an even greater mystery. Perhaps it was purely rage that kept his heart pumping and his brain functioning. He was, after all, a badass of the highest order.

In a safe house that was entirely private, one even Clancy hadn't known about, he stood in front of the bathroom mirror, naked and appalled. His body was a wreck. It all started where McLeod had managed to get a grab of his left ankle, and Stratton still reeled with the knowledge that he'd let that happen, distracted from the girl and let down by Dexter. The leg could barely support his weight, the muscles almost entirely wasted away, blackened flesh sucked tight to the bones. So thin, that skeletal limb, hanging off his hip like a broken tree branch. His foot a broken sack of black leather, the bones fallen apart inside where he'd run on it for a few yards before the destruction made him limp and drag the leg, a cumbersome weight.

He had stumbled several hundred yards, thankfully not followed, to where he had left his car in a lay-by on the dual carriageway. The trees and night-time shadows masked his progress and, by the time he was in sight of his getaway vehicle, he had been reduced to lying face down on the dirt, dragging himself along painfully slowly with his one good arm.

The blackness from his withered leg spread up over his hip, which stuck out like some grotesque giant ear, the curve of the iliac crest a mockery of a functioning body. It had yet to reach his genitals, but it was close, half his pubic hair greyer than the rest. The skin of his chest on that side was sucked in tight over his ribs, the darkness spreading halfway across, and he could feel it in there, slowly consuming his heart. Every breath was like a knife stabbing into his left lung, though fortunately his right seemed to still work efficiently. But his heart, his other organs, how long could they all hold up against this? The blight was spreading, ever so slowly, across his body. It was taking its time, but it would surely have him in the end. Had that Scots bastard actually managed to kill him after all? It was an atrocious possibility.

His left arm hung stupidly from the shoulder, but there was some muscle remaining, some ability to move it. The arm was weak as a kitten, barely able to manoeuvre its own weight. The hand could grab and hold onto nothing heavier than a half-full mug of tap water, but it worked. For now. And his thirst was brutal, he simply could not stop guzzling water.

Up the side of his neck and onto his face, McLeod's hideous death touch crept, and that horrified him more than anything else. Bad enough that his body was ruined, but to see his face half destroyed was soul-battering. Tendons in his neck stood out like ropes, his jaw and cheekbone sharp ridges through desiccated skin the colour and texture of beef jerky. Both lips on one side were withered to nothing, stretching away from his teeth, giving him half a death's head grin, and his eye was a shrivelled, grey nut in the round hollow of the orbit. He ran his right hand back over his scalp and more hair fluttered out, his pate darkened and dry.

He groaned, despair and agony, rage and regret. Whoever that woman was, she had given him an instant to prepare for that fucking lunatic Scotsman, launching himself through the air. Vince had got a shot in. The whole thing was laughable, and he had let himself down for half a second, laughing at the fool. He'd taken his eye off the ball for a tiny moment and let that crazy broad from the hospice crack him with a wooden fucking giraffe. Of all the insane, ignominious assaults to have brought him low. A sob pulsed through the groan. His life, his incredible professional life, destroyed by the evil touch of that tiny, insignificant man! The pulsing, incandescent rage was the thing keeping him standing, Vince knew. He would not waste it. If nothing else, he would see McLeod dead before the end. And he refused to give in just yet, refused to accept his fate. There may be a chance to save himself.

Slowly, wincing and gasping at the stabbing agonies, Stratton dressed. Though one trouser leg hung seemingly empty, it masked the horror of that limb. A sports sock covered the ruin of his foot. A long-sleeved sweat top and leather glove concealed his damaged chest, arm and hand. He tied a silk scarf around his neck and that only left his hideously deformed face on view. That would have to be concealed in some other way when the time came.

A tentative knocking sounded from the front door.

"About fucking time," Stratton muttered. And, more loudly, "I'm coming."

His voice was a rasping, broken version of his usual thundering tones. Aside from the pain and trauma, he imagined his voice box was slowly degenerating along with the rest of him. Using walls and doorframes, limping painfully on his good leg with the other almost dragging behind, he crossed the small flat and reached the front door. Through the spy hole he saw Gregory Wong, corrupt doctor-for-hire, standing nervously outside, his brown eyes darting left and right while he waited. His tan face was a network of wrinkles, his thin neck scraggly where it poked out the collar of his white shirt. His suit, as usual, was a strangely loose tweed arrangement, hanging off the doctor's bent, seventy-something-year-old frame.

"Brace yourself, Doc," Vince rasped through the door. "I am not a pretty sight."

Wong pushed in the moment Vince unlatched the door. "Shot or stabbed this ti—" he began then stopped dead, staring at Vince's face. Wong's mouth fell open, his skin paled as his eyes widened. "What in heaven happened to you?"

"It's a long story," Vince said. "But before I tell it, you better have that pain relief I wanted. I need that now!"

Wong nodded rapidly, unable to take his eyes from Vince's face. He bustled in, pushed the door closed behind him as Vince half-staggered, half-fell onto the couch in the centre of the room with a cry of pain. The doctor dropped to his knees and fumbled in his large bag.

"I'll give you a needle for the pain," he said, loading up a syringe.

Vince forced his eyes open, swallowing against the hurt. "Don't knock me out. Pain relief, but I got to stay awake."

"You clearly need to rest, Vince. I don't..." Wong shook his head, staring at Stratton's drawn mouth. "I don't know what this is!"

"I'm serious. Help the pain as well as you can without putting me out! I don't mind getting high, but I have to stay conscious."

Wong shook his head again, rummaged in his bag. He muttered about Pethidine and doses, his brow creased the whole time. With the syringe ready, he reached for Vince's left arm and gasped as his fingers closed on nothing until he hit bone. He sat back on his heels, horrified.

"Leg's the same," Vince said through gritted teeth. "Use this arm."

He lifted his right arm up and Wong pulled the sweat top sleeve back, tapped a vein in the crook of Stratton's elbow, and slid the needle in.

Vince leaned back again, revelling in the swift wash of the drug through his system. The pain took a step down to a dull roar, still horrendous, but no longer blinding. Wong was up on his knees, looking closely at Vince's face. He pulled up the left sleeve and examined the scrawny arm.

"This is dead, Vincent," he said, barely audible. "Dead flesh. Long-time dead."

"That right, Doc?"

Wong caught his gaze. "This tissue is long dead. Like it belongs to a corpse who died years ago and slowly decomposed in a very dry environment. You're mummified here, Vincent! This defies science!"

Stratton nodded weakly. "It does that. It was no natural thing that happened to me. Is there anything you can do about it?"

Wong went back to his examination, checking face, arm, leg, body. He palpated all over with his fingertips, used a magnifying glass with a built-in light to study the skin closely. He tapped on Vince's shin. "What does that feel like?"

"Can't feel a thing below the hip," Vince replied, his words slightly slurred from the drug. "Then the hip is a kind of deep aching burn. But my body, my arm, my face, they feel like… You know when something is so cold it burns? Feels like that, but beyond anything I thought possible."

"How did this happen?"

Vince ignored the question. "Inside my body it feels worse. Breathing is like being stabbed. I can feel my heart every time it beats, like it's been split open with rusty nails. What can you do about it, Doc?"

Wong stood and took a couple of paces backwards to an armchair, slumped into it. "Nothing. This is insane. I have no idea how this can happen to a person. This *can't* happen to a person. It's not like the flesh is necrotic, it's *years* dead. Your whole body is half dead and half alive."

"It's spreading."

"Is it?"

Vince lifted his jumper, pointed to his chest just in line with the nipple. "When I first got a chance to look at it, the blackness was about here." The blight was a good two inches past his fingertip.

"How long?"

"Few hours."

Wong shook his head, rubbed hands over his face. "At that rate it'll consume you whole in maybe twenty-four hours at most."

"And there's nothing you can do?"

"Nothing. If it was just in the leg, for example, we could treat it like gangrene, get the leg off quickly before it spread. But it's half your body, already inside you if your explanation is accurate. And spreading at the rate you're talking about, it seems unstoppable. Vincent, I ask again, what happened to you? Did you contract this like a disease? How long have you endured this before you contacted me?"

"It happened last night, about twelve hours ago."

Wong's eyes went wide. "What? From nothing to this in twelve hours? This is a medical marvel!"

"Glad to be of fucking service, old son. But it's not normal. It's some evil fucking magic."

"Magic?"

It took Vince about ten minutes and another shot of Pethidine to tell Wong all he could of McLeod and what had happened. The doctor was an old confidante and Stratton had no qualms about sharing the details, especially if he was destined to die very soon anyway. But even during the telling, and certainly after it, he could see Wong didn't believe a word of it.

"So what other explanation is there?" Vince asked after a moment's silence.

"None," Wong admitted. "I have no explanation for this. And your story is as good as no explanation."

Vince breathed deeply, savouring the succour the pain relief gave him. He was high, would happily close his eyes and drift off into unconsciousness, but knew he may never wake if he allowed that to happen.

"Definitely nothing you can do?" he asked again, though he knew damn well he was already dead. Even so, he planned to go on kicking for a little while yet.

Wong raised both hands, palms up. Shook his head. His mouth opened and closed once, twice, then he let his hands drop. "I can't even believe I'm seeing this. And if I am seeing it, I can't believe you're still functioning."

"Yeah, well, I need to go on functioning for a bit longer yet. Forgetting the spread of this shit, what can you do for me to keep me going? I need whatever drugs are possible to manage the pain, keep me moving. Adrenaline, amphetamine, whatever. It obviously doesn't matter if the cocktail kills me, as long as it doesn't finish me for a little while yet. I've got something I need to do tonight."

Vince had made some phone calls, checked with sources. He knew where McLeod was and that the fucker had survived the gunshots. Well, he wouldn't survive Vince's next visit, even if that was the last thing Vince ever did. He would extract a last victory and make sure McLeod went down before Vince himself descended into Hell.

Wong licked his lips, thought for a moment. "This is obviously not something I have any experience in. But I can get anything, legal or otherwise, you know that. Maybe I can think of some combination that might destroy your kidneys, your liver, but it should power you along for another twenty-four hours maybe."

"That's all I need."

"Planning to settle the score with the guy you claim did this to you?"

"Yep."

Wong sniffed, stood. "Okay. It'll take me a few hours to gather some favours and collect some things. The pain relief you've had should stay with you for now. I'll be back as quick as I can. I'm going to need big money for this."

Vince laughed, then winced at the pain of it. "That desk over there? Top drawer, take all you need. Fuck it, take all of it. You've been good to me."

Wong retrieved a wad of cash and thumbed through it. His eyebrows rose. "This is ten times what I need. More even."

"Like I said, you've been good to me."

"Can I ask one more favour?"

"Why not."

"When you've done for this guy, can you try to get back here to die? And can I have your body?"

Vince laughed again despite the pain. "Pragmatic fucking vulture, you are."

"You, this, is amazing. It's fascinating. I need to know more."

"I'll do what I can."

"Great! Won't be long."

Wong took the front door key Vince held up and let himself out. As the door clicked shut, Vince breathed deeply and settled in to wait, keeping himself awake with visions of the McLeod dragon and Vince the mighty, if wounded, knight, striking the fucker down again and again and again.

THIRTY-SEVEN

AMY DROVE TOWARDS the Sally Gentle Hospice in Matt's car, haunted by the look she'd seen in his eyes. Over and over she had managed to convince herself that Stratton must surely be dead, but even weak and broken on that hospital bed, Matt's gaze had held an equal conviction that the bastard lived. And he was right. If they didn't know for certain, they had to assume Stratton was alive and coming for Matt.

Amy had managed to send a message to work the night before, while they were making their plans at Steve's place, telling them she was unwell and wouldn't be in. She was due in for another shift tonight, in less than seven hours, though she knew she wouldn't be in any state of mind to work. But she needed things from the hospice all the same. Perhaps a small mixture of honesty and lies would be best.

She parked up and walked into the calm, quiet care home. Immediately the cloak of death settled around her shoulders, the mantle she wore gladly, had happily borne for years since she had discovered her talent. After witnessing Matt and his manipulation of the dark, she wondered if she wasn't perhaps as malevolent as him after all. Her talent had always been a gift in her mind, a service. Matt's was something altogether more full of malice and destruction. Was hers really any different? Especially now it seemed to be conjuring this presence that dogged her. That was no gift.

Regardless, watching him last night, watching the dark shroud around him as he attacked Stratton, she had seen a new methodology. New possibilities. From that one act, Amy had learned a lot. Whether she could come close to emulating any part of it was another matter. But to find out, she needed to gather more shadows of the dead. She had spent most of hers on Prentiss, saved some, but knew she needed more. And with that thought, she shivered again at the memory of the thing in her bedroom doorway that Carla had inadvertently saved her from. Would she awaken that thing again with these activities? And could she do anything about it this time if she did? Regardless, she had to try. They were preciously thin on choices.

Carol sat behind the reception desk and smiled as Amy entered. "You feeling better, love?"

Amy shook her head. "Not really. I'm feeling pretty awful, to be honest."

"Then what are you doing here? And you're not even supposed to be on until nine."

"I know. I'm not going to be able to work again tonight. I feel rotten."

"What is it? The flu?"

Amy winced inside. Everyone thought the simplest common cold was always "the flu".

"Not sure," she said. "Not flu. Some virus. I've been fatigued, headachey, no appetite." All those symptoms were true but for different reasons than a virus.

"You poor dear. You really have to be here?"

"There's a couple of people I want to see. I know we shouldn't get close but we always do. And they might not have long."

Carol smiled. "You're too soft-hearted for this job."

"It's how I'm made." Amy silently berated herself for that, thinking about what might be necessary. "We didn't lose anyone last night?"

"No." Carol checked records. "But a couple are weakened. Both Terry Stratton and Mary Sanders are marked here for close obs."

"Anyone in now?"

"Rounds finished about half an hour ago. Unless anyone calls, all staff are having a break."

Amy nodded, smiled, tried to maintain a presentation of weakness. It was not much of a challenge. If she lay down somewhere dark now, she'd be out in seconds. Only desperation pushed her through the fogs of fatigue. That and the constant throb and burn of her bullet wound. "I'll go around and have look in on everyone. Then I think I'll crawl home again."

"Okay, love. You really shouldn't have bothered to come all the way in!"

"Just in case, you know?"

Without waiting to endure more of Carol's understanding gaze, Amy turned away and headed for the rooms. She went to Mary Sanders first. The woman was only in her sixties, but looked ancient and withered as she lay there, eaten away by tumours throughout her organs. Amy laid a palm on Mary's brow, the woman's eyelids fluttered, but remained closed. The shadows were there, lurking very close to the surface, but not ready to rise just yet. Soon. Amy removed her hand, stood looking down at the sick woman for several moments, mind tumbling with terrifying thoughts. She refused to look over her shoulder, towards the gathering presence she imagined there, stalking towards her.

She left and walked further along to Terry Stratton's room. He was asleep too, the room dim, wan light leaking soft orange through the closed curtains. Terry looked worse than when she had last seen him only a couple of days before. The descent into the final fall was well underway. She laid a hand on his brow and frowned. His shadows were much closer to the surface than Mary's, he would definitely go first. But not yet. Maybe not for another day or two.

Amy glanced back out the door. Her best guess was that Mary might last until the weekend, another five or six days. Terry here maybe two days more at most. But she couldn't wait until then. If Stratton was coming, he would come soon. If the bastard wasn't dead yet, he was surely in a pretty bad way. Was there any recovering from what Matt had done? Would Stratton lay low, recover somehow over weeks and months, then come for Matt?

It seemed entirely unlikely given the image of the man in her memory, dragging himself one-armed over that wall, already half-dead. Having a long time to prepare, for Matt to recover, at least partially, was an encouraging thought, but not one on which she could rely. She needed to be ready now. She needed to be ready and by Matt's side. Even this delay, this distance between, filled her with dread. What if Stratton was in the hospital now, stalking Matt as she stood here indecisive?

"You've a lovely warm touch, love."

Amy jumped, looked back down at Terry. He smiled weakly at her.

She stroked his brow, ran a hand gently over his balding pate before she took her palm away. "How are you, Terry?" she asked, one side of her mouth twitching up in a smile.

"Oh, you know. Fucking dying." He grinned at her. They were silent for a moment, then Terry said, "I'm nearly gone, eh?"

"You think so?"

"Don't pretend, love. You know I hate that. Nothing hurts any more. I feel like I'm half somewhere else already."

Amy pulled a chair nearer, sat and took one of Terry's bony hands. "You've not got long now, no." His lucidity saddened her. It was unusual, but every once in a while there was one like Terry, mind focussed right to the end.

"I feel like I could just shut my eyes, go to sleep and keep falling. Never wake again."

"You could, Terry. You could do exactly that if you wanted."

He swallowed, hitched a breath. Amy grabbed a lollipop sponge, dipped it in water and pressed it to his lips. His tongue emerged, grey and mouldy looking, to lap at it gently. The sickly sweet stench of death on him was strong. "That's better. Thanks."

"You're welcome."

He faded for a moment, then pulled himself back. "Could I?" he asked. "Choose to just go away now?"

"I've seen it lots of times." Amy wasn't lying, it was so common as to be almost normal. "People know when their time is close. They see everyone they want to see, say their goodbyes and, once they're assured it's okay to go, they do just that. They simply let go."

Amy hated the part of her hoping Terry would take her at her word. Everything she told him was true, but guilt gnawed. She was encouraging him for her own sake. For Matt's sake. Then again, their situation was entirely the fault of Terry's son. There would be a strange karmic justice if things worked out this way. But none of it was Terry's fault. You couldn't hold the sins of the father against the children, or vice versa.

"I haven't seen Vince for a long while."

Amy swallowed, glanced away. "No?"

"I know time is messed up in here, I lose track. But it's definitely been a few days, hasn't it?"

"I'm not sure, Terry. I could check for you."

Terry tipped his wizened head, held her gaze with his red, wet eyes. "I'm ready to go. I've had enough. But I need to see my boy once more first. I'll hold on for that."

Amy tried not to let her frustration show. "Of course," she managed.

"Will you ring him? Ask him where the fuck he is? What's so important it stops him from popping in on his old dad, moments before I shuffle off this mortal fucking coil? And I want reassurance he's looking after his mum."

"I'll do that, sure. You rest and I'll give him a call."

Amy patted Terry's hand, hoping he would drift off for a moment. She didn't need go anywhere, just let him think she had. Her heart ached with the thought of the lies she would tell him next.

Terry closed his eyes and sighed, sinking into a light slumber. After only a moment, he started, eyes fluttering open. "Was it you?"

"Was what me?"

"I was talking with someone recently, about Macbeth."

Amy smiled. "We've talked a bit about you and Shakespeare before."

"Nah, nah. It wasn't you. Some young fella."

Amy stroked the old man's brow. "Sleep, Terry. I'll go and call Vince."

He closed his eyes again, his lips quivering. "The way to dusty death," he whispered, barely audible. His voice grew a little stronger. "'Out, out, brief candle! Life is but a walking shadow, a poor player, that struts and frets his hour upon the stage, and then is heard no more.'"

Amy gently stroked his hair. "Shhhh."

"It is a tale," Terry said. "'Told by an idiot, full of sound and fury, signifying nothing.' That's what I told that young man."

"Is it?"

"Yeah, and it's all true."

"Full of sound and fury, signifying nothing?" A tear stood at the corner of one eye as Amy considered the words. "I don't believe you, Terry. Your life has been a lot more than nothing. You were a teacher. You changed lives."

"Maybe," he whispered. "It all seems pretty fucking pointless from here though." His eyes opened and he tipped his head to her again. "There has to be something else, though, doesn't there?"

"Something else?"

"After this. After life. Otherwise, what's the bloody point of it all?" His eyes drifted closed again.

"Yeah." It was all Amy could manage. "What's the point?" Even though she knew in her heart the most probable answer was that there was no point. Asking the question didn't mean there had to be an answer. She'd always been a believer in being the best she could be in this life on the assumption there was nothing else. And if there was, well it was still important to live the best life possible. *Full of sound and fury, signifying nothing.* She knew those words would haunt her from this day on, but that last bit she refused to believe. Life wasn't for nothing. Life was for living.

Terry breathed evenly, sleep taking him again. His shadows swam languidly just below his surface, waiting to carry him down, but they were patient. No, Amy corrected herself, not even patient, just natural. Mindless, thoughtless, as indifferent as the universe itself. That thought disquieted her and she couldn't put a finger on why. She ignored the sensation of icy fingers on the back of her neck. Paranoia, that's all.

She sat in the gloomy room, the thick, sweet scent of death mixed with lilies heavy in the air. She let the tears come then. For Terry, for herself, for Matt and all they had been through. For the sake of sheer exhaustion. And for the compromise she was about to make of her most deeply held convictions.

She let Terry doze for several minutes, then gently spoke his name, squeezed his hand.

"You're here again?" he said, smiling weakly. His lips were like paper, cracked and peeling.

Amy gave him water off the small sponge, swallowed hard. "Yeah, I'm here."

"Is Vince coming?"

"No, he's not."

Terry's eyebrows quivered weakly up. "He's not?"

Amy closed her eyes, unable to bear that searching gaze. The things she'd been forced to do over the last couple of days were hurting her, but none more than this. She simply needed his shadows. Perhaps the stain of this act would stay with her forever, but she had to save Matt. There may not be another like him in the world and now she had found him, she could not let Vince Stratton take him away from her.

"I called and one of his boys answered. Clancy, I think his name was. He said that Vince had to go overseas on a business trip, very short notice, and wouldn't be back for at least a couple of weeks. Maybe more."

"I can't hold on that long," Terry said, his voice like a little boy's.

Something cracked in Amy's heart and she knew it would never heal. Vince wasn't coming back, surely. That part was no lie. She had to make that true for her own sake, and Matt's. But she needed to remove all hope from Terry, and that's what burned. Take away any last thread of connection to living he had left. He would die thinking his son was a bastard, and Vince Stratton was exactly that, the worst kind of fucker. But to leave Terry thinking so, his last thought of his son as he died, was a despicable act. "Clancy was supposed to come and see you, tell you himself," Amy said, the words like bile in her mouth. "But he hadn't had a chance yet."

"Vince didn't even have time to come and say goodbye?" Terry asked, though the question wasn't really directed at Amy. Tears filled the old man's baggy eyelids. "He's always been obsessed with his fucking business, but this… This is a new low."

Terry gasped for breath, from his weakness as well as the shock. He blinked long and hard, swallowed dryly. Amy gave him more water on his lips, but he let it roll off over his chin.

"He is not a nice man, my Vince," Terry said.

"Maybe," Amy whispered, struggling to hold back tears of her own.

"No maybe about it, love. He's not a nice man and doesn't do nice things. I'm not an idiot, I know something of his life. I've ignored it as best I can. A man is supposed to love his son, isn't he?"

"Of course he is."

"Well, I'm not sure I do. Sometimes I do, of course. And I certainly did, before. I remember his pudgy little arms and legs, the way he would run to me for cuddles when he was barely two or three years old. I remember the studious young schoolboy he was. So serious, but determined. But something else grew in him too, and I do not love the man he became."

The short speech exhausted Terry and he drifted off again. Amy sat and let her tears go. It might have been five minutes or half an hour later, in her exhaustion and grief she lost track, when Terry's eyes flickered open again.

"Overseas? I didn't dream that, did I?"

"No, I'm so sorry. He's not coming."

"And my Maisey?"

"Your wife? She's okay. Vince is doing the right thing by her. She's comfortable and safe." Amy made a mental note to ensure that wasn't a lie. She would make it true at her own expense if she had to.

"I wish she could come and say goodbye. But I know she's too weak, fading fast herself."

Amy nodded, lips pressed together.

"Fucking hell. Well, I've had enough."

Amy nodded again. She leaned down and gently kissed his forehead, pleased and appalled that her plan had paid off. "I'll go and see Maisey, tell her you love her. Tell her goodbye for you."

"Yes please, love. Tell her it will all be okay."

"I will. You're a good man, Terry."

"Well, I've tried to be. We all die alone in the end, eh?"

"I'm here. I won't go anywhere."

"You've got a job to do, haven't you?"

"I'm not going anywhere."

Terry smiled. "Bless you, love. One of the good ones, eh?"

Amy's tears still ran. "Well, I've tried to be."

Terry nodded, an almost imperceptible movement of his head. "Don't cry for me. 'On such a full sea are we now afloat, and we must take the current when it serves.' From *Julius Caesar*, that one."

Amy smiled, nodded, her throat too tight to allow speech. Terry was surprisingly lucid for one so close to the darkness, more so than any she'd seen before.

"Fuck, I'm tired."

Amy swallowed. "Go to sleep, Terry. I'll be here. You can let go."

His eyes shifted, held hers for a moment, and something in them stabbed deep into her soul. "Don't waste it," he whispered. "Whatever you take from this. Don't waste it."

She stifled a gasp. "I won't." Amy's heart hammered. Was he talking about the experience in general or could he somehow see far enough into her to know what she was doing? She would never know.

Terry closed his eyes and sighed, the breath coming weak and slow. It kept coming, his life leaking out of him as he sank into a sleep from which he would never wake. His shadows surged and writhed, pushed upwards, outwards. His chest hitched ever so slightly every ten or fifteen seconds, his body taking breaths his mind no longer cared for. It took him another two hours to fade away completely and Amy held his hand the whole time. When his final breath sighed out, she put her forehead to his and drew deeply against him, gathered all the shadows he had to give. She took every shade of death from him and planted it deeply inside herself. She sat for another several minutes, crying silently, letting the darkness settle in her. She ignored the sensation of something hungry circling, getting ever closer.

Eventually she went back to Carol, her feet dragging with exhaustion.

"He's gone?" Carol asked.

Amy nodded.

Carol smiled kindly. "I looked in when you'd been gone so long and saw you sitting with him. You're a good soul."

"Am I really?"

"Of course you are!"

"I had to stay with him, but I'm so tired. Still unwell."

Carol nodded, checked the clock and stood, moved to the staff room door. "Terry Stratton," she said to whoever was inside. "He just passed. Can you do the paperwork?"

Amy left them to the conversation. They would do all the necessary things. She didn't need to be there any more. It was dark and cold outside. She hoped she wasn't too late, all that for nothing. She had to get back to Matt and maybe she could sleep for just a little while if she knew Ben was there to watch over her and Matt both. She just had to get there. She climbed into Matt's car and headed back for the hospital, crying all the way.

THIRTY-EIGHT

AMY ARRIVED BACK AT THE HOSPITAL late in the afternoon, takeaway food bag in hand. A smell of overcooked vegetables and the savoury aroma of dried-out meat and thick gravy accompanied the antiseptic and sweet sickness in the linoleum corridors as porters wheeled tall metal trolleys around, delivering dinners. The front desk at ICU was occupied by a different nurse, who raised an eyebrow at Amy in a friendly gesture.

"Help you?" she asked in a soft voice.

"I'm Amy, er, Matt McLeod's fiancée." It sounded so weird to say such a thing, she'd never considered being engaged to anyone. Marriage was simply something that had never blipped on her life's radar. She could imagine it, in an academic way, but emotionally it didn't resonate at all. Her thoughts drifted momentarily to what it might feel like if Matt *were* her fiancé, even her husband. It was both ridiculous and strangely understandable. He was a good-looking guy, and funny and brave. Holy crap, what kind of thoughts were these? She hardly even knew him. But he shared something similar to her secret and that made her want to never let him go. Ideas of marriage could wait. She realised the nurse was looking at her strangely.

"I'm sorry, what did you say?"

"I said you're welcome to go right in. His brother is there too."

Amy smiled. "Thank you."

"Are you okay? You look very tired."

Amy's smile broke into a soft laugh. "Honestly, I've never been so tired in my life, and I'm a shift worker. But yes, I'm okay, thanks."

The nurse stood and reached out, put a hand over Amy's where it rested on the counter. "Times like these are very difficult and you want to do everything you can, of course you do. But you must remember to look after yourself too. The worst thing you could do now is get over-tired and have a car accident or something."

"Sure, you're right." A car accident seemed a strangely mundane likelihood in Amy's life. "I'll rest soon, I promise. I might catch a nap now, if Matt's sleeping."

"Good. You must take care of *you!*"

Amy left the counter, the nurse's concerned gaze an almost physical pressure on her back, and pushed into Matt's room. He looked about as awful as he had before, but maybe there was a little more colour in his cheeks. His eyes were closed, his breathing deep and even, the quiet pings from the monitors above his bed regular and somehow reassuring.

Ben sat in the chair by the bedside, a book on his lap. He smiled up at her. "Did you know they have a little library on wheels? Bloke came around offering patients and visitors books to read. Said he'll collect them later if we just leave them out."

She handed over the paper sack she was carrying, burger and chips. She'd eaten hers as she drove. "Nice idea," Amy said. "Sorry the food isn't more inspiring."

"No problem, I'm starving!" He tucked into the bag with fervour.

She looked back to Matt, sleeping peacefully. "How's he been?"

"He's doing all right." He went at the food with both hands. "He's woken a few times, seems to be fairly with it most of the time he's awake. The police came back about two hours ago."

"How did that go?"

"Matt was brilliant." Ben laughed, shook his head, swallowed. "He'd been awake already. We were chatting quietly when they came in, and he immediately acted half as conscious as he had been. He was all sleepy and kept wincing at the pain while they talked, made them right uncomfortable! He said as little as possible, but backed up that he was coming to Steve-O's for some quiet beers, got attacked by two blokes in balaclavas and doesn't really remember much of anything after that. Stellar performance."

"What about Farouk?"

Ben nodded, shrugged. "Abela Farouk, her name is. Homicide detective. I've picked that much up, but she still hasn't woken up. They don't know why but apparently it's like this sometimes."

"And the police were happy with all that?"

"They seemed satisfied for now. We still need a word with Abela if we can get it. Things might all unravel then."

"Yeah, I'm scared of that."

Ben shrugged again. "Nothing we can do about it yet. I keep checking in on her. Every time the nurse goes on obs rounds, I sneak into her room to see if she's awake yet."

"That's good." Amy dropped into a chair on the other side of the bed. "I am so tired I can barely see straight."

Ben's food was all gone and he picked up the book again. "Make yourself comfortable there. Here." He threw her a spare pillow from beside the bed. "I've had a few naps here and there while Matt's been sleeping. I'll watch him."

"You sure?" She wedged the pillow into the side of the chair and tucked her feet up. The chair wasn't big, but it was big enough in an ugly plastic armchair kind of way. As her head pressed into the softness of the pillow it was close to the most amazing feeling she'd ever experienced.

"Yeah, I'm sure. You clearly need sleep."

"Thank you, Ben. For everything."

"It's all good. You really think he's going to come back."

Amy drew a deep breath. "Matt thinks so, and I reckon he might be right. We have to assume so." The last word was lost in a huge yawn. She shifted her arm to ease the throb of the wound there.

Ben pursed his lips. "We still need to have that talk."

"We will," Amy promised. Or she wanted to promise. Maybe she just thought it as she tumbled into a deep, warm abyss of blessed unconscious.

THIRTY-NINE

AMY WOKE WITH A START. The room was dim, pale orange lights concealed behind the bedhead providing the only illumination. The machines quietly pinged, Ben snored softly, the book butterflied open over one knee, almost finished. The city beyond the window was dark, the glass mostly reflecting the gloomy room. Raindrops glittered on the outside, running races with each other to the sill below. Movement in the night made Amy start again.

Outside? They were several stories up. She twisted around in the chair, realising as her foggy brain woke up that the figure was in the room, reflected in the night-darkened glass. She sucked in a deep breath, heart thumping its way from her throat back to her chest, as the nurse at the foot of Matt's bed smiled gently. She held a clipboard in one hand and a cup in the other.

"Sorry, did I startle you?"

"Must have heard you. Didn't realise you were here." Amy smacked her lips, dry as paper and gummy at the corners. She couldn't imagine how awful her breath must be. With a wince, she slipped her legs out and put her feet on the floor, pins and needles flooding everything from the hip down.

"You can go home, you know. We'll take good care of him."

Amy smiled. "I know. You are taking excellent care of him. But I want to be here when he wakes for now. It's all so recent, you know?"

"Of course. Well, I have to wake him now to give him a tablet."

The nurse slipped the clipboard back into its plastic holder on the end of the bed and moved around to Matt's side. For a moment she blocked Amy's view as she gently tapped Matt's shoulder and he murmured groggily.

Amy rubbed her eyes, jumped up to see better. Matt caught her eye and smiled. "Hey," he said, sounding like an emphysemic old man.

"Hey yourself."

"Take this," the nurse said, ignoring them both. "Just a small pill. Don't swallow too much water at once."

"What's the pill for?" Amy asked, irrationally nervous about anyone giving Matt anything. Was there a chance this wasn't really a nurse, but some agent of Stratton's? Would he send an accomplice assassin rather than come himself? Was he too hurt by Matt's dark to come? He could send anyone, to do anything. Amy's heart raced again, sobs wanted to burst out of her.

"It's just a thing to help with the side effects of the morphine drip."

But was it? Really?

"Thank you, Julie," Matt said, and swallowed the tiny pill with a sip of water. He breathed out with a sigh and sipped again.

Julie?

"You remember my name," the nurse said with a grin. "You must be feeling better."

"You were very kind to me earlier," Matt said, and managed to look slightly abashed. "I won't forget that."

Nurse Julie patted his shoulder once and turned away. "Try to get back to sleep." She glanced at Amy. "You too. You all need it."

Amy noticed Ben was awake and he grinned, then closed his eyes again. The adrenaline rush of her panic sent waves of nausea through her. "I need something to eat," she said, suddenly aware of the gaping pit where her stomach used to be. The burger and chips earlier had not lasted long.

"Vending machine only at this time," Julie said. "Out the main doors, turn left and go about twenty metres. You can't miss it."

"Thank you. Hey, Ben?"

He opened his eyes again as Julie quietly let herself out.

"You want anything?"

"Nah, I'm good."

"Stay awake for a minute while I get something, yeah?"

"You feeling jumpy?"

"A bit."

Ben sniffed, pulled himself more upright in the chair. "Okay, no worries."

"I'm glad you're taking this seriously, Ben. Thank you."

"After what I saw? You're damn right I'm taking it seriously."

"I just need the loo first."

Amy let herself into the small *en suite* toilet in Matt's room and blinked against the harshness of the fluorescent light, cold and blue. Her face in the mirror was pale and drawn, her eyes puffy with dark swells underneath. But she had to admit she felt mildly better than she looked, thankful for the brief sleep. Or was it brief? She checked her phone for the time. It said 1:55 a.m. No wonder her legs were numb and she was hungry again, she'd been out cold in that chair barely moving for a little over eight hours. She relieved herself and flushed, then headed back out. With a pat to Ben's shoulder she went in search of the vending machine, hoping it held more than crisps.

An old man, dark skinned and grey haired, pushing a large plastic trolley full of dirty linen, passed her as she left the ICU. She held the door open for him and he ignored her as he limped through, one foot almost dragging as he went. She was too tired to feel very sorry for him, but had enormous respect for the people who were the tiny gears in the bigger health care machine. She knew the public's love of nurses and doctors, their hatred of the administration and government indifference. But so few people spared a thought for the porters, the cleaners, the orderlies, and all the others who kept hospitals running. The work was shit, the pay was awful, but someone had to do it.

She stared into the glass front of the vending machine, pleased to see some sandwiches in there, even if they did look a bit sad and dried out. She yawned, rubbed her eyes, then the bottom fell out of her world with a rush of adrenaline restricting her veins. What the hell was an orderly doing collecting linen in the middle of the night? And limping like that, as if his leg had been withered and almost destroyed. How could she have been so stupid?

With a cry of despair, Amy rushed back into ICU. The desk was unmanned, the dimly lit front office still and empty. A muffled grunt came from the direction of Matt's room. Amy rushed in and saw Ben bent backward over the foot of Matt's bed. The orderly, now clearly Stratton in blackface disguise, struck out weakly with one skinny, withered arm as he battled against Ben's grip on his right wrist. The bastard held a large knife that flashed silver in the wan light behind the bed.

"Fuck you, man!" Ben said through gritted teeth. "Didn't expect me, did ya?" He threw an elbow with his free hand that cracked Stratton's head sideways, but the big man shook it off.

"I'll fucking kill you too," Stratton said, and somehow pivoted his body, grinding Ben's back hard against the plastic foot of the bed. The clipboard in its holder cracked and fell.

Ben cried out in pain, and Stratton dropped the elbow of his good arm down onto Ben's arched ribcage. Something cracked and the air whooshed out of Ben's mouth. He grimaced against it, swung his free arm again, his fist balled up to hammer Stratton in the ear.

Matt was awake, eyes wide in terror, desperately trying to sit up but his battered body had barely the strength for him to lift his head.

Amy ran in, leaped onto Stratton's back, tried to haul him away. She managed to relieve some of the pressure on Ben, then Stratton was driving back with his good leg to slam her into the wall. Her back exploded in pain and the momentum slung her head to crack into the hard plaster. A million diamonds of a thousand colours burst out in her vision, the room turned over and spun quickly around. She felt impact and realised she'd slumped to the floor.

Ben yelled in rage and she heard something crash, the slap of flesh on flesh, a grunt of pain, though she couldn't tell if it came from Ben or Stratton. She struggled up onto her hands and knees, drawing in long deep breaths, trying to clear her head. Dizziness swept her, from hunger as much as from the blow to the back of her head. But she had no time to be weak.

She forced herself to her feet, swaying slightly, and saw Ben and Stratton struggling again. Ben's left arm bled from a small gash just below his elbow. How could Stratton be so damned strong and dangerous still, with only two properly working limbs?

She had one chance. She had seen what Matt had done with his dark. The way his shadows all writhed up and out, opening him to some stygian abyss. It was both incredible and horrible, so different to her gentle delivery of the shadows she collected. But their skills weren't so different. They both manipulated death, just in vastly different ways. She was full of Terry Stratton's shadows and she had to believe she could wield them just like Matt wielded his.

She bolted forward as Ben made a small space between them. Amy grabbed Stratton's face, her palms clasped either side, flat against his cheeks, one fat and sweating, one hollow and black. Ben grabbed the arm wielding the knife and together they ran Stratton back into the wall, him frantically hopping on his one good leg to avoid going down. When he hit the plaster, Ben slammed his knife arm against it and held it there, and Amy let all her shadows out in one hateful, voluminous rush, just like she'd seen Matt do.

Stratton's eyes went wide, bulging as the pain hit him. "Not you too?" he rasped, then his voice turned into a wail of agony.

Darkness swirled and writhed from Amy's fingers into his face, blackening the skin as pustules and tumours erupted from his flesh. The pain through Amy's body was almost unbearable, like someone was cracking open all her bones with pliers, but she refused to let go.

Ben stared, "Jesus fuck Jesus fuck Jesus fuck," over and over as he watched the necrotic wasteland of Stratton's head. But to his credit, Ben didn't let go of his grip on the assassin's sleeved arm.

The tumours grew, imposing over themselves, lumps upon lumps of mutating flesh, shrinking and tightening over the bone. Stratton's cheekbones rose like shark fins from tar, the right side of his face quickly matching his left, then even the bones began to fold and twist. His wail of agony and despair wheezed to a hissing escape of air as his chest collapsed in on itself. His good eye withered to a raisin and fell into the hollow of its orbit, then those orbits too corrupted and bubbled and buckled.

Ben yelped and staggered back as Stratton's arm became as thin and pliant as rope, and Amy followed the bastard to the floor, refusing to let go of his mushy, shrunken head until he was little more than a puddle of clothes and wet, blackened skin.

The hurt through her body was threatening her consciousness when she finally pulled her hands from the mess and staggered back. She bumped into Ben, who caught her and then sat into the armchair behind them, pulling her onto his lap lest they both hit the floor.

They sat there, gasping. Amy leaned forward, thankful for the solidity of Ben's knees as he panted, his head tipped back against the chair. She needed the pain to stop. How did Matt bear this? She realised his guilt probably made him consider it a just punishment, but how often had he subjected himself to it? Tears streamed from her eyes as her muscles burned and her bones ached. She would gladly take a solid hit to the jaw, anything, just to be unconscious now and end this agony.

"Make it stop," she begged between ragged breaths. "Make it stop, make it stop, make it stop."

"Just breathe, Amy. Try to breathe deep."

She looked up to see Matt, his own eyes wet with tears as he watched her. He tried to sit, fell back against his pillow, face twisted in pain, rage, frustration.

"It'll stop, Amy." Matt's voice was strained. "It will. But you have to push it away. Breathe deeply. Imagine you're gathering all the fucking black into a tight ball and push it back down, deep, deep down and away from you."

Amy sobbed, the pain like lightning through every inch of her. "I can't! It's too much!"

"You can!" Matt said, more force in his voice than she'd heard since before all this madness began. "You can and you *must!*"

Ben sat forward, put his arms around her. "I've got you. You're going to be all right. Do as he says. Breathe, Amy!"

She desperately forced herself to stop gasping and gathered one long, shaking breath. It rattled in her chest, stabbed pain through her limbs and out her fingers and toes. She writhed in Ben's grasp and he held her firmly, pressed his chest against her back. He sat back, pulling her upright from where she hunched over her knees.

"Sit up, Amy. Sit up and breathe."

"Do as he says," Matt said. "Please, Amy, push it away before it consumes you!"

The thought was terrifying enough to cut through the pain. She let Ben pull her up and sucked in a great lungful of air. It brought more pain with it, but a different hurt, and the darkness swirling around her like a predator subsided. Before it could surge back, she took another breath, and another. Something, somewhere, exulted, but she ignored it and breathed.

"That's it!" Matt said. "You're doing it. Keep doing it."

Amy took breath after breath, finally able to conceive of the idea of pushing the blackness away. Down and away, back to where she had drawn it from. The pain slowly receded with it, left her shaking and dizzy and crying, but only shock remained. The darkness had gone, and its agonising throbs reduced as its presence faded.

She found herself staring at the mess that Stratton had become, shining and oily, utterly corrupted but still thickly coalesced somehow. *You didn't like the adult he'd become*, Amy thought to the memory of Terry. *Well, you were instrumental in ending that man*. She wondered if he was anywhere to know what had just happened.

Silence but for ragged breathing and quiet sobs settled over the room. Tears ran over Matt's cheeks as he lay staring at the ceiling.

"You two are both some weird and dangerous fuckers," Ben said eventually.

Amy pulled herself off his lap, with a weak squeeze of thanks to his hand, staggered around the bed and fell into the chair opposite.

"You're going to be weak for a while yet," Matt said. "Stay sitting down."

"How did you teach her that stuff?" Ben asked.

Matt grinned crookedly, shook his head. "I didn't. She's already like me."

Amy pointed to the remains of Stratton. "But I've never done anything quite like that before. And I don't think I ever will again."

Ben looked from Matt to Amy and back again. "We've been mates for years. How did I never know about this stuff?"

"It's always been something I kept quiet. Not really warehouse conversation. I'm so sorry you got dragged into all this, man. But fuck me, I'm so grateful for your help."

"Definitely," Amy said. "I thanked you before, and I thank you again. I can't thank you enough."

Ben held up a palm. It shook slightly. "All right, enough. Mates look out for each other. I never anticipated anything like this, but you know what? I've seen enough. I'll always be your pal, Matt, but I'll be grateful if you never expose me to any of this stuff again, yeah?" He pointed at Amy. "Same to you. Happy to be your friend, but let's try to keep it all as normal as possible."

"Of course," Amy said.

"You got my word," Matt said.

Ben nodded, looked from one to the other. "I'm just a bloke who likes to earn a quid and enjoy a few beers. Go to the football on Saturday and have two weeks in Spain every now and then." His face folded up and he fell forward into his palms, sobbing like a child. Clearly everything had finally hit him like a wave.

Amy jumped up, unstable as she was, and grabbed him in an embrace. She sank to her knees and held him while he cried, whispering over and over, "It's okay. It's okay. It's finished now. It's finished."

Ben sobbed himself out, slowly stilling. Without looking up he sniffed hard. Amy found a box of tissues on the bedside and pulled a few free, handed them to him. She felt strength slowly returning to her limbs, but imagined it would be hours, maybe days, before she felt herself again.

"Sorry about that," Ben muttered. "I'm just… It's just…"

"Shut up, mate," Matt said. "It's entirely okay. Honestly, I'm surprised you held out as long as you did."

Ben looked up, a sheepish half-smile on his face. "Don't tell Gareth and Steve-O, eh?"

"Nope. I *will* tell them you were a fucking hero and saved our lives. I won't tell them anything else."

Ben sniffed again, blew his nose. He composed himself quickly.

"He really did come for you."

Matt nodded, his hair rustling against his pillow in the quiet. "He really did. Must have been hopped up on some mad stuff to still be that strong."

Amy dug around in the bedside drawer and found a gauze pad and some tape and bandages. She looked at Ben's arm, paused. "That's worse than I thought. Might need a stitch or two. Maybe you should head down to Emergency?"

"Just patch it up for now. I'll go somewhere else and have it seen to later." He looked around the room as she dressed the wound. The broken clipboard, furniture in disarray. And the puddle of what used to be Stratton.

"What do we do with that?" Amy asked as she finished.

"Maybe I can help," a weak voice said from doorway.

They jumped, Amy spun around. Abela Farouk stood there, bent and weak, holding a wheeled hospital stand with a bag of clear fluid hanging from it.

Amy licked her lips, lost for words, as Ben and Matt stared on, equally silent.

Abela nodded softly, then entered and closed the door behind her. She gestured to the window in the door. "I saw it all. I don't believe it, but I saw it."

"You fucked us," Matt said. "All this… It would have been over back there but for you."

Abela nodded, eyes haunted. "I know. I'm sorry. I needed to resolve Charlie's death. I *knew* Stratton did it, had to have been him." She glanced at the mess on the floor, then quickly looked away. "I followed Charlie's notes, tried to figure out the stuff about weirdly blackened corpses. It all made no sense. Then I followed him, saw you." She pointed to Matt. "I don't know why I warned him." She shook her head, looked at the floor. "I'm sorry, I do know why. Because I wanted Stratton for myself. I wanted to take him down, for Charlie's sake. And it cost you all so dearly."

"Aye, it did that," Matt said quietly.

Abela put a hand gingerly to her stomach. "Cost me too. But lying there, bleeding, I saw what you did. To him, to Stratton. I saw what I'd interrupted. I've been in that other room ever since, feigning sleep, trying to think of what the fuck I'd tell my superiors about it all. Then I heard this ruckus, heard Stratton! And I saw…I saw."

"What'll you tell your superiors?" Amy asked.

Abela smiled weakly. "What did you tell the police?"

"That muggers randomly attacked and shot him," Ben said. "And that he remembers nothing else."

Abela nodded. "And I just happened to be passing and got hit in the crossfire."

"You'll tell them that?"

"Yes. I'll think of a reason I was there. Because I don't know what the hell any of this is. I don't know how to even begin to process it. But you finished Stratton. And really, that's all I wanted. Fuck the rest of it."

Ben crouched and tentatively picked up Stratton's withered and blackened hand. "It's like jelly with a leather skin," he said, disgusted.

Farouk moved to one side. "A nurse is coming," she said.

Ben folded the corpse over on itself, using the clothes still wrapped around it to hold it together. Remains of bones snapped and popped like dry twigs inside as he made a large bundle of it. Taking a deep breath, battling against losing his dinner, he dragged it back across the floor and into the small *en suite* bathroom.

Amy had just managed to straighten the room, the bathroom door clicked as Ben locked it, then Matt's door swung open. Amy turned, the broken clipboard and its plastic holder still in her hands.

Nurse Julie saw the damage and frowned.

"I'm sorry," Amy said. "I tripped and knocked this down. I've broken it."

"Must have been quite a trip!"

"I grabbed for the bed, but collected this instead." Amy tried to look more contrite than guilty for lying.

"Not to worry," Julie said. "You really need to get a proper night's sleep, you know." She took the pieces and put them on her trolley.

She jumped, noticing Farouk in the room. "You're awake. You shouldn't be up!"

"I'm okay."

"Please, back to your bed."

Farouk nodded. "Come and talk to me. About him," she said to Amy.

Amy nodded, then sat. Farouk shuffled out and Amy stared at the line of light under the bathroom door as Julie checked over Matt.

"Your pulse and blood pressure are a little bit up," she said. "You feeling any different? Feel sick?"

"No," Matt said weakly, playing it up again. "I've had a bit more pain, that's all."

Amy didn't doubt that for a second.

"Don't be shy with that morphine," Julie said, and headed back out. She waved at the broken clipboard. "I'll bring a new one back later, if any doctors ask. When I finish my obs rounds."

Amy smiled. "No worries. Thanks."

She knocked on the bathroom door once she heard Julie enter the next room. "Ben, she's gone."

Ben emerged carrying a large black plastic bin liner, bulging in his arms. "Found a roll of these," he said. "Used half a dozen, one inside the next, just to be sure."

"Stratton's in there?" Matt asked.

"Yep."

Matt grinned. "In the fucking bin where he belongs."

Nervous laughter rippled around them. Ben was the first to become serious again. "So I'm guessing this is all over, apart from this." He hefted the bag.

"Aye, I think so," Matt said.

"Farouk said to talk to her about him," Amy said. "I guess she knows a way to be rid of him?"

"Okay. Then I'll talk to her and do you one last favour for now and get rid of this. Then I'm going home and I plan to get fucking drunk and stay that way for a day or two. I already rung in and told work I wouldn't be there for a while because I was looking after you, and they were good with that. I plan to drink instead."

"And I do not blame you, my friend. Thanks, man."

Ben squeezed Matt's shoulder, kissed Amy on the cheek, and left.

"I'm having trouble staying awake," Matt said.

Amy went to the bed and kissed his forehead. "I'm not surprised. I think we can finally have a rest."

She sank back into the armchair and watched Matt close his eyes. Her own fatigue was palpable, dragging at her, after the dark exertions. Her body felt like clay. When Matt's breathing became deep and even again, she let herself sink too. The memory of the pain still echoed in her bones. She just needed to rest. Stratton was gone, and she was so very tired. So utterly, bone-deep exhausted. She needed sleep.

FORTY

AMY WOKE TO THE PALE LIGHT OF DAWN leaking through the windows. The sky was overcast, grey clouds low and heavy, seeming to press down on the city. Rain still fell, gusting in a fitful wind. And it was cold. So very cold, her breath misted from shivering lips. Dread settled over her.

She turned her head slowly and a dark presence slipped into her field of view. It stood on the other side of Matt's bed. He slept on, oblivious. The shape moved in the shadows of the corner, tall and gangling, limbs too long, body too thin, the head shifting slowly left and right like a snake hypnotising its prey. And there was something altogether familiar about it, even through the uncanny proportions of its form.

Amy swallowed, her heart hammering again. The dark stalker she had set free before was back, as she feared it would be. Of course it was, but what choice had she had? If her previous activity had released it, then there was no doubt that what she had done last night would free it once more. Had she saved Matt only to die herself?

It moved forward, seeming to stretch both towards her and away at the same time. It emerged into slightly brighter light, and Amy screamed at the sight of her own face in shadowy monochrome between its reaching arms.

* * *

Matt snapped awake at Amy's piercing scream. His body was a field of a thousand different agonies, pulped flesh, broken bones, wounded organs.

He gasped as the pain hit his suddenly conscious mind, then hurt turned to panic when he noticed the presence reaching over him. The room was ice cold, the presence made of nothing but the dark, Death taken form. And its form was that of Amy Cavendish. She had told him before of the thing that had come for her, the entity she believed she had released with her use of the shadows. But realisation flooded him along with the cold and the dread. She hadn't released it. She had created it. And it would most certainly consume her.

Amy pressed herself back into the chair, face pale and twisted in terror. "It's too strong!" she wailed. "I'm sorry, it's too much. I should have known, but I'd still have done what I did to save you."

"No," Matt said, his voice cracked and weak. "No, I won't allow it to have you. You made this. Don't make it again."

Amy tore her eyes from the reaching figure to stare at him. "I made it?"

There was no time to explain. No time to do anything but finish it and that would certainly finish him too, but so be it. Let it end now, with everyone still alive. Maybe he hadn't brought death down on everybody after all, just on himself and Stratton, and that was how things should be. He would not let her die for saving him. "Think about it," he said, and when he was sure she had heard, he shot his uninjured hand up to grab the thing's arm as it stretched, almost reaching Amy where she cowered back in her chair.

He didn't hold anything back, didn't even brace for the onslaught he knew was coming. He simply opened himself and let everything go. He howled as the dark ripped through him, as though it shattered his bones and rent the flesh off in strips burning with icy cold. He was not an instrument of death, he was death itself, the very essence of entropy and decay. It was all so clear in his mind now, here at the end. Death was mindless, natural, inevitable. It cared no more for the living than the wave cares for the beach. Its effect was the simple consequence of its existence and it existed because it must. Universal rules at play, indifferent and unstoppable. He had opened himself to it while so young and innocent. Untainted by the vagaries of life or the hard edges of adulthood, he had seen death unadorned and stripped bare and become its conduit. What he always considered some malevolent darkness was just the unconcerned nature of living, the inevitability of death. And every time he had let it go, it had swamped him in its decay and corruption. Not through malicious will, but because that's what death did. That's what it *was*. A force, no more mindful or avoidable than gravity. Jump and you will fall. Open the dark and there is death.

And Amy had seen the same thing from another angle, some variant approach. Rather than delivering death as he had to his young brother, Amy had always seen death debasing others and her empathy had driven her to help. She had tried to ease their passing and, in doing so, redirected some of that inscrutable natural force. Never enough to save them, but perhaps enough to ease their suffering even a little bit. And that redirection she had learned to store within herself somewhere, some protected pocket where it couldn't devour her. And because she held it, she had the ability to let it go, gently and easily, unlike Matt's own agonising release.

But however gentle and empathic she might have been, she was opening herself to the energies of death, that force without compassion or concern. And where Matt had imagined death as darkness consuming him, she had seen it as a *creature* to be delivered. So Matt's darkness did indeed slowly consume him, while Amy manifested hers, a little stronger each time, and she created a malevolent entity out of an energy that was anything but. Through easing others' pain and delivering their deaths to those more deserving, she had created Death itself to wilfully stalk only her.

This almighty insight was all too late for Matt to save himself. But not too late to save her. If his manipulation of death was consuming, he would consume the thing she had created. Strip it away from her and hope she understood the last thing he had said so she wouldn't recreate it anew. She was smart, she would get it.

All this knowledge flashed through Matt's mind and then conscious thought was demolished by wave upon wave of agony, pulsing pain tearing him further and further apart, destroying the cohesion of his very being. But all worth it. All worth it as the thing Amy had created, the thing that bore a parody of her face, was enveloped in all the darkness Matt could imagine. All the death he could possibly draw on wrapped itself around more of itself, made manifest, like gravity closing in around a collapsing star and taking everything away, folding in and in and destroying all within its boundary, nothing, even death itself, able to escape its event horizon.

And then a blackness more total than Matt had ever known closed over his own mind and he was gone, taking it all with him.

FORTY-ONE

Amy's cries died in her throat as Matt's hand shot up and grasped the thing reaching towards her. Clouds of blackness flooded up around him and he howled in deathly agony, arching up off the bed. His lips pulled back from his teeth, his howl becoming a tight-throated wail as the dark billowed out and enveloped everything, the bed, Matt, the entity that looked like some hideous mirror of herself.

You made this. Don't make it again.

The realisation was horrible, the simple truth that she had indeed created this thing with her mind. With her rationalisation of what she did, the shadows she delivered. He was right, she had made it, giving it more strength every time she delivered her gift. And in the back of her mind, in some unconscious part, she had known that what she did to Stratton would give it more strength than ever. And it had. She had manifested it right here, and now Matt was giving his life to save her from it.

"No, no, no!" But her words were pointless.

Matt's machines went berserk, lights flashing, alarms ringing stridently in the dawn quiet of the hospital still sleeping. All the darkness Matt had created fell in on itself, like an explosion in reverse, collapsing down, and it took her entity with it. Matt flopped back into the bed, inert and wan. His body seemed more reduced than ever, flesh tighter to his bones. He was paler than snow, still and not breathing. All his machines flatlined.

The door of the room banged open and body after body in hospital scrubs burst in. They rushed a crash cart up to his bed and shouted at each other, yelling numbers and drug names, short, sharp, efficient.

"We're losing him," someone shouted.

"Clear!"

Nurse Julie inserted herself between Amy and the mayhem and took Amy's arm. "Come on, they need room to work."

"I can't leave him!"

Julie's kindly face became hard. "You're in the way!" As she dragged Amy out into the corridor, her face softened again. "I'm sorry, love, I really am. But they need all the space they can get to work."

"What's happening?" Amy asked, craning her neck to see back as Julie drew her away and sat her down near the desk.

"He's crashing, Amy. He was very badly hurt and his body is having trouble coping. But if anyone can help him, it's those people in there now. We have some of the best emergency and intensive care personnel in the business. Now you stay here and send every bit of energy you have at him. You tell him to live. Sit there and tell him to *live!*"

Amy stared after the woman as she jumped up and ran back to assist her fellows. Matt's door swung shut and Amy stared at the shadows of movement flickering around inside, listened to the muffled bleat of machines alarmed at the collapse of a life they were monitoring.

Julie was right that Matt was very badly hurt, but she couldn't know what else he had done. What he had just given to save Amy. Was there any returning from that? Despite Julie's instruction, Amy had nothing to pray to. That's what Julie had intimated. Pray for him. Whether she meant it religiously or not didn't really matter. But Amy had spent her life watching the most undeserving people rot away and die while others lived evil lives. She had done all she could to redress that balance, and now Matt was paying for it. How could there be anything in a world like that who might hear a person's prayers?

She remembered Terry Stratton's last words. *Whatever you take from this. Don't waste it.* And she remembered his summation of life. *Full of sound and fury, signifying nothing.* She shook her head. Thanks Shakespeare, you fucking nihilist. She had known those words, spoken in Terry's weak, dry voice, were going to haunt her.

Well, she hadn't wasted it. She had saved Matt, and she had saved anyone else from Stratton, others he might have gone after in the future had he lived. But her life and Matt's would not signify nothing. Whatever happened, they both stood for something. They had both made a massive impact in the world, even though it would never be formally recognised by anyone else.

She had no one to pray for and no reason to think Matt was going to survive what he had just released, but she put her head in her hands and, instead of crying, she wished over and over again that he had enough strength left to cheat that mindless energy of death once more.

FORTY-TWO

JULIE RE-APPEARED SOME FIFTEEN MINUTES later, her expression hard. Amy couldn't keep tears from her eyes at the sight.

"He didn't make it?" Amy asked.

Julie half-smiled. "He's tough, but I have no idea how he's holding on. He's died three times so far, right there under the doctor's hands. They bring him back and he crashes again."

"So he's still alive?"

"For now. If he was anywhere else he would be long dead, but we have the best staff and care here, so he has a chance. His heart is having trouble, his respiration is erratic, his blood pressure, not surprisingly, is through the floor." Julie sat behind the ICU desk and picked up a phone. "Give me a minute." She tapped a number, paused, then spoke animatedly, too quiet for Amy to hear.

Amy swallowed, looked again towards Matt's door. *Come on, you tough Scottish fucker!* She directed her thoughts like bullets at his room. *Do not let it end like this. We fucking won, you bastard. We beat him.*

Julie came and sat beside her, held out a few tissues. Amy realised tears were streaming down her cheeks. "Thanks. You don't need to be back in there?"

"No, not now. They're pumping him full of drugs, adrenaline and stuff, standing by to defibrillate again if necessary. He's intubated again, of course." Julie paused, caught Amy's eye. "You're a nurse, right? You want to know this stuff?"

"Yes, of course. Thank you. It helps to know what's happening."

Julie nodded, lips pursed. "Trouble is, I can't really understand what *is* happening. His responses are not what I'd expect from a traumatic injury, or many traumatic injuries like he's had. It's hard to understand just what…" She faded out, lost in thought.

Amy stared, unsure what to say. *He channelled so much death to destroy my hunter that he's lost his ability to hold onto life?* She didn't even know if that was right, but what good would it do suggesting such a thing to Julie?

Julie saved her from having to say anything. "Still, if ICU has taught me anything, it's that everybody responds differently. Seemingly healthy people drop dead, folk you're sure won't survive make a full recovery. It's weird."

Amy grinned. "I had a doctor in Sydney once save a patient from a crash. I congratulated him and he said, 'Don't tell anyone, but I have no idea what I just did. Sometimes medicine is as much art as it is science. And sometimes it's no better than fucking voodoo!'"

Julie laughed. "That doctor has it about right."

They settled into a companionable silence for several minutes and Amy realised the erratic movement through Matt's window had eased. As the thought struck her, the door opened and three doctors emerged. One of them was the bear-like Doctor Sturgess. She hadn't seen him going in. How could she miss a presence like his? As Amy looked up, eyebrows high, his beard split in a grin and he gave a thumbs up.

Amy sagged, tears coming again, and Sturgess moved to sit beside her. He put one huge, warm hand on her knee. "He's strong, your boy. He's not out of the woods, but he's not crashing any more. We've got him stabilised, but he's out cold. Likely to be in a coma for a while now and the real challenge will be bringing him up out of it in a day or two's time."

Amy hated that word, coma. "Is there any likelihood of permanent damage?" she asked. "Brain damage?"

Sturgess made a rueful face. "Always a possibility, but I wouldn't say it was necessarily likely."

"Julie said he died three times in there."

"Four. The last time I thought it was really over, but we got him back. Stay with him, talk to him, even though he's unconscious. We like to think that maybe people can hear their loved ones at times like this."

Amy smiled. "And it keeps the loved ones sane anyway, right? Gives us something to do."

"Of course, you're a nurse." Sturgess patted her knee. "You don't have to buy the bullshit, but as you know, there's no proof it *doesn't* work."

"I'll stay with him. And I'll get his friends in too."

"Attagirl." Sturgess stood and strode away.

Amy went back into Matt's room and lightly kissed his forehead. He was all tubes and blinking lights, stick-on sensor pads and drips. But she was used to that. And this time, she wasn't going to care for the patient until they died. She was going to work until he came back. For the rest of the day she sat beside his bed and talked to him, begged him to rise up.

* * *

Ben arrived around six in the evening. He contained his shock at how close they had come to losing Matt and stood by the bedside, watching the shallow rise and fall of his friend's chest.

"You don't get to do this, mate," he said quietly. "I won't allow it. And I should be at home drinking, you shitbag."

Amy stood beside him, put a hand on his shoulder. "I've been telling him much the same thing."

"After everything he got through? This isn't fair."

"Life rarely is."

They stood in silence for a while. Amy chose not to tell Ben about why Matt had crashed. The poor guy was already struggling with how much he had seen.

"What did you do with…you know, the bag?" she asked eventually.

Ben laughed. "That Farouk? She's dodgy as fuck. She set me up with this contact who runs a foundry and he let me into one of the furnace rooms while the rest were on lunch. In it went, not a molecule left from that fire. Farouk says the contact was actually from this other copper, Charlie Collins, but I don't know."

"She kept talking about a Charlie last night."

Ben nodded. "Farouk said it wrapped things up nicely that Charlie was instrumental in getting rid of Stratton after all. At least partly."

"Good enough for me," Amy said.

Ben grinned again and pulled out his phone. He dialled, then said, "Gareth? Hello, mate. Steve-O with you? Good stuff. Matt's slipped into a coma and I need you two 'round here now. We're all going to talk him up out of it. Amy's here too. Oh, and Gareth? Buy a One Direction CD on the way over." He laughed then said, "Exactly, mate!"

He hung up and leaned over Matt a little closer. "You hear that, ya bawbag? I'm gonna play One Direction at full bore until you wake up and turn it off."

FORTY-THREE

IT TOOK THREE DAYS FOR THEM to bring Matt around from his coma, and another thirty-six hours before the hospital was happy that his lungs and heart were working on their own as they should.

"Told you the threat of One Direction would bring him out of it," Ben said. "Surprised it took so long though."

"Maybe if you *had* actually played it?" Gareth said.

"Well, you didn't buy it. Besides, that might have actually killed him!"

Matt had to admit he was glad of that. He remembered nothing, but strange dreams had plagued his comatose period and all his friends had featured heavily in those visions. Further proof, Amy told him, that what gets through a coma is completely unknown. But also proof that people should continue to try.

He told the lads he owed them each a million beers and all three agreed that he most certainly did. They went off, promising to visit often. They all appeared to be moving away from the shock of what they'd seen. No further police action was forthcoming, except for the fine Matt's parents had copped for wasting police time. But they were home and safe, though more than a little angry with him, demanding explanations. It seemed the threat posed by Stratton had faded without further communication.

"So it's really all over?" Matt asked Amy weakly.

Amy smiled, brushed a hand over his hair. "Almost."

"Almost?"

"I can still see the dark around you," she said, eyes travelling his perimeter. "You see mine?"

"Aye. Beautiful as ever. You know you made your own stalker, right?"

"Yeah. I thought about what you said."

Matt smiled. "So you're going to stop personifying death? It's *nature*, Amy, nothing more. We can manipulate it a little bit, that's all. It's not out to get us."

"Are you listening to yourself? You can do the same. You can use yours a little more like I use mine and stop destroying yourself with it. Be more controlled and gentle."

"I suppose I need to consider that."

Amy looked up, watched clouds scud by out the window. Matt stared at her, mesmerised by her strength. He hoped she didn't plan to go anywhere, as he wanted to spend a lot more time with her. He hoped she shared that need.

"But honestly," Amy said, not meeting his eyes. "I wonder if we should do anything any more. Just because we can doesn't mean we should. We both got ourselves in a lot of trouble."

"And now we know more," Matt said. "I guess we need to think about it carefully, decide how to proceed."

"Yeah. And there's no rush. I don't think we need to be making any decisions or planning any hits for a long while yet. If at all."

"Right. So it's over. For now, at least."

Amy shook her head, smiled down at him.

She was clearly trying to make him realise something, but he was weak and still in a fair bit of pain. "What?" he asked.

"Your dark came to you directly from your guilt, yeah? You realise that?"

"And?"

"And you need to do something about that. Repair things."

Matt sighed, realisation dawning. "Oh, aye, my parents."

"Your life, Matt. You need to rebuild everything. When you're well enough."

"Holy shit, that's going to be a difficult thing to do. How do I even start to tell them what I did?"

Amy looked at him, squeezed his hand. "Just go there. Be with them. And find a way to talk about it once you're home."

Matt sighed, nodded slightly. "Will you come with me?"

"A holiday in Scotland, eh?"

"Yeah, I figure we've earned a break. Can you get the time off? Would you even want to come?"

"I think I can probably arrange that, if I had to," Amy said.

"So you will? You going to make me beg?"

Amy laughed. "Of course I'll come."

"Excellent."

Matt closed his eyes, unable to keep the smile off his face. For the first time in as long as he could remember, broken and hurt though he was, he felt whole. And there was a light on the horizon of his mind he had never seen before. He realised it was hope.

- END -

The novel *Devouring Dark* is a follow-up
to Alan Baxter's Australian Shadows Award Best Short
Story winner, "Shadows of the Lonely Dead",
which is reprinted here as a reader bonus.

SHADOWS OF THE LONELY DEAD

HIS EYES ARE TIGHT WITH PAIN as he turns away from me, buries his frustration in the pillow.

"Something I said?" I ask nervously. "Or did?"

He shakes his head, rustling against the duvet pulled up tight under his chin. "I'm sorry. It's not you… I can't… This has happened before, I… I don't know why."

"It's okay. We don't have to. No pressure, you know."

He sniffs, turns it into a humourless laugh. "Sorry. I'm damaged goods."

I put a hand on his shoulder, remove it quickly as he stiffens. "Oh, Jake, don't say that, it's okay. It happens to loads of guys, but no one ever admits it. Stay here, just sleep, you know."

He nods. "Maybe in the morning?"

"Sure."

* * *

I don't push for anything in the morning. Something difficult is happening and I like him too much to scare him off. I make coffee and bring it to the bedroom. He's beautiful, a wave of dark hair half obscuring his face, cheeks dusted with two-day's growth. He smiles softly as I creep up to the bed.

"I'm awake."

"Hi there."

We stare at each other for a moment, still getting used to how the other looks, everything so new.

"Sorry about last night," he says. "First time I stay and I can't…"

I hold up one hand, pass the coffee with the other. "Doesn't matter. We've got plenty of time, right?"

His smile comes back. There's an edge of melancholy that seems to live behind his eyes, but that smile pushes it away like a breeze behind clouds. "I guess so. Thanks."

"Take your time getting up, have a shower and stuff if you want. I need to get ready for work. I start at ten."

* * *

The hospice is quiet as I enter. Mary offers me a subtle nod from the reception desk and I push through double doors into the smell of carpets, disinfectant and death. Claire Moyer catches my attention, coming the other way.

"Mr. Peters last night," she says. "About three."

I nod. "Thought so. His family there?"

"No. No one."

I shrug and walk on, drop my coat and bag in the nurse's station. Poor old Mr. Peters, his daughters stopped visiting about two weeks ago, when he started to spend more time asleep than awake. It doesn't really matter. We all die alone.

Even people surrounded by loved ones are utterly alone as they slip away, the sea of grief around them unnoticed. Death is the only truly personal thing there is. No one can ever understand it, even someone like me. I've seen death take people hundreds of times, held their skeletal hands as the darkness closes in and their breaths stretch further and further apart until they don't breathe again. But I have no idea what it's like.

I check the roster, see who needs medication, bathing, feeding, simple company. I knew Peters was leaving last night. I hope he didn't realise his daughters had stopped coming, but it's surprising what gets through the haze of terminal illness. Even as their minds go and they forget the faces of people they've known their whole lives, moments of clarity spike through the deterioration like lighthouses sweeping the night and they ask, "Where's my wife?" "Where's my son?" And they know they're alone whether those people are there or not and the last of their resolve crumbles as they slide into that stygian unknown.

Edie Sutton is on my list. She needs a wash, and a feed if she's up for it. Doubtful she'll eat, she hasn't managed more than a couple of teaspoons of jelly a day for almost a week now.

I'm surprised to see her awake as I enter, eyes wet and frightened in the glare of spring through thin cotton drapes. I take a lollipop sponge, dip it in the glass of water beside her bed and gently press moisture to her cracked lips. Her chin quivers as the liquid rolls over her desiccated tongue. "That taste good?" I ask quietly.

Her eyebrows rise, the almost translucent skin stretched tight across her skull wrinkling like tissue paper. "Tired." Her voice is barely audible, but you get used to listening for their words, every syllable a struggle.

"Had enough, huh?"

Tears breach her red, sagging eyelids and she nods ever so slightly.

"You can go whenever you like, love," I whisper.

A moment of softening around her eyes. "Can I?"

"Of course you can. You've seen everyone you were waiting to see."

"My Damon?"

"He'll be here at lunchtime." Her son. Visits regularly as he works nearby, sits with her every evening for hours. "Another couple of hours."

She closes her eyes and her exhalation is slow and weak, like heat escaping a long summer day. She'll be gone soon, I'll have to keep a close check. I lift her hand, a collection of brittle sticks loosely attached to an arm like old bamboo wrapped in papyrus, check her radial pulse. Barely there and so slow. I let my mind pass through my touch, search out the decay and failing organs, take the shadows of her dying softly into myself. I can't cure her, but I can collect the scourge, its malice.

A dark stain spreads into me and I store it away.

* * *

The day goes slowly and quietly. It's usually quiet here, except those moments when someone cries out, sudden terror giving voice to weakened lungs as they momentarily face their mortality without the softening armour of fatigue or drugs. Or the howls of grief, sometimes from friends and family, sometimes from the sick themselves. Sometimes both.

I clean up Kathy Parsons, who's been uncontrollably shitting viscous blood onto plastic sheets for more than a week now, check her meds. She exudes the sickly sweet, cloying odour of death. She's terrified. Only forty-eight years old, eyes always wide in child-like fear, but she's got a little while to go yet. A little while to reach some kind of acceptance, though not all of them do. Some are gasping in disbelieving horror, even with their last breath. Almost everyone dies scared, especially the young ones. Some people are calm and accepting, content as they drift away, but they're rare, usually very old. Everyone has time to think as they lie here, suspended in the last darkening hours of their life. It's good that some find peace in that mortal dusk.

I reassure Kathy as much as possible, sit with her as a sedative soaks through her struggling veins.

Edie's pulse is almost gone when I check her again an hour later, breaths so far apart every one seems certain to be her last. I call her son to tell him he needs to get here, but his phone goes to voicemail. I leave a message imploring him to hurry if he can.

I pull the chair up beside her bed and take her fingers in my palms, rest my forehead against the back of her hand. Her frailty wafts into me and I soak it up, gather that insipid, creeping death into my cells. It can't hurt me. I don't know why, but it can't. So I collect it. I don't know why I do that either. Because I can. It doesn't heal them or ease their suffering, but at some level I like to think they know I share their pain and that offers some subconscious solace.

Edie's pulse weakens until I can't feel it any more. Her breaths are tiny, sharp intakes, almost imperceptible, more than ten seconds apart. Her exhalations are silent, air leaking from lungs little more than deflated sacks of inert offal.

Fifteen seconds apart. She's going.

Her life leaks into the air and the shadow of her sickness, her fear and loneliness, washes through me and she's gone. I shudder with the gift she's given me. My hands tremble as I stand and move away to mark her chart, dimness swimming behind my eyes.

Her son is hurrying along the hallway to her room as I emerge and his face falls when he sees me.

"I missed her?"

"I'm sorry. Only just. She passed moments ago. But she didn't wake again since this morning."

He barks an uncontrollable sob and tears tumble over his cheeks. We're all five years old when our mothers die. "I can see her?"

"Of course."

I'll send the counsellor down with the relevant pamphlets after he's had some time alone with her.

* * *

Not much else happens through the day, which pleases me. It's terrible when more than one patient dies in a day, as the first one feels somehow cheated of their time in my mind.

Jake is parked outside when I get home, an embarrassed smile twitching his lips. "Hi."

I'm so pleased he's there. "Hi." I had wondered if I might not see him again. Our few faltering dates that led to our first night together had been cautious but full of hope. When something got in his way last night, I worried it would frighten him off.

"Try again?" he says, holding up a bottle of red.

"I'd really like that. I have some steaks in the fridge, and wait til you try my potato rösti."

* * *

We gently fumble at each other's clothes, clumsy with nerves and the dull edge of the wine. Edie's death still floats around me, within me, but that helps. I embrace it. Nothing makes me hornier than death. Something about mortality reminds us at a level beyond thought of the importance of contact, of touch, of the life within lovemaking.

I'm not too proud to admit I usually masturbate a lot in the privacy of my home after we lose someone. It's unavoidable, the desperation to feel alive—to feel *life*—especially when I've absorbed the death into my marrow like I do. I hope Jake can see it through this time.

I'm as gentle as I can be, as caring as I know how. He shivers and stiffens with nerves as I run my hands across his shoulders. He looks into my eyes, a nervous smile. "It's okay, I'm sorry. I want to." He reaches back and unclips my bra, lets it drop beside the bed.

"You are so lovely," he whispers.

There's tension, fear, but he keeps assuring me I should continue and so I do and he eventually performs. It's soft and urgent, but electric. Afterwards he grabs hold of me and hugs me against his chest so hard I have to gently force a breath into my constricted lungs.

"That was wonderful," he whispers, his hot breath tickling my ear.

"It was," I say. "I'm glad."

He holds me tight and his breathing changes. He turns his face away. I push away to look at him and tears stand in his eyes.

"I'm sorry," he whispers.

"Are you okay?"

"Yes, really. It's hard to… This is difficult for me. But please, don't feel bad. I just can't help it."

"Anything I can do?"

He smiles, leans down to kiss me. "Just keep being so nice to me."

"That's easy."

I settle beside him and turn to let him spoon me, push myself back into the curve of his body. He's so warm and strong and vibrant—the opposite of poor Edie's hard, cool, frailty, all jutting bones and oxygen tubes.

"Was someone less than nice to you?" I ask, biting my lip the moment it's out. Probably not the thing to say.

"Something like that."

I stroke his hand, not game to risk saying anything else, ask for any more of his secrets.

"I'll tell you one day," he says, voice thin with pain.

He holds me tight until we fall asleep. It's good to have someone so alive to hold on to, a beacon against the shadow of all the death in me.

* * *

The days at work pass slowly and my hours rotate to nights. I prefer the solitude and peace of the night shift, and most deaths happen then. It's strange how people who have been unconscious for days or weeks almost always seem to slip away in the depths of the night, like they know somehow that leaving while the sun shines is unusual. I remember Edie dying in the middle of the morning; her shadow still drifts through me, the echo of her disease. It's all that's left behind, her life and body far away now.

We haven't lost anyone for nearly a week. The orderlies are taking bets on how much longer it'll be. Sam's aiming high, reckoning another few days. Marek is less confident, thinking Mr. Patel will die tomorrow. They're both wrong. Jack Oswald will die tonight, maybe in the next two hours, three at the most. I can *feel* it. I've always been drawn to death, always offended by the hopeless indignity of it. And I've always sought to care for the dying, take into myself something of their pain, a memory of their suffering. I was destined for this career.

I pad into Oswald's room, put a hand against his cheek. It's very cool, his eyes flickering gently behind thin, pale lids. I was wrong, it's happening already. No one to ring for old Jack, he has no one to come. "Last of a line and good riddance," he said to me when he arrived three weeks ago.

"You can't be all bad," I'd said, and he laughed.

"Not bad, really. Just not much good either. Never had kids, wife died twelve years ago. Worked fifty years for fuck all and here I am being tucked away in a corner to die alone."

"We all die alone, Jack," I said, an attempt to soften his hurt.

"Yeah, but there's alone and alone, ent there."

Darkness swells up in him. He hasn't woken in five days. He had a drip in his arm feeding him a bare minimum of hydration, anti-nausea medication and painkillers—a poor simulation of normal life while he dies—but we took that out a few days ago. He's a skeleton under linen stamped with the name of the hospice.

He'd asked me the week before to speed it up for him. "Can't you jab me wiv somefing, make it happen? What's the fucking point in hanging on?"

I'd told him I wished I could, and I meant it.

We wouldn't let our dogs and cats suffer like this but we'll happily put our own parents away to wither and waste into ignominy and despair. They deteriorate to frightened babes again as everything they've ever been deserts them, and we think it's the humane, moral thing to do, to let that happen. To watch it happen while we tell them everything will be okay. Which is the worst line of bullshit we ever try to sell in a world powered by lies and deception.

Jack's eyes pop open, a flood of panic blanching his already ivory face. After a moment he focuses on me and nods, a tiny movement of understanding and he's gone. His darkness swells into me, the entropy of his illness drawn up through my hands where I hold his. It adds itself to the blackness I carry inside, that I've carried for so long. Will I fill up one day, no room for any more, and then what?

With trembling fingers I close Jack's eyes and fill out the paperwork. Marek will win the bet. His guess was closer even though they were both wrong.

* * *

"I want to tell you why sex is so difficult for me." Jake's face is creased with what looks to me like grief.

"You don't have to."

"I know, but I want to. We've been together a couple of months now and it feels serious. It is, isn't it?"

I nod vigorously. "Oh, I hope so." I really do hope so.

Jake draws a deep breath that shudders on the way down. "I never knew my real dad. He left when I was too little to remember."

I open my mouth to say something, I'm not really sure what, and Jake holds up a hand.

"Let me get this out in one, or I may not make it."

I nod and he smiles, squeezes my hand across the table.

"I don't mind not knowing him. My mum was young and irresponsible. She's always been fucking useless, so I can hardly blame my dad for leaving. It's what I did, first chance I got. She should have protected me, but she couldn't even protect herself." He draws another breath, sips wine. "My mum shacked up with Vic when I was about six years old. She'd knocked around with guys before then but never for long. She did her best by me, even though her best was bloody rubbish. But when Vic came along, everything changed.

"He drank heaps, was always on the edge of violence. Mum told me how much she loved him, but it was clear she was terrified of him too. She said how we needed him to pay the bills and he wasn't such a bad guy. Even with two black eyes and a split lip she'd tell me how he wasn't such a bad guy."

Rage flares in me and Jake can see it in my face.

"Let me finish." He reaches out, strokes my cheek. "You're such a good and decent person, the way you care for the dying, you're so good to me. You couldn't be less like Vic *fucking* Creswell." He drinks more wine, his hand shaking. "Anyway, it wasn't long before Vic started…touching me."

I let out a soft sound, part growl, part moan of dismay.

A tear breaches Jake's lashes. "I'm sorry, I need you to know this."

My knuckles creak as my fists clench in my lap. "I want to hear. You shouldn't carry this alone."

Jake nods, sips. "Anyway, he went from fondling and making me do things to him to raping me in very little time."

"You were six?"

"I was probably eight by the time he started that."

He says it like that makes it somehow better than if he were six. "What a fucking—"

"He ruled my mum and me, did what he liked to us. My mum should have protected me, but she was trapped too. He would beat her if she tried to intervene. Beat me if I threatened to tell. We lived in terror. When I was fourteen I told mum we had to go, we had to run away. She said we had no money, where would we go?"

"There are shelters," I start to say and Jake nods again.

"Of course, but that wasn't the point. You know what she said to me, after years of beatings and sexual assaults?"

I sigh and shake my head. "She told you she loved him."

"Yep. So I ran away. I have no idea what they're doing now. He could have killed her for all I know. I haven't spoken a word to her since I left. I was on the street at first, then in shelters and care. A foster home took me in when I was sixteen and I was a bastard, doing all the things my mum did and worse, acting like her boyfriends, thinking I was different."

"You're nothing like that," I say. "You're amazing."

He smiles, but it's not enough to chase away the melancholy this time. "My foster mother is a lady called Glenda Armstrong and she fixed me up. Wouldn't take my shit, made me finish school. I was lucky. She gave me direction, I got a job, turned myself around. Twenty-five now, finally feeling like I've got it somewhere near together. And then I met you. For the first time I feel something real, instead of just angry fucking because I thought that's all I deserved." His tears have stopped and there's anger in his eyes.

"You should be so proud of where you've come, given where you started," I tell him.

"But I'm scared and you mean a lot to me and that's why it's so hard for me to be intimate, emotional. It's always been an act before, an act of defiance more than anything else, a show of power. But with you, I have no guard and it's terrifying."

I stand, move around to hug him and kiss his hair. "I'm honoured," I whisper. "I'll never hurt you."

"I know."

The shadows of all the people who have died with me mask my vision, make Jake a distant blur. "So many wonderful people die every day, struck down by disease or age," I say. "And yet fuckers like that Vic get to live."

Jake nods against my chest. "There's no justice in the world. We have to hang on to our luck when we find it, because that's all there is."

* * *

After nearly a week of no deaths we get two in a day. The darkness wells inside me, that delicious blackness I can't help but gather. Sometimes I think it's going to overwhelm me, but there's always room for more. The journey home is muffled by the circling presence of their passing.

Jake comes around not long after I get home, bag of shopping in hand. "I'm going to make us a great dinner tonight. Special recipe! Something Glenda taught me."

"Great! I'm glad we're having a good dinner. I have to go away for a couple of days."

"That's sudden." His brow is creased in concern and it breaks my heart a little.

"There's a two-day course Claire Moyer was supposed to go on, but she's come down with something. Someone needs to go, it's about a new drug administration practice, and they asked if I'd step in. I head off early in the morning to Newcastle. I'll be away overnight, back by dinnertime the next day. Sorry."

He smiles. "Don't apologise. Work is work. Let's enjoy tonight then, eh? Maybe you can lend me your key when you leave and I can get my own cut? Then I can have something ready for when you get back on Thursday?"

I raise my eyebrows, give him a crooked smile. "Your own key?"

"If you think…"

I sweep him into a hug. "Of course I think. I'd love that."

* * *

It took a lot of searching to find this place, but hours of free time in a palliative care hospice can be put to good use with a search engine and access to hospital records. Hints from Jake about where he grew up and a keen eye. Plus friends in social services to join the dots. The idea, the realisation, hit me like lightning when Jake told me his story.

There's a broken-down car on the front lawn, leaking oil across the dirt like black blood. The house is peeling, the paint reminds me of the skin of a dying woman's lips. I knock on the door, heart hammering against my ribs.

A large figure shimmers through the frosted glass panel and the door swings open. A man stands there in shorts and a stained shirt. He's a tall bastard, muscular, but a beer gut mars anything close to a good physique. He has muddled tattoos on his arms and legs, grey and black stubble across his face like a TV tuned to static. His eyes are dark and mean. "Well, hello, darlin'."

"Victor Cresswell?" I ask.

His eyes narrow. "What?" He glances to my hands, probably checking for a summons.

"*Vic* Cresswell," I ask.

"Yeah."

I hold out my hand. "It's nice to meet you."

His lip curls in a sneer and he takes my hand, squeezing too hard to assert his dominance as he puffs his chest out. "Nice to meet you too, sweetheart. What the fuck is this?"

And I let my darkness out. It rushes through my palm, desperate to escape, and races into him. I feel it gust up his arm, into his chest to nestle in his lungs. It wraps shadowy arms around his liver and coats his gallbladder in an inky embrace. It snakes through his intestines, finds his prostate and slips down into his balls.

A shudder ripples through him as I break our grip and smile, turn away.

"What the fuck was that all about?" he yells as I make my way back to the waiting taxi, a tremor in his voice.

As I tell the taxi to head back to the station he stands in the doorway, one hand rubbing absently at his throat. There's a patina of fear across his face. How much does he suspect? I give him a month at most before the decay begins to set in. Before the tumours start to blossom through his organs. Black, flowering death.

I'm empty inside, somehow hollow but with whiteness swelling into the places where I've collected all that dark over the years. Perhaps I shouldn't have let it all go, should make it last. It's disconcerting, I'm a little lost without the shadows of the lonely dead inside me. I'll have to start collecting again. No matter, at least three at work have less than a week left.

I knew I gathered it for a reason. A shame it took me this long to realise what my purpose is. I have a mission now, giving this unfair blackness to bastards truly deserving of it.

I'm going to be busy.

* * *

Jake is watching television and looks up in surprise as I enter the house. I'm glad he decided to stay at my place, not his. When the moment's right I'm going to ask him to move in.

"I thought you weren't back until tomorrow," he says, smiling. It's genuine happiness on his face and that warms me.

"We got through the training in one day and finished up in time for me to get the last train back. So here I am." I had taken into account that Vic might be harder to find, maybe not home. It had all been much easier than I anticipated.

"Well, that's a lovely surprise," Jake says, gathering me into a hug.

I breathe deeply of the clean smell of his skin. "Yeah," I say. "Maybe there is some justice in this world, after all."

- END -

ACKNOWLEDGEMENTS

No BOOK IS ONLY THE WORK OF THE AUTHOR. A team of people are involved, to varying degrees. When I wrote the original short story, "Shadows of the Lonely Dead", I knew there was more to explore in that subject. A lot more. But the story had pushed me. It was the hardest thing I'd ever had to write, because it came from such a personal place. When it won an award and was reprinted in two different Year's Best volumes, I figured other people felt that resonance too, and perhaps I should explore the themes more deeply. It took a long time to eventually write this novel, but I'm glad I did. Hopefully it resonates as deeply.

So I firstly want to thank editor Simon Dewar for buying "Shadows of the Lonely Dead" for the *Suspended In Dusk* anthology, and thanks also to Anthony Rivera and Grey Matter Press for taking on *Devouring Dark*.

Everlasting thanks and love to my parents, John and Gloria, and my brother, Steve, for always believing in me. I wish you guys could be around to see this, but if you were, perhaps it wouldn't exist. Life, and death, is damned weird.

Eternal gratitude to my amazing first readers, Angela Slatter and Jo Anderton, for helping me to knock this manuscript into better shape. And I owe a debt of gratitude to friend and fellow writer, as well as genuine lifesaver, Doctor Brendan David Carson, for double-checking all the medical and surgical details contained herein. Should any errors remain, they are entirely my own fault.

To all my friends and colleagues in the writing and horror communities, thank you for being there, for reminding me we are tribe. It's so important to know we're not alone in this strange thing we do. I won't attempt to name you all, mainly for fear of missing someone out, but you know who you are and you rock. Yes, you.

And my undying love and gratitude to my wife, Halinka, and my son, Arlo. You two are shining beacons of love, hope, goodness, and empathy, and you keep the shadows from me. I love you both more than I can ever sufficiently express.

Lastly, thanks to you, Reader. I hope you enjoyed this.

Alan Baxter, NSW, November 2018

ABOUT THE AUTHOR

Alan Baxter is a British-Australian author who writes supernatural thrillers and urban horror, rides a motorcycle and loves his dogs. He also teaches Kung Fu. He lives among dairy paddocks on the beautiful south coast of New South Wales, Australia, with his wife, son, dogs and cat. He's the multi-award-winning author of several novels and over seventy short stories and novellas. So far. Read extracts from his novels, a novella and short stories at his website – www.warriorscribe.com – or find him on Twitter @ AlanBaxter and Facebook, and feel free to tell him what you think. About anything.

MORE DARK FICTION FROM
GREY MATTER PRESS

"Grey Matter Press has managed to establish itself as one of the premiere purveyors of horror fiction currently in existence via both a series of killer anthologies — *SPLATTERLANDS, OMINOUS REALITIES, EQUILIBRIUM OVERTURNED* — and John F.D. Taff's harrowing novella collection *THE END IN ALL BEGINNINGS*."

- FANGORIA Magazine

GREY MATTER

P R E S S

MANIFEST
RECALL
ALAN BAXTER

"GRABS YOU BY THE NECK AND NEVER LETS GO."
— JOHN F.D. TAFF, BRAM STOKER AWARD-NOMINATED AUTHOR OF
THE END IN ALL BEGINNINGS

MANIFEST RECALL
BY ALAN BAXTER

Following a psychotic break, Eli Carver finds himself on the run, behind the wheel of a car that's not his own, and in the company of a terrified woman he doesn't know. As layers of ugly truth are peeled back and dark secrets are revealed, the duo find themselves in a struggle for survival when they unravel a mystery that pits them against the most dangerous forces in their lives.

A contemporary southern gothic thriller with frightening supernatural overtones, Alan Baxter's *Manifest Recall* explores the tragic life of a hitman who finds himself on the wrong side of his criminal syndicate. Baxter's adrenaline-fueled approach to storytelling draws readers into Eli Carver's downward spiral of psychosis and through the darkest realms of lost memories, human guilt and the insurmountable quest for personal redemption.

"If you like crime/noir horror hybrids, check out Alan Baxter's *Manifest Recall*. It's a fast, gritty, mind-f*ck." — Paul Tremblay, Bram Stoker Award-winning author of *A Head Full of Ghosts*

"Alan Baxter's fiction is dark, disturbing, hard-hitting and heart-breakingly honest. He reflects on worlds known and unknown with compassion, and demonstrates an almost second-sight into human behaviour." — Kaaron Warren, Shirley Jackson Award-winning author of *The Grief Hole*

"Alan Baxter is an accomplished storyteller who ably evokes magic and menace." — Laird Barron, author of *Swift to Chase*

GREY MATTER
P R E S S

greymatterpress.com

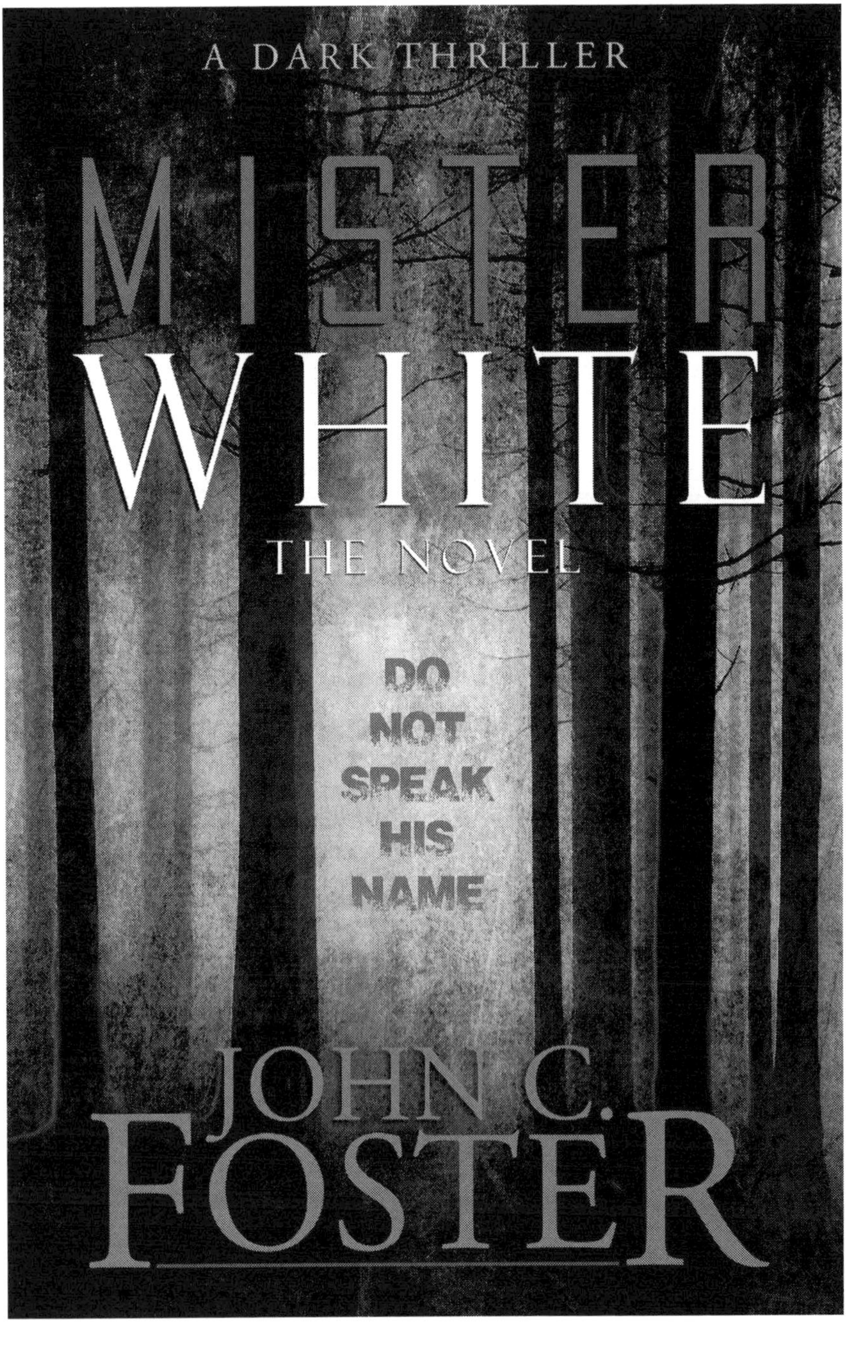
A DARK THRILLER
MISTER
WHITE
THE NOVEL
DO
NOT
SPEAK
HIS
NAME
JOHN C.
FOSTER

MISTER WHITE
BY JOHN C. FOSTER

In the shadowy world of international espionage and governmental black ops, when a group of American spies go bad and inadvertently unleash an ancient malevolent force that feeds on the fears of mankind, a young family finds themselves in the crosshairs of a frantic supernatural mystery of global proportions with only one man to turn to for their salvation.

Combine the intricate, plot-driven stylings of suspense masters Tom Clancy and Robert Ludlum, add a healthy dose of Clive Barker's dark and brooding occult horror themes, and you get a glimpse into the supernatural world of international espionage that the chilling new horror novel *Mister White* is about to reveal.

John C. Foster's *Mister White* is a terrifying genre-busting suspense shocker that, once and for all, answer the question you dare not ask: "Who is Mister White?"

"*Mister White* is a potent and hypnotic brew that blends horror, espionage and mystery. Foster has written the kind of book that keeps the genre fresh and alive and will make fans cheer. Books like this are the reason I love horror fiction." – Ray Garton, Grand Master of Horror and Bram Stoker Award®-nominated author of *Live Girls* and *Scissors*

"*Mister White* is like Stephen King's *The Stand* meets Ian Fleming's James Bond with Graham Masterton's *The Manitou* thrown in for good measure. It's frenetically paced, spectacularly gory and eerie as hell. Highly recommended!" – John F.D. Taff, Bram Stoker Award®-nominated author of *The End in All Beginnings*

GREY MATTER
P R E S S

greymatterpress.com

"Paul Kane is a first-rate storyteller."
—— Clive Barker, Bestselling author of
The Hellbound Heart and *The Scarlet Gospels*

BEFORE

PAUL KANE

BEFORE
BY PAUL KANE

In 1970s Germany, a mental patient at the end of his life suddenly speaks for the first time in years. A year later in Vietnam, a mission to rescue a group of American POWs becomes a military disaster.

In present day England, the birthday of college lecturer Alex Webber sends his life spiralling out of control as a series of disturbing hallucinations lead him to the office of Dr. Ellen Hayward. And things will never be the same again for either of them. Hunted by an immortal being known only as The Infinity, their capture could mean the end of humanity itself...

Part horror story, part thrilling road adventure, part historical drama, Before is a novel like no other. Described as "the dark fantasy version of Cloud Atlas," Kane's Before is as wide in scope as it is in imagination as it tackles the greatest questions haunting mankind—Who are we? Why are we here? And where are we going?

"Paul Kane is a first-rate storyteller, never failing to marry his insights into the world and its anguish with the pleasures of phrases eloquently turned."
— Clive Barker, author of *The Hellbound Heart* and *The Scarlet Gospels*

"I'm impressed by the range of Paul Kane's imagination. It seems there is no risk, no high-stakes gamble, he fears to take... Kane's foot never gets even close to the brake pedal." — Peter Straub, author of *Ghost Story*

GREY MATTER
P R E S S

greymatterpress.com

BRAM STOKER AWARD–NOMINATED

JOHN F.D. TAFF

"A dark descent into
the world of the contract killer.
Taff hits this one out of the box."
— JOE MCKINNEY

KILL-OFF

WHEN DEATH IS A WAY OF LIFE

KILL-OFF
BY JOHN F.D. TAFF

Would you kill someone — *anyone* — if you knew you could get away with it?

David Benning's life is unraveling. Unemployed, running low on cash and with the responsibility of caring for a father struggling with Alzheimer's, he finds himself blackmailed by a shadowy cabal with mysterious and deadly goals.

Known only as "The Group," David quickly learns they breed killers. Turning everyday people into accomplished assassins with unusual targets. As he's dragged farther down into this dangerous world of secrets, guns and payoffs, their true motives are slowly, chillingly revealed.

With nowhere to run, David can trust no one, not even the woman he's been sent to kill...and has grown to love. Can they work together to free each other from the deadly grip of this lethal game?

Kill-Off is a tough, no-nonsense and inescapable thriller in the vein of Richard Stark's *The Hunter* or James Cain's *The Postman Always Rings Twice.*

"John F.D. Taff took this reluctant hitman story in a direction I was not at all expecting. This is a believable everyman who happens to be pretty okay at killing people and has a sufficient motivation to do it. Taff blazes a fresh and innovative trail along familiar thriller territory to craft this nailbiter."
— Bracken MacLeod, author of *Stranded* and *Come to Dust*

"*Kill-Off* has its roots so deeply dug in reality that the ensuing contrast to crime, violence, and assassination plots paint a vivid picture. An everyday person...gets sucked into a twisted game of assassin, [and] the reader is sucked along with him." — Mark Matthews, editor of *Garden of Feinds*

GREY MATTER
P R E S S

greymatterpress.com

AVAILABLE NOW
FROM GREY MATTER PRESS

Before — Paul Kane

The Bell Witch — John F.D. Taff

The Devil's Trill: The Ladies Bristol Occult Adventures #1 — Rhoads Brazos

Dark Visions I — eds. Anthony Rivera & Sharon Lawson

Dark Visions II — eds. Anthony Rivera & Sharon Lawson

Death's Realm — eds. Anthony Rivera & Sharon Lawson

Devouring Dark — Alan Baxter

Dread — eds. Anthony Rivera & Sharon Lawson

The End in All Beginnings — John F.D. Taff

Equilibrium Overturned — eds. Anthony Rivera & Sharon Lawson

I Can Taste the Blood — eds. John F.D. Taff & Anthony Rivera

The Isle — John C. Foster

Kill-Off — John F.D. Taff

Little Black Spots — John F.D. Taff

Little Deaths: 5th Anniversary Edition — John F.D. Taff

Manifest Recall — Alan Baxter

Mister White: The Novel — John C. Foster

The Night Marchers and Other Strange Tales — Daniel Braum

Ominous Realities — eds. Anthony Rivera & Sharon Lawson

Peel Back the Skin — eds. Anthony Rivera & Sharon Lawson

Savage Beasts — eds. Anthony Rivera & Sharon Lawson

Secrets of the Weird — Chad Stroup

Seeing Double — Karen Runge

Splatterlands — eds. Anthony Rivera & Sharon Lawson

Suspended in Dusk II: Anthology of Horror — ed. Simon Dewar